Spectacular Praise for
ANYWHERE

"*Anywhere for You* is a gorgeous story about hope, healing, and human connection—one of those rare novels that is as elegantly written as it is emotionally raw. Greaves's words will stay with me for a long time."

—Emily Henry, #1 *New York Times* bestselling author
of *People We Meet on Vacation* and *Beach Read*

"*Anywhere for You* by Abbie Greaves will break your heart and then put it back together again. . . . A love story full of mystery, heartbreak, and maybe, just maybe, a chance for a happy ending."

—POPSUGAR

"I very much look forward to seeing what she writes next."

—Jojo Moyes, *New York Times* bestselling author

"Poignant and moving . . . standout love story . . . and one that shines a light on some very important issues. Exceptional."

—*Sun* (UK)

"A beautifully crafted, tender love story."

—*Sunday Express* (UK)

"A moving tale of troubled souls who join forces to help each other."

—*Daily Mail* (UK)

"It's a pleasure to read such a stylish and confident new voice—readers are going to love discovering Abbie Greaves."

—Louise Candlish, internationally bestselling
author of *Our House* and *Those People*

"Both a love story and a mystery, this tender and moving tale raises so many issues, including the importance of family and community."

—*Woman's Own* (UK)

"Just as she did in her debut novel, *The Silent Treatment,* Abbie Greaves again demonstrates with *Anywhere for You* . . . that she has an incredible gift for delicately opening up interpersonal relationships and putting them on full display, for better or worse."

—The Nerd Daily

"If you like your mysteries with a whopping side of heart, and your characters intense and raw, Greaves is the writer for you. Readers of *The Silent Treatment* will be struck by the way she has enhanced her talent for plotting, and newcomers will marvel at the emotional intensity of her prose."

—Book Reporter

"Absolutely incredible read. . . . The author has provided the perfect balance of humor and heart-rending sadness and has produced a thoughtful and emotive read. . . . A book that can make me both laugh and cry is an absolute winner. . . . It will be one of my books of the year."

—*NB* magazine (UK)

"Fans of Jojo Moyes will love this intricate tale of a woman searching for answers about a lost lover."

—*New!* magazine (UK)

Anywhere for You

Also by Abbie Greaves

The Silent Treatment

Anywhere for You

A Novel

Abbie Greaves

WILLIAM MORROW
An Imprint of HarperCollinsPublishers

P.S.™ is a trademark of HarperCollins Publishers.

ANYWHERE FOR YOU. Copyright © 2021 by Abbie Greaves. All rights reserved. Printed in the United States of America. No part of this book may be used or reproduced in any manner whatsoever without written permission except in the case of brief quotations embodied in critical articles and reviews. For information, address HarperCollins Publishers, 195 Broadway, New York, NY 10007.

HarperCollins books may be purchased for educational, business, or sales promotional use. For information, please email the Special Markets Department at SPsales@harpercollins.com.

Published by Cornerstone in the UK in 2021.

A hardcover edition of this book was published in the US in 2021 by William Morrow, an imprint of HarperCollins Publishers.

FIRST WILLIAM MORROW PAPERBACK EDITION PUBLISHED 2022.

Designed by Kyle O'Brien / Art by WladD/Shutterstock, Inc.

Library of Congress Cataloging-in-Publication Data has been applied for.

ISBN 978-0-06-293388-1

22 23 24 25 26 LSC 10 9 8 7 6 5 4 3 2 1

For Mum and Dad, whose patience with me is inspirational, to say the least.

Anywhere for You

2018

Mary O'Connor has become part of the furniture at Ealing Broadway station. Like most items abandoned on the roadside, she is overlooked and underappreciated. But that is where the similarities stop. There is nothing scruffy about Mary—quite the opposite in fact.

Her hair is neatly pinned in a bun at the back of her head, the dark strands shining with the luster of a horse chestnut. Mary hasn't had a haircut in years, sees it as an indulgence she does not deserve, but there are good genes at play that keep her hair in prime condition regardless. They are the same genes that also lend her symmetrical features, high cheekbones, and a neat, aquiline nose. Without so much as a trace of makeup, her eyes are wide. Searching, someone observant might say. That, or haunted.

Every evening Mary power walks here straight from work, after stacking the shelves at the supermarket down the road. There isn't time to head home and change, what with her shift finishing at five thirty and the rush to get to the station and not miss a minute of the people traffic. Instead, she will button a cardigan over the branded yellow polo shirt provided by her employer. It may not be a fashionable look, but Mary's beauty is enough to eclipse even the most heinous of sartorial crimes.

Once Mary reaches the station, her body slips into autopilot. She finds her position, under the concrete entrance porch, a few yards ahead of the ticket barriers and to the left of a kiosk offering watery coffee. Then, satisfied with her spot, she will reach down for the sign. She carries it with her at all times, slotted into the back pocket of her hiking day pack and folded in two along a central crease that is becoming weaker with age. *Not the only one,* she thinks, pursing her lips as a sharp twinge runs along the bottom of her left shoulder blade. And to think she turned forty just last week. The emotional toll of the past few years has left Mary feeling at least twenty years older.

She is tall, touching six feet, so she will take a second to ensure that she has positioned the sign at what she estimates to be Average Eye Height. Then she pulls the two sides of the cardboard apart and unveils her message to the world. She'll adjust her fingers, when they begin to cramp, but she is always careful to avoid obscuring even half an inch of the wording: *COME HOME JIM.* Every word matters and every syllable is ingrained in her heart.

"Jim?" she asks the commuters as they trudge past, their heads bent over their phones or one of the free local newspapers that end up collecting at her feet. In the last year or two there has been an alarming rise in the number of people she thinks are responding to her. In actual fact they are speaking into those buds, the little white apostrophes in their eardrums that are almost invisible, not a wire in sight. Very disconcerting. And to think they look at *her* like she is the one unhinged from reality.

On a busy day, one or maybe two people will stop and ask after her or Jim. The first will usually be a concerned do-gooder, someone who assumes she has fallen on hard times (or perhaps her head) and is in need of a moment or two's conversation. Despite her tidy appearance, there are always a couple of people a month who will try to slip her some money too. But how to explain that she isn't so much homeless as without the one person who should be her home? They always move on before Mary has begun to find the words.

In winter, she calls it a day when her hands are so numb that she begins to drop the sign—after two hours or so in her thin woolen gloves. This always leaves her with a fresh sense of guilt. Is she packing up too early? What if Jim comes just as she has her keys in the door to the flat? After nearly seven years of this routine, six full cycles of winter, spring, summer, and autumn, she has reconciled herself to the niggling sense of negligence that accompanies putting the clocks back.

But now, in early August, she can be out until ten o'clock at night. That gives her another hour, according to her watch, silver on a slim chain, a treasured gift from him. Mary will weather the pain in her feet and her shoulder and her heart because she has nowhere else to go and no desire to face the flat, still as a mausoleum and the silence stifling.

She will wait out that hour, and even then she knows she will wish she could stay outside the station forever. She will wait until her knees buckle and her ankles give way. She will not move on or get over it or end-stop this. She will not give up. No. She will wait and wait and then wait some more. After all, wasn't that what she promised Jim?

To the ends of the earth, or Ealing. Always.

1

2018

Ten P.M. Mary twists her neck from side to side. There is a crack, followed by a series of small crunches like leaves underfoot. Whoever said standing was the key to good health doesn't spend over twelve hours a day on their feet. Mary folds the sign and tucks it back in her rucksack before taking one last look around. Although she should be inured to disappointment by now, the sight of the station concourse, empty of the one face she wants to see, bites.

As it is a Tuesday, Mary does not have time to head home before her 11 P.M. TO 3 A.M. shift at NightLine, the local crisis call center. She does the same slot on Thursday nights too and would do more, were it not for the fact that Ted, CEO and rotation supervisor, put his foot down over fears that Mary would overexert herself. The reality is that she is so exhausted—emotionally, physically—that she has forgotten what it is like to feel otherwise. She hopes that the fifteen-minute walk from the station to St. Katherine's primary school, the charity's headquarters, will perk her up enough to be coherent on the phone tonight.

When Mary first started at NightLine, it was three months after everything that had happened with Jim and, while she had already established her vigil at the station, somehow that was not enough. His loss had left a void in her life, a great gaping crater to swallow her whole. Even though it seemed it would never be filled, Mary knew that she had to at least *try* to do something to cling to whatever shreds of a future she had left.

So when the advert for new volunteers went up on the Community Noticeboard on one of her first days working at SuperShop, Mary tore down the leaflet on instinct. She stuffed it into her trouser pocket. For a day or two that was as far as she got. Every time she thought about emailing the inquiry address, one of Mam's favorite phrases would pop up in her mind, puppet-style, before she could click Send: *You can't help anyone until you can help yourself.*

There was logic in that aphorism, as there was in most, but if it was only people beyond the need for help who offered it, then surely there would be nobody working for charities at all? Besides, Mary fitted most of the volunteer criteria—she was committed, reliable, a strong listener. She had a slight question mark over her ability to remain "confident in crisis situations," but Mary told herself that NightLine could provide as good an opportunity as any to learn.

She had never been as bombarded by information as she was during her first few training sessions. Ted started off flagging the most important pages in the hefty handbook but he soon abandoned that; perhaps he could sense that Mary was conscientious enough to scour it from cover to cover anyway. All that reading, and still there was only one phrase that Mary took to heart, emblazoned on the paper file as the organization's tagline: *Space to Speak.*

It made her think of Jim, which in itself was nothing new, but now the tagline flipped her thoughts. She had spent so long reliving every conversation she could remember between the two of them. But now she realized that, even with perfect recall, those strings of words couldn't tell the full story. Mary promised herself that she would give her Night-Line callers all the space she could possibly afford.

Although her self-esteem has come close to collapsing in recent years, she knows that she is a good volunteer. And, despite the grueling nature of the role, she has come to realize that she feels more comfortable at NightLine than she does almost anywhere else in the world these days. There is the sense of purpose that grounds her after the emotional upheaval of the daily vigil. There is the solace of the classroom walls. And then there is the company of the other volunteers, whom she has grown very fond of indeed.

Of them, Mary has known Ted the longest, although he doesn't strictly count as a volunteer. Not since his wife died two years ago and he made the decision to take himself off the phones while he grieved. He works in a managerial capacity now—rotation, setup, the boring nuts and bolts. The two of them used to pass like ships in the night, until last year when his youngest went off to university and he confided in Mary that he was feeling rather at a loose end.

That makes two of us, Mary thought, before drawing out of herself enough to ask if he fancied a walk sometime. Now, a Sunday-afternoon stroll has become something of a habit for them both. A few weeks ago they popped down to Kew together to celebrate his fiftieth birthday— if two scones at the café can be called such.

"Evening," Mary calls as she enters the classroom.

Ted has his back to her. He is wearing his usual polo shirt and khaki shorts and is standing under the light fixture, his shaven head glowing like a bulb. Mary can see that he is in the middle of filling the tea urn. It, however, does not want to play ball. The stainless steel drum wobbles on the table edge.

"Mary!"

In his enthusiasm to greet her, Ted releases the hand that is cradling the metal, and the urn falls to the floor with a crash. They both flinch.

"Bloody nightmare, this thing," he says as the drum rolls under the table. Mary is always surprised by how neutral his voice sounds to her Northern Irish ears. Not a trace of accent, even though he has the Jack-the-Lad disposition of an East End geezer.

"Did you have a good trip?" Mary asks.

Ted nods and Mary notices his tan. He has always been sun-kissed—one of the perks of being a gardener, she supposes—but he is positively bronzed after two and a half weeks of visiting his elderly parents in Dorset. It takes ten years off him. "Fine, thanks. Hard to see them getting frailer, though."

Mary tries not to think of her own mam, getting on now, her ankles like tennis balls swollen above her carpet slippers. A dutiful daughter, she reminds herself, would spend her evenings helping her mam ease them off, not posing outside a station five hundred miles away. She pushes the thought to the back of her mind.

"I ought to be off." Ted's voice cuts through Mary's reverie. She must have been silent for longer than she thought because, when she refocuses on the room, she can see that Ted is wavering, unsure of whether to go in for a goodbye hug. Mary offers her most convincing smile instead.

When he is gone, she takes her seat, winding the phone cord around her index finger as she awaits the arrival of the other two regular volunteers at NightLine.

It isn't long before she clocks Kit and Olive crossing the road through the window. Kit—a twenty-something with the boundless energy of a schoolboy—is mid-anecdote. His sandy hair keeps falling into his eyes, and Mary can imagine that it is all Olive—a retired chiropractor—can do not to offer him an elastic band for it. Kit has the chiseled handsomeness of a boy-band lead but with a slapdash approach to the specifics of his appearance, which means that he looks, perennially, like he has just returned from a festival. To think that he works in an investment bank by day, too.

"It seems a little far-fetched to me . . . ," Olive says as they enter the room.

She turns and gives Mary a wave before heading for the teacher's wheelie chair. She undoes the Velcro on her sandals and slides her feet out of them. Olive is an old friend of Ted's and has been at NightLine since its inception. It goes some way to explaining why she treats the place like her own front room.

"How are you, *amigo*?"

Last thing any of the volunteers heard, Kit had taken up a Spanish app. Now, it seemed, they would never be hearing the end of it.

There is a silence until Mary clocks that he is addressing her. "Me?"

"What's new?" Kit prompts.

"Not much." *Nothing* would be more apt. But how to explain to Kit that her life never veers off the same course of supermarket shift, station vigil, and two evenings a week of volunteering here at NightLine? She can only imagine the sort of work-hard, play-hard city existence he must lead. The last thing she wants to be is pitied.

"Any summer holiday on the horizon?"

Before Mary can go through the ordeal of a response, the phone nearest Olive burbles.

"Park yourself!" Olive barks at Kit. "We're starting."

Soon the room settles into silence as the three begin to take the calls in turn. Mary's first is a long one, over two hours. It is a young man whose wife has left him, with the twin toddlers in tow. It never does get easier, hearing someone say they aren't sure what there is to get up for in the morning, and there is no doubt that Mary has far more sympathy for the sentiment than most. Not that she can let on about that. Volunteers are anonymous and cannot give so much as a hint of their own personal lives. It is comforting, she finds, presenting yourself as a void. It comes rather more naturally to her than she thinks can be healthy.

Mary has a few moments to herself after he hangs up. She digs into the Twix that Ted left for her and makes a fresh cup of tea. Looking back, she will marvel at how the most extraordinary events always seem to coincide with the most ordinary of moments. But for now she swallows down a mouthful of her biscuit, then picks up the receiver.

"Good evening, you are through to NightLine. Before we begin, I ha—"

"Hello?" The male voice on the other end of the line is crackly, as if a hand is being moved across the microphone.

"Hello, good evening, it's NightLine. There are a few questions that I have to ask fir—"

"I wanted to say that I missed you."

At first Mary doesn't trust her own ears. She's been here long enough that she thinks she has heard it all.

"Are you still there?" the voice asks. The sound is muffled but there is a detectable slur between the words.

"Yes, yes . . ." Mary rests her free hand on the desk but she can see that it is trembling, regardless of the complete tension in her bicep. For a second she tries to focus her mind on the here and now. But it is futile; she is already spiraling years back, to the moment they met. It couldn't be, could it?

"Did you hear what I said?" The man's words seem to fall on top of one another, the effect of a half bottle of whiskey no doubt, if not more. Her pulse thunders.

"Yes. I did, thank you. You, er . . . missed me." The last words stumble out. What started as a trickle of hope down Mary's spine has now flooded through every cell and fiber of her body.

"I missed you."

Mary flicks her eyes over her left shoulder to check that neither Olive nor Kit is eavesdropping. She feels at once as protective as a tigress and as vulnerable as the prey within inches of its claws.

"This has been one of my worst days in years. I've felt so alone, like there's no one who will listen. It's hard to find the will to keep going when you haven't got anyone to turn to. Except you. You've always been there for me. You've never given up on me. You're my safe—" The line crackles. Mary misses the last word, but she mouths the syllable she knows will be there.

Place

When she puts a hand to her forehead, it is sticky, the sort of clammy warmth that appears before a virus takes hold. Another crackle jolts her fevered mind into action.

"Where are you?" Mary manages. She needs an answer. Even if she doesn't get a location or coordinates, or anything traceable, just one word would do. One word, that is all she needs. *Okay.* Because if he is calling, after so long, then there must be a reason. Because, oh God, what if he's in danger, or sick or . . .

"I can't tell you that. Not now. I wanted you to hear me, Mary."

Her breath catches.

"You know my name," she whispers, more to herself than to anyone else.

"What?" There it is again: the rustling on the other end of the line that distorts the voice with the sound of an untuned radio.

"Are you there? Hello?" Mary will make her own voice heard over the uncertainty of the line. She will drown its weaknesses with the force of her desperation. "Hello?" She has that same horrible sense of having said the wrong thing. She can't lose him, not now. "Hello?"

Before she has a chance to say another word, the line goes dead.

Mary stumbles across to the door. She can barely see, let alone look where she is going, her mind a freight train of worst-case scenarios. Seven years of nothing have crumbled in the space of a minute. Why? Why now? She leans her burning forehead against the glass pane, the handle jabbing into the soft flesh of her belly. What does it all mean?

In the reflection she stares deep into her pupils, as if there will be something there to anchor her.

But all she sees is Jim, that first night together, his voice like gravel and his face like home.

2

2005

Mary can remember exactly where she was standing, the moment she first saw James. Not because of fate or the fixing point of Cupid's arrow, or some other nonsense she didn't have the head or time for. No, she remembers it because that was the very spot where, seconds before, she had knocked half a casserole dish of coq au vin down her best white shirt.

The timing couldn't have been worse. There was less than half an hour to go until the bride and groom arrived for the reception, and they had paid more than enough to ensure that their head waitress wasn't dressed in their wedding supper. Plus, the sauce was scalding. It was bad enough working a July wedding in full uniform without adding a burn into the equation.

Mary pulled the cotton away from her bra to cool her skin, aware that half her breasts were now on show—she was wearing one of those absurdly skimpy balconette ones that Moira had persuaded her to buy. She glanced up to check no one was about.

"You alright there?" the man in the doorway called.

Who on earth was he? Not one of the caterers. Mary would have clocked if one of them looked like an off-duty model. Was he a wedding guest? No—he was far too early and he wasn't dressed for that, in slacks and one of those shirts purposefully manufactured without the collar. Who knew men's catwalk fashion could make it as far as the Stormont Hotel, Belfast? Certainly not Mary.

There was an ungainly plop as a plum tomato toppled from its temporary perch on her left breast and onto the carpet.

The man suppressed a laugh and flicked his tongue to the corner of his lips. He had the sort of stubble that Mary had heard the girls behind reception describe as "designer," in whispers, after the well-heeled stag parties had been checked in. She had never seen the appeal, until just now.

"Can I help you?" she asked. She felt embarrassed, yes, but her indignation was tempered by a ferocious curiosity about the stranger who was making his way toward her. He hadn't broken eye contact once.

"Me?"

"Yes, you. Who else would be watching and not saying a word?"

He smiled again, wider, this time with a confidence that suggested he had seen plenty of women with their tops soaked through before.

"I didn't mean you had to help." Mary suddenly realized she had overstepped the mark—after all, who was she to be asking a guest here to clean up? "It's my fault anyway."

"Well, I'm early."

An English guest too.

"For the wedding?" Mary nodded her head in the direction of the seating plan, perched on an easel in the corner of the function room.

"I wish! I'm here for a conference. Surgeons? ENT specialists."

Really? He looked a bit older than Mary herself, who, at twenty-seven, thought she had more than enough life experience to be able to age a man accurately. He could be midthirties, at a push? That might explain the confidence. Maybe also that knowing look, the crinkles at the corners of his eyes. He was still staring, his gaze hungry. It was almost savage.

"I'm afraid I don't know anything about that . . ." Mary trailed off. Her brain had ceased to function. "You could, er . . . try the front desk."

"But I like the view here."

What was that he said? Mary hoped she hadn't started hearing things in the midst of whatever mania had come over her.

The man took a couple of steps, stopping in front of an errant chicken thigh and about six feet away from Mary. It was a long time since she had seen eye to eye with a man; most local Belfast men tended to come up to her shoulders, or thereabouts. She estimated that this Englishman had a good three inches on her: perfect height to do up his top button, if only he had one.

"Are you sure you don't want a hand?"

Mary allowed herself a second or two to look him in the eyes— pools of rich, warm hazel that reminded her of licking a chocolate-spread knife. There was something playful about his features too. A scar sliced through the hair on his left eyebrow. She was desperate to find out how he had acquired it.

Her hands trembled around the oven mitt. "No, sure I'm grand. But thanks for your trouble all the same."

"James. It's James."

"Yes, well, thank you, James."

"I'll be off, then."

For the love of God why had she said that? Mary didn't want this to be the last she saw of him. It couldn't be. But what was the alternative? She had a function to prepare for and a shirt to change.

He made to move. But instead of leaving, he picked up the stray chicken thigh. He tore into the meat with all the relish of a dog lost for a week in the wilderness.

"Delicious."

Mary was so shocked that, even as he made his way to the exit, she didn't move an inch. She was so shocked that when he turned, just as he rounded into the corridor and poked his head back around the door-frame to ask her name, she answered.

The wedding passed Mary by in a blur. She had worked so many by now that they often did. But that afternoon was different: every time she saw a guest with a shock of dark curls, she felt her abdominals tense in the hope it might be James; every time she adjusted her spare shirt so that it wasn't pulling so tightly across her bust, she couldn't shake the hot feeling of his gaze on her.

She stayed to clean up once the reception had wound down. It was double pay and every little bit helped the family accounts, although Mam always tussled over Mary's envelopes of cash. Mam wanted her to have enough left over to, as Mam would say, "live her life" too. For the first few years that meant a couple of sneaky vodka and Cokes when Mary went out with the rest of the girls from work.

But when school ended, those nights started to thin, until there was no one but Mary and her best friend, Moira, left. Everyone else had gone to university or started courses for beauty or accountancy or, in the case of Ciara Campbell, welding. That was one good thing about drifting from the old gang; it was harder to tell just how quickly everyone else was moving on with their lives.

Mary swept up the remaining cutlery, trying not to think about how circumstances had conspired to trap her in a job she had thought would be temporary. Eleven years she had been at the Stormont, ever since she finished school at sixteen. It was easy enough to know you should move on; far harder without a sense of what else you could do. There were the fabric maps she made in the pockets of her spare time, but they were a hobby, nothing more. Mam had framed one of Belfast in the hallway—her best to date—but still it did little more than re-mind Mary of her failure to pursue an artistic career. Living at home wasn't helping matters; comfort never encouraged anyone to spread their wings.

She began to collect the glasses. One looked as if it had been cracked and she stopped, holding it under the light to examine if it really was damaged. In the reflection, Mary could see that she didn't look altogether that much older than when she started working here. It was the big eyes, she thought. She had always been aware that she was pretty, in a conventional sense, but that was as much as she would ever admit to herself. It was far from vanity that she was raised and, as Mam always said, good looks will only get you so far in life.

"Mary?"

Her eyes flitted to the door.

"Good wedding?"

"Not mine."

"Yes, I gathered as much." He was even better looking than she remembered. He had untucked that ridiculous shirt of his and had rolled up his sleeves so that Mary could admire the tone of his forearms. "What about a hand now?"

Round two, then.

"Go on," Mary said, after her heart had dislodged from her throat. "You can start stripping the linens over there. They go in the far laundry bin."

James took his orders, and Mary had to stop herself from staring, drinking in the fact that he had come back. She needed to know why—but how to ask without seeming desperate or trying too hard? She decided to come straight out with it. Chances were she'd never see him again.

"So what brings you back here? Can't be the love of cleaning."

"You."

"I beg your pardon?"

"You heard me." James looked up this time. There it was again, that smile. She didn't know how it was possible to feel such camaraderie with a stranger, how it was possible to feel so at home. "You," he continued. "There's something . . . enigmatic about you. Quiet but fierce. Yes, maybe that's it. Beautiful too, which helps, but that's not it. I want to figure you out. I missed you these last few hours."

Mary had no idea how to respond. Weren't Englishmen known for being the silent type? Or was that just some nonsense that came from films? Either way, Mary knew no one this upfront with their thoughts and their compliments. She ought to thank James, but that seemed so transactional. Best not to do anything that could ruin the moment.

James returned to his linens.

"Do you want a drink?" She picked up a half-full bottle of wine and two untouched table glasses.

"I thought you'd never ask."

James took the seat next to Mary, his leg brushing against hers. "Cheers," he said, tipping his glass. "To weddings and conferences and surprise . . . encounters."

Mary flushed. She had never been one to get ahead of herself. Besides, it had been so long since she'd been with anyone like that. Dean was the last, and it had been three years since they had broken up. Moira thought she had cobwebs growing down there. Mary couldn't really disagree.

"So where are you from?" she said, wanting to change the subject before the process of her thoughts registered on her face.

"Ealing. West London. Have you been to London?"

Mary shook her head. She'd been on a school trip to Calais just before she left, but that was the sum total of her traveling experience.

"It's great—as a tourist, at least. To live, it's pretty mad. Expensive too. But I grew up there and now I can't seem to leave."

Mary could sympathize with that. James riffed a bit about the sights in his local area, asking whether she traveled much—would she like to?

It was a conversation that Mary felt she could have indefinitely with such an engaged audience, but she felt oddly impatient throughout.

"And you live alone?" Call her cautious, but she wanted to check she wasn't treading on any toes. She had nothing by which to judge this man's integrity, bar her own gut instinct, and right now her stomach was churning with such aggression that she worried it was audible.

"Confirmed bachelor." James put his hand on his heart. "I'm a one-woman man, with the right woman; and in the absence of the right woman, I'm . . ."

"Alone," Mary finished.

"Charming."

"I mean you're staying here, alone, tonight?"

James's eyebrows shot up and Mary willed herself not to undercut her own confidence. It was so unlike her, this forwardness, yet it somehow felt as if it suited her. When would she get an opportunity like this again? The man would be back at work on the other side of the Irish Sea, come Monday.

"Yes. That I am."

Mary knew it would have to be her to make the first move. "Maybe we could check it out."

At the front desk, it was the night porter on duty, the low-level hum of the revolving doors broken only by the occasional snuffle as he toppled into sleep. As they waited for the lift, James slipped a hand onto the small of Mary's back. When the doors opened, he pushed a fraction harder, guiding her in so that the two of them stood, her back against his chest, their reflections thrown into wobbly distortion in the metal pane.

The lift moved slowly and Mary wondered if he would kiss her there and then, like he would have done in a film or in one of those confessions in *Cosmopolitan,* where women are paid fifty quid to admit to all manner of strange sexual proclivities. But no. Mary had never known reticence to be quite so frustrating.

He was staying up on the fifth, the "posh floor" as she knew it, with its larger rooms and the fancy suite at the end. *Often reserved for honeymoons,* Mary thought, with a shiver of anticipation. Just before they reached his room, James broke off, sliding the room card out of his front pocket. The door opened on the first try and he stepped forward into the darkness as he waited for the lights to kick on.

Mary followed him, nudging the door closed with her hip. She went to walk further into the room but Jim's lips were already on her neck. As he kissed the skin there, he ran his hands along the waistband of her skirt, releasing her shirt and pulling it off over her head in one deft movement. He unhooked the one working bra clasp and she dropped her arms, waiting for the bra to fall forward. It struck Mary that she should probably do something about her tights, but before she could figure out the logistics of that, what with James's body now pressed firmly against hers, he stooped to bend and slip them down for her, bunching the nylon in two pools at her ankles that she could kick aside. He picked her up and carried her to the bed.

Mary watched James undress himself. He didn't look directly at her, which made things easier, she supposed, so she didn't have to check her expression or imagine herself at the agricultural show, sizing up a prize specimen. That's not to say that she didn't notice, though—his shape, the way his chest hair began an inch below the shelf of his collarbone, the two lines in V-formation at the base of his stomach, which seemed to be carved from the shadows of the room itself.

When he came to bed, his body arched over Mary and, with the calluses at the base of his fingers grazing her nipples, then hovering at the very top of her thighs, it struck Mary that maybe she had met him before. He hadn't said it was his first time in Belfast. Could she have seen him in the hotel? Perhaps in a bar further into the city?

She never got too far with her inventory of possibilities. With his head between her legs, her hands in his hair, and a pillow pushed beneath her hips, for once her mind went blank.

After Mary finished, her body was shaking, and when James laid his head on her breast, his ear pressed against the flushed skin there, the two of them quivered together like the twin propellers on a two-man plane.

Mary traced her finger along the gap in his left eyebrow. How was it possible for a person to be at once so familiar and yet so entirely new?

She could already feel herself falling.

3

2018

After seven years at SuperShop, Mary should have the tasks down to a fine art. In the morning she's assigned shelf-stacking and the odd spot of product rearrangement (if required), and in the afternoon she'll hop onto the tills, scanning customers' groceries until her shift finishes. But today the routine is shot, and Mary's nerves with it.

There is an incident where she is unloading loose cabbages, heedless of the capacity of their carton, only to realize there is an overflow when the surplus begins to collect at her ankles. Later there is another, where a customer extends her loyalty card for swiping for a minute before Mary notices. Eventually the woman coughs and Mary slams back into the room, as apologetic as she has ever been, although it doesn't reassure anyone in the queue as to her sanity.

Janet, the manager, takes Mary off the tills after that, under the pretense of needing her in the stockroom. When she stands, Mary totters. She has made it through the best part of the day on no sleep and no food, but still the cogs in her brain show no sign of slowing their chaos. She has not stopped reeling through snatches of last night's garbled conversation, every memory of the warm familiarity of Jim's voice undercut with pain.

"What's up?" Janet hisses, the moment they find an unoccupied corner by the overflow freezers.

A forlorn-looking bag of peas sits, forgotten, at Mary's feet. She nudges the soggy packaging with her shoe and fiddles with her badge. The upside-down letters of *Here to Help!* are beginning to swim.

"Mary, come on, you've got to tell me. I want to make things easier for you but you have to let me in. Otherwise it's hard, you know . . ." Janet raises her hands in vague circles to take in their surroundings.

Mary knows what she means. Janet is the reason they've kept her on here, even with the question marks raised by anyone in senior management who has seen her vigil. Apparently, she should be representing the SuperShop brand at all times, inside working hours and out. She had no idea people paid so much attention to the morality of the workers bagging up their groceries.

"I know . . . I know," Mary murmurs. "He called. Last night." The words tumble out and now, in the air between them, they start to feel terrifyingly real. This is all Mary has hoped and dreamt of, and yet she cannot shake the sense that there must be some trauma prompting him to reach out now. The thought of him hurting, and her not there to comfort him, makes her chest cave.

"Mary . . ."

Janet doesn't need to be told who. It always comes back to him. She smooths a strand of eye-popping bright-red hair back behind her ear. There's a discount on hair dye at the moment.

"It's so strange, I know. All this time when I didn't hear a peep— not a word or a postcard or a letter—and now this?" Mary glances up, detects the skepticism in Janet's eyes. "I know you think I'm mad. And maybe I am. I feel like I'm going crazy most of the time anyway, but not then . . . not when I heard his voice again. Janet, honestly, this was him. I know it. He said I was his *safe place*. Jim always said that about me."

There is a lurch in Mary's voice, and Janet leans in to hold her. Like everyone else, she lives in the dark when it comes to Jim—where he has gone, the circumstances of his disappearance—but anyone with eyes can see the toll it has taken on Mary.

"I just want to know that he's safe and well. Not in trouble or . . . what if he needs me? I couldn't stand—"

"Come on now. Don't run away with yourself. Let's start at the beginning, shall we?" Mary tries to stifle a sob. "How did you know it was him? Did he say it was?" Janet lowers her voice, as if she were speaking to a child in the middle of a night terror, unable to hear anything but the softest of sense.

"It was his voice. And he missed me and he reached out, because he said I had always been there for him, that I was the person who would never give up on him."

"And this was at home?"

"No, at NightLine. So he must know I'm there—or have found out. Maybe he's nearby and he's seen me there or . . . I don't know why, but I know. *Here*." Mary thumps her chest so fiercely that Janet worries it will bruise.

She extracts Mary's hand and holds it in both of hers. "Alright, it's okay." Janet pulls a crumpled tissue out of her pocket and passes it to Mary. "Look, sweetie, I'm not sure what to say for the best. I've always known you have a sure head on you, so I'm not going to start doubting it. We'll talk more tomorrow, but for now I think it's best you go home. I'll sign you off sick—that's no problem. Just get home, put your feet up. Stay in tonight, please?"

Mary chooses to ignore the question and presses her knuckles under her eyes to blot the tears.

"Thanks. And I'm sorry about this."

"No worries—what are friends for, eh?" Janet squeezes Mary's shoulder. "Now, I've got to get back. You slink out, and, er . . . don't mention this to the others, please? I don't want a riot on my hands! Anyone asks, it's a migraine. Nasty bastards, those."

Mary tries her best to minimize the time spent in her own flat. It's closer to a studio, dimension-wise, but it was the most she could afford on her wages. There is a kitchen-cum-living-room, a single bedroom and a bathroom with the world's loudest extractor fan. It suits her needs fine, given that she doesn't have much in the way of personal effects, but every so often she will look at the rental-gray carpet or the chipped, textured wallpaper and wonder how she ended up alone here at forty, when thirty looked so very promising indeed.

Since Jim left, Mary knows that she has herself to blame for her isolation. Mam calls every now and again to check in, but Mary keeps her voice bright and breezy and finds every excuse to avoid her visiting. Each of her three younger brothers, none of whom she is close to, has his own kids now; and even former party girl Moira, her oldest friend from Belfast, is married with children. It is a good excuse for losing touch but, deep down, Mary knows that the occasional text response at her end wouldn't go amiss.

In London, Mary has acquaintances—the NightLine volunteers, Janet—but they are all very much circumstantial. That's not to say there aren't invites here and there, but Mary will turn them down. Most fall in the evening anyway, when everyone knows that she will be at the station. At first they would try and persuade her to miss the odd day. Janet was particularly vociferous—she wanted Mary to abandon the sign altogether.

Initially Mary felt defensive. Who was Janet to dictate how Mary should or shouldn't handle her loss? But she has grown to see that Janet's ardor comes from a place of concern. Once, Mary came close to explaining to her the reasons for her vigil. In her head they have always felt clear, the framework supporting her existence in a world without Jim at her side: *Because I need to be doing something; because I promised that I would always be his safe place, no matter what; because love is nothing if not patient.* But then her throat closed up and she mumbled the same refrain that she always used to bat away the question: *We all have to get by.*

Now Mary slams the front door and heads straight for the bathroom to splash her swollen face. When she looks in the mirror, she is almost unrecognizable from the girl who used to turn heads on a Friday night, the one who stopped Jim in his tracks, stole his heart, and set him on a whole new path in life. He always called Mary beautiful. But it is one thing to tell someone that and quite another to make them feel it. Every time Jim's hands lingered when he fastened the catch at the top of her dress, when he teased out a matted clump at the back of her hair with the comb, she grew a little more confident in her own skin.

The thought of his hands running down the nape of her neck now is enough to make her ache with longing. She stumbles into the corridor to snatch up her bag again but, in the hurry, she knocks the rickety cabinet sideways. The contents spew onto the ground, among them every note that Jim ever wrote to her, in a shoebox with edges flimsy from years of tender handling.

Mary drops to her knees. If ever there was a time to tumble down memory lane, then it is certainly not now. Jim called, and until she knows what that means, she must double her vigilance. In fact she should be at the station already, sign in hand. What if he were to turn up there, just like the old days, expecting to see Mary waiting for him by the ticket gates, at the end of a long shift? The chances now must be higher than ever. Not to be the first person to see him—to hold him—is unthinkable.

She shuffles the fallen mementos together, but the majority are postcards and the laminate slips between her trembling fingers. Jim used to pick one up from wherever he went, in the UK and further afield, writing them on his return while Mary dozed, and then leaving them for her to discover around the house. There are postcards from the Giant's Causeway; every tourist site in London; one from a conference in Singapore and another from Washington, D.C. She turns over the card that lies on top. Brazil, it would seem:

I've seen Copacabana! Sugarloaf Mountain! The conference centers too (as dull as they sound). In short, I've traveled halfway around the world and still there is nowhere I would rather be than with you.

Yours always,
Jim xxx

Mary already knows the words by heart. In the early days, when she couldn't sleep for missing Jim, she would come here and read each postcard in turn as if, strung together, they would form a bedtime story of happier times that could soothe her to sleep. In recent years she has been stricter with herself. She tries not to look in the shoebox more than once a week, and only then when she is worried that she might be forgetting Jim's turn of phrase.

"Where are you, Jim?" she mutters, tracing her finger along his signature.

She does not know how long she has been transfixed on the spot, languishing in the thought of his warm hand in hers, the cowlick from where he had slept, the shy smile and wink when he saw she had found one of his missives. Eventually she brings the card to her lips, then releases it before her hands refuse to let go. Tidying up can wait. She heads out the door, rucksack bouncing with newfound urgency.

For seven years there has been no break in Mary's daily routine. She has prayed for a postcard, a text, an anonymous email—*anything* that suggested Jim was safe. But nothing. A call almost seemed too much to hope for, especially when Jim was never keen on the phone. It didn't help that he was so intensely private too. So to be reaching out, now, in such a stark manner . . . it was a cry for help, wasn't it? It had to be. Mary squeezes her eyes shut for a second and tries to blink away the small spark of hope that last night's call could mean Jim will come home. If you wish for too much, nothing will come true.

She can hear the station before she sees it. In fact when she does catch sight of the bright-blue frontage, it is impossible to make out anything in the entrance hall through the mass of sweaty commuters packed into it. There must be a problem on the line, because no one seems to have advanced through the ticket gates and there are a few rogue arms with camera phones trying to capture a video of the chaos in a bid to explain to their loved ones why they are delayed.

She could do without this, today of all days. Mary can't see through the sea of bodies, so how on earth will anyone see her? If Jim were to arrive . . . well, then at least he will know that she tried, Mary thinks, hurrying across the road. It is time to enter the fray.

Unsurprisingly, no one is happy to be elbowed aside by a broad-shouldered woman muttering her apologies. Mary is used to having a certain amount of vitriol directed at her, for daring to assert herself in the harsh free-for-all that is the station, but today is particularly bad, or so it feels to her—fists and fingers jabbed into her sides, expletives, aggressive shoves. But she will not be cowed, not when there is so much at stake. After significant exertion, she reaches her spot. She wipes the beads of perspiration from her brow and takes a few deep breaths. She is still penned in and, while she wouldn't usually say she is claustrophobic, she is starting to feel that way now.

Suddenly there is a rush. The bodies pressed on either side of Mary surge forward. She twists her neck to try to figure out what is happening. It looks like a train has just opened its doors, but the ticket barriers are still shut. *Eejits!* Why open the doors now, when there is nowhere for this swarm to go? All that it has done is cause a stampede.

Mary tells herself to ignore the chaos and focus on the task in hand. But how? With all these people slamming against her, it is an effort to extract her sign from the bag. She can feel the sweat pooling under her arms and at her hairline. Worse still, her fingers are clammy. They slip against the sign. She can't let it fall. It will be crushed under all the impatient, unfeeling feet.

She digs in with her nails. Better to damage the cardboard than to lose it altogether. Sign blessedly secured, she raises it to its usual position with trembling biceps. Even to hold it, she has to keep her arms pinned to her sides. Still, people think she is taking up too much space. "Jesus!" one mutters. "Not the time, yeah?" a suit shouts, close enough to Mary's face that she can feel the smack of his saliva on her flushed cheek. "MOVE OUT OF THE WAY."

Part of her wants to do just that—to move right out of the way, back to her flat, away from this horrible tornado of a crowd. It's the crush, the heat, the noise. It's too much. All of it is too much. But then the thought of Jim, last night, on the phone comes to her again. *You've never given up on me.* Well, she isn't about to start now. As Mary straightens her spine, an elbow catches her right in her rib, jolting her from anguish into anger. She removes one hand from the sign and uses the other to snatch the offending arm.

"For the love of God, will you give me some fecking space to breathe!"

Mary's voice comes out at triple her normal volume, silencing the concourse. But she does not realize that, because her ears are ringing and the room is spinning, the pinpricks of white light that flash before her eyes interspersed with the beady red eye of a phone camera, catching it all on film.

Just like that, Mary O'Connor becomes an internet sensation.

4

2005

Mary swung her bare legs to one side and brushed a thread from her denim skirt, a casualty of an unsuccessful morning's work on her latest fabric map. On the right of the bench, a four-pack of lager and a sharing packet of crisps. Was it . . . a bit laddish for a second date? There was a fine line between looking casual and dampening the romance by accident. But Mary had panicked in the supermarket—which wine needed a corkscrew?—and she had snatched the first thing in sight. She was stuck with her choices now; James was in a taxi en route from City Airport and she didn't have time to rush back and try to return her refreshments.

Second date—that was the real pressure point, and Mary's nerves could well feel it. The morning after the night before, two weekends ago, had had its own challenges to navigate (no change of clothes, nothing to freshen up with) but then everything had felt so natural with James before he had rushed off to catch his flight. He took her number, kissed her goodbye, and then, before she had even exited his hotel room, there was a text from him. I meant it—I want to see you, soon. Jx

A day later he called and, without dallying too long in pleasantries, told her that he had booked a flight over to Belfast again, a week from the coming Saturday: *I said soon, didn't I—if you're free? Don't make a man beg, Mary. There's so much more of you to unravel.* Mary felt her whole body tingle at the sound of his voice. She told herself to get a grip. Nothing to put a man off like an inability to cop ahold of your emotions. *I should be free,* she replied, before promptly hanging up and screaming into a pillow.

Moira was happy enough to cover her shifts, although she was like a bloodhound, sniffing out the excitement in Mary's tone. She tried to play it down, but still Moira looked fit to fall over in her shock—*You, with a fella? Are you feeling alright?* As if Mary needed any further reminder that she had skipped her footloose and fancy-free years and fast-forwarded straight to middle age.

Underneath the thrill there was a sense of guilt too. Ever since Da had stopped working five years ago, when they found the tumors in his lung, Mary had felt dreadful being away from the house for as much as an hour. What if something were to happen and she wasn't around? It didn't bear thinking about. But James would be here for only two days, and sure she wasn't going to be far away from home. Mary would never forget that she had duties—as a daughter, as a sister, as a friend—but for the first time in a long time she was starting to hope she might also find a life outside them.

"Now there's a sight for sore eyes."

Mary's heart lurched. She hadn't thought he'd get here so soon, but now here he most definitely was—as handsome as she remembered him under the summer sun, a leather holdall thrown over one shoulder. He dropped it at her feet and Mary stood to kiss him. This was it—their one chance to find out if the spark was still there.

James leaned in, easy as anything. His bottom lip was chapped, and Mary found her own settling against its grooves. She ran a hand through the curls at the nape of his neck and drew him in deeper, caught up in the smell of him—smoky, with a hint of pine. It was intoxicating. His tongue brushed against hers. Mary could feel the chemistry between them lifting her out of the park, out of herself, in a way that was eminently unsuitable to a public space.

She pulled away. "So, welcome to Victoria Park."

James wasn't taking in any of their surroundings; rather, he sat at the far end of the bench, one arm hooked over the backrest so that he could face Mary. "You look gorgeous."

"Oh, yes, er . . . thanks." Mary had never taken a compliment well. She had chosen an emerald-green silk blouse with short sleeves and a ruffle around the neck, as feminine an item as she could bring herself to own. The neckline was too risqué for work but it seemed to have found an appreciative audience at last. "How have you been?"

"Busy. The usual. Every ear, nose, and throat complaint under the sun."

Mary opened her mouth to ask more about his professional life but James cut her off.

"Work is the last thing anyone wants to talk about." He raised an eyebrow and Mary prayed that he didn't want to discuss her performance last weekend. "Tell me what you want to be doing instead."

"Pardon?"

"The end goal. The one you dream about when you're working the real job. I always find that very telling."

"I don't know."

No one had ever asked Mary that question before. It was as if James could see straight to the heart of her; she had felt it over the spilled chicken supper and she felt it even more keenly now. Maybe he knew, contrary to what she had just said, that she had an answer too. But she had never mentioned it to anyone. It had never seemed relevant and it wasn't important, what with everything else going on. But for the first time since Da's diagnosis, Mary felt like she was able to look to the future, in James's presence. He asked because he wanted to know; her vision mattered to him.

"You do. Come on? What's that blush, otherwise?"

Mary took a deep breath and turned, slightly, so that she could only catch sight of his response in her periphery.

"I'd like to be an artist. A fabric artist. I make these maps." Mary wiggled her phone out of her pocket. She opened up the photo reel and found the gallery of images she had never shown to anyone. Now that she had said it, she felt she needed something to prove this was more than a whim.

For a minute or two James didn't say anything. Mary watched as he clicked through the fuzzy collection of images. Without a proper camera, she had to make do with the low-grade resolution of her Samsung.

"Those are amazing, Mary. Do you take commissions?"

"Not really. I've just done them as gifts. For family—no one else."

"You could make money from those. A lot of money, selling them to the right people. Set up your own business, the recommendations come pouring in . . ."

"Hey, hey, I think you are getting a bit carried away here."

"I won't push it—yet. Scoot over."

"What?"

"Over here. Now I've got ahold of your phone, you'll be wanting a picture of us both, I'm sure. Print it out, stick it up on your wall . . ."

"In a border of hearts, no doubt."

James smirked. "Get over here." He wrapped his arm round her waist and the camera flashed. Mary shuffled away before she got too used to the proximity of his hand on her knicker line.

"Gone so soon?" His face was still less than six inches from hers.

"Before you make a scene."

James licked his bottom lip. "Spoilsport." He kissed her cheek instead. "So maps are the big plan—but what brings you to the hotel?"

"I've always been there." Mary attempted a shrug that looked more absentminded than resigned. It wasn't inspirational, was it? A job organizing other people's events and clearing them up afterward. "I started part-time when I was sixteen. Full-time once I left school."

"A lifer?"

"Close enough."

Mary had expected to feel judged. After all, James came from money. You didn't need a degree to work that out. In the grand scheme of things, maybe he wasn't even that well off. But it was still enough to feel like he came from a whole different world. That he spoke a whole different language. To Mary, it looked like not worrying if your salary would last until the end of the month or whether one unexpected expense would send the whole family under. She had wanted to resent James for his relative fortune—the way it bought him so much more freedom—but somehow she couldn't.

"My dad's sick," she added.

"I'm sorry."

She had no idea why she had blurted that out. It sounded so odd, out in the air, a prognosis that cast its horrible spores among the dandelion clocks.

"No, I'm sorry. I don't know why I said that. I don't want you to pity me."

"Don't worry—I don't. You're far too hardy for that."

Mary lifted the corners of her mouth in a small half smile.

"You can tell me about it, if you want. But if you don't, then we can talk about something else. Like the map you are going to make for me."

That was all it took for Mary to unburden herself. She liked that James didn't interrupt, that he let her get upset and say the things that she had been so scared of admitting to herself—how she loved her family, but sometimes felt that she was trapped at home with three boisterous brothers while the best years of her life passed her by. How she couldn't stand to be without Da, but she didn't know how long Mam could stand the strain of the caring. When she cried, Mary didn't worry about the face she made or the way her makeup ran sideways. She took the tissue James offered and the space he opened up for her to speak.

"He's lucky to have you. They all are."

A group of teenagers barreled past, faces obscured by hoodies, and, in one case, the sort of hi-fi system Mary hadn't seen in years, not outside the secondhand stores in Newtownards. When the racket had died down, Mary was back on an even keel. She offered James another lager, his third. It saved her drinking them and making a fool of herself.

"So, what about you—what's the bigger plan? Now you've seen mine," she asked.

"I'm afraid I don't have one."

"Bullshit!"

James looked up with palpable surprise. This sort of feistiness had always been a part of Mary but she spent most of her life suppressing it, trying to keep everyone else happy. James had a knack for unearthing the sharper sides of her personality. She was enjoying having an outlet for them.

"Honest, officer! I'm not kidding you there. Nothing good at least, not like your maps."

"Nothing at all?"

"I don't want to be doing what I'm doing—I know that much."

"Medicine?"

James nodded. "It's not easy. But it is what it is. I like helping people. But most of the time, it's not that. It's cock-ups and paperwork and pain. Still, I can't see myself giving it up. I'm thirty-six, it's not the time for a career change."

Mary had wondered how old James was, but hadn't found a polite way to extract that information yet. So, he had nine years on her—not that it was a problem. She had always felt and acted older than she was. Did that mean James was looking for an end to his bachelor days or should she be worried about why he was still on the market? Better not to ask at this juncture, she decided.

"You don't like London?"

"Never have," James replied with a shrug. "But it's where my parents are. And now the job. If I could, I'd be out there, in the fields somewhere—a couple of big dogs and some sheep, I'd be happy. Do you reckon I'd suit it?" Before Mary had a chance to answer, James adopted what she guessed was an attempt at a West Country accent. "Farmer Jim."

The idea was so farcical—so incongruous of the man sitting in front of her, in his pressed shirt and jacket—that Mary couldn't help but laugh. Her head fell forward, brushing inappropriately close to his crotch.

"Steady on—it's that mad an image, huh?"

"Pretty much, *Jim*."

Mary leaned in, eager to kiss him again. She had never known that sharing vulnerabilities could kindle a spark—not to this extent. It suddenly struck her that there was one place she needed to show him, and she needed to show him it now, while this intimacy was still so fresh.

"Let's get out of here."

It wasn't dark yet but there was a chill in the August air. By the time they reached the park gates, Mary was shivering. She knew she should have worn something with more substance than her gauzy blouse, especially if they were about to head down to the Lagan.

"Are you warm enough?" Jim had one arm wrapped around Mary's biceps, no doubt feeling her goose pimples. "Stop a sec." He pulled her to a halt. "You're freezing—you should have said." He untied the arms of his jacket, which were crossed over his shoulders. He stepped behind Mary and waited for her to extend her arms into it. There was something square and hard in the breast pocket—a hip flask or maybe a box of some kind. "Suits you."

Mary led them away from the Waterfront Hall with its throngs of concertgoers, down toward where the new developments petered out and the silence of the riverside settled. When they were far enough away from the rest of the city, she wove herself through the metal barriers that kept drunk pedestrians from falling into the water. A small cross that had been hatched into the pavement with a shard of flint glowed in the pink dusk light—the work of many hours that she had spent alone there.

It was a place Mary had never shared. Not with Moira or Mam. Certainly not with Dean during the ill-fated course of their eighteen-month relationship. He would have drowned out the sound of the waves with all his incessant chatting—a seagull in a pair of Pumas and whatever hoody he'd found knocked off the back of a lorry before his shift at the petrol station. No. This was somewhere just for her. It was somewhere she came to think, to dream, when the world got too much with its needs and its insistences and the ties that bind.

Mary was determined not to over-think the significance of inviting Jim here. All she knew was that it felt right and, since the moment she met him, trusting her instincts had paid dividends.

She sat with her back to the city, ankles dangling over the six-foot drop below, and beckoned Jim to do the same. He shuffled next to Mary so that their shoulders touched. The lightest of pressure, but still it thumped through her. She turned to kiss him, and what was meant to land as a peck grew deeper and more insistent until she had to force herself to pull away before they caused a public-order offense. Who knew how much time had passed, who had seen them like this? She'd be mortified if she was caught hot under the collar by a neighbor or a colleague.

He wrapped an arm around Mary's waist. "Nice spot you got here. And the company's not too shabby, either."

"You big flirt."

"Only with you."

"I doubt that."

"Why?"

He'd got her there. "Course you're like this with the other girls."

"Which other girls?"

"The ones you must have in London."

"Ah—yes. I hope someone is feeding them this weekend."

"You know what I mean."

"And I know there is only one woman I have eyes for."

Mary's breath caught in her throat.

"So, when are you coming over, then?" Jim asked.

"To London?"

"Where else?"

Mary avoided his eye. What was there to say? She couldn't afford it, even if she saved for months. And besides, the family needed that money. She was hit by the sudden realization that this had all been a dream—a silly, happy dream. A two-week dream that had enriched her and would eventually leave her, like every other guest who came to the hotel or anyone who took root in her heart.

"A fortnight, then. I'll book."

Mary turned and opened her mouth to object.

Jim kissed her to the sound of those same objections floating ever further out to sea.

5

2005

Neither Mary nor Jim woke up until the cleaning staff knocked the next morning. Mary took in the oak desk in the corner of the room, the holdall thrown across it, then glanced down at the starched white sheet pulled over her chest. This wasn't her bed at home, that was for sure. Duvet covers with pile that thick were hard to come by in the O'Connor home. *The Stormont Hotel. Their second date.*

Mary shouldn't have been surprised they had ended up back here. The two of them had been like teenagers at her spot by the Lagan. He'd had his hand up the front of her top and she'd had hers . . . well, that was not for thinking about on a Sunday morning, the Lord's day no less. Mary couldn't believe that it had been her, acting so, so . . . *wanton* in a public place. Much as she might have scorned another person making such a scene, she couldn't seem to get ahold of herself around Jim. She had known him barely three weeks, met him twice, and already she could feel everything she thought she knew about herself—about the world—shifting on its axis.

There was another knock, louder this time.

"Shit!"

"What's going on?" Jim was lying on his front and he raised his head an inch from where it was squashed against the pillow.

One more knock, accompanied by a cough and a sentence Mary couldn't for the life of her make out. She rooted around for her shirt, his shirt—anything to recover a semblance of dignity and avoid her colleagues getting more from the room's servicing than they had bargained for. There was nothing nearby. She caught sight of her lacy bra dangling down from the curtain rod—too high even for her to reach. What the hell had they been up to? She gave up and crawled into bed, pulling the sheet right up over her head.

"Leave it, leave it." Jim stumbled out of bed and shoved his legs into the trousers thrown over the desk chair. He cracked the door open. "How much for late checkout?"

Mary couldn't hear the answer but she knew it was far too much extra to be paying. That was how they made the real money here, off people too lazy to stick to the rules. She couldn't remember ever having lain in this long.

"I'll settle up downstairs then. Thank you both, you've been very helpful."

She could only imagine the sort of smile he was shooting them and the effect it must have had.

Jim shut the door and made his way back to bed. He peeled the sheet down off Mary and placed one hand on the inside of her thigh.

"Embarrassed of me, are you?"

"Embarrassed we're still in bed more like." Mary tried to ignore the finger tracing up her skin. How was James so energetic at this time of day, anyway? There had been the lagers at the park, another couple from the chippy where they had got their supper. She wished that she too functioned as well on a hangover. "It's expensive—the late-checkout thing."

"It's on me."

"It always is."

"Is that a complaint? I take those very seriously, you know." Jim pursed his lips in an expression of mock solemnity.

Mary hoped he could manage something better for his actual patients.

"I want to contribute. For this . . . the room."

With the missed shifts, things would be even tighter than usual, but she would be able to figure something out. She could dredge the bottom of the overdraft, if she had to.

"Okay. I appreciate that. But, just this once, let me? And our next weekend in London. And maybe a few other bits . . ." Jim began kissing from the broken, frizzing strands on her hairline, down onto her neck and chest.

It didn't sit quite right with Mary or, rather, it wouldn't have usually sat well with her at all. But somehow, with Jim, there was never that edge of obligation. Not from him, and not from her, either.

Jim ran his tongue around her nipple and grazed it with his teeth. Perhaps late checkout was value for money after all.

A quick text to Moira confirmed what interesting activities a Sunday morning in Belfast had to offer. Judging by the relish with which James had polished off fish and chips last night, Mary had him pegged as a foodie. Once he'd checked out, she decided they could fill the remaining hours before his flight home at St. George's Market.

Last night had left Jim with the appetite of a horse. He ordered from almost all the stalls that sold food—more than he could hold, even in those huge hands of his—offering Mary a bite of each bun and box and bap from his fork, until she wondered whether he might be one of those men Moira read about in the magazines, who get a kick out of feeding up women. Mary reckoned she could live with that.

Crammed side by side on one long picnic bench, hemmed in by locals chowing down their brunch, Mary marveled at the fact that sitting here with Jim, in a spot she had visited a hundred times before, she felt as if she was seeing it all through a new lens. The roof-tiles and cobbles came into fresh focus. The heckling of the sellers played out in high definition. By contrast, every other aspect of Jim's company left Mary feeling drunk, giddy in the certainty that the feeling was mutual. For the first time ever, she felt as if she was letting go of her anxieties and expectations and obligations. For once, she was living.

Walking off all the food they'd eaten, they discussed both everything and nothing. Mary had an inexhaustible stream of questions for Jim but she didn't manage to ask so much as a tenth of them; Jim was focused on asking Mary about herself and, more than that, hanging on to the most mundane of her answers. Mary had never thought herself special in any way. Until the moment Jim walked into her life. Interest like his couldn't be feigned. As he saw it, she had grit and gumption and fire. The longer she spent in his presence, the more she started to see those qualities in herself too.

They wandered down to the old shipyard, now partly obstructed by the scaffolding of new developments. Sunlight refracted off the hulls, making them both squint.

"The *Titanic* was built somewhere around here," Mary offered.

"Somewhere around here . . ." Jim pulled Mary in so that her back pressed against his chest. She had to stop herself from envisaging what it looked like, under another of those strange collarless shirts of his. It was firm enough to double up for the ironing. "That's very specific." He brought the thumb and index finger on both hands together into a square, forming a viewfinder that he slotted over Mary's left eye. "Any further improvement on *somewhere* around here?"

"Away with you!" Mary wriggled.

She snuck a peek at his watch on the arm that was pressed around her shoulders. He would have to go soon. Her heart hurt just thinking about it.

"Million-dollar question, though." Jim kissed beneath her ear and, in the moment of impact, Mary knew she would give up a check for that much if it could buy another day together, in the sun, right as they were. "Would you trust me to offer you the last spot on the lifeboat?"

Yes, Mary thought. *Yes, yes, yes.* She'd stake her life on it. But she couldn't be running away from herself. They were two dates in; three, if you counted out the separate days. The man still had to work for this.

"I'll have to see about that," she replied. "You may yet turn out to be a wrong'un."

6

2018

"WILL YOU GIVE ME SOME FECKING SPACE TO BREATHE!"

The words spit out across the heaving station concourse. Everyone stops. Everyone stares. It is as if the hundreds of irate commuters have drawn a collective intake of breath and are waiting for one woman's command to exhale again. Whoever she is, there is no doubt that she has the crowd under her spell.

It takes a lot to bring Alice Keaton out of herself but this has certainly done the trick. She rises onto her tiptoes to try to make out the source of the sound. It was a woman's voice, with an Irish lilt to it. Fire too. Where did that come from? Anger? Hurt? From experience, Alice would wager both. To respond like that, in such a public space . . . she must have been desperate. Alice can't remember the last time she heard someone *speak* on the London transport network, let alone shout.

It's no use. At just five feet, Alice still can't see anything beyond the crumpled shirt of the man in front of her. The voice—the woman—remains an enigma. Before Alice even has the soles of her ballet pumps back on the ground, the impatient passengers press forward. She is carried with them in the direction of the ticket gates, now finally open, and the waiting train beyond.

Alice flings her right arm out, like a rogue cyclist's attempt at signaling. She isn't a commuter, like the rest of them; she is here on business! She is already late for her appointment with the station manager. The sooner she can meet Neil, the sooner she can leave and spend her evening in the way a self-respecting twenty-six-year-old should (faceup on the sofa, large glass of wine in hand), not in pursuit of yet another inane article.

Neil Bloom is the longest-serving member of the Underground network and, as such, the chosen interviewee for this month's "My Ealing" column, which fills the back page of the *Bugle*. As a junior reporter there, it is Alice's job to source, collate, and write up his take on such scintillating topics as "favorite spot for a dog walk" and "best coffee in the borough."

Alice had joined the *Ealing Bugle* fresh out of university. They'd offered her a position after a month's internship and she had jumped at the opportunity. Everyone knew that entry-level jobs in journalism were akin to giant pandas in the wild—increasingly rare. But it didn't take long for the novelty to wear off. The most exciting piece in her current portfolio covers infighting at the local Women's Institute. As she shuffled that gem to the top of her CV a few weeks back, she was tormented with a fresh wave of self-doubt. If her professional highlight of the past five years involved investigating a septuagenarian's jam-recipe theft, then something had gone wrong with her life plan. Make that *very* wrong.

But still, journalism is the only career Alice has ever wanted to pursue, that goal the one good thing to come from her teenage years, she thinks, with a kick of sadness. To fourteen-year-old Alice, journalists had the tools and means and tenacity to hunt down the truth. Where the authorities couldn't or wouldn't help, reporters stepped in. Where unanswered questions trailed into oblivion, writers could pick up the strands—and people—left behind. Alice dreamt of writing that mattered. She wanted her career to be meaningful. So then, how the hell has she ended up here, en route to an interview with the world's most lackluster local celeb?

Enough of the crowd has now thinned for Alice to get a proper view of the station floor. Bodies slam in and out of the ticket gates, oblivious to the scene just minutes before. *Will you give me some fecking space to breathe!* The words are still ringing in Alice's ears and she shakes her head to try and buy some mental clarity before meeting Neil. To the right, she clocks the acrylic screen that shields the control room of Ealing Broadway. Neil should be in there right now.

So should she. If it wasn't for what, or rather *who,* Alice spots on the far side of the station.

A lone woman is swaying on her feet, like the last bowling pin left standing at the alley.

There is absolutely no doubt in Alice's mind that this is *her,* the woman who only minutes earlier had the station in her thrall.

She is midthirties, perhaps—tall and broad, dressed in black nylon trousers and a burgundy cardigan that clashes with her yellow polo shirt. So far, so ordinary. Until Alice glances at her face, that is. Now *that* is a contrast. The woman is stunning: there are no two ways about it. She has wide green eyes and cheekbones straight from the pages of a magazine, lips that look as if they have been permanently stained.

Alice's gaze drops to the woman's hands and she reads the sign: *COME HOME JIM.* Who knew that three little words could be suffused with such yearning, such pain? Something near Alice's breastbone seems to crack. All thoughts of the interview drop from her mind. She has to say something to this woman. She just *has* to. It's empathy, yes. But this also goes beyond extending basic human kindness. It is familiarity. Alice knows how it feels to be abandoned.

"Hi there. I wanted to check you were okay?"

The woman lowers her sign and turns toward the voice. There is nearly a foot's difference between them in height, and Alice imagines that her scalp is being subjected to particular scrutiny. She smooths her hands over her blunt chin-length bob, then runs a finger under each eye to check that her mascara hasn't slid halfway down her cheeks.

"Er . . . yes. Well, no. I don't know what came over me."

"Maybe we should get you a seat . . . a drink?"

Alice looks over at the control office. There is no sign of life inside. That decides it—screw the interview! She'll email Neil and apologize tomorrow. Say a personal situation came up. It doesn't feel altogether far from the truth.

"No, honestly, you get on. I'm fine here." The woman tries to hold the placard up a centimeter or two higher, with conviction, but her biceps are quivering.

"I'd like to."

Alice can't leave her in this state. She could keel over, and clearly no one else around here would care.

"I ought to . . ."

The woman trails off, seemingly lacking the energy to finish her own sentence. Call Alice forthright (it wouldn't be the first time), but this is the proof she needs to push this stranger to abandon her position. She needs to sit down. That much is obvious.

"I insist." Alice watches as the woman's grimace wavers. "You need to take care of yourself, or I'll have to do it for you!" The last words were meant as a joke, but instead they seem to cause a flash of pain to cross the woman's face. Alice places a palm on her forearm. "Please, for me?"

"Okay," she says finally, with a sigh. "But it will have to be quick."

Alice hadn't thought much beyond extending the invite. The cafés she knows are closed by now and the lady with the sign doesn't seem the type to hit the bottle. In contrast to her outburst, she is well put together. She is already pinning back a few escaped hairs that mar an otherwise flawless face. Alice can't believe it took a scene like that to get the woman noticed, but then again, people can get so absorbed by their own thoughts.

Just like Alice now, too busy scrutinizing her companion to realize that she has walked them to the nearest pub. She will have to hope hard liquor doesn't offend the woman's sensibilities.

"Here, what can I get you?" Alice asks.

It isn't too busy, it being midweek, but there are still a few glances in their direction from the regulars ferreted away in the corner nooks or bunched on barstools.

"A Coke for me, please." The woman fishes out a fiver, which Alice promptly refuses. "I'll go get us a seat, then. There might be something outside."

When Alice has sourced their drinks, she follows her companion through to the garden. It is sweltering and she slips the glasses of iced water off the tray first. "I'm Alice, by the way."

"Mary."

"Well, it's nice to meet you, Mary. I'm sorry it's, er . . . not in better circumstances."

Alice wonders if Mary will take the bait and explain herself. No such luck. She swirls her straw and nods toward the drink. "Thanks for this."

"Not at all. Thirsty work, what you are doing."

This time a more direct approach. Alice can't see the sign and imagines Mary must have stashed it away in her absence. There is silence while Mary sips her drink and focuses on the wood grain of the bench. Still nothing. She looks like a tough nut to crack, but Alice's nosiness is starting to get the better of her.

"What happened back there?"

Mary is still fixated on the table. "It's been a difficult week," she says, eventually.

"Do you want to talk about it?"

Alice does not expect a response to that. She knows how hard it can be to open up, even at the best of times and to the kindest of people. It doesn't look like she will be able to penetrate Mary's fortress of intense privacy, however much she wants to let her know that she is not alone.

Alice downs half her drink, expecting that they will be on the move soon. When Mary answers her, Alice is so surprised that she coughs up her slurp of gin.

"I had a call last night. From Jim."

It takes a second or two for Alice to cotton on. She stares at Mary, who is now looking straight at her. She looks terrified. Alice gets the impression that the words slipped out before Mary could stop them.

"No. No, I didn't mean that. Ignore me, I don't know what I was thinking . . . I'm not the sort of person to go blurting out my problems to strangers. I'm just tired and unsettled and it was probably your kindness that set me off. I know you only asked to be polite and I'm grateful for that, really, but you know what"—Mary reaches down for her bag—"I ought to be off."

"Jim from the sign?"

The sound of Jim's name, said with such tenderness, stops Mary in her tracks. She nods, tears smarting in her eyes.

"Hey, come on. What's the rush?" Alice flaps at Mary to sit down again. "You can talk to me. A problem shared is a problem halved . . . or, well, if it's not halved, then you can get it off your chest. It might make you feel better. And don't worry about me. I've got nowhere else to be."

"Jim called," Mary says, quietly, as if testing out her confidence.

The longer she spends with Mary, the more Alice wants to get to the heart of her. She's compelling. One of a kind.

"I mean I think it was him. He sounded so afraid. Or . . . I don't know. Maybe ashamed to be reaching out? It was so hard to tell, because we weren't speaking for long before the line cut out."

"Did you ring him back?"

"No, I couldn't. He didn't call me on my mobile, you see. It was at the call center where I volunteer. NightLine. It's this crisis call place—a local one. But it's all anonymous, so you can't trace calls or set a redial or . . ." Mary's words are tumbling over one another, a stampede of garbled word endings and hurried breaths.

"Here, it's okay. Have some of this." Alice uses one of her immaculately painted nails to tap the straw in Mary's drink with enough pressure to turn it back round to face her. Mary takes a gulp that empties half the glass.

"Sorry."

"Not at all."

"It's odd, isn't it?" Mary asks.

"It sounds it."

"Hmm . . ." Mary begins to pick at the shredded flesh on the side of her left thumb. Alice tries not to recoil at the sight of the skin there, raw and flecked with splinters of crimson. That is years' worth of damage. It will take as much time to heal.

"So, who is Jim? If you don't mind my asking."

"A man I know. Knew, I suppose. He disappeared."

Disappeared. Alice's heart leaps into her throat.

"It was seven years ago," Mary adds, in a whisper.

"I'm sorry. Can I . . . can I ask what happened?"

"I wish I knew. No one knows where he is. I don't. His parents don't. Not that I have any contact with Richard and Juliette anymore . . ." Mary swirls her straw around the melting nuggets of ice in her glass. "The police closed the case. That's why I started going to the station, with the sign. I had to be doing something." She screws her eyes shut. The next words seem to gut her. "It gave me a reason to go on."

Alice reaches across the table and places one hand over Mary's clenched fist. "I'm so sorry, Mary. Genuinely."

Mary still cannot meet Alice's eyes. She does, however, manage to summon some semblance of a smile, the flesh of her lips turned in as if to trap inside all the emotion the smile should convey. Alice imagines the fear and the exhaustion tumbling back into Mary's tightened chest, rounding her shoulders that fraction further down. Something has hollowed Mary out—something that runs deeper than pain alone. Alice is too scared to ask anything more, lest she loses herself in it too.

"So, tell me more about this call place—NightLine?"

Mary's eyes lighten a fraction.

"I started going a few months after Jim disappeared. I suppose that I needed to do something useful. Help people who were struggling. Maybe work on my own listening skills."

Alice cannot fathom how, in the depths of her own nightmare, Mary had it in her to reach out and try to catch others. "It's impressive. I should be doing something like that."

"We're always looking for people. If you google it, you'll see there's a website. It's not much to look at, but it does the job." Mary pauses, conscious of the fact that she has talked exclusively about herself. "What do you do anyway? Outside of this?"

"Er . . ." Alice's mouth dries up. She can't tell Mary what she does for a living, can she? No one trusts a journalist. And Mary is beginning to warm to her. The last thing Alice wants is for Mary to feel that she has walked into an ambush, on the pretense of kindness.

"It's online stuff. Digital. Content creation mainly."

The words appear to have gone right over Mary's head. Is that strictly a lie, Alice wonders? If so, then it is just a small one.

If only Alice knew how it was about to snowball.

7

2005

"Rise and shine." Jim set two mugs on the bedside table next to Mary. She dunked her little finger into the nearest one and sucked up the frothy milk coating. She had concluded that it must be witchcraft, the way Jim managed to make the drinks like a professional barista. "Back in a sec, there's something on the stove."

Once he had bounded out of the room, Mary took a moment to soak in her surroundings. She had never been in a flat like Jim's—never been in a flat, full stop—and it had taken a while to get used to the glass and the metal and the scrupulous lack of clutter. To Mary, it seemed a tad impersonal but then again, if you had no one to share it with . . . Plus, the local area made up for the lack of character inside. From the little she'd seen of Ealing, it had plenty of cozy cafés and pubs, all packed out with young couples with disposable income to burn.

Mary could see herself living here, picking out a few soft furnishings in the secondhand stores or in the fancy boutique she'd spotted further down the High Street, if Jim was the sort to turn his nose up at a used cushion set. *Stop it, stop it, stop it.* She was running away with herself, again. This was only their third weekend together, her first in London, and while things couldn't have gone any better, she could still scarcely believe how keen Jim was on her.

Keeping her inherent cautiousness in check was far from easy. There had been a moment, after Jim had sent through the booking confirmation for her flights, when he'd had to call her to get her middle name and check the spelling of her surname. *Was it one* n *or two?* The minute Mary hung up, she flew into a tailspin of panic. Was she mad to be flying over for a third date? Worse yet, was she mad to be falling in love with a man who lived five hundred miles away?

Fortunately, when her own confidence wobbled, she had buoys other than Jim. Mary had been so worried about how Mam would take the news of a man in her life, especially one tempting her across the sea when she ought to be at work. But when she finally stammered out the words, Mam was so thrilled for her that Mary couldn't wrestle herself out of a bear hug. *I'm so pleased for you,* Mam kept saying. *You deserve to put yourself first for once.* Mary had never realized her single status had been such a cause for Mam's concern.

And then there was Moira—good enough to cover a third weekend shift, but only in exchange for answers to her most prurient questions about Jim. Mary was saved from the shame of it all when Jenny, their manager at the hotel, interrupted Moira brandishing three different lengths of paper tube. That ended Moira's investigation, temporarily at least. Just before Mary had dashed off to catch her Friday-night flight, Moira had chucked a sealed plastic bag in her direction: another balconette bra.

Now, though, there was absolutely no doubt in Mary's mind that the logistics, and the hassle and the anxiety, had all been worth it. Never in a million years would she have imagined that she would be sitting waiting for a handsome Englishman to deliver her breakfast in bed. She could get used to it. That and the rest of Jim's ministrations. Jim had bought toiletries for her that didn't smell like a bloke's and picked up a box of Barry's so she could have a proper Irish cuppa. Even when they popped out to buy milk for it from the shop round the corner, Jim took the side of the walkway nearest the main road that bisected Ealing. Gallantry indeed.

It was still early days, Mary reminded herself, and things could change. But she prayed desperately they wouldn't.

Jim stuck his head around the door. "Hungry?" He squeezed the rest of his body back into the room, his focus honed on a plate balanced on a velvet cushion. "Sorry, I don't own a tray."

"Unbelievable." Mary pretended to swat away whatever he was delivering, but her stomach growled. "Something smells grand."

"You flatter me." Jim placed the cushion on Mary's lap. "Homemade. The bread—not the eggs. Still a little way to go until I get my farm."

"And a rose?"

"Nicked it from next door when we went past yesterday and you were busy daydreaming about me."

Mary shot Jim her most withering look. "Flowers are for apologies, and apologies are for men who have done something wrong."

"Ah—that's my girl. The great romantic herself."

Mary took a bite. The eggs were 50 percent butter. She wiggled a little further under the duvet. "Confess."

"It's a small thing that slipped my mind."

"I was joking." Her hand tensed around the fork. She had no idea what was going to come out of his mouth next. She'd asked the first time they met, but what if he'd lied? Was he dating someone else? That was it—he had a girlfriend. A wife. Jaysus, Mary, and Joseph, what if he had a *wife*?

"We've got people to see later."

"Oh. Who?"

"My parents."

Mary's mouth dropped open, giving a good view of the seeds from his sourdough lodged down the side of her molars.

"It'll be great. I want them to meet you. It's a quick lunch. Then it'll be back to us two, before you head home . . ."

Was this all happening a bit too soon? Needless to say, they'd ask about how the two of them had met—what they saw in each other. Mary felt her tummy muscles cramp at the mere thought of that pressure.

Jim continued, blissfully unaware, "They'll love you. You just need to be yourself." When Mary didn't respond, he slid the plate and pillow to the side and forced his face into her eyeline. "I'm sorry I didn't tell you before. I didn't want to freak you out, but seems like I've managed that anyway. If you want, I can cancel? I'll say I'm sick."

Mary mulled over the offer. But if she pulled out on this, what sort of message did that give about her faith in the two of them—in herself too? "No. I'll go." Jim's face lit up. "You can finish this while I have a shower." She gestured at the nibbled food, going cold already.

"Or I could join you?" Jim scooted close enough that Mary could feel the heat radiating off him. He tugged off his T-shirt and slid his hand under hers. "I appreciate that I have a lot of making up to do."

Mary hadn't been anywhere like the restaurant Jim had chosen for lunch with his parents, with its exposed brick walls and fat metal tubing where the picture rail should be. Suffice to say, she wouldn't care to come again. The water jug had half a plant in it. Jim laughed as Mary pushed the stem to one side to try and serve herself.

"Over here!" he hollered.

Mary stood and smoothed the skirt of her dress against her thighs. If she had known she was meeting his parents, she would have brought something nicer, certainly something longer. She didn't want them thinking she was a hussy, that she wasn't good enough for their son.

"Hi, it's nice to meet you."

"Mum, Dad, this is Mary."

"Richard." Jim's father stepped forward, pumping her outstretched hand and giving what she was sure Da would confirm as a "strong hand-shake." When he was done, Mary kept her arm outstretched and twisted at the waist to extend it to his mother as well. She was rummaging in her handbag, oblivious.

"Mum," Jim reached out to touch her on the wrist. She looked up, slowly, as if startled from an unexpected nap.

"Sorry, sorry, it's a pleasure." She dodged Mary's hand—by now hanging like a plastic bag from a tree—and kissed her on the cheek. "I'm Juliette, and I know that James will have told you many terrible things about me already." When she smiled, it was too weak to look convincing.

As they sat down to consult the menus and Jim fielded some questions about the clinic, Mary tried to align both of his parents with the feeble array of half-baked ideas that she didn't feel were sufficiently developed to constitute expectations. Juliette was slight, neat, and quiet, a little wisp of a woman in comparison to her larger-than-life husband.

"Anyway, son, nice to see you with a girlfriend for once. We were starting to think there was something wrong." Mary's eyes must have bulged because Richard clapped a conciliatory hand on her shoulder. "Joking, joking! It's been a while since he's brought anyone home. When was the last time, Juliette? Our James was twenty, wasn't he? How is Evie these days anyway? Up to brilliant things, no doubt. She was always such a go-getter." Mary noticed Richard's eyes light up. "Do you hear from her much?"

Mary looked down at her napkin. She knew Jim didn't have much by the way of recent or serious exes (something of an oddity in itself, she thought, given what a catch he was) but she could envisage the sort they were. Blond and leggy, probably bred like racehorses.

"No, not at all. That was such a long time ago now, things were . . . different. Anyway, there's just the one woman for me now." He reached over and squeezed Mary's curled hand.

"Good to hear it," Richard said, topping up the wine glasses. Jim was already one ahead of the rest of them. "And, Mary, Jim says you are in the hotel business? Is that his way of saying a receptionist?" His laugh boomed around the room. No one else joined him.

"Dad!" Mary could see Jim about to berate him and she wished he wouldn't bother; somehow tackling that sort of comment only ever seemed to entrench the snobbery. Didn't rich people want that anyway: to think you could get in on their jokes?

"I started off in housekeeping, actually," Mary interjected. "Worked my way up from that to reception, and now I'm doing events. It's the Stormont, in Belfast—do you know it?"

"No, can't say I do. But our James was full of praise for it." Richard seemed chastened. Mary gave herself a mental pat on the back. She could handle this—one prejudice at a time.

"Ah, he would say that. But to be fair to him, though, it's nice. Well-kept, you know. Popular with weddings." Mary hoped the mention of nuptials might draw Juliette into the conversation. It wasn't so much that she seemed bored, but that her mind was evidently elsewhere. She was staring into the middle distance, her fingers splayed around the stem of her wine glass, rotating its contents.

"Very nice. Very nice. And what else do you do then—when you're not working?"

"Mary's an artist." Jim placed a hand on her thigh, alarmingly high up. Mary sat up an inch or so taller, in the hope it would drop. "She makes amazing maps, in fabric. You have to see it to believe it."

"Sounds very impressive." Jim's gesture of intimacy served to remind Richard of his own wife. He stroked the exposed skin on her forearm, and she looked up at Mary.

"We'd love to commission something. Maybe we could do Skye . . ." Juliette petered out and both Jim and Richard looked down at the table. Jim pressed his finger hard into the center of his bread plate and picked up a scattering of crumbs.

"Not now, darling," Richard said, dropping his hand again. Mary tried to meet Jim's eye but he was fixated on crushing a slippery oat under his thumb. She never thought she'd say it, but she would take Richard's supercilious snipes over this hush. It was eerie. Entirely alienating for a stranger.

It was a relief when the food came. Mary was able to move the conversation on from Skye and the resonance it so clearly held for them. They discussed Jim's job; some cousin's children, who weren't enjoying the start of Michaelmas term at what Mary gathered was a boarding school. But Skye lingered, a specter at the table that Mary found herself consciously and constantly dodging around. When the plates had been cleared, Richard signaled for the bill straightaway and, despite Mary's protestations, wouldn't hear of her contributing. He'd already made it quite evident that he thought her card would bounce.

Jim marched them both out. Mary didn't so much as have a chance to use the loo.

Outside the street was loud, with a busking brass band playing to an appreciative crowd. It was a while before either of them had a chance to make themselves heard over the noise.

"So?" Jim asked, as they walked back to his flat. "You survived?"

"Just about."

"You did well. And look, I'm sorry about what Dad said, about your work and stuff."

"I'm not ashamed of it, James. Unless you want me to be?"

"Christ—no! Whoa, what gave you that idea?"

"The fact I'm not Evie, for a start. I work in a hotel, I'm hardly a 'go-getter.'"

Evie's name had been spoken—what, twice? And still Mary knew that whoever she was, whatever degrees and pedigrees she may or may not possess, she was the daughter-in-law the Whitnells truly wanted.

"I didn't want to be with Evie. I never will—okay? You're what I want. The only one I want."

Jim dropped Mary's hand and barreled her into his chest instead. She could smell the red wine on him, now more ethanol than fruity, his cologne beneath. For a minute the world navigated around their pressed bodies, as Mary tried to separate the man holding her from the cruel assumptions of the people who had raised him.

When she was confident her voice wouldn't shake, she ventured, "What was the issue with Skye? Why did you all go so . . . quiet?"

Silence.

"Huh? What happened there?"

Jim gazed, spacey, out over Mary's shoulder, somewhere beyond the parked cars. He had that same faraway look that his mother had all through the meal. Eventually he shook out his neck and kissed her forehead.

"Let's talk back at home."

8

2005

The short Tube journey back to Jim's flat gave Mary an opportunity to study the subtle shifts in the man beside her. He was holding her hand but, unless she was imagining it, the grip seemed looser. They sat in silence, bar the odd observation that she threw in to break her own sense of unease. Up until this moment their time together—just the two of them—had been nothing short of amazing. It was snorting laughs and in-jokes and the sort of covert looks over coffee or cocktails that dulled the rest of the world entirely. Now, at the mention of Skye over lunch with his parents, Mary could feel a strangeness seeping between them.

"I'm sorry," he said once they had got through the front door.

Jim poured himself a whiskey from the sideboard, then slumped on the sofa. Mary took the armchair opposite. She'd been right—he was avoiding her eye. He didn't even have the decency to offer her a drink too. Surely she was the one who needed it. Was this it? She couldn't see how it was worth the airfare for the pleasure of calling things off in person.

"About my mum, I mean. I should have told you before. It wasn't fair to spring it on you. I thought she'd be better. That *it* would all be better. Maybe once I'd brought someone back, she'd have to act normal."

"Wait—*what* would be better? You're not making any sense."

"Her . . . everything."

"You're going to need to give me more than that." Mary surprised herself by how firm she sounded. She had flown over here, missed out on a weekend's wage. She was not about to have her time wasted with flimsy excuses. "You spring your parents on me. I'm as uncomfortable as all hell while we talk about your ex—the *wonderful* Evie—and now you're going to keep me in the dark about this too?"

Jim glanced up. "You want to know about Skye?"

"Yes."

Mary watched as his gaze dropped again. Jim had previously seemed so candid. But then, she supposed, he had never dug into anything more personal than a sense of discontent at his chosen career path. This new level of openness was causing significant distress. He was shredding the skin on his bottom lip, struggling to find the words. "It's where Sam died," Jim said, finally. "Sam, my brother."

"Oh God, Jim, I'm so sorry." Mary could have kicked herself for not being more patient with him. There was no way back from her tone. Speak first, think later—that was her all over. It would be the undoing of her.

"It's fine. It *should* be fine. It was so long ago—two decades. Doesn't feel like that to Mum, though."

Mary was about to open her mouth to apologize again but managed to stop herself just in time. The last thing she needed to do now was make this about her. She'd made matters bad enough already.

"Tell me about him."

Jim startled. Had she said the wrong thing again? But then, slowly, his countenance started to change, a little warmth coming back into the lines around his mouth. Maybe it wasn't so much the wrong thing to say as a thing that was so rarely asked.

"He was eighteen," Jim began. "Two years older than me, so we were always competing, whether we admitted it or not. I idolized him.

Sam was the smart one, the funny one. The good-looking one. We couldn't go anywhere in school, out of school, without a whole train of girls falling at his feet." Jim gave a small huff of laughter. "He was my parents' favorite too, although they'd never admit as much. He had a place at university, two months away. Oxford: medicine."

"He sounds amazing," Mary ventured.

"He was. And I wasn't even jealous, strangely." Now that Jim had started, the process of opening up seemed to be a little less torturous to him. Mary noted that this was the way into Jim's confidence—with the softest tread. "He took the pressure off me. I could be the wayward youngest. A bit hopeless, but I'd figure it out. I felt invincible when I was with Sam. It probably looked like teenage arrogance, but you never see it like that at the time. I thought I would always have him. Until I didn't, of course."

"Can I as—"

"What happened? Yeah, I wish I knew." Jim drained his glass, set it on the table, and clenched his hand around the armrest. The veins on his forearm bulged. "None of us were there. He was in Skye, on some big hurrah up in Scotland with his school friends after they had finished their exams. Mum got the call. In the middle of the night."

Mary could see Juliette in her mind's eye, bleary and confused as the phone rang, kneecapped when she picked up.

Jim swallowed. "He had been driving and the car had flipped. When we heard, Sam was being airlifted to the hospital. We drove all through the night. Dad floored it up there. God knows how fast he was going. No one cared. That whole way up, I prayed that he'd be there. I'd never prayed before but if anything was going to turn me to it, it was that. I promised anything, just so long as Sam would be okay.

"Only it wasn't. By the time we got there, he was gone. He hadn't lasted the night. We went in to see him, and by that time the tubes and the machines had disappeared and he was lying on the bed. Gone."

Jim finally glanced up from the floor, not so much looking at Mary as through her. "No one ever gets over that, do they? Mum never came close. Dad said it, once."

"Said what?" Mary whispered.

"That she's a dead woman walking."

At her feet, Mary's phoned buzzed. Her alarm. She hadn't trusted the two of them to get her to the airport on time, what with the way the last two days had gone—the endless mornings in bed and their body clocks ticking completely out of sync with the hours in the day. It seemed a lifetime ago already.

"Sorry. Sorry." Mary hit the snooze button.

"No, *I'm* sorry. Do you need to go now?"

She shook her head. She hadn't a bag to check in anyway. Jim was sitting forward in his chair, leaning over to touch her knee.

"Really, Mary. I mean it. I'm so sorry. That wasn't the way today was meant to go. It wasn't the way I wanted this weekend to end. I wish it didn't have to end, full stop. Do you know the worst thing about it all?"

She had no idea where else this conversation could possibly take them. All she wanted to do was reach out and hold Jim, the thirty-six-year-old man in front of her, transported twenty years back in time to a scared, rudderless teenager. "I think it should have been me, not Sam, to die. He would have done a better job at living. I spend most of my life wishing this was all at an end. That I could escape it all."

How could he think that? If Jim had died in Sam's place, then they never would have met and Mary would still be a shadow of the woman she had become in the space of a month in his company. She shuddered. Whatever was going on here, she had no doubt that it plumbed something far deeper, far more troubling, than restlessness.

"It sounds so ungrateful, right? But that's not it. It's the pressure. The expectation. From my parents, now Sam's gone, yes; but it's at work too, with my friends. I can't let a ball drop. Sometimes I wonder what life would be like if I could show that things were less than perfect. That sometimes it's hard enough to get out of bed in the morning, let alone keep up appearances."

It was all Mary could do not to clutch at the hand on her knee and whisper, *Then don't.* She knew then that she loved him. That she would always want him—appearances or not.

"And then I met you," Jim said.

"P-p-pardon?"

"Then I met you. I know it's early days—I know that. I'm the last person to get my hopes up when it comes to . . . things like this. But it's the first time in a long time that I felt I can be myself, that there's something worth sticking around for."

"Ach, I don't know about that." Mary hated herself for trotting out an automatic brush-off. But to say how she really felt? It was too soon, much as she might wish it wasn't.

"You're different, Mary." She mustn't have done a convincing job of hiding her expression because Jim quickly added, "In a good way, I mean. You're so . . . principled. Fierce, when you stand your ground and keep me in my place. I need that. But I feel like you don't need me, not at all. No, it's more, I don't know, that you *want* to be with me. There's no expectation to be someone other than who I really am. I feel free when I'm with you. Well, *freer.*"

Jim smiled. Or rather Mary thought he did. No sooner was it there than it was gone again.

"We could escape."

"What?"

Jim shot back in his chair, frowning. Mary had the awful feeling of having put her foot in her mouth.

"Why don't we get away?" she suggested. "That's what you said you wanted, right?"

Jim narrowed his eyes at her, as if figuring out how committed she was to her own sudden outburst. Mary still hadn't come to terms with the intensity of his gaze.

"Go on then—surprise me."

The words were still ringing in her ears when she landed back in Belfast later that night.

9

2018

When she arrives at the office, Alice dodges the kitchen chitchat and heads straight for her desk, a large takeaway coffee cup in hand. She is not pleasant company before the caffeine hits her bloodstream and, with less than an hour's shut-eye behind her this morning, it is a wonder that she is alive, let alone functional enough to be at work.

Since Alice parted ways with Mary outside the pub last night, her mind has been in pieces. She spent a good hour or so worrying if Mary had made it home okay. While Mary may have appeared hardy, ferociously guarding her personal space, Alice saw another, more vulnerable side to her over their drink. She wouldn't do anything stupid—would she? Alice ought to have taken a number for Mary, but she was too consumed by the mystery of Jim's disappearance to think straight.

When that anxiety eventually began to dissipate, curiosity snatched its place as the main obstruction to Alice's prospect of sleep. She didn't extract many details from Mary but that does not stop Alice from itching to know what happened to Jim. Alice is achingly aware that there are some losses too large and too unwieldy to move on from, and it is clear that Mary is merely shuffling around hers. If only Alice could get her hands on a bit more information, maybe she could start to pull together the full story, bring Mary some closure . . .

"There you are!" Jack, editor in chief and Alice's boss, pokes his head over her cubicle. There is a smear of what looks like dried baked beans on the corner of his lip. She considers pointing it out but then decides against it. He's easily embarrassed. "Can I have a quick chat?"

"Of course." Alice pulls out the adjacent desk chair. They haven't had a new intern in yonks.

"In my office?"

Her stomach plummets. Has she ever been called into Jack's office in her whole five years here? Sometimes she'll drop by of her own volition, if she's done some good work that she wants to waggle under his nose in an attempt to secure a pay rise, but she's never been ordered there. What can she possibly have done wrong?

"Just a quickie," Jack says, once the door is shut. "Take a seat."

He looks nervous. Flustered too—much more so than usual. Whatever this is, it's bad news. Alice has a radar for it. The air-conditioning has been broken since she joined, so she can't blame the chill down her spine on that.

"I'm afraid the paper isn't doing too well, Alice." Well, *that* wasn't news. Who actually bought the *Bugle,* besides a couple of local pensioners with nothing else to do? "We're entering a phase of cuts, come the beginning of September, and you are our most junior reporter."

"The cheapest, right?"

Jack doesn't take the joke. He squirms in his chair. "Which means that your job is on the line."

A little of Alice's morning coffee comes up the back of her throat. She can't lose her job. There is nothing in her savings account. She won't be able to afford the rent, and there'll be no option but to move back to Slough with her mum. Her palms begin to sweat. The last time they lived under the same roof without awkwardness was when she was twelve. That was fourteen years ago! It would dredge up everything.

"I'm so sorry, Alice." Jack bows his head. "A redundancy is not yet confirmed. It won't be until the shareholders come down in a few weeks' time, but I wanted you to have the heads-up, in case it does go that way."

"Is there nothing I can do? I can work longer hours, take on more responsibility . . ." Alice stops short of saying she could take a pay cut. There isn't much less cash that she could live on.

"If I were you, I'd be working up my CV, so that you're in a good position. Put your best pieces online, maybe."

"I don't have any!" Her voice comes out far louder than intended and, in the uncomfortable silence that follows, Alice is reminded of Mary's outburst last night. The hush that follows unleashed despair.

"You've got some time." Jack glances at the calendar on the wall. "They're not coming until the very start of September, which is still three weeks off. I'll do all I can for you. If you can get me a great story, I will push it to the front page. Top of the online stuff. If you can get something good—really good—to me by the end of August, I will run it. You have my word on that, Alice."

"I appreciate that," she says, trying to control the scratchy feeling in her throat. She mustn't cry. Not in a professional context. Not when she needs to be taken seriously.

"Let me know about the story you want to run. I'll hold the last August edition for you."

In any other situation Jack's kindness would be worthy of a smile, but Alice does not trust her wobbly bottom lip. Instead she lets herself out of his office and rushes back to her desk before anyone can ask what their chat was about. She takes three deep breaths and tries to get a handle on her panic. *Get it together, Keaton.* There must be some hope to cling on to here, Alice thinks.

Well, to offer her the front page: that's big. Alice has wanted the opportunity to step up for so long. Only she never expected it would come with this high a price. Besides, are there any local stories powerful enough to convince a bunch of corporate big dicks that it shouldn't be *her* neck on the line? Nothing ever happens around here. Take it from a woman who has covered the opening of four separate dental practices in the last two years.

Alice unlocks her phone and, out of habit, goes to open Twitter. The home of breaking news—for her generation at least. She doesn't know what she wants to find there. An inspiring quote? A fitting meme? Inspiration for her last-ditch article?

She is about to get all of them at once.

The first item on Alice's timeline is a video—popular, by the look of things. She checks her phone is on mute, then presses Play. At first it is hard to make out what is going on or where the footage has been shot. It's low-grade, something from a camera phone probably. To begin with, all that is visible is a press of backs, bags, and coats and the odd rumpled hairdo. There must be hundreds of people in the enclosed area, close to a thousand even. They are all jostling for the same few centimeters until, suddenly, they freeze.

Two seconds later, space has miraculously opened up in front of the camera. Alice recognizes the station. And there in the center of the image? Her heart thunders so loudly that she wonders if Erika, on the other side of the partition, can hear it.

It's Mary—her sign in full view.

It's her outburst last night.

Alice drops her phone to her desk, and her head into her empty hand. For Mary's moment of private despair to have been shared in such a public way: it's awful, unbearable. It's a violation, that's what it is. How has this happened? Alice snatches her headphones from her handbag and plugs them into her desktop. While she tries not to be seen on social media at work, she'll make an exception this time. Thanks to Jack's announcement, she clearly doesn't have much left to lose.

The initial post that Alice saw on her timeline belonged to an old school friend, a beauty blogger, who had retweeted the original video and captioned it "QUEEN." Alice now clicks through to the original post. Who the hell thinks they have the right to broadcast Mary's meltdown without her knowledge? Someone called Simon Seager, that's who. The rat. Above the footage he has written: "Saw this on my way home last night. Now THAT'S how you get the job done." It has two hundred thousand retweets and is growing by the second.

And what's worse? *Twenty thousand comments.* Alice feels her breakfast beginning to rise up the back of her throat. She hovers the cursor above the comment icon, bracing herself. The internet attracts the bowels of humanity, its anonymity the perfect backdrop for vitriol of the worst kind. Can she do this? She has to. Better her than Mary, seeing all this. Alice feels protective of Mary, despite having only met her once, but that's the nature of being welcomed into the confidence of a woman who does not open up much at all. If any of these people have said anything rude . . . Alice clenches her left fist in fury under the desk and musters up the courage to click with her right.

The first comment is anodyne: "gets shit done"; the second, more of the same vacuity: "work mood." The third makes Alice gag. It's a half-baked innuendo from an anonymous alias. She imagines Mary opening it, the color seeping from her face. That can't happen. It just can't. She has suffered enough. If Alice has to spend the whole day reporting thousands of creepy, faceless men, she most certainly will.

Fortunately she is running ahead of herself, as always. Rude comments are, on closer inspection, very few and far between. For the most part, people have added variations on "jkz." "lol." "legend." The more observant among them have mentioned the sign: "what's all that about?" And some are already asking after Jim: "where's he at, then?" Alice's mind flashes back to Mary's face, crumpling as she told Alice how Jim had reached out on the phone, less than forty-eight hours ago. It manages to make even the most well-meaning commentators sound hollow in comparison.

Will Mary have seen this video yet? She'd be so embarrassed that her momentary lack of composure had been caught on camera, no doubt; not to mention the fact that there are now countless strangers commenting on her private life. Maybe the news will never make it to her? A quick Google search for "Ealing station lady" shows up that the video is so far contained to social-media platforms and Alice can't imagine that Mary has a profile on any of those, or is much bothered with checking them, if she does.

She returns to Twitter and the original posting of the video, which has amassed in excess of a hundred comments since she last looked at it. She begins to read the latest batch:

"Why would anyone leave a woman like that?"

"Where did Jim go?"

"#FindJim"

"BRING HIM HOME."

"There a story in there."

Yes, Alice thinks, *yes, there is.* And if anyone is going to find it, it is going to be her.

10

2005

"Here we are!"

Mary kept her back to Jim as she spoke, her voice tight. This was not the cottage described online. It could barely be described as a cottage at all. More of a shed, although that was unfair to gardeners everywhere. A shack, then.

For the first few days after she landed back from London, Mary was paralyzed by the responsibility of planning an escape for herself and Jim. What had she been thinking, volunteering for the task so briskly? Nothing could dampen the chemistry between them quicker than letting her inner Girl Guide out. But it wasn't as if she could back down. Every time she thought of Jim in his flat in Ealing, admitting that he thought it should have been him instead of Sam, Mary could feel her heart break all over again. She had to incinerate that thought from his head, one good thing at a time.

Unfortunately the reality of Mary's finances meant that an escape downgraded to a holiday, the research for which she took to doing every evening after work, at the public library not far from the Stormont. The library was far from private (the clue being in the title) but it was still a darn sight better than using the clunky desktop that was perched in the corner of the O'Connor family sitting room—Mary's business subject to the scrutiny of whoever happened to be lounging around. As far as she knew, none of her brothers were aware that there was a man on the scene, and she wanted to keep it that way. She'd only met Jim a little over six weeks ago and their happiness still felt too precious to share.

Mary calculated that she had £200 for this trip, and even that would strip the savings pot bare. The funds didn't leave her many options in terms of location, and in the end she settled for somewhere she had been before: Portrush, a seaside resort town on the Antrim coast. It would be quiet enough now that the schools were back, off the beaten tourist track, wild by the sea. Cheap too, although she should have known that a rental with a rock-bottom price had a catch. Mary tried to remember the description that had accompanied the series of well-shot, well-lit photos—the words *romantic, cozy, unique* all sprang to mind.

But there had to be a difference between positive messaging and false advertising. She surveyed their accommodations for the next five nights. It consisted of a single room: at the far end, a small double bed was hemmed in by cupboards on either side and above the headboard; the kitchen table was close enough to the foot of the bed for an average-sized guest to graze their toast with their toes. The bathroom was no-where to be seen.

"I've always liked an outdoor piss, myself."

Jim wrapped an arm around Mary's waist and attempted to turn her round. She stood firm. How had she managed to mess this up? And when the stakes were so high too. Her anger at the cottage-company charlatans had morphed into the urge to cry. She'd disappointed Jim, not that she could show it when she needed to be strong for them both. No good holiday ever began with the architect in chief sobbing on a shoulder. Even if Jim's were the perfect shape for it.

"I'm sorry, it didn't look . . ." Mary fumbled for her phone. If there was any signal here, then she would prove that she hadn't been remiss in her research.

"No! I'm not hearing a word of it." He planted a kiss on her cheek. "Back to basics—isn't that what they say?"

He went to drop his holdall in the corner and kicked his shoes off. One hit the radiator and the valve toppled off onto the floor, unleashing a flurry of chalky residue. Mary hoped that asbestos wasn't a heating thing. Not that it looked like they would be warming up anytime soon. She shivered. It had reached the midway point in autumn when the novelty of horse chestnut and golden leaves underfoot had given way to a distinct desire to see the sun again.

"Bloody hell!" Jim was standing on the mattress in his socks, stumbling under the weight of blankets that were cascading down from the cupboard above. "Do you think it's a sign that we're going to be cold, then?"

Mary picked up a navy tartan rug that had drifted to her feet. It smelled even mustier than expected and there was an alarming hole in the center, its edges singed.

"You know you want to laugh. Come on." Jim jumped down and slid over to her, an unfinished patchwork quilt wrapped around his waist. Loose threads tickled the linoleum floor tiles. "Just a little chuckle." He prized the rug from her hand and fashioned her a sarong too.

It was ridiculous. Absurd. Undeniably awful. But there they were, laughing until their stomachs were sore and it was an effort to get in a breath at all. Each time they stopped, all it took was one look at their fancy dress, so grim it should come with a health warning, to start them off all over again. How did Jim manage to do that? To unravel the knots in Mary's mind and remind her of what was important in the world.

That night they slept in a duvet fortress of Jim's creation. While Mary had torn herself away from his arms for long enough to cook supper, he had fashioned a four-poster from the discarded bedding they discovered crammed into every conceivable pocket of storage. He had wedged three miscellaneous bicycle lights in among the drapes. If Mary didn't breathe through her nose and squinted, it was almost luxurious.

"You did your best with a bad lot," she said, nestling further onto Jim's chest.

"I could say the same about you."

"Well, I didn't make the soup."

"I meant with me," Jim replied.

He took a swig from the open bottle of red wine and passed it to Mary. She had been a bit concerned when he had loaded a crate into the boot of the rental car—was her company really bad enough to require all that drink?—but now that she had seen where they would be staying for the next few days, she couldn't be more grateful for Jim's unorthodox packing.

"Yes, that too. You are a terrible, terrible lot."

She still hadn't quite got used to the bulk of him next to her, the heat of his naked body, the feel of his skin beneath her palm. And yet, at the same time, she had never felt quite so comfortable with anyone else. Every so often Mary had to stop and remind herself that they had only met on four separate occasions—less than twenty days spent together. In total. The line between madness and brilliance seemed very fine indeed, especially when it came to Jim.

"I could hide out here," he said, propping himself up on his elbows and peering through the curtain of sheets, out of the window. The blinds were broken and the rain whipped the glass.

"It doesn't look like we'll be going anywhere anyway," she mumbled.

She didn't trust herself to say it, but there was nothing Mary wanted to do more than lie there, exactly like this, until the landlady threw them out. There was nothing else she needed. No one. She wondered if this was what it meant to be in love. If it felt like being at peace. If so, she hoped it wasn't as fragile a state as the rest of the world made it out to be.

Jim lay back and rolled Mary onto her side, his chest against her spine. The drive had exhausted her, and she could feel herself drifting off.

"This was just what I needed," he murmured into the nest of her hair. "I think *you* might be just what I needed."

Mary quickly learned what it meant about a holiday being as good as a change, or vice versa. To be fair, she hadn't much experience with vacations, breaks—whatever you wanted to call them. But for the first time in years she felt rested. And while, meteorologically speaking, the holiday in Portrush was a washout, physically and emotionally it had been nothing but a success. Mary had slept for more than ten hours every single night. Jim claimed he had too, although the two times she'd been up in the early hours to brave the outdoor toilet, she could have sworn she'd seen his eyes open, staring at the ceiling.

Aside from that, there were no signs of the pain she had seen in Jim's eyes on her last afternoon in London. That weight seemed to have lifted off him, dissolved, she hoped. She made no mention of Sam or his parents and avoided the topic of work whenever possible. Not everyone needed to integrate the various aspects of their life. If she could be the sole good thing in Jim's, then, sure, that was an honor. She no longer felt the need to be worrying all the time. Not when everything was so promising between them.

On their last day the sun made its first appearance. Auspicious, Mary thought, as she packed up her toiletries bag in the bathroom stall. It had taken some effort to rouse enthusiasm for a spot of tourism from Jim but now, at least, he was in the shower, drumming the melody to a song she didn't recognize on the emptying plastic toiletry bottles.

"We're leaving in five. Don't make me drag you out of there," Mary shouted over the racket.

"Then don't make me an offer I can't refuse."

She tossed a towel over the top of the shower door and went back to their cabin to pack a day bag before her self-restraint went out the window.

An hour later Mary pulled in at Dunluce Castle car park. Up ahead, a frazzled teacher wielding a clipboard was trying to coerce stragglers into the back of the ticketing queue.

"A school trip, then." Jim raised an eyebrow as the engine purred into silence.

"It's a site of great historical interest."

"To whom, exactly?"

"You. Soon. Out you get."

Mary took his hand and dragged him through the entrance exhibits, outpacing the kids on the bridge, a group of whom were jumping up and down to see how much force it took to rock it. They found a secluded corner at the water's edge, looking down at the waves shredding on the sheer cliffs below. In the sunlight, the foam around the rocks seemed to spark and the Causeway Coast stretched, majestic, as far as the eye could see.

Jim nudged his hip into Mary's. "Fine, I'll give it to you. It was worth the trip."

"I knew it would be. And to think if I'd succumbed to your charm we wouldn't be here at all."

"It was a close call, wasn't it?"

She gave a wry wisp of a smile. Men like Jim didn't need the ego boost.

"You're full of it, you know that?" She went to wriggle her hand into his back pocket but he twisted to position himself out of reach.

"Keeping something in there that you don't want me to see?"

"Maybe."

Mary dodged to reach for his pocket again. But then something akin to a grimace flickered across Jim's face, which stopped her in her tracks. Before she could say anything, the moment was interrupted by the same group of boisterous kids from the bridge. They slammed their tiny frames up against the railings to the right of Jim, waiting until the spray spat up into their faces before they sprinted back onto dryer land, squealing.

"It's enough to put you off, isn't it?" Jim said.

He was back to smiling, whatever frustration Mary had detected lost already. She wondered whether it was healthy to have quite such elastic moods or whether it was only the sort of thing that *she* would find odd, given the success with which she had nursed some schoolyard grudges over the course of ten-plus years. Now, with a much more important conversation afoot, she shrugged off his rebuff quickly.

"Off what?"

"Children," Jim replied.

"Ha—that bad, eh?"

"It's not for me," he admitted.

"Having your own kids?"

"Yeah."

"Fair enough. It's not for me, either." Mary had never given much thought to having her own family, and now that simple fact seemed to confirm the answer for her. She wasn't bothered either way.

"Really?" Jim pulled back by an inch to scrutinize Mary's face. If he was looking for signs that she was joking, he was coming up equally blank. "What about the brood back home—doesn't that make you want a family?"

"Jaysus, no. Makes me want something else. Why? Are they not for you, I mean?" This wasn't a conversation that she expected to be having, and certainly not so soon. But seeing as they had started, she might as well finish with some firm answers. "If you don't mind me asking."

Jim didn't seem perturbed. "It's a lot, right? That responsibility. You, responsible for someone else's life. You can't put it down and pick it up again. Yeah, the responsibility. It's not for me."

Mary didn't know what to make of that. After their conversation, back in London, she should have expected as much. Jim had a free spirit, or rather he craved one. Children would never fit with that. But a family and a relationship were two separate things. She told herself that it changed nothing about the prospect of their relationship becoming the anchor in his life.

"You seem fine to me."

"Must be doing a good job at hiding something then." Jim grinned. He wrapped both arms around her waist. "Or maybe I'm good with you. You make me want to be better, at least."

Before she could deny it, Jim had pulled Mary in, his hand at the base of her neck guiding her toward him. He was insistent, his tongue searching and drawing her deeper. For a minute there was nothing. Just Jim, Mary, and the warmth of his mouth on hers. Then, from behind, a wolf whistle accompanied by thirty tramping feet.

She went to pull away but Jim caught her, his hands clasped at the small of her back.

"I'm not ashamed to say I love you. And I never will be."

11

2005

Mary was so blinded by joy that she drove them the wrong way to the pub. Twice. *Jim loved her too.* She'd had an inkling, sure, but to have it confirmed was another matter entirely. It meant more to her than any label on their relationship ever could. It meant that they had a future.

Playing house for the past week, it had been impossible *not* to imagine what it might be like to wake up next to Jim every morning, his face on the pillow and his stomach pressed firm against hers as they waited for the kettle to boil. She could imagine them ten, twenty years from now, coming back to Portrush for their anniversary. They might even stay in the same hellish cottage for the novelty, if it was still standing.

"I take it you don't fancy a ringside seat for the news?" Jim said as they entered the pub. On the television, the presenter with a sharp suit and a grave sense of his own self-importance drummed a pen on the table in impatience at his evasive interviewee. One of the men at the bar gave a yawn that transformed midway into a belch. "Looks scintillating," Jim added.

"Shush, you!" Mary slapped him on the arm. "Go get us a seat. The best ones are round the back, there."

It had been two decades since Mary had been here, a nipper barely up to Da's waist. Mam was pregnant with Gavin then, so it was just the four of them on holiday, piled into a tiny one-bed apartment behind the train station. Clearly it had all become a bit much for Mam, swollen up like a balloon and exhausted from the constant bickering between Mary and Terry. She'd demanded the house to herself for two hours and kicked the lot of them out, although it seemed unlikely that a pub visit was what she had in mind.

Da had bought them both a half-pint of lime and soda and there was a packet of crisps to share, the foil torn down the center so they could see the spoils inside spread out in front of them. Normally Mary would have taken great pleasure in ensuring the exact division of the crisps. Terry was a guzzler, had been from the minute he emerged from their mam, a whole twelve pounds and with a remarkable capacity for storage in those gummy paws of his. But that day Mary was transfixed, her mind far from the snack.

She had her wide, infant's eyes glued to the walls of the back room, every inch covered in maps. From floor to ceiling, pages and pages of large survey grids and guides had been overlapped in the most mesmerizing wallpaper she had ever seen. It wasn't that the locations lined up, rather it was the opposite: somewhere by her left ankle, Leeds ran into Fife, which in turn was pushed up against a pin-sized black dot that marked Belfast. Mary traced her finger up the network of pink and yellow veins that led into and out of cities, hopping across the rings of faint green fields and along the pale-blue trails that marked the rivers.

Up until then, geography had been a subject in the school timetable. Not a very important one at that, more the preserve of a few hours before the long summer break, when the rest of the maths and the science and the spelling had been covered. It was dry and it was fixed. All Mary had gathered from the rushed lessons was that every man had his place on the atlas. A predetermined one too. It was the luck of the dice where you had come from and, for most, you'd be lucky to end up anywhere else.

But this? Well, it was something else. For the first time in her seven and three-quarters years of life, Mary had really felt there was a world beyond Belfast and one that maybe wasn't as out of reach as she had previously been told. Over the years that followed, she returned time and time again to the image of the map room. If it could be as simple as cutting up the map and making something new—a patchwork of possibility, a home perhaps—then maybe her horizons weren't as immovable as she had first thought.

Twenty years on and life had got in the way. Da was sick, Mam needed the help, and, if Mary was honest with herself—as honest as she could only be in the dark, on her own, in bed at the end of a shift—she would say the real problem was her. Da's diagnosis was a convenient excuse to avoid the true reasons why she hadn't moved out or found a different job. In reality, routine had ground down her drive. Some days it was all she could manage to be ambitious enough to change up her choice of biscuit in the staff room. It had taken Jim to remind her what else was out there for her, how high she could yet fly.

"Wow," Jim said, as Mary landed their pints on the nearest table. "You didn't mention this bit."

"I didn't know if it would still be here."

He beckoned at the seat next to him, which he had pulled right up to the back wall.

"You reckon you can find us on the map? I'll race you."

It didn't take long for Mary to emerge victorious, although she kept tight-lipped on the muscle memory that drew her finger right back to the spot she had lingered on all those years earlier.

"What about me, then?" Jim asked. He had already finished his drink. Mary hadn't managed to take so much as a slurp from hers.

"What about you?"

"Where am I?"

"Tough one, that." She squeezed Jim's thigh.

"Is there a London map in here? Let's find my flat. I'm feeling terribly homesick." Jim pouted in a parody of sadness. "Loser buys the next round."

They worked in a competitive silence. In the next-door room there was a flurry of consternation, followed by the rhythmic thumping of plastic, which Mary took to mean the television had given up the ghost.

"Got it!" Jim hollered, after what couldn't have been more than a minute. Mary weaved through the strewn chairs and peered over his shoulder. He draped his arm around her waist. She could feel the hair on his forearm tickling the line of skin above her jeans. "Right here."

He was, infuriatingly, right.

"It's an awful long way away," Mary sighed.

It was the first time either Mary or Jim had alluded to the elephant in their relationship. No sooner had Mary said it, than she wished she could have gulped the words back. She didn't want to sound needy or to ruin the memory of their perfect day. She wanted still to be fierce and independent, *different,* whatever other qualities Jim had seen in her, and which she had struggled to see in herself before they met.

He began to trace his finger in a curve around Ealing. He closed the circle over the crosshatch that represented the train station. "You know that doesn't matter. You know that, don't you?" Mary didn't have a clue what she knew anymore. The last two months had thrown the rest of her world on its head. It had been amazing, exhilarating, dizzying. Anything but certain. "I want you to know that I'll be there for you, wherever that is—the ends of the earth, Ealing . . ." He underlined the word on the map. "Always. I mean it. I hope you know that."

Mary froze. Did that mean what she thought it did? It couldn't. Hope for too much and you end up with nothing.

"Seriously, Mary. Here, look at me." Jim tipped her chin up and kept one hand propped under it. "I've always wanted to run, to disappear. But with you, for once, I don't." There was so much Jim could have told her—how Mary felt like stillness in the chaos of his life; how, until he met her, he had never known it was possible to feel so tethered to someone, without them applying so much as a single gram of weight. That perhaps he hadn't been broken after all, he just needed to find her. "There is no one else who could make me say this, trust me. I want to be there for you. Always."

It was on the tip of Mary's tongue to ask him to repeat himself. She must have heard wrong. This was the sort of romance that happened to other people. It didn't happen to her, in the shabbiest boozer that Portrush had to offer.

"Move in with me."

"I beg your pardon?"

"You heard me. Move in with me. You've seen the space—there's definitely enough for us two."

Mary scoured his face for signs that she was being had, but Jim was as earnest as he had ever been.

"I'm tired of this back and forth. I want this. I want you." Jim leaned forward, kissed Mary's forehead. He was the only man she had ever been with who was tall enough for that. The only man who was tender enough, too.

"Yes," she whispered. Then louder, with her newly unearthed conviction, "Yes."

12

2018

Mary hesitates outside the door to the classroom. She is terrified of making her return to NightLine and has been since the moment she heard Jim's voice on the end of that awful, staticky line two nights ago. Terrified, yet still so hopeful. A good way of describing the state of suspension in which she has lived for the past seven years, she thinks with a sigh.

Yesterday, after returning from the pub, Mary was confronted with the sight of Jim's notes scattered across the hallway floor, and whatever relief confiding in Alice had provided dissolved in a second. She sank to her knees and began picking up the postcards at random. *Remember dinner round the corner from here? I had the best date in all of London town.* She knew she shouldn't be doing this. It was not so much picking at a scab as stabbing a weeping wound. *Belfast's finest export—and to think she's mine! I'm the luckiest man on the planet.*

Jim always did have a way of opening up the world to Mary. Before she met him, Mary believed that life was about doing enough to keep afloat—at home, at work, in whatever small semblance of a personal life she could carve out. But Jim showed her that she could get on, not merely get by. He opened her horizons. He encouraged her to dream big, then bigger again. For the six years they were together Mary never doubted that Jim would have given her the world. She was sitting among the proof.

And all the while that Jim was pushing her to imagine what lay beyond her feet, in the seas of possibility, Mary remained the safe harbor for them both. He had said as much on the phone. She broke everything down into manageable pieces. She was measured. Calm. Of course she had blips—everyone did.

Last night at the station was a perfect example of that. The memory sent a hot rush of shame up Mary's spine. But she quashed it; a momentary lapse in control didn't change her character. Jim knew the real Mary better than anyone else. He must—or why else would he be reaching out now, after seven long years of nothing? If he has worked up the courage to phone once, then surely there's an even greater chance that he will call again tonight.

Mary pushes open the doors to NightLine.

She heads straight for her seat. There's the usual half-melted Twix from Ted, along with some clippings on what appears to be a wetlands walkway.

"You alright?" Ted waves, the other hand buried deep in an industrial-sized sack of teabags.

Mary always marvels at the depth of the smile lines carved into the stubble around his mouth. *That's positivity for you,* she thinks. Ted has rebuilt himself after his wife's death as well as anyone could and, even in the early days, he still found time to ask after all the volunteers. People this considerate aren't two-a-penny. Mary wonders, fleetingly, if she has ever told him how grateful she feels to have his friendship in her life.

"I left you a piece about a new walk I thought we could try," he continues, when Mary doesn't respond. "Bit further afield than we normally go. North of the river, I think it said, but maybe we could do it when you've got a clear day? I'm a bit slammed with clients at the moment, but it isn't as if the marsh is going to up sticks—"

Ted is interrupted by Kit, bursting through the door. Olive is nearly knocked out by the force of it flying back toward her.

"It's the señorita of the hour!" Kit shouts, with a mouthful of what appears to be a granola bar. "NightLine's very own online darling." The grin on his face is at odds with the look of utter bafflement that is shared by Ted, Olive, and Mary.

Kit clocks their expressions. "Come on—you must have seen this." He pulls his phone out of his back pocket and flicks open an app. Ted, Olive, and Mary shuffle closer. It's Twitter, not that Mary has any personal experience of it. She has never had any sort of profile on social media, not so much as an ill-advised Facebook account. The self-promotion, the notifications, the narcissism of it—just thinking about it is enough to break out in hives.

Kit scrolls, locates a video, and then presses Play. The first few seconds show a tinny recording of a disgruntled crowd, location indistinct. But then comes a voice that Mary would know anywhere. It's like nails down a blackboard.

It's her.

"FOR THE LOVE OF GOD WILL YOU GIVE ME SOME FECKING SPACE TO BREATHE!"

Mary's chest feels punctured. There is an unbearable pressure on her upper ribs and, somewhere underneath, her lungs are struggling to get in any air at all. Forget last night; it's now that she needs space. Why is everyone so close? She battles the urge to lash out with her hands, bat the phone away from their horrified eyes. Instead she tries to force herself to focus on the video, which has now finished. The shapes in the final shot seem blurred. Mary blinks, the image clearer second time around. Christ—the sign! The sign is in there too.

"What . . . what is this?" Mary's throat is closing up around the burr of panic that has lodged there. "Who? How?"

Kit's mouth drops open. "I thought you would have seen or heard . . ."

"Here, come on, take a seat," Olive says. "Make yourself useful and get Mary a tea," she snaps at Kit.

Mary grabs Kit's wrist before he can comply with Olive's order.

"Er, well, someone obviously caught this . . . scene on camera." Kit may be choosing his words carefully but Mary still feels shame washing over her in waves. "And they uploaded it to Twitter. People like it, though!"

"What do you mean, *like* it?"

"They're saying all sorts of nice things about you. You're a legend—you stand your ground. You get stuff done, that sort of thing." *But not the one thing that really matters,* Mary thinks, with a stab of pain. *Bringing Jim home.* "Lots of lovely comments actually, which is a shocker for the internet . . ."

He opens his phone again, as if to illustrate, but Olive snatches it away before he has the chance.

"Had you seen this?" Mary fixes on Olive and Ted in turn.

They both shake their heads.

"Honest," Ted adds. "Hadn't heard a peep."

"I don't do the internet," Olive says, wrinkling her nose in distaste.

"It doesn't seem to have migrated anywhere else—into newspapers, or whatever you guys read." Olive looks affronted at even the most oblique allusion to her age. Over thirty-five is evidently still ancient to Kit. "I mean, this is classic online fodder," he continues. "Clickbait. Loads of people watch, retweet, find the next thing. Attention is already moving on and it's barely been up for a day."

Kit's last addition, although designed to soothe Mary's angst, is ignored.

"How many is *loads of people*?"

Kit bites his bottom lip. "A million views?"

Mary's head collapses forward. She can't picture that many people. All of them sitting behind their screens, judging her, mocking her. It's a mob. A swarm. If she thought she had felt her fair share of powerlessness in this life, then she had been naive. Did nobody think she might not want some internet notoriety? Did they not think this might gut her? How could anyone be so selfish?

They didn't even think to leave Jim out of it. His name is on the sign, and the sign is there for anyone who cares to see. Will Jim have seen it? He wasn't on social media, not back when she last saw him, but if he is still out there, then perhaps he will know someone who will show him? Of course Mary wants Jim to know that she still cares, that she will wait as long as it takes for him to come to his senses and return home, but she doesn't want him to find out through some stupid internet sensationalism. The shame of it!

She looks a mess in the picture—stray hairs and a horrible pallor to her skin, made all the worse by the pixilation. What if one of her brothers saw it and showed Mam? Then the question would be what on earth she was doing there, outside the station. The vigil is not something she has ever found the right words to explain to Mam. Jim's parents wouldn't be able to see it, would they? They have at least ten years on Olive and were never much up on technology, so maybe she's okay on that front.

"People don't remember anything they see online, I swear," Kit says, when the silence is surely becoming unbearable for the rest of the volunteers. Ted and Olive have shuffled a little closer, as if wanting to hold Mary but yet afraid she might ask them for some *fecking space* too.

"But why?" Mary mumbles. Then, louder, "Why? Why would anyone take note of that . . . scene at all? I just wanted them all to stop with their pushing and shoving and their goddamn elbows." No one responds. "Why?"

Kit shrugs. "It's unexpected, I suppose. Saying anything to a stranger on the Tube might as well be front-page news. Then there's the sign . . ."

"What about it?" Mary snaps. She has had enough of people not minding their own business or, rather, appropriating it for their own entertainment.

"Nothing!" Kit's hands shoot up. "It's intriguing, that's all."

There is a knock on the door. Olive, Kit, Ted, and Mary all look toward the source of the noise at once. A woman's head is visible, a crisp mahogany bob with a neat fringe framing the features of it. In the circle of laminated glass, the image is blurred, but her icy blue eyes pierce through.

"Hi, all! I'm Alice."

A few seconds pass before anyone responds. "Ah, yes, we were expecting you," Olive says, finally. The scene could not look less expectant, or welcoming, for that matter. Olive struggles to fish the timetable out from the embroidered purse that is slung across her chest. "Alice Keaton, yes?"

"That's me."

"Hi again," Mary tries to muster up a smile. "Nice to see you've come."

"You know her?" Kit is brushing down the front of his T-shirt, where he has been collecting crumbs from his cereal bar. Mary has never seen him move quite so fast in all his life.

"Yes, we met briefly yesterday. Mary actually suggested that I sign up. And, well—here I am!"

"So, Alice." Olive pronounces her name with a distinctive hiss. "If you grab a chair . . . Yes, one of those little stacking ones, you can sit next to me tonight. Kit, you'll need to be on the first phone—can you get Alice set up with a headset?"

Once again the world moves on, while Mary stands frozen in time. Stills from the video flash through her mind like the outtakes of a horror movie. When she touches a hand to her forehead it is clammy. What was it that they called it—*going viral*? It makes sense. Mary can barely recall the last time she felt this nauseous. The call, and now this? It will be the end of her.

"Should you be here?" Ted risks a hand on Mary's shoulder, a light touch but still enough to make her shiver in the unbearably hot classroom.

"Yes. Honestly. I think it's best for me. Not to be alone . . ."

In reality, all she wants to do is to collapse into bed and never get up again. But she can't do that when the stakes are so high. If Jim calls again, she must be there to hear him, to help him.

"You know yourself best," Ted replies. "And where I am, if you need anything at all."

The line opens shortly after Ted leaves. Kit takes most of the first few short calls, passing the odd one over to Olive or Mary. The traffic gets heavier toward midnight, as it always does—not so much the witching hour as the time of terror: lonely widows who would do better to try the nonemergency services for concerns about the loitering outside their windows; Gerald the trucker, who is convinced that the water pipes are speaking to him; Aurelia, who is struggling with the isolation on her maternity leave, despite getting out and about as much as she can.

"Mary, I'll need you to take this one." Kit has his hand cupped over the speaker of the phone, the mute button long since nonfunctional. "Olive's had a call cut out, so I want to try this one on yours, in case her machine's gone skew-whiff."

"Good evening, you are through to NightLine." Nearly seven years here and the patter has become a comforting second nature to Mary. Surprising, really, how the words march out in perfect formation, even as her own world is falling apart.

"Good evening."

"Before we begin, I have to ask a few questions. Are you having thoughts of suicide?"

"No."

"Are you currently in a safe space?"

"Yes—I suppose you could call it that."

"Right, thank you. Those are all the questions for now, and we're free to continue. How can I help?"

"Mary, is that you?"

With the agony of the video, her body in self-preservation mode, Mary hadn't registered the voice on the other end of the line. The familiarity of it.

"I didn't know if you'd still be there."

"Why?" Mary lowers her voice. "Why wouldn't I be?"

"After I called . . . you seemed so distressed. I wanted to reach out, but the last thing I wanted was to upset you in the process," The line, already dodgy, falters. It is as if the microphone is being rubbed against an abrasive surface. *Has he grown a full beard?* Mary wonders. "Look, I don't know what I was thinking, calling . . . I didn't want you to get the wrong idea. It was late, I'd had a drink." Her eyes flicker shut. She should have known. "I was at the end of my tether; I didn't know what else to do. I'm so sorry."

"That's okay. That's why I'm here. How are you feeling now?"

"Lost."

Mary cannot believe her ears. It is as if the last seven years have dissolved in the space of that one, tiny word. Her humiliation at the video too. It doesn't matter. Not really. Not if it means that Jim will finally come home.

"I'm so lost. I made an awful decision and I need you to forgive me or . . . I don't know what I'll do."

At NightLine they are trained for the worst—the darkest calls, the worst imaginable confessions. It is never easy, *never,* and yet with the anonymity there is that small fraction of distance that makes the role possible in the first place. But when you are hearing someone you know in those dire straits? Mary has never had to consider how paralyzing that would be until now.

She needs to dig deeper into what he is saying, but it is hard when she is sitting close enough to Olive to reach out and touch her broderie blouse. She cannot afford to make Olive suspicious and, at the same time, Mary finds that she is craving retreat, in the way she always has when it comes to Jim. Just the two of them, blind and deaf to the rest of the world.

"Did you hear that? I'm sorry. I'm *so* sorry." There it is again, the scraping sound that muffles the voice.

"Yes. You're not alone. I'm here." Then, almost whispering, Mary adds, "I can come get you." She needs more privacy than this. "Bear with me one moment. Hold on—just a second. Can you hold?"

She doesn't wait for an answer. Instead she dives under the desk for her bag. She rummages in the front pocket for her mobile and jabs her thumb on the Home button, twisting it every which way to get the damn thing unlocked.

"One more minute, please," she mutters.

Mary types her mobile number into the desk phone to transfer the call. She keeps her eyes fixed on the desk, making herself as inconspicuous as possible; if Kit or Olive saw, they would cut the call. She knows this is against every rule in the NightLine book, but she can't bear to lose him again. In her fervor, she is oblivious to the actions of everyone around her.

Including, that is, Alice, who at this very moment is staring at Mary wide-eyed, too absorbed by the scene unfolding in front of her to make notes in her reporter's pad.

The beeps start up, a Morse code of pin drops that are her lifeline to Jim. It can't be more than thirty seconds before they end as abruptly as they began.

"Hello? Hello? Are you there?"

There is a whistling over the line, a high-pitched buzz that cuts right through her ears. Mary looks up at the dashboard.

Call disconnected.

13

2005

Mam was at the door before Mary had even got halfway up the drive with her suitcase. It was dark and she was silhouetted by the kitchen light behind her. Mary inhaled the smell of stew, almost caramel-rich, and tuned in to the sound of the horse races and Da cursing over the top of them.

"Here she is! Ah, we've missed you!"

"It's not been a week, Mam."

"I know, I know. But we want to hear all about your holiday in Portrush. Come in, tea's nearly done."

Mary had just dropped Jim at the airport to catch his flight back to London and already, his absence felt like a draft in her chest. No one seemed to notice though and, bar Mam, there was little interest in her time away. Gavin and Conor were on their usual raucous form, offering competing renditions of whatever had happened at the Brown Derby last night—some tall tale about Jamie, two doors down, throwing a punch and the two of them stepping in like the King's Road's answer to the A-Team. It was comforting, the joshing and the joking and at least two glasses taken down by Gavin's flying arm, mid-gesture, but still Mary's anxiety sat like a lead loaf in the pit of her stomach. She had no idea how Mam would take the news that she was leaving.

"We're not so bad, are we?" Mam asked as she wiped down the table.

Mary was scouring the bottom of the saucepan, trying to figure out which stains were worth her time and which were staying put. In the next room, Da gave a cough loud enough to wake the dead. When she didn't respond, Mam came and placed a hand on her back. It was cold and Mary could feel the slight damp of the J-cloth she had been holding through her thin blouse.

"What is it?"

"I'm moving."

Mary made herself turn round. It was one thing to announce you were leaving your family, quite another not to do it to their face.

"Out—of here and out of Belfast. James asked me to move in with him."

Mary watched as Mam's eyes widened. The hairs at the far corners of her brows were starting to go gray, and she noticed that Mam hadn't gone far enough with the pencil to color them in.

"Oh, Mary. That's wonderful!" she managed.

"I'm sorry, Mam."

"For what?"

"Leaving you."

She had no idea how Mam would cope without her in the house. The boys were . . . exactly that. Boys. They still tried to jump Da for the TV remote, even when he was just in the door from a chemotherapy treatment.

"As soon as I'm set up with a job out there, I'll send my usual contribution." Mary was already panicking about what she would do for work and money. Jim had said he could spot her for a few weeks, but she hated relying on him and that arrangement couldn't last forever. "And I'll come back as often as I can, if there's an . . ."

Mary couldn't bring herself to say the word *emergency* because that would be to admit the reality they were all trying to block out: Da wasn't getting any better. She hated the fact that she was leaving him in this state, but if she didn't go now, then when?

"It's an hour by plane. Two, door-to-door."

Mam hadn't said anything but Mary could see it was because she was swallowing down a lump in her throat.

"It's your time, you know that?" Mam reached out and wrapped an arm around Mary's shoulder, squeezing her against the side of her own body. "I'm so happy for you."

Mary blinked back her own tears. "I meant it, though, about the money."

"I won't take it. You've done more than enough and now it's your chance to be happy, yourself. And I know it's awful sudden—these things often are."

Mary had known Jim two months, met him on just four separate occasions. Mam must be about to caution that this was all happening too quickly, and what would Mary say to that? She had thought the same thing herself; would have believed it too, had it not been for the sheer force of their connection.

"You don't think it's too soon?" Mary knew her own mind but she still wanted Mam's approval—everyone did; it didn't matter if she was seven or twenty-seven.

"No! Wherever did you get that idea from? I haven't said as much, have I? Besides, when you know, you know. I had it with your da. We were engaged after six weeks, and look at us now." Mary glanced at the half-finished sweater Mam was knitting for Da, which was draped over the kitchen chair. He was always cold, now that he'd lost so much weight. Herringbone stitch too—that sort of devotion was inspirational. "When you meet the right person, you need to be with them, no matter what. Through thick and thin. I have no doubt you'll do that for Jim, Mary." She paused. "There is the one problem, though."

Mary's pulse lurched. They'd already discussed work, money, Da—she had no idea what other possible issues there could be.

"We haven't even met your young man."

"Oh." Something surmountable at least. "Will you come with me? For the move?" Mary blurted out, before she had the chance to worry about the cost. "You and Da both. That way, you can see where I'm living."

She could see her mam turning the offer over and over in her head, scanning Mary's face for a sign that she was about to retract it. "Go on, then." She smiled. It had been a long time since Mary had seen one so genuine from Mam. "It would be nice to see the two of you together. See the man who stole your heart. I'll look into the ferry."

The hotel was gobsmacked she was leaving. Mary tried not to take it personally. Jenny, her manager, reacted as if someone had suggested taking the foundations out of the building. *Eleven years' service,* she repeated over and over, *no one coordinates an event quite like you.* When she asked who the lucky lad was, how long she'd known him, Mary mumbled something about him being an old friend, and Moira gave her a sharp kick in the shins.

"Why the feck did you say that?"

"What else was I meant to say? I don't want to sound unhinged."

"For shacking up with a stranger."

Mary could feel a fine sheen of sweat breaking out along her hairline. Trust Moira to put it like that. It was true: there was no way you could say you were relocating on the back of meeting a man four times and have it sound sane. But that didn't change the way she felt, nor Jim; when they spoke every evening his excitement crackled down the phone, even after a twelve-hour shift at the clinic.

"Lighten up, girl." Moira smacked Mary with the back of the guest book. Mary would miss Moira something rotten. "It's the ballsiest thing you've ever done and I won't let you back out of it."

Moving day came round quickly enough. Somehow Mam had found the money for the ferry, justifying the expense on the basis that they would be there to help Mary with her bags. Never mind that the treatment had left Da breathless beyond the end of the road, or that Mary didn't have enough stuff to fill more than two big sports duffle bags. Mam had chosen the night crossing on her less-than-scientific conjecture that it was possible to sleep off seasickness. An hour in, and the sole hope Mary had of dodging a night with her head stuck over the loo was to lie stock-still on the floor of her cabin.

Jim had insisted on picking them up from the port, in spite of Mary's protests. Mary wondered if this was his own penance, for not meeting her parents earlier. When she explained what had happened—what Mam had said about her moving in with a man they'd never met—he'd felt awful. The last thing he wanted was for her parents to think they were handing over their daughter to a stranger, let alone one who had no interest in them, either. Not that it was his place to apologize; it was both their faults, she supposed, for being so wrapped up in each other that they hadn't thought how their infatuation could read as selfishness.

It was still dark when they disembarked—Mary shouldering one bag, Mam the other. Da was reaching out to hold one handle of it, but Mam shuffled away every time he tried to take some of the weight.

"Why don't I?" At the bottom of the ramp, a hand appeared to scoop up the bag. "Good morning, Gorgeous," Jim said, loudly enough for Mary to hear, but not her parents.

Mary did the briefest introduction she could muster. "Mam, Da—this is Jim. *James.* James, my boyfriend." She couldn't believe she'd never called him that before.

"Her boyfriend," Jim repeated. "And very sorry I am, too, that we haven't met until now."

A family with huge four-wheeled cases had backed up behind Da, and Mam took his arm, pressing them both against the railings so the others could pass.

"Shall we?" Jim said, when the rumbling of the wheels had quietened down, bending his thumb in the direction of the car park. "I thought it might be a bit tight, but it looks like our Mary packs light."

They talked the whole four-hour drive down—Mam and Jim. Da even chimed in a lot more than he was known to do, about rugby and, crucially, the way he'd petitioned the oncology department into upsizing their screen, so he didn't have to miss a minute of game-play during treatments. Jim had bought a couple of teas from the service station (lukewarm but still welcome) as well as croissants, a luxury Mam wouldn't stop thanking him for as they sped down the motorway. It was a miracle that she didn't get a crick in her neck, the way she kept poking it round the corner of the driver's seat, trying to catch Jim's eye.

"It's a long time since we've been in London, isn't it, Stan?"

"1976—the first Hong Kong Sevens. Before your time, no doubt?"

"Too young to remember, I'm afraid," Jim replied. He flicked the indicator and slowed the car into a spot outside the flat. "Here we are, then! Home, sweet home."

He collected both bags from the trunk and slung one on each shoulder. He opened the car door for Da and the two of them walked up to the flat together, deep in conversation. Before Mary could follow, Mam reached out and clutched at her wrist.

"He's perfect," she breathed.

"Alright—steady on there."

"You're a lucky girl, Mary O'Connor."

Thirteen years—six together, seven apart—and not one minute would go by when Mary would even come close to forgetting how lucky she was.

14

2018

Ten minutes past midnight. There is a snap as the desk phone falls from Mary's hand and lands on the desk. She fumbles to catch it before it does any more damage. "Sorry, sorry."

Alice can see that Mary is trying to ferret her mobile away before Olive notices that she has it out in the first place. Maybe she should create a diversion? Luckily, Olive is tied up on another call, a lot of affirmative *hmm*s but not much chance for her to get a word in edgewise.

"I take it the caller hung up again?" Kit asks. "We keep getting cutouts—I could swear it's the same person. *Aie!*" He doesn't wait for Mary to either confirm or deny his hypothesis. "You ready for your next, then? Hopefully someone will be there this time. Mary?"

"Actually, Kit, I need to go." She is already snatching up her belongings. She doesn't meet anyone's eye. Alice hopes that Mary isn't about to cry. She looked so fragile when Alice entered the room, and if whatever she just witnessed was Mary taking another call from Jim, there's no doubt that she will be broken.

"Oh, no problem. And, look, I'm sorry again about earlier. As I say, it's blowing over already . . ." Mary isn't listening. She's off. "Hold on!" Kit bounces out of his seat. Mary turns. "Are you okay to get home?" Kit, who has looked over at Alice on average five times a minute since she arrived, gives her a particularly pointed glance. "Budget probably won't stretch to a taxi but maybe Alice could walk you? You're close, aren't you, Mary?"

"Of course. I'd love to." Alice leaps in before Mary so much as has the chance to refuse.

Mary looks both uncomfortable with the attention and irritated by the intrusion. But it's futile; Alice is already on her feet and chasing Mary out of the door.

"You alright there?" Alice calls to her back.

Stupid question. The call, and perhaps now two of them. Then the video. Alice knows that Mary is aware of its existence; Kit mouthed "video" at Alice once she realized she had walked into something of a NightLine emergency earlier.

It is not until Mary comes to a standstill, five minutes later, that she says anything at all.

"Right, well, here I am." They are standing outside a fish-and-chip shop on a road where Alice once viewed a rental flat herself. She passed on it. "Above here, I mean," Mary mumbles. She steps over the threshold and goes to shut the door.

Alice shoves her foot in the crack. "I'll make you a cup of tea, will I? I could do with one."

"Actually . . ."

"Just a quick one. It's been such a night." Before Mary can protest, Alice has slipped into the corridor. "Up here, then?"

Alice feels somewhat bad about forcing herself on Mary but if their first encounter taught her anything, it is that Mary is backward about coming forward. Which explains in part why Alice is here now; Mary is never going to ask for someone to help find Jim. But, as Alice can attest, closure is everything. If Mary doesn't see that now, she will, once she has reached it. And the fact that these could well be answers that furnish a story—the big one that could help Alice save her own skin at work? Well, that's a bonus, too.

Mary turns the key for her own front door and heads straight for the sanctuary of the sofa, feet curled up under her body like a frightened child. Alice takes charge of the kettle.

"So," Alice begins, settling two mugs of tea on the three-legged stool that passes as a table. She takes a seat on the chair opposite Mary. "Are you okay? Really? You know you can talk to me."

Mary's emotions are written across her face as clear as a bloodstain on a freshly laundered white sheet. A gift to a journalist, Alice thinks. Right now, she can tell that Mary is weighing up the ordeal of repeating the night's events against the relief that might come from sharing them. Mary bites down on her bottom lip, as if willing the words to stay inside. Then, finally, she relents.

"He called. Jim. Again."

"Tonight?"

"Yes."

"What did he say?"

Mary takes a deep breath, the exhale trembling on her bottom lip. "He said he was feeling lost. He was sorry as well, because he hadn't meant for his reaching out to upset me like this. Not that it matters, and I tried to tell him that, but it's so hard, there, at NightLine. Especially because Jim's always been so private. So I went to transfer the call to my mobile. I know, *I know,* you're not meant to, but I couldn't speak to him there. Not with everyone else. And I told him to hold on, that I'd put him right through. And then the moment I got my mobile to my ear . . . he was gone." She shudders.

Alice has a hundred questions dancing around her mind but they all die at the base of her throat, in the face of Mary's sorrow. Only a few words escape. "I'm sorry. Really I am."

"I just . . . I just don't know what to do. I can't lose him again."

Alice knows that exact feeling—the powerlessness of those left behind. But now, hearing shades of her own darkest days articulated? It is all she can do to keep her mind on the reasons why she is here: to find Jim for Mary, and to get the story that will keep her in a job.

"Is this him?" Alice asks eventually.

She points at the sole photo frame on display in the kitchen-cum-dining-cum-living-room, propped on an otherwise empty mantelpiece. In it, Jim's face occupies two-thirds of the image. He is tall, dark, and classically handsome, like the lead in a Sunday-night period drama. Alice is finding it hard to locate so much as a single flaw, aside from a chip in his left eyebrow like a knife's slice through the hair. Mary's face pops over his shoulder, either being piggybacked or following a few paces behind in the selfie. Wherever it was taken had a stunning landscape: flat, overlapping stones rising up out of a raging sea behind the couple.

"Yes, that's him. He was my partner. My boyfriend, I suppose. He was nine years older than me, though, so it always felt silly to call him that."

"You look so happy."

Maybe Alice has pushed it too far. Mary's eyes flutter shut. "We were," she says. "*So* happy. I didn't know what the word meant before I met him. Not properly. I've never felt so alive as when I was with him. Sorry, will you excuse me?" She stumbles off the sofa and toward what Alice imagines must be the bathroom. She hears the lock being drawn, then muffled sobs.

Alice wishes more than anything that she could comfort Mary, but experience has shown her that some sadness can only be self-soothed. When Mary comes out, it will be Alice's cue to leave. But she will be leaving empty-handed. Unless there is anything else she can glean from inside Mary's flat . . .

Before Alice's conscience has a chance to object, she snaps a picture of the photograph on the mantelpiece with her phone camera. She has no idea when she'll need it, but it is of much better quality than the video from last night. Plus, this one features Jim. *Jim.* Jim who? Alice hasn't even got a surname for him, sorry excuse for a journalist that she is.

She stands and heads to the sink. There is a bunch of papers stuffed between the radio and the drying rack. Alice flicks through a few bills and leaflets, scanning the text. They are all, unsurprisingly, addressed to Mary. Alice starts to stuff them back. She doesn't want Mary to appear and catch her red-handed. In her hurry, a passport photo falls out.

It's Jim, again, but here his handsomeness has suffered in the same way that other mere mortals do, when faced with renewing their official documents in the overpriced photo booths. Although she knows she isn't fit to pass judgment, he looks rough in this one, especially compared to how attractive he was in the other image. Eye bags. Lank hair. In need of a shave. What happened to him?

Alice turns over the photo. *James Whitnell, July 2011.* So it's Jim for James. This should get her started.

When Mary reemerges, Alice is already by the door. "You don't deserve any of this—you know that, don't you?" She cannot stand the thought that a woman as kind and loving as Mary would blame herself for any of what has happened. She hasn't even touched on the issue of the online video. Probably for the best, Alice thinks, handing over a receipt, her number scribbled on the back. There is only so much a person can bear to discuss in one night. "Please, call me if you need anything. Anything at all. I want to help."

She hesitates. This is the moment to tell Mary what she has in mind—an investigation that could uncover what happened to Jim and salvage her own career, all in one fell swoop. But although she has not heard about it, Alice has *seen* how badly Mary responded to the exposure brought on by the video. Mary wouldn't want a news story, not even a local one sensitively handled by someone she knows. How would Alice begin to phrase her plan? She has already lied to Mary about her occupation two nights back, at the pub.

Better to seek forgiveness than permission, Alice thinks. Besides, if Alice can only show that the ends justify the means, if she can find Jim . . . Well then, there won't be any forgiveness needed.

"I should let you get some sleep. Night, Mary."

Outside the air is still warm, despite the fact it is past one in the morning—the preserve of just a few nights in the short, sharp London summer. Alice's flat is only a ten-minute walk away, but somehow she doesn't have the strength to put one foot in front of another. She cannot deny the echoes of her own experience any longer.

Since meeting Mary, Alice has tried to stifle the sense of kinship she felt with this woman, a stranger with a sign that speaks to the worst period in her own life. One that Alice has never spoken about—for fear that the shame and the sadness will return to undo all her progress over the years. *Disappeared.* Is it worse if it is a romantic partner who vanishes or if it is a family member, someone genetically programmed to stay?

Alice will never forget the day her dad went missing. She had just turned twelve. A week before, he'd been at the center of her birthday party, playing the role he loved best—the clown. Pulling faces, cracking rude jokes. All Alice's pals adored him. But none so much as her. They were the thickest of thieves, the best of friends.

Once the party had wound down, the two of them curled up on the sofa to watch *Match of the Day,* hot chocolate in hand. Alice was already sick from all the sugar—the cake, the ice cream, the party-bag sweets—but she would always find room for tradition, and this was theirs. While Alice glazed over at the scores, her dad would pretend not to notice the cream she siphoned off the top of his drink. When she dozed off against his stomach, he pulled over the blanket, tucked it under her feet. Alice knew she would always be safe and secure with him by her side.

But then came Monday, March 15, 2004—a date forever ingrained in her memory. Alice woke up and he was gone. She could tell her mum was trying to put on a brave face for her, but not even the world's greatest actors can plaster a mask of confidence over the earth-shattering realization that their family has been destroyed. Alice remembers slamming her hands over her ears. If she didn't hear it, it wasn't true. She could believe instead that her dad was sleeping in or working late, that he would be back with them soon.

But as days became months and months became years, Alice had no choice but to accept that their family of three had now become an uncertain bond between two. That didn't stop her wondering, though—whether there was something she did to cause her dad to go, or if there was anything at all she could do to bring him back home again.

Eventually everyone else's interest in him waned. He was gone and that was that. Even Alice's mum was so paralyzed by sadness that she headed to bed the minute she got home from work. To Alice, that was defeat. Not that she could say as much to a face drawn with the dull hand of grief. But what could Alice do to make matters better or to prove there was still hope for her dad? She was so young, in her first year of secondary school. She had only just started walking home alone from school. No twelve-year-old can conduct an effectual investigation.

A decade and a half on, Alice is now old enough to be in a position to help, albeit this time it is someone outside her immediate family. It strikes her that, of all people, her mum would know what to say to Mary. But would she approve of Alice pursuing Jim's story, without Mary's blessing? Deep down, Alice knows the answer to that.

And it is not one she can afford to hear.

15

2006

Mary heard Jim before she saw him. Or rather she thought it was Jim. If she wasn't mistaken, he was doing some DIY. Not that there was anything she could think needed fixing; in the six months since she'd moved in, she had yet to come to terms with how pristine he kept the Ealing flat.

It took a few attempts to get the key into the inside door. Mary was loaded down with bags from the sewing shop on the Uxbridge Road. She was starting to wonder if she was their best customer; after she had set up a website at the end of last month, Mary had received a deluge of commissions and now found herself needing to top up weekly on threads and calico.

Eventually Mary was in. She dropped her parcels by the door and left her sunglasses on the side table. The racket was far louder here— incessant hammering that seemed to be coming from the living room. Since when did Jim own a toolbox? Unless he'd bought one recently in a pique of madness. Wasn't he a tad too young for a midlife crisis?

In the doorway it took a while for Mary to work out whether Jim was mid assembly or mid destruction, never mind what the object in question was. His shirt had ridden up, his lower back covered in a fine layer of dust. Above his left hip there was a small screw-shaped indent.

It was a particularly warm spring day and it looked like he was working up a sweat. Her beautiful, competent professional of a boyfriend, floored by a flat pack.

Mary cleared her throat. Nothing. He was in his own world. She didn't want to startle him but surely a light tap on the shoulder would be safe enough.

Jim jumped, his shout muffled by the sound of the hammer clattering to the floor.

"Sorry, sorry." Mary placed her hand on his bicep. "But I have to say, it's nice to see you doing some hard work. For once."

She bit her tongue, relishing the look of indignation that passed across Jim's face. He had been working twelve-, even fourteen-hour shifts recently, which made her grateful for the all-consuming nature of her own new job. With her head at the sewing machine, the rhythmic *tip-tap* of the needle as it punctured both the calico and her consciousness, she couldn't find the time to pine for him. She kept her phone on loud, though, so that when Jim texted to say that he was leaving the clinic she could head out to meet him. Seeing him making his way through the gates at Ealing Broadway station was the highlight of her day. Some of Mary's best moments since moving to London had been on those five-minute walks home together, hand in hand.

"Can I ask what this, er . . . is?" Mary watched Jim's chest deflate. "I mean, it'll be lovely looking when it's done."

"It's for you."

"Ah. Wow! Yes, well, I've always wanted a . . ." Mary squinted to try and read the small print of the instruction manual that was strewn worryingly far away from the carnage of planks and nails in the center of the room. Trust Jim to think he knew better. Or was that all mankind?

"A desk. For your sewing. It was meant to be a surprise."

Mary crouched down. The fabric on the knees of Jim's jeans was shredded, another casualty of the project, along with the floorboards.

She took his face in both hands and kissed the sawdust away. She had thought she couldn't love him more than in that moment in the doorway, seeing him sweat over an installation designed for amateurs. And now this—a selfless surprise. That was the beauty of what they had together, Mary realized: every time she thought there was no further to fall, she fell a little bit deeper.

"I wanted you to have a workspace of your own. I thought we could put the desk over there." Jim gestured to the side of the kitchen table, which was colonized by Mary's ongoing projects. They had been eating lap suppers every weekend for months now. "And I also wanted to do something to make sure that you knew this was your home as much as it is mine."

"Jim," Mary began. Half the syllable caught in her throat and she willed herself not to cry. She didn't want him to think she was unhappy or uncomfortable here, not when he had done nothing whatsoever to make her feel that way. But still, Mary never forgot the place that had been her home for the previous twenty-eight years. Calling Mam was never the same as catching up on the sofa with her.

"No! Let me finish! One more thing . . . I suppose it's also my way of making you take your business as seriously as I do. You're cautious by nature. A worrier. And I get that. But this is going to work out, Mary. It is."

There was no holding in her sobs now. No one had ever had as much faith in her as Jim. No one came close. Of course her family wanted the best for her but it was a different sort of best, the kind that comes from being content, not pushing yourself to reach out for your highest hopes and dreams. Jim had shown Mary that her sense of familial duty and her own ambition weren't mutually exclusive, that putting herself first didn't have to be egotistical.

"Thank you," she managed. She had no idea what she had done to deserve a man this kind, this generous, this supportive. Making a living from her maps had been a dream, but so was experiencing a love that made her feel as if she could rise to the challenge of it. Mary felt a flash of selfishness, as if she had somehow conspired to hoard all the good luck. "Will I give you a hand finishing this? Looks like you need it."

With her at the helm, following the steps to the letter, the desk soon took form.

"I feel like we should celebrate." Jim was perched on the edge of the finished product, Mary beginning to sort her workstation around him. "We could order in from the Indian place that's just opened near the station—you know the one? Get a bottle of wine, finish that box set—we're nearly on the last DVD."

"Aren't we meant to be at Gus's housewarming do?"

Jim shrugged. "I don't feel like it."

Neither did Mary, to be fair. She'd met Gus and his fiancée Jillian at birthday drinks a few weeks after she had moved to London. Everyone had gawked at Mary when she'd arrived, Jim's hand in hers. *The girl who managed to steal James's heart,* Jillian breathed. *Someone to finally set him on the straight and narrow—in the nick of time!* That one had gone down particularly badly with Jim. They only stayed for one drink and, since then, Mary got the impression that Jim had been dodging invites from his wider friendship group.

"Don't you want to see your friends?" she ventured. It wasn't her place to get involved but she hated the idea that Jim was closing himself off from the people he had known since university. More than that, she hated the idea that they might blame her for Jim's recent isolation.

"I want to spend time with you."

"We always do. Day after day after day . . ."

"Bored of me, already?"

"Never." The truth of it stopped Mary in her tracks. Jim took the opportunity to draw her in, until she was nestled between his legs.

"So what's the problem then?"

Was there one? This would be typical of the old, pre-Jim version of Mary, finding problems where there were none. The last six months in Ealing had been the best of her life, far better than she could ever have envisaged when they played house back at Portrush. No major incidents or arguments; their weekends slipped by in a happy haze and they were forming a new routine to their days, which Mary could live with until the very end of hers.

But Mary did sometimes wonder if this seclusion that they lived in was entirely healthy. Moira hadn't had the chance to visit, and Jim and Mary had yet to sit down and book plane tickets to Belfast themselves. Jim's friends had all but got the boot, and that left his parents. Since Mary had moved in, Richard and Juliette had been round only once, for a cup of coffee. Not so much as a biscuit to accompany it. They didn't seem to have thawed much to Mary.

Jim's hands crawled into the back pockets of Mary's jeans. He smelled the same as ever, smoky. "Fine. But I won't share my peshwari naan."

"That's my girl. I wouldn't expect anything less."

"Will we go get it together?"

"Nah." Jim was already on his feet. It was already past six and Mary's stomach growled in anticipation. "I'll go."

"I'm happy to." Mary followed him into the hallway and went to grab her coat.

Jim caught the hood and placed it back on the hook. "You stay here. Sort out the desk. Get yourself all set up. I'll only be gone a half·hour."

He pecked Mary on the cheek and was out of the door before she could protest.

She had no idea what all that was about. There he was, telling her that he wanted a date night, but he didn't want company for the trip to collect the food. It wasn't as if there could be another surprise. Unless there was a call he wanted to take, or he didn't want her tagging along to look, horrified, at the cost of the wine he bought or the amount he was purchasing or how fast he got through—

The phone made a welcome interruption into Mary's catastrophizing. She hadn't wandered down the slippery path of worst-case scenarios in months now, and rarely regarding Jim. The man had just built her a desk—there was nothing to worry about.

"Hello?"

"Mary?"

She knew, as soon as she heard the tone of Mam's voice, that she had been worrying about the wrong thing.

It was Da.

16

2018

Alice switches on her office computer and yawns while she waits for it to load. Another evening with Mary, another sleepless night. She can no longer deny that she is doubly invested in finding Jim—personally as well as professionally—and while she had hoped she would be able to skirt around her past, that's never possible, is it?

The day her dad disappeared changed everything. Alice's relationship with her mum has never been the same. They don't text beyond the perfunctory and never speak on the phone unless it is a matter of life or death. Of course Alice knows that her mum loves her, would do anything for her, but it is as if there is a tent pole keeping the two of them a safe distance apart. If they started to speak openly about what had happened, the illusion of normality that it had taken them both so long to construct would collapse. If Alice said how she really felt about his loss, then it would kill her mum all over again.

Because it was not just Alice's childhood that was stolen abruptly; it was her future too. What would it be like, she wonders, to have her dad in her life now? She could talk to him about work. Although she does not feel proud of how she has stagnated at the *Bugle,* a father wouldn't care. Not a good one. Would he beam at all her nonsense articles, or share the links with his friends and colleagues? She could get his advice on her predicament here—the looming redundancy. And he'd take a view, no doubt, on her personal life too; any boys she thought fit to bring home. Not, of course, that there has ever been much of a chance of that . . .

The computer burbles into life. *Eyes on the prize, Keaton,* she reminds herself, sitting up a little straighter in her desk chair. It may be too late for her, but if the last few days have shown her nothing else, it is that it is not too late for Mary. Jim is reaching out and there has to be some reason for that. She begins to search "James Whitnell" online.

Turns out there are quite a few of them, worldwide, so she has to narrow her search term almost immediately, adding combinations of "UK" and "London." On the property records, she finds details of a flat he once owned nearby, sold seven years back for a small fortune. A far cry from where Mary is now living, Alice thinks with a flash of indignation. As if she hasn't suffered enough, left in the dark like this.

She finds James's full name listed on the alumni page of an Oxford college, no other details included; a similar situation with a posh school in central London. It shouldn't surprise Alice, given how refined he looked in the photo on Mary's mantelpiece, but Mary doesn't look as if she comes from money. They must have been worlds apart. Fancy flat, loaded family, adoring partner—it looks to Alice like Jim had a pretty nice life. So why the hell would he disappear?

Did he even need to work? Alice scrolls through a further four pages of search results until she hits a return for "Dr. James Whitnell—ENT" on the swanky website for a doctors' clinic that definitely isn't NHS. Alice clicks. *Error 404—not found.* Well, no surprise there then. Neither was Jim. If he had fallen off the face of the earth, he wasn't likely to be consulting on some rich person's nasal passages.

But he must have been good at what he did, to have landed a job somewhere like that. Wasn't there someplace where doctors were tracked anyway? In case they turned out to be psychopaths? Alice could find out more there about where else he could have worked, maybe.

She opens a new tab on her internet browser and brings up the medical register, types in James's name. *Sorry but we cannot find a record that matches your search.*

So he's ghosted here as well! Alice lets out a grunt of frustration and returns to the stylish, neutral tones of the private practice where Jim's profile is now defunct. She can't imagine that staff turnover is high in a place with cream leather sofas in reception. Someone there will have known why Jim vanished from their page. Maybe why he vanished, full stop.

Alice jots down the address. It's time for a field trip.

Eldridge Health Centre is located in a town house on a side road in Kensington that is leafy and quiet. Alice hovers on the threshold and checks her teeth in the polished bronze knocker. While she always dresses smartly for work, this area is much more haute couture than high street, and she doesn't want a rogue biscuit crumb upsetting an already fragile appearance of belonging.

Confidence will be key. Alice throws her shoulders back and walks into reception as if she owns the place.

The woman behind the desk is touching thirty, she would guess, with a long, sleek brown ponytail and the bored expression of an employee who ought to have moved on long ago. Alice should know.

"Can I help?" she asks.

"Yes. I'm here to see Dr. James Whitnell."

The receptionist's jaw drops, revealing impressively straight bottom teeth. Her eyes widen, moving from shock to confusion and then to something else that Alice can't quite place. One thing's for certain, though: she recognizes the name.

"I'm afraid Dr. Whitnell no longer works with us," she says, considering each and every word. "May I ask what this is regarding?"

"Oh—I'm an old friend."

The receptionist frowns. Jim was nine years older than Mary, and Mary is—what, thirty-five, forty? So Jim could well be twenty years older than Alice. *Shit!* "I mean, I'm here on behalf of an old friend. I didn't know he'd left. . . . Well, thanks anyway. I'll be off."

She turns on her heel. The minute she is outside the clinic she shoots down the side of the building and crumples behind the garbage cans. She doesn't want the receptionist to follow her down the road and ask any more awkward questions. What the hell was she thinking, claiming to be an *old friend*? This was a monumental error on her part. Anyway, it wasn't as if the receptionist was about to impart some vital information about Jim's whereabouts to a bloody stranger, was it? Alice wonders if her brain has short-circuited or if she is intrinsically dim. She needs a minute to compose herself before she braves walking past the window. This has been an epic waste of time and—

The front door slams again. There are footsteps—two sets, it seems—first on the concrete steps and then, alarmingly, on the gravel that covers the side alley. Alice drops to the ground. Peering round a trash can, she can see the receptionist and another woman who is younger, with auburn hair layered to her shoulders. The receptionist offers her colleague a cigarette. They both light up.

"Strangest thing just happened, Em," the receptionist says. "This girl walks in. You wouldn't have seen her from your desk, but she was about your age. I dunno, maybe twenty-five? Pretty little thing, neat bob. Anyway she comes in and asks to see Dr. Whitnell."

"Who?"

"Exactly. He's before your time. He was here—what, ten years ago? Maybe a little less. You'd remember if you saw him, though, I'm telling you. He was gorgeous, Em, drop-dead. Everyone was after him but he was very much taken. He had this long-term girlfriend. Mattie? I think that was her name. I met her once. She was as stunning as him, annoyingly. Bit of an odd air to her, I thought, but the whole situation was weird when I saw her."

"Wait, I'm lost . . ." The second woman is doe-eyed. It doesn't look as if it would take much to confuse her.

"Oh, yeah—so Dr. Whitnell. *James,* as he insisted we all call him." The receptionist drops her northern accent in favor of some Queen's English. "He left ages ago, and this woman's looking for him now? Weird, if you ask me. Especially given the circumstances *James* left in."

"Which were?" Auburn-hair perks up at the thought of gossip afoot. Alice too, only her heart is hammering so hard it is making it difficult to hear anything else. *Focus, Keaton. Focus.*

"We never knew for sure. One of the PAs overheard their boss say that he jumped before he was pushed. That it was only a matter of time before James was shown the door, what with the way he was . . ."

There is a crunch as the receptionist stubs out her cigarette on the gravel.

"Wow!" her colleague says, leading the way back inside. "I didn't know things like that happened round here."

"But keep it to yourself," the receptionist adds. "I don't want to get a reputation for stirring scandal."

17

2006

Mary was in no way prepared for losing Da. It didn't matter that there had been so many years between the diagnosis and his death; no amount of time could help her reconcile herself to a life without him. He was their rock. The house would surely collapse without the sound of the races as the backdrop to her brothers' bickering. And Mam—what about her? They had married at twenty-two and spent more time together than they ever had apart. It was Da who showed Mary what to look for in a man: honesty, consideration, and the sort of adoration that made Mam feel like a queen, even in an overcrowded semi.

Jim had known what was wrong the minute he walked through the door. Mary still had the phone in one hand. He dropped the takeaway bag, popadams spilling across the floor, and bundled her into his arms. But try as he might, he couldn't squeeze out the pain in Mary's chest at the thought that she would never hug her da again, never have him tell her again how proud he was of her gumption at moving to England and of her talent with the maps.

Mary couldn't see straight, let alone work in the week before the funeral. A cabin strike meant there were no flights available before then, and Jim couldn't get away from his consultations to be at home with Mary, much as he kept saying that there was nowhere he would rather be than in the flat with her, providing company in her distress. To make matters worse, there was something wrong at work. Jim wasn't getting back until the early hours and, when Mary asked him directly, he didn't deny the existence of an issue. *I'll tell you about it when it's sorted,* he'd said, and Mary had accepted that, knowing her grief had crowded out space for any other emotions in the foreseeable future.

At the wake there was a turnout just shy of a hundred, and Mary was strung out between accepting condolences and keeping the sandwich trays filled. Her brothers had been delegated the role of looking after Mam, but still Mary kept half an eye on her at all times. Then there was Jim, who knew next to no one. Mary had briefly introduced him to Moira and her new boyfriend, but they had other people to talk to and soon Mary was losing track of him. Sure, he was a grown man, but his behavior had been so off in the last week, what with the stress at work, and Mary didn't want to make matters worse by demanding that he stick by her side when he might need a breath of fresh air.

In a rare five-minute window of respite, Mary had gone looking for Jim. It wasn't a big house and she quickly found him in the kitchen with her brother Gavin. Each had a can of Guinness in hand and, behind them, a row of what she assumed were empties. Could neither bother to clean up the place? And why wasn't Gavin with Mam?

Mary took a few deep breaths to try to calm herself. If ever there was a time for an argument, it wasn't now. Besides, Auntie Carol was calling: *More Scotch eggs—did Mary know if the caterer had done any?* By the time Mary had located them and spoken with three cousins clustered in the hallway, she wasn't in the mood to check in on Jim again. She tried to stifle the thought that he didn't deserve it anyway.

Instead she climbed the stairs to the one room that was out-of-bounds for the wake. Mam and Da's. It looked exactly as it had the last time Mary had seen it, nearly seven months ago, just before she moved in with Jim. She didn't know what she had been expecting to have changed.

Da's clothes were still folded on the chair in the corner, his puzzle books on the dresser and loose change from his holey wallet scattered alongside. She collapsed on his pillow and stared up at the ceiling, wondering what he had been thinking in those last moments. She prayed that it had been something nice—Mam, her, the boys, maybe their own holiday in Portrush over twenty years ago.

"I put your man in my room to sleep it off." Gavin poked his head round the door.

"What?"

Mary sat bolt upright. She had no right to be lying here, but at least her brother had the good grace not to mention it. If anything, he looked embarrassed for himself. That was a first.

"What?" she repeated, when an answer wasn't forthcoming.

"Your man—James." Gavin cocked his thumb and little finger and tipped his dish-shaped fist toward his mouth, in what Mary imagined was an impression of Jim's afternoon drinking.

"Are you sure?"

"He's the most well-spoken drunk in here. The only one with that accent too. He, er . . . spewed in the downstairs toilet."

"Jaysus!" Mary swung her feet off the side of the bed and pinched the skin at the back of her neck. The knots only seemed to work themselves deeper. To think she'd come up here for a break, too. She should have tried to find him again. She should have kept a closer eye. "And you say he's up here?"

"Don't shoot the messenger."

In Mary's old room, Jim was lying on his side, his body curled in Gavin's attempt at the recovery position. Mary straightened him out and laid a cold palm across his forehead.

"My beauty," he croaked, releasing a wave of acrid breath with the undertone of whiskey. It was part of the smell of him, albeit usually without the tinge of vomit. "What did I miss?"

"Most of the wake, by the looks of things."

"I needed a little something to help me through."

"To help *you* through?"

"Don't be so sensitive. You know what I mean."

Mary could feel the anger rising, the pressure in her head and the heat of it all sticky under her arms. She stood up to leave.

"Come on," Jim slurred. "What's got into you?"

"It is my father's funeral," Mary hissed. "You are a fecking disgrace."

As she shut the door, one palm flat against the wood to dull the sound, Mary bit down on her knuckles to stop herself from crying. What the hell had just happened? This wasn't the Jim she knew. There had been a few minor tiffs in the nine months they'd been together—over the chores, a sharp word in the cocktail of agitation that was the stress of starting up her new business and Jim's high-pressure role—but never anything like this. Was their first proper argument going to be their last, too? Of all the times and places for it. If she wasn't allowed to be *sensitive* with Da's body barely settled in the grave, then when? Mary needed Jim, today more than ever, and there was no denying how he had let her down.

She had never expected Jim to disappoint her like this. She had never expected him to disappoint her, full stop, although, she supposed, that was far from realistic. Mary suddenly realized that she'd been so swept away by Jim, their chemistry and the brilliance of him that she hadn't had the chance to assess the pedestal she'd strapped him to, the nicks and notches that made him as flawed as everyone else.

How much had he put away? The Guinness she saw him with, some others by the looks of things, whiskey judging by the smell. There had definitely been moments since Mary moved in when she had registered her own surprise at how much Jim could drink. But then he so rarely showed the effects of it, not swaying or slurring or slowing down like anyone else did, so it couldn't really be a problem, could it?

With a jolt, Mary remembered the jacket she had borrowed from Jim on their second date. It had been a hip flask in the pocket. She knew it. And then there was the shameful state of their recycling bin back in Ealing. She always tried to put a cereal box on top, lest the neighbors wonder how they got through so many bottles.

"There you are!" Mary jumped and her chest slammed into the door, making it rattle. She heard Jim burbling on the other side. "Sorry, love, I didn't mean to startle you. You alright?" The skin under Mam's eyes was sunken, purple like deep bruises in the dim light that made it out from the tasseled lampshade above.

Mary took Mam's arm and steered her into the boys' bedroom next door. "It should be me asking if *you're* alright, Mam."

Mam gave her a weak smile that barely stretched to the corners of her lips, let alone the rest of her face.

"Stupid question," Mary mumbled.

"Big drinker, is he?" Mam tilted her head in the direction of Gavin's bedroom. "Auntie Kay says he was putting it away from a flask. Can't say I blame him."

"Sorry," Mary's voice came out as a quiver. "I . . . I didn't know or I would have—" What? Not brought Jim? Said something about his drinking before? She had no idea why she hadn't mentioned the booze earlier, but then again, it didn't seem like a serious issue. Mary herself enjoyed a drink, just never to this extent. Or perhaps it was the case that a certain degree of willful ignorance was a condition of their blissful bubble of a life together—keeping shtum was the only way it could stay intact.

"Ach now, I'm not here to judge, am I? God knows your own father had his vices. Probably would still be here, if he hadn't." Mary's childhood had played out against a backdrop of her parents arguing over Da's twenty-a-day habit. "I wanted to check in that you two weren't having a spat or something like that."

Mary shook her head. "He's never like this."

"Then nothing to worry about, love. None of us is perfect."

Mary gulped. This was a far cry from what Mam had said when she helped Mary move into Jim's place in Ealing. Mary was reminded of how swiftly Mam's opinion of people could shift, especially anyone with the propensity to hurt one of her children. She felt the sudden urge to protect Mam's good opinion of Jim, of the happy relationship she used to think they shared.

"I'm no saint myself and maybe that's it—the stress of me moving in—and then he said that there had been an issue at work, last week. I don't know what, but maybe a complaint or . . ."

"It ain't you, doll. Sounds like the young man has a lot on his plate and today has probably tipped him over the edge." Mam stopped and fixed Mary right in the eyes. "And if there were to be a real problem, you'd tell me, right?"

"What are you saying?" Mary's voice trembled.

"Just that I'm on the end of the phone, anytime you need me. You're never too old to come home."

Mary couldn't get Mam's words out of her head as she flew back to London the next day, the seat belt pulled tight across her lap and the atmosphere between her and Jim stretched even tighter. There was a slight vindication on her part when Jim woke up with a pounding headache, crashing about in the dark on the hunt for the aspirin that Mary very well knew was in the front pocket of his bag and guzzling down water like a man lost in the desert for a week. She had pretended to be asleep until ten minutes before their cab arrived.

Overhead, a subtle beep announced the seat belt sign turning off. A split second later and Jim had snapped the clips on his belt loose and turned ninety degrees to face Mary, blocking the businessman in the window seat out of view.

"I can't say how sorry I am." He still reeked of booze.

"I don't want to talk about this now."

"Well, I do." Across the aisle a teenager dropped the earphone nearest them, with little to no subtlety. "I cocked up. Big-time."

"Do you even remember what you said?"

Jim set his jaw. Mary would take that as a no, then. "I embarrassed myself, I know that much. But more importantly, I embarrassed you. I wasn't there when you needed me—"

"Let me help, then," Mary interrupted. She detested the idea of a scene, and even more the reality of it, but there was no way she could stand down on this. "You told me I was sensitive, about my own father's death." She knew she shouldn't be goading him. She needed to reel herself in before she lost her upper hand—and maybe Jim—forever. But somehow she couldn't stop herself. "Is that what you think? Huh?"

"Of course not! I don't know why I said that. It doesn't sound like me. Not that I'm denying it." Jim raised his hands in surrender. "I was drunk but that's no excuse. None whatsoever. Mary, please." He reached for her hand and she whipped it away.

"What's with this drinking anyway?" Mary asked.

"I had a bad week at work." Jim rubbed his fingers across his forehead with a worrying amount of force. "I didn't want to tell you about it because you had so much else on your plate. You were grieving. One of the patients made a complaint about my . . . work. I didn't want to worry you. There's nothing to what they said and it's blowing over already. But still—"

"It wasn't just yesterday, was it, though?" Mary thought about all the evenings when Jim poured himself a whiskey the minute he walked through the door from work, or anywhere else, frankly. The crate of wine they had demolished in Portrush, although in terms of consumption it was nowhere close to a fifty-fifty split. "Do you have a problem with drink?"

"No!" Jim looked horrified. "Maybe I drink a bit too much now and then, but everyone does. And yes, maybe it's been too heavy, recently. I've used it to unwind, though. Not as a crutch or anything. Look, Mary. Mary, please, will you look at me?"

The front wheel of the refreshment trolley had caught in the end of Mary's scarf, which was trailing on the floor, a great big cable knit that had flopped out of the minuscule net on the seat in front of Mary. It took a few sharp tugs before she could set it free, straighten up and face Jim. He looked contrite, there was no denying that. But she couldn't get sucked back into the safety and security of him, not until she got the answer that she needed. She wasn't the sort to set an ultimatum, but as she had tossed and turned in the early hours of this morning, she knew that she couldn't go on in this relationship without one.

"Will you give it up? The drink. For me?"

Jim recoiled in his seat. He was being honest, then, when he said he didn't register it as a problem for him.

"Yes," he replied, when the shock on his face had faded into resigned acceptance. He paused, and then, "You know the worst thing about all this? When I met you, for the first time since Sam died I started to like who I was again. You have no idea how you saved me. None. And I've repaid you like this. I know I need to make it up to you." Mary could see her own reflection trembling in the gloss across his eyes. They were bloodshot, more so than she had ever seen them before. "And if going dry is what it takes, then that's what I'll do."

"Thank you." Mary leaned over and took his hand in both of hers.

"And it goes without saying that I'll quit it too. It'll be a health kick for the both of us." She could smack herself for saying that. It made it sound like a detox, not a solution to the one problem that she could see had the potential to split the two of them apart. "I'm grateful that you're doing this, for me."

Jim shook his head. "That's what it means to be on the same team."

18

2018

On the bus back from the doctors' clinic to Ealing, Alice's head is fit to burst. What scandal? What could Jim have done to merit nearly losing his job? Does Mary know about any of this trouble at work? Alice can't well ask, not without explaining why she was nosing around his former employers' in the first place. If she had to say, she'd guess Mary didn't know. Mary said it herself: she and Jim were happy. *So* happy. But while Jim wouldn't be the first person in the world to feel more content at home than at work, there was evidently more conflict between the two spheres of his life than in most people's.

Alice is so consumed by her thoughts that she nearly misses her stop. Her arm catches in the automatic doors. Rubbing the sore spot as the bus pulls away, she realizes that she has got off too early. She is now in the midst of the rush-hour traffic outside Ealing Broadway station. After everything, Mary is still there, sign in hand. She hasn't even taken a day off, despite the video. Not that most people seem to pay her any more attention than usual.

Mary's head is bowed. What is she thinking? About the calls, Alice imagines; whether Jim is out there somewhere, thinking of her. If he is hurting. If he needs her. If there is something else she could be doing to bring him peace. Alice could go up to her now, but she can't imagine

Mary wants that. What Alice needs to do is provide real, tangible help for her, in the form of finding out what is going on with Jim. Tracing the calls would be a good start.

But how? Alice learned a grand total of zilch about the mechanics of NightLine last night. Olive was preoccupied and kept insisting that Ted could cover more of the detail at the training session he runs at his house for all new volunteers. Alice can't remember when Olive said that would take place; it could be weeks away, for all she knows, and she can't wait that long. She has to get this story by the end of the month or she'll be out of the *Bugle's* doors, pink slip in hand.

What she needs is someone to talk her through how the back end of NightLine works, and the sooner, the better. Mary is out of the question. Olive came across as snappy. Ted would tell her to wait for his talk. That leaves Kit. On-another-planet Kit. Would he be of any actual use?

Before Alice can fully question the logic of what she is about to do, she has wandered into a side street and is searching for Kit's number in the volunteer booklet she received last night.

"*Hola!*" He answers on the first ring. "Kit speaking."

"Hi, Kit, it's Alice. Alice from NightLine? I started yesterday . . ."

"Alice, of course. How are you?" If Kit is confused as to why she is calling, he has the civility not to let it show in his voice.

"Can I come round?"

"What? Oh, er . . . yeah—er, sure." There is a pause, then, "Why?"

"I think it might be quicker if I tell you when I'm there?"

"Be my guest." Kit reels off an address on the other side of Ealing, and Alice grabs a pen to scrawl it on her hand.

Thank God, Alice thinks, *for the trusting people of this world.*

K it's flat is on the sixth floor of a concrete housing block, the lift out of service. By the time Alice makes it to his door, she is sweating— and not in a dewy, attractive sort of way.

"Welcome!" Kit says as he beckons her through the front door and past a bin filled with odd shoes. "*Mi casa* is *su casa* and all, so make yourself at home."

Alice hasn't had time to consider her expectations of Kit's *casa,* but she didn't think it would have visible damp on the ceiling or wallpaper peeling like an orange rind.

"Can I get you a drink?" Kit is wearing a checked shirt, the front tucked in, the back flopping out. Alice wonders if she interrupted him getting ready for a party—a date even. It's a sharper look than the sketchy band T-shirt from last night.

"No, no, I'm fine, thanks." Alice can see a lot of dishes piled by the sink and none on the drying rack.

There is a silence when she knows that Kit is expecting her to explain why she has turned up, out of the blue, at the flat of a man who is pretty much a complete stranger. He doesn't seem dangerous at least, a fact for which Alice cannot be grateful enough.

"I suppose I should explain why I'm here. . . . Last night was all a bit manic. Lots going on. And I was quite confused by everything, so I wanted to find out a bit more about NightLine."

Kit's eyebrows knit together in perplexity. They are thick and a little unkempt, the odd hair long enough to curl. *Charmingly.* Would that be the word she would use to describe it? Not that she is here to profile Kit, Alice reminds herself.

"Okay. Very conscientious of you." He gestures at the sofa, littered with crumbs. "Fire away."

"So, when the call comes through—to you or whoever is lead caller—we don't see anything on the dashboard. A caller ID or similar?"

"Yep, that's right. That's all deactivated. Not sure how, but that does the anonymity bit for us."

"And there's no way to trace callers?"

"Not our job." Kit flicks his palms upward as if to suggest logistics are something that fall from the sky.

"Even if you think they might be at risk, or if they say something bad—you know, like *dangerous* bad?"

"Why are you asking all this?"

Alice pretends to jot down a few extra lines to buy herself some time. "It wasn't explained very clearly," she says, when she looks up. "And it's so important to get all this correct, don't you think?" Kit strikes her as the sort of person who would reply to any question, rhetorical or not, so she presses on. "To confirm, there is absolutely no way to trace these calls?"

"You *are* a regular Nancy Drew, aren't you?"

Alice avoids his gaze, looking instead at the small tear in his shirt sleeve, the skin underneath of which he seems to have colored in with a blue pen. Suddenly he seems like more of an overgrown teen than a man who must be in his midtwenties. She has never met a person quite so hard to pigeonhole.

"Very funny. No, I mean, like, how does that work? They scramble the calls . . . somewhere?"

"Yeah, I think so. I'm not the expert, though. Ted would be your man for that."

"We wouldn't even know a caller's location?"

"Not unless they told us. Are we doing Twenty Questions or something?"

Alice fixes Kit with one of her more scathing looks.

"I mean, can't you wait until your session with Ted tomorrow?" Kit continues.

"How do you know it's tomorrow?"

Kit's cheeks flush. "Sometimes Ted needs a hand . . . so I offered," he stumbles.

"Right." Alice narrows her eyes. "So back to the calls: they're not logged?"

"What's this *really* about, Alice?"

Her breath catches in her throat. Can she lie her way out of this one? Does she even want to try? It would be nice, wouldn't it, to have someone to share the load with? Plus, Kit has an in with NightLine, a real one. Not the flimsy connection that she herself forged in the name of getting to the bottom of the Jim mystery. It's a risk that she's prepared to take. "I want to find Jim."

Kit looks confused. Then it drops. "Jim, off Mary's sign? Her boyfriend? Or, I mean, that was who I always assumed he was . . ."

"Yes and yes."

"Why?" Kit looks a little taken back but at least he's not angry, or affronted, or anything else he might be, when faced with Alice's nosiness.

"Because Mary is hurting, and she won't stop until he comes back. Because living in a cloud of mystery can't be healthy. Because, I don't know . . . don't you want to do something worthwhile for once?"

Something in Alice's last appeal seems to twig with Kit. He presses together his lips, tempted.

"Is this what *Mary* wants?"

Alice tries to quell the unease churning in the pit of her stomach. Mary will thank her, one day. She knows it. "Why wouldn't she, Kit? She isn't the sort of person to ask for help herself."

She watches as Kit turns her answer over in his head. His eyes are suddenly clouded. It looks as if he is tuning out of the conversation and into a place beyond these four walls. "I can understand that."

"But I still think we ought to . . . keep this to ourselves?" Alice continues, quickly. She needs to keep Kit onside. "We can't get her hopes up. If we find Jim, then great, we'll tell her. But if we don't, then, well . . . I think it ought to stay as our secret."

"No, we shouldn't get her hopes up. You're right about that. Disappointment's a shitter." Kit says the last word with real force.

"So you're in?"

"Fine." He is back in the room. He shakes his head, as if to clear a bad dream, and gives a small smile. "But I still don't get it—why this fascination with the calls? Jim hasn't . . ." His mouth drops open.

Did he notice something earlier this week, at NightLine? Alice has seen firsthand how distraught Mary was in the wake of the calls; it must have been visible to the other volunteers, however much Mary hoped it wouldn't be.

"Mary has had two calls now that she thinks are from Jim." Alice feels a twinge of guilt, sharing this information with Kit. But she needs backup if she is to find out what's going on at NightLine. "But you can't tell anyone any of this, okay? Mary told me in confidence when I first met her. She'd hate it if she thought anyone else knew."

"Fine. I won't. But I don't see why she'd tell you and then not want anyone at NightLine to find out. We've known her for longer. Actually, you know what? It doesn't matter." Alice is pleased to see that Kit is capable of checking his own entitlement. "But I will say that you're going to have a problem with these calls. They're meant to be impossible to trace. So if you are serious about finding Jim, then you are going to have to get other intel."

"I've already made a start," Alice begins. "I have Jim's full name—James Whitnell—and I've run that through some searches at wor—" She comes to an abrupt stop. If she tells Kit that she's a journalist, he'll suspect an ulterior motive.

"Procrastinating on the boss's time and dime, eh?"

"Quite."

"What is it you do anyway?" Kit asks.

"Digital. Sales . . . ," Alice freestyles. "But back to Mary. Look, it's not like the police will help us. They closed Jim's case and it will take years to reopen it, if they agree to."

Kit nods. Alice guesses he is around the same age as her. A year might as well be an eternity.

"And Jim has been missing for seven years now," Alice continues. "So we won't get far with mobile-phone data, CCTV, car searches—even if we could access that information."

"What about the people who know him? Other than Mary, I mean. They must still be around. What about his parents?"

"According to Mary, they cut her off."

Kit rolls his eyes.

"My thoughts exactly."

"Do we at least have their names?" he asks.

"Somewhere in my notes." Paper scatters out of Alice's pad. "Richard and Julia . . . or does this say Juliette?" Alice twists an index card up to the light, dated yesterday. It contains a scribbled summary of their initial conversation at the pub.

"Why do I have the feeling this is going to be a late night?" Kit mumbles, heading out of the main room.

Alice bristles at the assumption. He doesn't think their working together means that . . . No, he couldn't possibly. "Excuse me—where do you think you are going?"

"The bathroom. Unless you want to join? I imagine you'll be timing my loo breaks from here on in."

O nce Kit has made himself comfortable, he returns, wiping his hands on his jeans. "I have it! It came to me whilst I was on the loo."

Marvelous, Alice thinks; she is in the presence of the sort of genius that thinks best while relieving himself.

"What about all this stuff thrown up by the video?" Kit asks.

"You mean the online comments?"

"Maybe. But also the hashtag—*FindJim*."

Alice hadn't realized they had managed to get a hashtag trending, or, if not trending, at least going to the extent that there might be some useful information to gain from it.

"I'm happy to get started there." Kit's stomach growls. "But I will need sustenance. What would you rather do: spaghetti or search?"

"Spaghetti," Alice replies without hesitation. It's been a long day. The lacuna of Jim's online presence, the near miss at the clinic, finding out about the strange cloud under which he left that practice . . . She hasn't even begun to tell Kit about that, but it can wait for now. He's already got Twitter open, his eyes fixed on the screen.

Alice goes to fill the pot and locates some pasta in the cupboards. They are concerningly sticky.

"What were Jim's parents' names again?" Kit asks, just before the spaghetti is done.

"Richard and Juliette."

Kit returns to his typing. There is a pause, then, "Aha!"

Alice's heart is thundering. Maybe there's a message from Jim. A geolocation. She flies from the stove to the sofa, angling herself so close to the screen that she can feel Kit's body warm against her side. "Who's Gus Driddlington-Hodge?"

"Your guess is as good as mine." Kit zooms in so that the tweet fills the screen. "Read it."

It doesn't take long for Alice to absorb the words. "In light of the recent video, James's parents, Richard and Juliette, ask for their privacy to be respected. #FindJim."

"A friend of the family?"

"I'd say."

Kit has already copied Gus's gobstopper of a surname into Google.

The first result is for a website called McAvery Asset Management and a headshot there matches Gus's Twitter profile picture. Two clicks later and Kit is emailing Gus directly.

"I didn't know you had the funds to invest." Alice is struggling to find anything to accompany their supper. There are some anchovies in the fridge but the best-before date was two months ago.

"I don't. But he doesn't know that." Kit finishes his message, releasing the whooshing sound of a sent email. "Not until Monday at 10 A.M., that is. You can get time off work, right?"

Alice nods. If she's in the firing line for redundancy, then she can't be that essential to the team. Besides, Jack would never notice a brief absence. She dropped him an email to say that she might have a story—one that would justify the front page—but hasn't said anything more specific, including its subject matter, in case she jinxes it. Jack's awkwardness surrounding her job insecurity has made him remarkably trusting.

But what about Kit? Olive muttered something about him being a banker and, if that's the case, then it will be *him* struggling to get a day's leave. Which means Alice will have to fly solo. "Hold on—you *are* coming too, aren't you?"

"I've got a backlog of holiday to take," Kit replies, a little too quickly. But before Alice can question that, he adds, "It's a date, then. A plan, rather." He smooths down the front of his shirt. "We're off to meet our new friend, Gus."

19

2018

As Kit predicted, last night was a late one. Once they had set up their appointment with Gus, Kit and Alice sat side by side on the sofa, slurping spaghetti as they trawled through the other Twitter comments under Mary's video in forensic detail, on the off chance there might be another clue hidden among the reams of randomly strewn emojis.

There were a few men by the name of Jim who had been tagged in the original post, but no luck there. It was a rogues' gallery. None of them bore so much as a passing resemblance to the man in Mary's mantelpiece photo.

By the time Alice left Kit's, it was past midnight and she was starting to doze off on his shoulder. He insisted on calling a cab.

Still, no rest for the wicked. Alice is awoken before 10 A.M. (criminal on a weekend) by a text from Kit: Lest you forget, Ted's NightLine training session is at 12 P.M. TODAY. We'll be expecting you. KIT. Alice still thinks she made a good call letting him in on the Jim investigation—after all, he did find the Gus lead—but hopes he isn't going to bulldoze the next steps with his incessant enthusiasm and inability to text at socially appropriate hours of the day. She drags herself out of bed and into the shower.

Ted's house is about ten minutes' walk from the school where Night-Line is held, in an area that is popular with young families. The cheaper supermarket that Alice relies on is nearby, but she still always takes a longer route there and back, despite being laden with groceries, rather than risk seeing fathers help their children navigate the sidewalk without bicycle training wheels or toting infants aboard their shoulders.

Today, however, there is no way to avoid confronting her own discomfort. She keeps her eyes fixed on the map on her phone and focuses on the task ahead. If Ted has any way of tracing the NightLine calls, Alice needs to find out what that is. And fast.

The door at number 25 is open and she can already hear Ted somewhere beyond it. She is about to press the bell, for courtesy's sake, when Ted emerges, beckoning her in. "Alice! Lovely to see you again. I've just been hearing a bit more about you." He is wearing a polo shirt, his biceps bulging around the cuff on the sleeve. *Attractive,* Alice thinks. *For an older person, that is. He must be—what, fifty?*

"Good things, I hope!"

"Of course—I'd expect nothing more from this chap." Ted claps his palm on Kit's shoulder, a great meaty slab of hand that sends a vibration through Kit.

"That's a relief, then." Alice looks up at Kit, who doesn't seem to be able to meet her eye. There is a bashfulness about him that she hasn't seen before. "And thank you for having me here." She adds, "You've got such a nice place."

She hasn't actually had a chance to take it in yet. They are standing in the living room, which is carefully decorated, an intricate floral wallpaper with matching carpet and a three-piece leather furniture set.

"Thanks. Not often in here anymore. Most of the time it's just me—my kids have both moved out. Tim's at university and Rachel's graduated, but living with friends somewhere out east. 'Cooler,' she tells me." Ted gives so much energy to the air quotation marks that they bounce like bunny ears. "Usually when she's avoiding her old dad visiting."

"Sounds about right." Alice smiles, through a flash of pain. She hopes Tim and Rachel know how lucky they are.

"Thought I'd leave the front door open to get a bit of a breeze in. I don't normally come in here during the day. Never bother doing the curtains at night." Ted waves a hand toward the heavy, pleated drapes and Alice imagines the dust caked between the folds. It strikes her as unbearably sad. "It's stuffy, isn't it? We haven't had an August this warm in a while." He leans one hand on the telephone table in front of the window and uses the other to reach out and check that it can't be pushed any further ajar. "Right, so, shall we?"

Ted takes a seat in the armchair. Kit and Alice settle on the sofa opposite, only Kit's spatial awareness seems to be lacking, as ever, and Alice has to shuffle right back against the cushions to avoid his bobbing knee.

"As Kit knows, I do this with all the new volunteers. Nice for me to meet them. I know Bev would have liked it too. Bev was my wife," he clarifies. "She passed two years ago now. Pancreatic cancer. It took her in a matter of weeks after the diagnosis. She was only forty-six. She should have had so much more time. *We* should have had so much more time."

"I'm sorry to hear that," Alice says, careful to look at Ted directly. There is nothing worse than an awkward shift-eye when acknowledging someone else's grief.

"Thank you." There is a small crack in Ted's voice, which Alice wishes she could plaster. "Bev was a real life force. I can't say how difficult it's been, going on without her. A brave face takes one hell of an effort to apply in the morning, let me tell you that. But I have to try.

Some days are easier than others—for the loneliness and what have you. Anyway, NightLine was Bev's big legacy and she'd love that we're getting so many brilliant young volunteers, like you two. Where was I? The most important thing—Kit, you'll know this. Old hand, isn't that what they say? Or is it 'old hat'? I never quite worked that one out. . . . As I was saying, the most important thing about volunteers is their empathy. Good, honest communication."

Alice swallows. Her reasons for being at NightLine aren't entirely honest. She wouldn't be here if it weren't for Mary and the prospect of what finding Jim might mean for her own career, as much as for Mary's peace of mind. When Alice zones out of her guilt and back into the conversation, Ted is still rambling on about the qualities in an ideal volunteer. She needs him to cut to the chase.

"I think the thing I'm really interested in is the mechanics of the operation," Alice interrupts. She turns to Kit for support, but he looks as startled at her interruption as Ted. *Shit!* Alice can never work out what is the right amount to push: too little and you end up trapped, like her at the *Bugle*; too much and it gets people's hackles up, especially if you're a young woman.

"Oh," Ted adds, with a smile. "Well, we always welcome interest! Funny thing is, though, I know nothing about that myself."

Alice glances over at Kit. He is frowning.

"For real?" he asks. "I didn't know that. Who does, then?"

"It's all contracted out now. Software." Ted flaps his hands above his head, as if the technology that has outsourced Alice's best chance of finding Jim might be floating through the air.

It is all Alice can do not to scream. "Could I use your bathroom?" she asks, worrying that the urge might tip her over onto the *too much* side of the spectrum.

"Course, of course," Ted replies. "You'll have to go upstairs, bit of a plumbing issue with the one down here. First door on the left—it's my bedroom, but don't mind that. It's the door by the wardrobe."

Compared to the living room, Ted's bedroom feels spartan. There is none of the surface clutter that characterizes the downstairs, just crisp white sheets and a wicker laundry basket with shirttails trailing through its cracks. It reminds Alice of something, and it takes her a second or two to remember what. *Mary's living room*. That same functionality, the way any small personal touch seemed to reflect the underlying emptiness and amplify it tenfold.

Alice sits on the edge of the bed, the pillow still dipped from the imprint of Ted's skull, where he hasn't bothered to plump it. How is it possible that he doesn't know how the back end of his own bloody organization works? Nice as he is, this incompetence is infuriating, to say the least. Maybe Bev was the brains of the operation? A fat lot of good that is to Alice now. She isn't likely to extract answers on geolocating anonymous calls through the medium of a séance.

There is a single photo on the bedside table—a wedding shot. Bev is a little imp of a thing next to Ted, her sparrow's chest held in by a tight bodice of embroidered satin. She looks shrewd, the sort of woman who would have NightLine running like clockwork. She also looks ecstatically happy. There is so much private joy in that shot that Alice feels she is overstepping the mark by looking at it.

She drops her eyes from the photo. A lanyard is sticking out of the top drawer of Ted's bedside table, obscuring the otherwise clean lines. She opens the drawer a fraction to release the lanyard and tuck it back in. However, a strand of the nylon has got caught in the hinge and she ends up pulling the whole thing out, the tray heavy with junk.

In the commotion, a sheet of paper on top slips over the lip. Alice picks it up. It takes a good minute or so for her to realize what it might be.

It can't be, can it?

She takes a photograph on her phone and then tucks the sheet away, back where she found it.

There you go, love," Ted says, passing over a mug and extending a packet of custard creams with the other. "We were starting to worry about where you'd got to!"

"Sorry—I have an awful headache. I'm a bit dizzy."

Kit springs to his feet with at least twice the alacrity he has ever previously demonstrated. "Here, take a seat, Alice."

"Can I drive you home?" Ted already has the car keys in one hand. This is the last thing she needs in her state of shock.

"No, no, I'll be fine. You can carry on."

"Absolutely not," Ted says, shaking his head. "You ought to get home and lie down."

Alice nods, as much to end the conversation as anything else. "Maybe Kit can walk me?"

"Yeah, I'd love to." The opportunity to step up in service seems to have brought Kit's inner puppy dog to the fore. He makes a great show of taking Alice's arm, stroking at its inside.

"I'm dizzy, not geriatric, Kit," Alice says, rankled. She can feel his grip loosen and almost immediately regrets it. "Sorry," she mumbles.

"Not at all. *Grumpy,* not geriatric."

"Get her home safe, now," Ted says in the doorway. "We can re-schedule your shadowing until you are feeling more like yourself, so don't push it. Hope to see you both at NightLine's Annual General Meeting next week, though."

Once they are out of sight of the house, Alice doubles her pace.

"I thought you weren't feeling well?" Kit is tall enough that he hasn't had to break his stride to keep up.

"Hmm."

"Is it a headache? I have these patches back at mine . . ."

What is she meant to tell Kit? She can't tell him what she just saw. Not when she doesn't understand it herself. He'll confuse matters. He might blab. Christ—is he still talking?

"Reiki! You'll never believe how good it can be for tension-related migraines. Solutions often come from the most left-field places."

Kit might be right about that.

20

2007

Although she knew she had no right to, Mary still felt disappointed that Jim hadn't come to pick her up from the airport. Two years in, the throes of early romance had all but worn off and, besides, it wasn't as if she had much luggage from her weekend trip back to Belfast. It was so out of the blue from Jim, though; he'd said just the day before that he would be there to collect her. Then, when she texted him before takeoff, it was as if he'd forgotten that promise, in favor of better plans. Apparently he'd been tied up in town, whatever that meant.

Mary tried to suppress the queasy sense that something was awry as she wheeled her case through the maze that was Duty Free in Heathrow Terminal 2 Arrivals. It seemed that every stand was devoted to alcohol—huge vats of gin and vodka and whiskey at knock-down prices, enough to drown a man. Probably for the best that Jim wasn't about. He had been sober over twelve months now—Mary too in a bid to support him—but she still wanted him at arm's length from temptation.

When they landed back from Da's funeral more than a year ago, Jim still with one foot in the doghouse, he had turned over his new drink-free leaf with surprising ease. They chucked away whatever was lingering in the cupboards and swapped pubs for restaurants when they wanted a date-night out. In fact it seemed so easy for Jim that, at first, Mary wondered whether alcohol had been that much of an issue at all. Had she overreacted? Had the wake simply fallen at the end of a bad week, as Jim had claimed, and had not in actual fact shined a light on a longer-term problem?

Three months later they had been at Gus and Jillian's wedding, and Mary found her earlier conviction verified. Gus couldn't believe that Jim was "off the sauce," as he put it. He almost choked when he saw Jim was putting away elderflower cordial instead of white wine. "She saved you, just in time, sonny boy," Gus said, one arm wrapped around each of them. While the sentiment may have been nice, Mary couldn't help wondering what, exactly, she had saved Jim from. She spent the rest of the night sipping from the same glass as Jim, to make sure he had stuck to the soft drink.

Jim, however, had taken that encounter in good humor. In fact the old Jim, who had been conspicuously absent at the wake, had now returned with a vengeance. A year on and he was the same confident, gregarious man that Mary had fallen for at the Stormont. She had also, for the first time, noticed the restlessness that Jim had spoken about soon after they met. Only now it didn't seem to be the negative quality that Mary had imagined it might be. In the first few months of sobriety, Jim planned no fewer than five separate weekends away for the two of them: Paris, Dublin, Amsterdam, and Berlin (so good they went twice), relishing the extra downtime Jim had now that he had switched to a private practice, and the cash Mary had recently earned, with an influx of big-money commissions.

They even braved a trip to Sussex with Jim's parents, at the holiday home they owned on the coast. Mary had been reluctant, not that she had said as much; in the eighteen months or so that they had been living together by this point, they had seen Richard and Juliette no more than a handful of times. Maybe it was the sea air or maybe it was Jim's calmer disposition, but the three nights went without a hitch.

A week before this trip, one of Mary's maps had been featured in an article on up-and-coming artists in the *Evening Standard*. Jim had been fit to bursting with pride. When Mary had walked down to collect him from Ealing Broadway station on the evening it was published, he had insisted that they pick up as many copies of the newspaper as they could carry between them. Their flat was stuffed with the newspapers and, suffice to say, one copy of the piece had even put an end to Richard's comments about Mary's career. Since then they were getting along, if not well, then comfortably enough.

As for Juliette, it was clear that she appreciated the opportunity to dote on her son. Seeing her head resting on Jim's chest, however, couldn't help but make Mary think of her own mam. She got the sense that Jim was avoiding trips over to Belfast, since his drink-related misdemeanor. He hadn't come this weekend, or on an earlier trip. Mary didn't want to begrudge him for it—after all, you dated the person, not their family, or so she hoped—but that didn't mean she didn't wish he had a better relationship with Mam.

Mary imagined that Jim was ashamed of his behavior at the wake, even if he hadn't explicitly said that, since their reconciliation on the plane home. Well, that made two of them. She flew off the handle whenever Gavin tried to make a joke of it and, even with Mam, she found herself skirting around the issue. She would never forget the concern in Mam's eyes. But it was more than that too; it was Jim slipping from pole position to last place—the golden boy seen without his varnish. Mam didn't try to bring up Jim's performance at the funeral, either, but Mary knew her well enough to conclude that it didn't mean her worries had subsided in the slightest.

So instead of telling anyone the real reasons why they weren't drinking anymore, they stuck to excuses like health and sleep improvement, and vehemently played down any suggestion that they were trying to conceive. Neither of them had changed their opinion on the subject of kids, or marriage, for that matter. And it was easy enough to believe that lifestyle factors were to blame when their sobriety was yielding such impressive results; Jim, in particular, was sharper and brighter than he had ever been before. Whenever Mary caught him whistling as he rustled up brunch, she felt a fresh wave of adoration rush over her. He had given up the drink without so much as a grumble of complaint. He had meant it—he really would go to the ends of the earth for her.

Mary had reached the front of the taxi line now. Her suitcase stowed in the boot, she rummaged through her bag, looking for her phone to text Jim and tell him she was en route home. Part of her didn't know if he deserved the courtesy, after standing her up, but the greater part just wanted to see him again.

Looked like Jim had got there first: Meet me at the end of Arnfield Road—you have a date. Jx

W hat's all this about?"

The juxtaposition between Jim in his good navy jacket and the crumbling wall he was sitting on was quite something, alright. He had on one of his signature collarless shirts too. It was always so hard to hold on to her annoyance in his presence. If he had been too busy to get her from the airport, then she ought to let that go and not allow the bad air to infect their evening.

"I said a date, didn't I?"

"But you could have said I needed to dress up." Mary was makeup-free. Some of her lunch was smudged on the neckline of her sweater. "Do I have time to drop my bag off and change?"

Jim shook his head. "Sorry—but not to worry. We've got places to be, and we're cutting it pretty fine as it is. You always look gorgeous."

He stood up to kiss Mary. Good thing she'd thought to pack gum, she mused, as she felt his lips lingering for a second or two longer than seemed appropriate for Ealing's neighborhood watch. He was forgiven there and then. "Right, well, I'll save the rest for later." Jim winked. "Shall we?"

He took Mary's hand as they weaved down the main road, pulling her to a stop outside the new restaurant that had just opened between the park and the pharmacy. Mary had glanced at the menu on her way past last week; it was eye-wateringly expensive and looked like it would most probably shut down within the month. People in the area had money, but most of them had a modicum of sense to accompany it.

"After you."

"Are you sure?" Mary hissed as Jim held the door for her.

"It's on me."

"Come on—halves. Please?"

"It's a special occasion."

Was it? But before Mary had a chance to ask, the waiter was with them and, not long afterward, a bottle of sparkling water and two menus.

Jim slipped a box across the table before Mary had even read through the appetizers.

"For me?"

"Who else?" Jim smiled.

This couldn't be—could it? They had made it clear from the beginning that nuptials weren't in the cards, but Mary was still a woman and, as such, had been long conditioned to think that a square jewelry box came with more than simply a large receipt.

"Go on," Jim coaxed. "Save the card for after."

Taking a deep breath, Mary cracked the hinge. Inside sat a watch on a delicate silver chain, the strap bunched twice around a crimson cushion.

"I mean—what . . . what's this for? It's too generous, it's—"

Jim slipped the postcard from where it sat underneath the box and slid it toward Mary. The front showed the industrial cityscape of Berlin, their last trip away together.

> *Happy 2nd Anniversary! You have no idea how much you have done for me. Thank you for always being the calm in my storm. Thank you for loving me, no matter what.*
>
> *Here's to another two, four, six, eight—it'll be great! Christ, scrap that, it's terrible. Ruins the sentiment. What I mean is—here's to many, many more brilliant years.*
>
> *Yours always,*
> *Jim xxx*

There were tears in Mary's eyes before she reached the sign-off. The fact that Jim was hers for now was almost too much of a blessing for her to fathom, let alone the fact that he had written he would be hers, always.

And to think she had forgotten it was their anniversary, too. She'd been so busy being annoyed that he couldn't collect her from the airport earlier in the day, worried about what it must mean, that there was no space to consider anything else. She thought briefly about trying to talk her way out of her predicament, and then settled on the truth. It was the very least he deserved after setting up all this.

"I'm so sorry, I forgot it was our anniversary. Belfast must have scrambled my brain or something . . ."

"It doesn't matter," Jim replied. He didn't look offended in the slightest. Mary wondered how she had managed to get so lucky with a man this forgiving. "It's a nice excuse for me to treat you, and for us both to have an evening out." He went to slip the watch onto her wrist.

"I knew it would suit you. I spent hours in the jeweler's today. It was overwhelming in there, trying to decide what you might like. That was why I couldn't get you from the airport. But I hope you think I made a good choice. I hope you think it was worth it."

"You're always worth it," Mary replied. "Always."

21

2018

"Wow, you've, er . . . scrubbed up well," Alice says when she clocks Kit, bounding up the stairs at Green Park station. He is wearing a three-piece suit for their meeting with Gus, their Twitter find—and a friend of Jim's, if their suspicions are about to be proved correct.

Kit smooths the fabric on his pinstripe waistcoat. It strikes Alice as one step too far, but that's Kit for you. "Thanks." Alice can see him trying to control his smile. Chuffed doesn't quite cut it. "As do you, *milady*. Are you feeling a bit better?"

It takes Alice a second or two to work out what he is talking about. Of course—her abrupt exit from Ted's house, two days ago. Kit checked in on her by text, but she was too overwhelmed to reply.

"Yes, thanks; not sure I was sick so much as . . ." Alice's mind hasn't stopped reeling through the options for even a second. Bewildered? Shaken? Scared of what her discovery meant for everyone—herself, Kit, Mary? *Especially Mary.* She settles for: "Tired. I think it all might have caught up with me. So, what's the plan of attack for today?"

They are walking deeper into Mayfair, judging by the caliber of the cars that are cruising by. A builder wolf-whistles Alice and she shoots him a withering stare.

"I'll introduce myself to Gus as the potential client, investor, or what have you." Kit adjusts his tie. "Chitchat until we get in the office, door closed. Then . . ."

"We just go for it?"

"I think that's our best bet. I mean, what's the worst that can happen?"

Alice mulls over the question in silence. Has it already happened? *No*—she doesn't know anything for certain yet. She needs to put the afternoon at Ted's house out of her mind, at least temporarily, and focus on combing Gus for whatever leads he might be able to provide regarding Jim's disappearance.

"This is it," Kit says. They are standing outside a huge town house with freshly painted iron railings. "You ready?"

She nods. The soles of her ballet pumps slap up the marble stairs. At the front desk, she keeps herself tucked behind Kit, scared lest someone senses the extent to which she doesn't belong here.

Alice's teenage years were characterized by continual anxiety about money. After her dad disappeared, they only had her mum's wage as a teaching assistant to live on. The paper route Alice took on provided little more than petty change. It was one thing not to have her dad there to take her to the cinema, quite another to know that there wasn't the sort of money to pay to go alone, either.

"Christopher Ripton?"

"Speaking." Kit stands and takes the hand of a man with the swollen complexion of a television chef. He wears a ring on his little finger and another on his fourth, the flesh sprouting out over the gold.

"I'm Gus Driddlington-Hodge and it's a pleasure to meet you . . . both?"

"My partner, Alice," Kit supplies.

Alice is too anxious to cringe at the assumption.

"Please, come through."

Gus's office is palatial. Fully air-conditioned too—what luxury! They take two upholstered chairs on the far side of his large oak desk and wait until he is seated, a glass of sparkling water in front of each of them.

"And how may I help you today? Your message mentioned a midlevel inheritance portfolio—the desire to invest in Asia, perhaps?"

"Yes, that's one thing. But before then, I wanted to ask . . ." Kit digs an elbow into Alice's side.

"We wanted to ask about this."

Gus looks puzzled, waiting for Alice to fumble with her phone. She brings up a screenshot of the tweet and turns her phone around.

"We're looking for Jim."

Gus glances at the screen, his expression inscrutable, before swiveling in his chair so that he is looking at Kit and Alice out of the corner of his left eye.

"Journalists?"

"No!" both Kit and Alice shout over each other. "Friends of Mary's," Alice adds. "Hoping we might be able to help her get some closure."

"I should still have you thrown out by security."

"Can we at least explain?"

Alice is acutely aware of how shrill she sounds in her desperation. This man knows Jim. Better than his colleagues, perhaps better than anyone in the world, other than Mary. He must know something that can help them find Jim, and the answers that Alice knows, from experience, will enable Mary to rebuild her tattered self-esteem.

"I thought this had blown over." Gus sighs. "That was what that message was all about. James's parents didn't want Mary making a scene. I didn't know whether or not I should alert them to the existence of that video, but in the end I did. I thought they had a right to know. It only ended up distressing them—Mary's behavior, not to mention all the speculation in the comments section. *Why did he leave? Where's he gone?* Well, it's none of their business. James's parents asked me to say something to that effect online. If you're friends of Mary's, then maybe you can make her read that tweet too."

"But you must agree that Mary has a right to know where he is?" Alice presses.

"She does."

Alice brushes over his words. "Don't you want to know that he's okay too?"

"Of course! But it's unlikely. To be honest, I wasn't altogether surprised when Jim vanished. Most people who knew him felt the same way. Apart from Mary, it seems. She never got it. In her eyes, it was all Happy Families. Some people choose to see what they want to see."

"And you have no idea where—" Kit starts.

"I've said enough." Gus spins back around and plants his fists on the table. "Too much, probably. I'm going to have to ask you to leave."

Alice does not want to get up from her seat. What did he mean about Mary seeing what she wanted to? Alice has never met a woman more firmly grounded by the reality of her situation.

She opens her mouth to speak but Kit is already on his feet, one eye on the panic button by the bookshelves and Gus's hand wavering above it. He tugs on her sleeve. "Come on, Alice."

Kit steers Alice into a café near the Tube station. While she stews, he procures two iced coffees and a large cookie, peppered with raisins.

"Sulking time is *terminado*," he says, winding his index fingers as if wrapping up her discontent.

"But he could have had the answers."

Kit tilts his head. "We won't get anywhere clutching at straws. Anyway, Gus gave us some helpful intel."

"Did he?" The investigation so far seems to constitute long, loose threads. Alice is already far too tangled up in them.

"Well, apparently Jim wasn't too happy. Or maybe he and Mary weren't that happy *together* . . ."

"We don't know that," Alice snaps. "She never said as much to me. In fact she said the opposite: they were devoted to each other."

"No, it was just Gus's suggestion," Kit concedes. "But no couple is perfect."

"Jim wasn't happy at work, either," Alice volunteers. When Kit frowns, she adds, "I went to check out his last employer, some private doctors' practice. Long story short, I overheard a conversation where someone working there said he'd left under a cloud."

"Meaning what?"

"They didn't say."

"Annoying." Kit takes the prize for understatement of the century and then breaks into the cookie. He passes Alice the larger half.

"My sentiments exactly." She slumps down in her chair. "I don't know where we go from here."

She isn't expecting an answer to that. But if Kit can be counted on for anything, it is his ability to continue a conversation in even the most inclement of circumstances.

"My hunch is the forums."

"Forums?"

"For missing people."

Alice freezes, unable to swallow her mouthful, but Kit is oblivious, already sliding his laptop out of the briefcase that he modeled for their appointment. It looks like an exhibit from *Antiques Roadshow*—and not one with a decent price tag, either.

"Are you sure? I mean, there will be loads of people on those sites. More recent cases—" Much as Alice wants to find Jim, she cannot fall down this particular rabbit hole. Not again.

"Nah, they go back years. I found the thread on Jim last night. It's very short, a couple of entries in the first week or two after he disappeared. Nothing useful there that I can see, but I reckon that's because the information is all so dated now. You said he'd been gone—what, seven years? We need to, you know, freshen up this page." Kit drags his chair adjacent to Alice's, the legs scraping along the floorboards. Alice squeezes her eyes shut. "You alright there? Early start, I suppose."

"Fine." *It was so long ago, Keaton. Pull yourself together.* On the screen there is a series of blurry CCTV images and photos shot across petrol-station forecourts.

"To start with, we're going to need a proper picture of Jim," Kit mutters to himself. "Face-on or something. Alice, are you paying attention?"

She stares down at her coffee, which is still untouched. She can't bring herself to look at the forum page.

"I said we need a photo of Jim. That might attract some legitimate information."

"I have one," Alice says quietly. She finds the image she took in Mary's flat during her first and only visit there and sends it via Bluetooth to Kit, her mind still elsewhere.

"Wow! Nice-looking pair. Where did you get this?"

"At Mary's flat. I thought it might come in useful." She neglects to mention that it is not an image that was shared willingly. She needs to get out of here, before Kit starts digging into the missing-persons forum in detail.

"That looks like the Giant's Causeway." Kit is too absorbed in examining the backdrop to interrogate Alice's response. "Do you know, I nearly broke my ankle there on a school field trip. I was running amok and the sea appeared from nowhere. I'm telling you, Allie, the topography is next-level. Ragged as a sheep's back end." Alice has stopped listening, but he is merrily oblivious. "I'll get this up now, will I? I bet we'll have a heap of fresh responses within a few days. In the meantime there's still the calls, aren't there? Not that good old Teddy boy was much help on that front."

Argh. That was the worst thing about problems—they never traveled solo. Rather they moved en masse, ready to trample Alice in the stampede. "I think I'll save that one for another day."

"Oh—you mean you have something? Do you want to check it out together?"

"No!" The word slips out and Kit looks crestfallen. But Alice knows this will be nothing on his response if her hunch about the calls is proven correct. She shoves a handful of coins on the table. "I've got to go, Kit. I'll let you know if it comes to anything."

She sincerely hopes not.

22

2018

Alice drains the last of her coffee, the fifth of the day, and wonders how she ended up here. *Here* being the *Bugle* offices. At 10.30 P.M., too. Although, that said, she is no stranger to staying late at work. It would explain why she hasn't seen her flatmate, Maia, in the best part of a month and why she hasn't been on a date in—what, a year? Has it really been that long? Regardless, it's a sorry state of affairs by anyone's standards. Alice herself cannot understand why she is devoting so much of herself to a job that has given her very little in return. Soon there might be nothing to show for her sacrifices at all.

That is why it is so important that she starts to make connections with the information she has gleaned about Jim, and that she starts *now*. When it comes down to it, what did she learn from their conversation with Gus yesterday? Things with Jim might not have been as dazzling as Mary led Alice to believe. Plus Gus wasn't surprised when Jim vanished. Add the scandal at work, and the only conclusion about Jim that Alice can so far draw is that his life was unraveling at its perfectly stitched seams.

She presses the lead of her pencil so firmly into her pad that it snaps. She chucks it across the room, relishing the hollow *thwack* as the pencil hits the floor in an otherwise empty building. She has never felt quite so frustrated in a professional context. Whereas previously Alice could go through the motions with her articles, making surface-level refinements to pointless assignments that did nothing more than fill column inches, now her work is, finally, starting to mean something.

Even the most pointless articles have never stopped Alice believing in the good that journalism can do. She wouldn't have put herself through the long hours and the low pay and the blows to her confidence otherwise. When a career advisor asked Alice, at fourteen, what she wanted to do, she replied simply: *Uncover the truth.* The advisor shuffled through a sheaf of leaflets and then selected one booklet. Investigative journalism it was.

Her first forays into her chosen path came only days after that brief, perfunctory career chat. What's more, they took place on the very forum that Kit landed upon yesterday, in the café. Twelve years back, the site was a lot more rudimentary, but that didn't stop the teenage Alice from setting up a page for her dad—*Nick Keaton: Missing.* Her sleepless nights returned. This time, as Alice tossed and turned, not in sorrow, but in hope. There would be a flood of leads. She began to imagine what a reunion might look like—a park somewhere, apologies uttered and accepted among the first blooms of spring.

Poor, naive Alice. The most she ever got were a few condolences. And there she was, disappointed all over again. The thought of that forum is enough to make her feel sick, even now. Seeing Kit open the site yesterday with the same misguided teenage hope was another kick in the teeth. She didn't want to crush his idea, but she didn't have the strength to involve herself in that particular strand of the investigation, either.

That makes Alice sound like such a snowflake. She isn't, not really. She could take a look at the forums herself, if she wanted to. In fact she could do it now, while she has a decent internet connection and time to burn. No time like the present to prove how far she has come.

She opens a new window on her browser and breathes out through her mouth.

"You're here late! I thought it was just me."

Alice's head whips round so quickly that she catches a nerve. She exits the internet and brings up a Word doc at random. In her panic, she has ended up clicking on a piece from three years back, something about a flurry of food-poisoning cases at the local kebab shop.

"Ha! Didn't expect to see you, Jack."

He looks exhausted. There are several heavy ring binders in his arms, all labeled *Accounts*.

"Lots to sort before September," Jack mumbles. "I need to find a way to balance the books but they're looking a little, er . . . wonky shall we say?" When he laughs, the top binder teeters and slips off the pile. Alice picks it up and places it back on the tower. "By the way, how is that story coming along? You sounded like you had something exciting on your hands."

"Yes . . . well. Working on it." She feels reluctant to say anything more. She knows that Jack deserves to be let into her confidence—he did offer her the lifeline of the front page—but the piece feels so fragile right now. Subject it to even a drop more pressure and the whole article could collapse.

"What sort of thing is it? I know I said a feature would be good, but an interview could work as well, provided it's big. An exclusive, ideally."

An interview with Jim . . . That would be the ultimate end goal, but is that really the story Alice is trying to tell?

"More like an exposé," she says.

Jack tilts his head, intrigued. "Now that would be *brilliant*. Long time since we've had one of those. Popular with the readers, and a nice way to up your profile when the shareholders . . . just generally."

Alice knows that he means well, but a reminder of everything she stands to lose is the last thing she needs.

"Thanks. Actually, I've got to be off." Alice powers down her computer and snatches up her bag before Jack can ask what the subject of this exposé would be. "There's a lead I need to follow up now."

"Now? Well, I won't hold you up. Must be urgent if it's happening at this hour. Good luck! And with the rest of the exposé." Jack lingers a little too excitedly on that last, exotic syllable.

Alice does not have time to correct her ill-advised word choice before he has scurried off and out of earshot.

There is, as Alice can now confirm, no comfortable position to loiter in behind a bush. She is struck by a strong sense of déjà vu. First, the bins at Eldridge Health Centre—and now this. She can't imagine that this is how proper journalists spend their time. If this story does manage to propel her up the career ladder, she'll be happy to forget this aspect of her origins, that's for sure.

Her patch is illuminated by a streetlamp overhead, so Alice is glad that she took some time in the bathrooms at the *Bugle* to make sure she looks as inconspicuous as possible. She's swapped her tropical-patterned shift dress for head-to-toe black. Somewhere down the back of her desk drawer she located a bandanna, which is now holding her characteristic thick bangs back, and her bob is tied in two miniature French braids.

What is the penalty for loitering with intent? Hopefully not jail time. She looks awful in orange. A fine, perhaps? It's unlikely that the current state of Alice's finances would stretch to covering it. Crowdfunding, then. *Mind on the matter, Keaton,* she reminds herself before uttering a brief prayer to every conceivable deity that she isn't about to be carted off by the police. She's come out here on the basis of Saturday's discovery and a troubling hunch about the source of the calls.

Part of Alice wants to be right about this; it would validate her instincts and bring an end to Mary's NightLine torment. But a greater part of her wants to be wrong. Because if her intuition is spot-on, what then? Alice gulps. That is not a conversation anyone would want to have. Mary would be crushed. Alice can see her face now—those big green eyes filling first with shock, then horror, then realization. It would be better for Mary to find out now, though, Alice thinks, than after any more calls. Much as Alice would rather trash this plan and flee as fast as her feet can carry her, she needs to push on. For Mary's sake.

She checks both sides of the street for stray pedestrians or curtain-peepers. The coast is clear as far as she can tell, but she keeps her phone to hand in case she needs to pretend to be taking a call. She finds a spot at the end of the hedge that allows her an unobstructed view into the living room, while still protecting her from clear view of the homeowner, were he to look out. True to his word, the curtains are wide open.

The armchair nearest the window is facing away from Alice but she recognizes the shirt, the fit around the arms. She wouldn't have pegged him for a crap-television fan, though; the TV opposite splits and splices between videos of people paid to submit their videotapes of pranks gone wrong, for public consumption. If she squints, Alice can make out a small megaphone with a diagonal line hatched through it in the bottom right of the screen, announcing that the show is on mute. For that, Alice can't say she blames him.

How long will she wait? Half an hour? An hour? More? At some point she will have to go home. *Come on,* she thinks, *don't make me leave empty-handed.* Her strategy pays off; she doesn't need to wait more than five minutes for her answer. Once the adverts come on, he picks the phone up from the cradle. Alice takes a photo. It isn't much—the back of a bald head, the phone, and the furry blur of pixels from the screen beyond. It is, however, time-and date-stamped.

A minute later she takes another shot, for good measure. No sooner has the second snap been taken than his head drops into his hands. The phone falls to the floor.

Alice has never hated the feeling of being right quite so much in all her life.

23

2009

Mary had been waiting for so long on the doorstep of Jim's clinic that two other patients had arrived in the time she had been standing there. When the third showed up, a woman with a small quilted handbag on a metal chain, she at least had the good grace not to barge right past Mary.

"Are you going in?" she asked, rummaging around for some paperwork tucked in the pocket of her camel coat.

"Yes, yes, sorry. I was just checking I had the right place."

She should know, given that Jim had worked here for over eighteen months now. That said, Mary had only been here once before. It was shortly after Jim had first moved to the private practice, at an after-hours drinks party held by the partners. The months that followed had felt light, like the air of celebration had been blown right through them both. Jim was so excited about the new job—as he put it, the chance to do his work without the pressures and the impossible targets that his previous role had put on him.

With a wince, Mary remembered the mention of the complaint that had pushed him over the edge at Da's funeral three years back. It was little wonder that his career made him so anxious. There was no margin for error, and it couldn't help that patients looked up to doctors as if they were gods—infallible. It made running your own business look like a piece of cake, although with more map projects coming in by the day, Mary was starting to wonder if she had bitten off more than she could chew as sole proprietor and employee of her own business.

She stepped aside to let the other woman access the buzzer. The door clicked open and Mary walked in after her, trying to avoid being thwacked in the thigh by her handbag. The reception area looked different now, during working hours. It was quiet; a woman in a starched trench coat flicked through a glossy magazine while, on the other side of the room, a man with a badly disguised tonsure tapped his pen against the clipboard, trying to conjure up the answers missing from his patient survey.

There was a muffled drag of wheels on carpet as a young receptionist with a long, chestnut ponytail moved out from behind her computer to greet Mary.

"Good morning, can I get you checked in?"

"I'm here to see Dr. Whitnell," Mary stammered. His portrait was straight ahead, a string of letters beneath his name. Almost four years together and the mere sight of him, looking gorgeous even as a two-dimensional cutout, was still enough to turn her into a gibbering wreck.

But was it that or was it the nerves? It dawned on her that she had absolutely no idea how Jim would react to her turning up unannounced at his workplace. The picnic was a spur-of-the-moment idea. It was Jim who had brought out Mary's sense of spontaneity, back when they first met, but as time went by, things settled. Or rather, *they* settled—which would have been fine, had it not been for the fact that Mary had stumbled down an internet rabbit hole last night, ending up on a questionnaire in an online women's magazine entitled "Steady or Stale?"

After answering a few too many questions with the letter C, Mary had convinced herself that the contentment of their four-year relationship was, in fact, complacency. At first she couldn't see the issue with how things stood between herself and Jim. There had been no major issues since the wake, although he was no longer off the drink. The odd, mutually agreed glass of wine with dinner had snuck back into their lives. Still, things were nothing like before. They never kept alcohol in the house and Mary had never smelled it on Jim, either.

As far as Jim had told her, this position was a vast improvement on the old one, and the worst that either of them could complain of professionally was not having enough hours in the day. In the last few weeks Jim had seemed a little tetchy, though. The insomnia that Mary had first noticed in Portrush had returned, and she would often wake to the sound of Jim creeping to the spare room, where he could scroll through his laptop in peace. In the morning his energy levels would be on the floor.

Mary had wondered if it might have something to do with her. She'd never been one to make the first move, romantically, had never needed to, either. But then she started to wonder how long it had been since the last time they had sex, and she needed the calendar to hazard a guess. She was secure enough in their relationship not to jump to the conclusion that Jim was cheating but it wouldn't hurt for her to step up to the plate, maybe make more of an effort in bed. He did still fancy her, didn't he? Or was his mind elsewhere?

The questionnaire might have had a point. If so, it claimed they were doomed, unless Mary could reignite a spark. The article, unfortunately, didn't give many family-friendly suggestions on how such excitement could be reignited, and Mary's independent thought had only stretched as far as the unexpected delivery of two cheese sandwiches for lunch today. She had thought they could celebrate the start of spring in style.

"And can I take your name please?"

"I'm Mary O'Connor—his girlfriend. His partner, I suppose. So it's not an appointment as such . . ."

A look of shock flashed across the woman's face before she caught it and replaced it with a smile, smoothing one hand down her glossy ponytail. Mary could feel the weight of the two Tupperware lunch boxes pulling at her right shoulder joint. She could hardly sit in the park and eat both alone.

"I'm afraid he's out today. He hasn't been in the office all week." She lowered her voice but it did nothing to salvage the embarrassment rushing up Mary's spine in a wave of heat that was beginning to spread across her cheeks too. "Dr. Parry will be finishing his current appointment in the next five minutes, if you'd like to speak with him?"

"No, no. Er . . . that's fine. Jim asked if I could collect any post of his?" Mary could see the cogs whirring in the receptionist's mind. Clearly there were no notes in the staff handbook to prepare you for the unexpected arrival of unwanted girlfriends. "Personal post, I mean. He mentioned an online order?"

"Just give me a sec, I'll be right back." The receptionist went into the side room. Mary thought she could make out the low hum of voices beyond it. She could feel panic beginning to take over and thought about leaving before the young woman returned, although that wouldn't have done anything to help Jim's career. "Do you think it's this he was after?" She poked her head round the door and shook a small brown cardboard box in Mary's direction. It gave a loud rattle.

Mary looked down at her phone, pretending to check. Her chest contracted as the image on the background came into focus—Jim in an Italian restaurant near Newtownards, pizza sauce slopped on the side of his mouth. It had been taken last year, on a rare occasion when she had coaxed him over to visit Mam. It had been a brilliant evening out, even if Mary had felt the rest of the trip was strained. Ever since Da's funeral, Mam seemed wary of Jim. There was no beer in her fridge and every time Jim was in the toilet, Mam would ask, pointedly, if Mary was alright—if she would tell her otherwise. Surely maternal protectiveness had an expiry date. Mary would be turning thirty-one soon.

"Yes, yes, seems to be." She clicked the screen off and shoved the phone back in her pocket.

The receptionist handed the parcel over, no further questions asked. "We hope James will be back in next week," she said, as if by way of consolation. "Send him our love."

Mary stumbled outside, her head spinning. She had seen Jim that morning. He had looked knackered but mumbled something about not sleeping well and then kissed her, as usual, before heading off to work. Or so she had thought.

He hasn't been in the office all week. How was that possible? For the last four evenings Jim had arrived home by 7 P.M. at the latest. Mary had been so overwhelmed with commissions in the last few months that she hadn't the time to fetch Jim from the station at the end of the day. She missed that routine, sure, but they were still spending time together and that was what mattered, right? All week they had eaten supper together, then curled up on the sofa to watch TV. Mary always asked after his day at work. Always. And while it may have been a routine question, she never got anything other than the routine answer from Jim, either. *Fine*—the assumption being that he had spent his days in the clinic, not wherever he was hiding out now.

In the Tube station she jogged onto the first train she saw, listing every possible explanation for a situation that seemed to defy all reason: he hadn't wanted to tell her he was sick; maybe something had come up with his parents and he hadn't wanted to worry her. But for a whole week? Unless it was an affair . . . but Jim wasn't the type. Not the Jim she knew and loved. Mary pressed her head into the dimpled handrail ahead, as if she could press some more convincing conclusion out of it. It took ten minutes for her to realize she had been traveling in the wrong direction.

She had half expected Jim to be sitting at the kitchen table when she walked in, his bag slung on the sofa and an explanation on his lips, but as soon as she got through the door, Mary knew the house was empty. The detritus from preparing the picnic was still on the chopping board, a gift for the christening they were due to attend tomorrow still perched on the hallway table. What if he wasn't back for it? Mary thought her legs would give way.

Before she lost her resolve, she sent him a text: Hope you're having a good day at work x. Her thumb grew sore from checking to see if it had been read.

Nothing.

Should she even be at home? If something bad had happened, then she should be out looking. But what could have happened to Jim, Mary wondered, that was so bad on the previous four days, yet meant he could still find his way back to the flat, come evening, leaving Mary none the wiser that anything was wrong? He was skiving work all day, then returning home for his supper—why? A crisis of conscience? A pang of longing for his girlfriend of four years? It didn't add up.

In the absence of anything better to do, Mary put the television on for some background noise. She lay on the sofa. For the first time she realized how many shows centered around couples—buying houses abroad or arguing on talk shows or hosting excruciating dinner parties for strangers. She settled on horse racing. Her eyes stung from holding in tears. When she closed them, she could see Da squatting in front of the box when he was well enough, in his chair later on, shaking his paper at the screen and cheering for whichever steed was riding with his bet that day. Had he ever lied to Mam?

That was a different relationship. But just because Mary and Jim had decided not to go in for the wedding and the yoke of four kids, it didn't mean they were any less *happy*. The minute Jim walked into her life, he redefined Mary's own sense of what the word could mean. It was more than not worrying, more than not expecting the worst. It meant waking up excited for the day that followed and the potential of what it might hold. Mary wandered to the kitchen noticeboard, where every postcard Jim had ever given her was fanned in a border, in some places three cards deep. It meant being together, the two of them.

What had gone wrong then, this week? Was Jim not as happy in their relationship as she was? Or was he not happy, period? Mary's mind spiraled back to their third date together, the mention of Skye during her first time visiting him in London. She had never forgotten what Jim had said then—that he thought it should have been him instead of Sam—but she had hoped that was the musing of a younger, grieving man. If there had been something more sinister at play—a long-term mental-health condition underlying all this—then wouldn't he have said? He was a doctor after all. He was the expert.

Mary went to check her phone again. It wasn't unusual that he didn't reply to texts during the working day, but then again, he wasn't at work—so how would he explain that when he came home?

If he came home.

24

2018

"I thought we'd have our AGM in the garden," Ted says. "Make the most of this weather. The others are already out there."

Mary tries to catch Ted's eye, but he is seemingly fixated on a spot of scratched paint on the doorframe. He doesn't look himself today. There are heavy shadows under his eyes and the effect of the Dorset tan has all but worn off, leaving him sallow and puffy. She should have realized that something was up when he didn't ask for help with the refreshments today, but then again, she has had so much else on her mind.

There was another call from Jim at NightLine this week. Or so Mary thinks. It was even less coherent than the previous two and it lasted no more than a minute in length. The line was poor. All Mary could hear were sobs, interspersed with apologies. It was torment. Jim was never one to show much of his emotions, preferring to bottle his stresses until they exploded in an uncharacteristic mess. The second the call ended, Mary's mind began to spiral through a hundred worst-case scenarios. Was he sick? In some kind of trouble? *Please, Lord, at the very least let Jim be somewhere warm, with a good roof over his head.*

By some miracle Mary made it to the end of that shift. But between calls she wasn't in the classroom. Rather she was back in their old flat, her head on Jim's chest, her arms wrapped around him, in the happiest place of all. "The fortress," Jim used to call it, when Mary pulled the duvet up over their heads. Whatever issues the day had thrown up at work or with family, they belonged to another world outside the covers. Mary would give anything—*anything*—to be back in the fortress now. She could still make everything alright for him, for them both.

"Mary?"

Ted gives a light cough but it develops into a bark. They haven't been for a Sunday-afternoon walk together in weeks now, and Mary suddenly feels awful for not checking in on him. Ted does so much for everyone else and never thinks about himself. Reaching out for help doesn't come easily to anyone, but Mary has always found that men can be especially reluctant in that regard.

"Are you alright there?" She scrabbles in her bag and produces a battered aluminum water bottle.

Ted flaps it away. "Better not be the summer flu. It can take me— but not before the AGM is done!" He raises a fist in what Mary guesses is a weak impression of a superhero. Acting isn't his forte. That, or something is off with him. "Do you want to go out back? We're just waiting for Alice now."

Mary takes a seat next to Olive on one of the high-backed dining-room chairs that Kit is carrying out of the house and onto the lawn. Both greet her, but Mary finds herself struggling with the small talk. It is an unwelcome return to the days before Jim, when she felt more like a spectator peering in, rather than a participant in her own life. These calls have thrown everything out of kilter.

"Hiya!"

Alice has arrived, slightly out of breath. For a few seconds Mary watches Alice waver, uncertain whether she should come and speak to Mary more privately.

Mary hasn't seen Alice in over a week now, since she invited herself up to her flat after the second call from Jim. Alice wasn't on the shadowing schedule, and Mary wondered whether she had abandoned the volunteering altogether. She couldn't shake her disappointment, however irrational she knew it to be. Alice is the only other person who knows about these calls, and Mary appreciated the chance to share their emotional load in her hour of need.

Although competition is stiff, this could well be one of the worst weeks in Mary's life. The impact of the calls, one after another, topped off by that god-awful video on the internet. Mary hasn't heard from Mam, which is a blessing, she supposes; none of the rest of her family, either. From what she heard last Christmas, child-rearing has absorbed her brothers' entire attention and, between work and bedtime stories and bath time, they aren't keeping abreast of the nonsense online in the way they used to.

Mary herself hasn't looked up the footage since Kit showed it to her on his phone at NightLine. She hasn't the strength, what with everything else going on. All she can do is pray that it has blown over, as Kit promised. She would feel most comfortable asking Alice to confirm that, but no, Alice is staying put where she is, on the far side of the circle.

"Is there anything else I can bring through?" Alice asks.

"No, no, you're fine, love," Ted replies.

Mary watches as Alice's jaw seems to clench. *Or did it?* No sooner is the tension there than it is gone again. Mary tells herself she is being hypersensitive.

"Looks like we have everyone," Ted says, emerging with a jug of squash, a stack of paper cups, and a handful of papers. He sets the refreshments on the grass in the center of the circle and passes Olive the sheets to hand out. "Quite the team we have here, eh? I'm so glad everyone could make it today. Has everyone got a copy of the AGM agenda? I thought we'd work through it point by point, unless anyone has anything they'd like to raise before we crack on?"

"I do," Alice announces.

"Go on then." Ted's smile is warm and welcoming, in comparison to the steel in Alice's gaze.

Mary shifts in her seat; she knows that Alice is kind, but she has also seen a sharper side to her too, when she elbowed her way into Mary's flat. Why is she staring at Mary? *Oh God, she isn't—is she?* Mary told Alice about the calls in confidence, and if she is about to out Mary for not flagging them with Ted as a potential safeguarding issue, then she might be kicked out of NightLine. And if that happens and Jim calls again . . .

"It's Ted," Alice blurts. "Phoning you, Mary. The calls to NightLine that you thought were from Jim? They weren't from him, I'm sorry. They were from Ted."

Mary feels her stomach plummet. In the circle there is silence, but in Mary's head there is a cacophony. What is Alice saying? Ted was the one calling. *Ted.* It can't be. Is this true? How would Alice know? Mary forces herself to look at each of the volunteers in turn. Olive is baffled and Kit looks as if he has been slapped. Alice is as forthright as ever. But Ted? He is looking at his feet.

A wasp, swollen and plump with feeding, lands on Mary's hand and crawls down her ring finger. She doesn't move to bat it away. The time for Ted to refute the allegation is ticking down.

"Is it true?" Mary asks, eventually. Her voice is quiet but firm. She has lived in the dark confusion of an unknown for so long. She cannot shoulder another. She simply cannot.

Ted grinds the heels of his palms into each other. Next to him, Alice is fumbling about on her phone. God only knows what she has on there. More fecking videos? Mary does not want to know. Not now, when her humiliation is already being broadcast to an audience consisting of the closest thing she has to friends.

"Well, is it?" Mary stands. Her voice is louder this time. The anger is biting at her ears, blood flooding to her head. She does not know how much longer she can continue this show of strength.

"Yes," Ted says.

And with that, Mary's legs go weak. Her knees buckle and she falls back into the chair, her upper body crumpling. All the tension in her muscles evaporates. It doesn't make sense. None of it. How? Why? The caller never did explicitly say he was Jim, but she was so convinced. *He said he missed her. He said she was his safe place* . . . Or did she imagine it all? She's delusional. Better that, though, than to admit she has forgotten the sound of Jim's voice. *Her* Jim. How was that possible?

"Mary, I didn't mean for it to come out like this," Ted begins. "I was going to tell you. I tried to apologize." His voice is splintered and tears are pooling in his eyes. "I never thought you would think it was Jim. I didn't mean to mislead you, that was never the intention. I promise. I don't know what I was thinking."

He reaches a hand across the circle, toward Mary. She doesn't notice it.

She has never really listened to Ted, the quality of his tone, its depth. It's just . . . a voice. Nothing distinct about it. He can't be more than a year or two older than Jim would be now. She only has herself to blame—the stupid, hopeful, delusional eejit that she is. She has made herself look like such a fool.

"I never meant to hurt you." Ted's jaw is shaking. "I wanted you to notice me, Mary. And you never would. Then, when I called, at first it was a mistake; I'd had a drink and I was lonely and desperate. I wanted you to listen, even if you didn't think it was me. After that, I found myself calling to apologize. It escalated. Awfully. I can't tell you how much I regret it."

A drinker, too. Mother of Christ, must they all be at the bottle? Of all the times that Mary has craved oblivion, she has still never once turned to that excuse. Because that is what it is to her. An excuse. And she has had enough of them. Maybe Ted is to blame, maybe she is, but what else is there to say?

She looks up, fleetingly. All of the volunteers are staring at her, unsure what she will do next.

Mary herself has not the faintest clue. All she knows is that she has to get out of here. Fast.

She snatches up her rucksack and runs out onto the road.

25

2018

"Did it really have to be like that?" Ted whispers.

It is just Alice and Ted, alone in his garden. In the small section of lawn between them, two fruit flies circle the spare AGM agendas and the jug of orange squash that acts as a paperweight.

Alice has nothing fitting to reply. *Yes*—because what other way was there to tell Mary that her highest hopes were pinned on a hoax? *No*—because no one would ever plan to inflict this sort of pain on two people whose lives have been forged from the harsh coals of hardship.

Ted is trembling, although it must be touching thirty degrees under the midafternoon sun.

No one would willingly believe that it was Ted—kind, friendly, *genuine* Ted—making the calls to Mary at NightLine. But the evidence was incontrovertible. First, the timetable that Alice found in Ted's bedside drawer, with Mary's hours highlighted. Then Alice's trip to his house, on a Tuesday night, to catch him in the act of calling. Alice had photographs of both exhibits ready to present at the AGM, in case Ted tried to deny his involvement. She hadn't expected him to own up so readily.

"Don't try and make this out to be my fault," Alice says.

She'd practiced those words in the mirror before setting off for the

AGM today. In rehearsal, they were delivered with fury. But now they feel crumbly and weak. Ted's con may have cost Alice half of her already tight deadline. It may have unsettled the delicate fabric of Mary's routine. But within touching distance of the broken man in front of her, Alice suddenly realizes that her anger was myopic, to say the least.

Because Ted never pretended to be Jim. What's more, listening to him trying to explain himself, it struck Alice that he was every bit as lonely and desperate as Mary. He had stumbled in his bid to make a connection and got in over his head, making things worse when he tried to backpedal.

"I'm not—" Ted stops almost as soon as he begins.

His voice is cracking and although there is a part of Alice that wants to short-circuit that response, to hold him before the heaves of guilt arrive, she also knows that she is not the right person to absolve him. He needs Mary's forgiveness, no one else's.

Mary. Alice hopes she is okay. A woman in that state, running into the road . . . Alice has been here before, after the first night she met Mary, worrying that she might do something stupid. But that is not the person Alice has grown to know. Mary is far stronger than she looks. She will weather this, even if the disappointment soaks through to her core.

Still, Alice ought to be looking for her too. Do Kit and Olive know where she lives? The sooner she is found, the sooner Alice can appeal to her mercy. It isn't just Ted whose conscience is desperate for relief.

"I ought to go and help them look for Mary."

Ted nods. He still has not looked up at Alice, his gaze focused instead on the patch of grass in front of him, shaded by his hunched chest.

"Tell her I'm sorry. Keep telling her that, please."

Once Alice is out of the house, she collapses on a wall at the end of the road. Maybe it is the heat, maybe it is the trauma of the last few minutes, but she is so disorientated that she can't work out which way Mary's flat is from here. She clamps her head between her knees but it only makes the dizziness worse. What was she thinking, springing her findings on Mary in such a public fashion?

The truth was that Alice was so caught up in the moment of revelation that the more sensitive approach she had constructed and practiced went right out the window. Although she doesn't regret setting Mary straight on the source of the calls, Alice knows she needs to apologize for the manner in which it was done. She knows, from personal experience, how soul-destroying an ill-considered delivery of the truth can be.

The way Alice found out about where her dad had gone was far from public, but the thought of it now, over ten years later, makes her feel even more faint. She was sixteen and it had been more than four years since the day he disappeared from her life. Four long years of tormenting herself over what could have happened to him—whether he was dead in a ditch or sleeping rough in a city center just miles away. Four years in which she had drifted from her mum and isolated herself from friends whose biggest concern was procuring a fake ID in time for Friday night.

But then salvation dropped. Through her letter box, to be exact. Alice will never forget the warm flood of anticipation when she saw her dad's handwriting on a card, in the post, two weeks after her birthday. It had the uncomfortably straight lines and crabbed joins that she had dreamt of, a thousand times or more. She opened the envelope with trembling hands. Out fell a twenty-pound note. *Happy Birthday, Alice!* it began. *Hope you have a wonderful day.*

Whatever small sentiment that held was soon lost beneath the note below, which explained that she had two half-siblings now. He had met someone else and made a whole new family. Alice had never felt so vulnerable, so deluded by the hope he might come home. She shoved the money in the back of her sock drawer. Then she snuck downstairs and returned with a matchbox. The card went up in flames, together with the last of her childhood innocence. Life didn't always have a happy ending—did it?

And while the arrival of that card tipped Alice back into grief all over again, at least the clarity helped her find a different path, once its veil had lifted. That is all she has ever wanted to provide for Mary: a chance to move on.

Alice is no longer quite as light-headed and she stands, pulls out her phone to check the map.

Kit calling.

Alice prays he has good news. "Hello?"

"Are you okay?"

"Yeah." Alice lies. She can't go into the memories that today has dredged up. "Did you find Mary?"

"Olive spotted her going into her flat, but we just missed her. And we tried calling up but there was no answer. She shut the curtains. I think we leave it for a while and hope for the best."

Alice gulps. "Okay . . . I'm sorry about Ted, by the way."

"What about him?"

"For not sharing my suspicions, I suppose. It was so much to take in, and I know that you're close to Ted. I didn't know how you might react."

There is silence on the line. Kit is clearly struggling to find the right words for the NightLine chaos that Alice uncovered.

"Ted's a good guy," Kit says eventually. "A good guy who made a mistake. I hate that he's upset Mary, I really do, but I also hate how upset he must have been to have called her like that in the first place. I hate myself for not doing something to stop it."

"Sorry—what?" Alice chokes out. "I mean how could *anyone* have stopped that?"

Kit shrugs. "I don't know. I could have spoken to Ted a bit more, maybe asked him out for a drink. We all knew that he was struggling. After Bev died, he took some time off NightLine but it wasn't even a fortnight. He had the kids to look after, and his day job. He's always been one of those show-no-weakness types. That can be pretty lonely."

There is more authority in Kit's voice than Alice has ever heard before. She wants to ask where it comes from, but Kit continues before she has a chance. "If he was calling Mary like that, then he must have had nowhere else to turn."

Alice knew Kit was smart, but this level of emotional intelligence is startling. She could learn a lot. "I was pretty insensitive at the AGM, wasn't I?"

"I can imagine that it was impossible to know what to do for the best. Besides, I'm sure Mary will forgive you. And if you manage to get her some answers about Jim . . ."

And there was Alice thinking *she* was the tenacious one. They still have leads about Jim—the scandal at work, the personal unhappiness implied by Gus—but without the calls to trace, what hope of finding him? She isn't predisposed to throwing in the towel, but she will need a day or two to compose herself before she finds a new avenue into her investigation.

"Alice, are you still there? Alice?"

"Yes."

"Good, well, I need to get on to the real reason I called, before my minutes run out."

Panic seizes Alice's chest. Isn't there some statute that says how much bad news a person can endure in a day?

Kit continues, "I have something you are going to want to see."

"What is it?"

"Can you come round now? I have to show you in person, to explain. But trust me, Alice: you will want to see this. The calls might not have led us to Jim, but this . . . well, let's just say I'm pretty confident that it will."

26

2018

Kit's flat is no cleaner than the last time Alice set foot in it. If anything, it is more of a mess. Two bowls with what looks like cereal crusting on the lip sit by the side of the sofa. There can't be any clean mugs or glasses left in his cupboards. Alice can't work out why he doesn't bother to tidy up or pay for a cleaner with that banker's salary of his. She would ask, if it weren't for the fact that, as per his call fifteen minutes ago, there would appear to be far more urgent matters at hand.

"So what's the 'something' you think I might want to see?" Alice asks, before Kit has a chance to say a word.

Kit flaps her toward the sofa. "Hold on, just let me get my notes."

"Notes?"

"I've been learning from the best."

"You charmer." Alice smiles. Kit returns with two slim piles of A4 paper, each bound by mangled paper fasteners. If he has brought her here to unveil an adult's take on a primary-school history project, she will scream. Does she look like she has time for this? But Alice's impatience has already cost her—and Mary—today. She keeps a smile fixed to her lips. "Go on then: shoot."

"Well, that photo did the trick." There is a pause while Alice tries to pinpoint what Kit is talking about. "The one you sent me to put up on the forum when we were at the café near Gus's office. Of Mary and Jim at the Giant's Causeway?"

Watching Kit open up the missing-persons forum had unleashed such blind panic in Alice that she completely forgot she had given him that stolen image to upload. *Oh shit!* As if she hasn't put her foot in it enough already. That photo was never hers to share, but then again, Mary won't have seen it—will she? If it turns out to be as effective as Kit seems to think, then Alice's subterfuge will have been worthwhile.

"It has had so many responses, Allie, I can't tell you. But good ones, too. The people on this missing-persons page are actually invested, you know?" *Only too well,* Alice thinks. "None of the people piling on the social-media bandwagon. These people have been sharing sightings. Proper, legitimate ones."

Kit holds up an index finger, keen to stop Alice's imminent interruption.

"Now I know this is a bit of a change of tack. But I was never sure that the NightLine calls would lead anywhere. Even before this afternoon, I was busy examining the other information we had gleaned. And then it struck me—with Gus and the scandal at Jim's work, we have some ideas about *why* he disappeared." Alice nods. That much is true. "But what about *where* he might have disappeared to? If Jim is out there and we can find him, then we can ask him to his face what happened, and that's killing two birds with one stone, right?"

"Okay . . ." It is never clear to Alice where Kit's brain is going next and never has that been truer than at this exact second.

"What the people on the forum can do, and have done, is try to pinpoint *where* on the map Jim might be right now."

"But he left seven years ago."

"Can you cut me some slack, please? I'm talking about *recent* sightings here. I'm working with the last twelve months. There's five, all of

them backed up by at least two witnesses. Some by a lot more. Here."
Kit hands over one of his booklets. "I've plotted out our route and attached that as an appendix too. We would be heading north; it's a lot of
ground to cover and I reckon it will take a week minimum."

Alice opens Kit's dossier and flicks through ten pages of text, interspersed with high-quality images. After the map appendix, there is a
second, which contains a packing list. It reads: "*Spaghetti*." Last page
aside, this is far from a primary-school history project. There are no
words for how deeply she has underestimated him.

"What do you think?"

"Kit, this is so much work. You didn't have to . . ."

"I know. But I wanted to. There's a big difference."

"Why?"

"Why what?"

"Why did you want to do all this? It must have taken hours. You
must have so many better things to be getting on with."

"I wish." Kit sighs. "No, but honestly, it was you who said it. I
wanted to do something worthwhile. And I haven't done for a long, long
time. That's been my problem, I suppose." He has the same tone that
he used on the phone earlier, when he talked about Ted's strong-man
bravado. There is a pause where Alice would, previously, have burst in.
But if NightLine has taught her one thing, it is that sometimes people
need space to speak. "I've known Mary for months now, and never have
I thought of finding Jim for her. Maybe I thought I didn't have the skills
or the time, but now I realize that they were all excuses. It took you to
show me how to get my priorities in order."

"Well, I'm grateful, really. And impressed and . . ." *Hopeful,* Alice
thinks. Her heart rate hasn't stabilized since she started turning the
pages of Kit's booklet. The very detail is compelling. He's right, it's a big
change of tack but it does sound promising.

"We could leave on Monday and start on the route I've suggested, to visit each of the five places with recent sightings. I've got a mate with a car who says he can lend it to me for a week. But only a week—then he needs it back. According to my plan, it's manageable if I keep my foot down at seventy. All you have to do is chip in for petrol."

A week. If they were to find Jim, that would still give Alice just enough time to write up her story and make the promised front page before her neck is on the redundancy chopping board. But what of Mary? Alice hasn't even apologized to her yet, let alone sought her blessing for the trip. Although Mary would surely agree that Kit's research provides a brilliant opportunity to find Jim.

"What do you say?"

Alice hesitates, tells herself she must focus on the greater good and nothing else.

"Yes," she says, "Monday it is." Sometimes in life you have to make a decision. Alice hopes that she won't live to regret it. "Let's not tell Mary for now, yeah? If I see a good moment, I can broach it with her in person. I think it would be best coming from me."

"That makes sense. Great, well, we're all set then! Do you want to stay for an early supper? I was thinking—"

"Spaghetti? I'd love some."

While Kit busies himself by the stovetop, Alice starts a new email.

Hi, Jack,

Have some promising leads for my article. Will be taking next week as annual leave to investigate them. I'll be back next Monday, with my copy for the end-of-August front page.

I won't let you down.

Best,

Alice

She clicks Send before her confidence falters. Now there's no way she can back out of this trip.

"Can you come and help me serve?" Kit calls. Alice drops her phone into her bag and heads to the kitchenette, plucking two stray bowls at random. She squeezes past Kit to reach the sink, and the muscles in her bum contract on contact.

"Sorry." Kit shuffles backward, but now the two of them are pressed up against one another, like standing spoons.

It feels good and wrong—it's Kit!—and . . . *Not today, Keaton.* Alice lurches forward, unsettling what looks like two months' worth of recycling, which is tucked down the side of the fridge. Flat sheets of cardboard sail out onto the floor. It looks like the streets in central London, after a rally.

And then it hits Alice: how she will make it up to Mary. A chance to seek her approval for their upcoming excursion, too.

"Kit, do you have any paint?"

27

2018

Sunday early evening and the station is quieter than usual. It is easy to pick out Mary, in her usual spot. She looks exhausted but still her posture is rigid, proud. Alice reflects on how Mary didn't miss a day of her vigil, even after the video did the rounds online. Formidable doesn't come close.

"Alice?" Mary says, without moving her sign.

Alice doesn't reply. Instead she takes the paving square next to Mary, rummages in a large plastic bag and produces her handiwork. Her script is not as neat as Mary's and there was a wobble on the J, which she had to overcompensate for, making the curve at its base double the width of the rest of the letters. Still, it does the trick.

Mary reads it: *COME HOME JIM.* For a second she doesn't respond and Alice can feel her anxiety kicking in. Messing up once looks clumsy; twice looks spiteful.

"At least you spelt everything right," Mary says, at last. Her eyes are watery and there is a slight tremble in her voice, which is hard to disguise.

Last night, while Kit was finishing the paintwork on the extra signs, Alice emailed the other NightLine volunteers to detail arrangements. What she had in mind was a stunt: part apology, part show of solidarity.

And for the latter it really was a case of the more, the merrier. Still, she didn't suggest an RSVP—better not to find out how much Ted and Olive hate her right now. If Alice is doing this alone, then it won't be ideal, but so be it. The most important thing is that she shows Mary that she still cares, both about her and about finding Jim. Alice firms up her footing.

It isn't long before there is a commotion at the traffic light ahead. Kit is bounding across the road, seemingly ignorant of the honking cars that he has dodged between, with Olive tutting in his wake. Alice feels a rush of relief, even if Olive has yet to make eye contact. This is for Mary, Alice reminds herself; it is not about her own ego. She nods at her bag between her feet and Kit produces two more signs from inside.

Standing in a line like this, it strikes Alice that they could be mistaken for a small flash mob or a poorly managed pop group. Commuters walking past are starting to slow down, rubbernecking like the first drivers after a car crash. It's hard work, standing in imitation of Mary's impeccable posture. Under such scrutiny too. Alice's sandals are beginning to rub and she bends down to release the sore point. Just as she is about to stand up, a hand reaches for her carrier bag. It has large, dark hairs on the back of the fingers. The nails are stained, dirt dug deep into them.

"I didn't think you'd come," Alice says.

"I didn't think I would, either." Ted doesn't look well. His eyes seem to have shrunk over the course of the thirty hours or so since the AGM. She wonders if she should send him home but decides it's best to bite her tongue.

Alice glances across at Mary, who is looking straight ahead, out past the triangle of park, beyond the traffic lights and toward the row of shops with their flaking paintwork. Ted sets himself up on the far side of Kit.

They can't have been there for long, the five of them, before an onlooker takes a photo. In her peripheral vision, Alice can see Mary shudder. The last thing she needs is a reminder of the video or a scene that could attract the same level of online attention again. Alice curses herself for not considering how they might look to others.

"Shall we call it a day?" Alice says, turning round so that she is facing everyone, shielding Mary too.

Four pairs of eyes zone in on Mary. She gives a small nod.

Before anyone has a chance to object, Ted pipes up, "Mary, could I walk you home?" His voice is uncertain. "I've got a lot of explaining to do."

Buses heave and wheeze along the Broadway but no one else seems to be breathing.

"Okay," Mary replies. It is hard to tell how she is feeling about the offer. Then again, that is for her to know and for Ted to find out. Alice tries to check her curiosity—it will be the end of her, someday. "Will you give me a minute first? I'd like to speak to Alice alone."

"Of course," Ted says.

He and Olive shuffle further down the road, toward the coffee cart. Kit is already wandering in the opposite direction, peering at something on his phone. He looks shaken, and Alice wants to check in on him but she can't, not now.

Despite the fact that they are in a public space, Alice suddenly feels very alone. She is about to be told that she is a terrible person, that Mary wishes she had never met her . . .

"Thanks, for this. For everything." Mary places a cool hand on Alice's forearm.

"Oh." The words are choking in Alice's throat. This was not what she expected. "I mean, I should be apologizing."

"I appreciate it," Mary says, repinning a stray hair into her bun. "The trouble you went to, looking into the calls. For one thing, it confirmed it for me."

"Confirmed what?"

"That sometimes it is better not to know."

"Really?"

Mary nods. "The unknown isn't always the worst thing in the world. Not when the truth can crush you."

Alice cannot believe her ears. Mary can't mean this. She doesn't understand what she's saying. That sixteenth-birthday card might have been the worst surprise of Alice's life, but at least it set her free from stumbling in the darkness of uncertainty. It dampened her anxieties. It set her on the path to acceptance. If only Alice could find the words to tell Mary that.

"So I'm asking that you stop looking now, for Jim."

"What—wait . . . what do you mean?"

Alice thinks of Kit's dossier on her bed, at home. She hasn't even begun to broach the issue of their upcoming investigation.

"I've said my piece, Alice. You have to stop looking."

With that, Mary power walks off toward Ted before Alice can stop her. She is soon swallowed up in a crowd of passengers disembarking at the bus stop.

"Shit!" Alice kicks a pile of free newspapers at the corner of the station entrance. This was not the result she wanted. The apology was important, but that doesn't mean Alice wasn't also hoping that it might act as a means of readmitting her into Mary's trust, to get her blessing for the trip that might secure the story. There was one message she did hear, though, loud and clear: Mary does not want her to keep searching for Jim.

But why? What does Mary mean when she says the unknown isn't always the worst thing in the world? It must be her fear talking. Alice knows that the routines of ignorance may be comfortable, but they aren't sustainable. Not when your sanity is at stake. In this situation, Alice does know better than Mary. Mary will come around to her way of thinking, Alice knows she will. It is impossible to see what you need when you are blinded by confusion.

Alice looks down at the sign in her hands. *COME HOME JIM*—the message says it all. And here she is, about to embark on a journey that could cause just that. That decides it. Alice will go without Mary's approval. When she brings Mary the closure she knows that Mary needs, Alice will be forgiven. Besides, she can't back out of the trip now. She has told Jack she'll be away from work, returning with her article. Kit has the logistics all planned.

Speaking of which, where is he? Alice needs to find out what time they are leaving tomorrow. She scours the road and sees that he has wandered further down the street, his eyes still glued to his phone. She has no idea what is going on with him.

"You alright?"

"Good job, there," Kit replies. It is clear he isn't listening.

Not the question I asked, Alice thinks, *but fine.* If Kit isn't going to engage with her, then she will settle for the answers she needs in order to get home and pack instead. "What time tomorrow?"

Kit shrugs. "Eight A.M.? The sooner we hit the road, the better." He clicks his phone away and rubs a hand over his eyes. When it falls to his side again, he looks less tormented, as if a cloud has passed across his face, obscuring his true feelings. "I saw you speaking to Mary—I take it you're forgiven then? What did she say?"

Alice averts her gaze. In a split second she decides that she won't— *can't*—tell Kit that Mary asked her to stop searching for Jim. Kit's moral compass is a lot better calibrated than her own and he would withdraw his help if he knew, no doubt about that. He doesn't understand Mary like she does. He doesn't understand that Mary's instinctive dread of the truth will be outweighed by the long-term relief of its reveal.

"Oh, er . . . not much. Well, I'll see you tomorrow morning to start the investigation."

"*Investigation?* Is that what we're calling it now?"

"That's what it is, Kit."

"Alright, alright."

"I'm not giving up on this," Alice continues. She tries to fight the memory of Mary just minutes ago: her demeanor forgiving, but her instructions to end the inquiries firm. "It's in Mary's best interests."

"You're like a terrier, you know that?" Kit manages a small laugh. "Has anyone ever told you that you're wasted in digital sales? You should be a journalist."

Now it is Alice's turn to force some jollity onto her face. *How much strain can her conscience bear?* Kit cannot find out about her day job. Not before they find Jim. And then? She hopes he can find it in his preternaturally large heart to forgive her.

"I'll keep that in mind."

28

2018

Mary and Ted walk to the park in silence. There is an unspoken assumption that the explanations that will follow are too unwieldy to be broached over the sound of buskers or the hullaballoo of weekend drinkers spilling out of the pub. When they arrive, Mary chooses a bench on the far side from the gates, secluded enough that she doesn't think the two of them will be interrupted. It's a particularly leafy spot too—maybe that will help clear the air.

Alice's revelations yesterday had not so much pulled the rug from under Mary's feet as tipped the ground one hundred and eighty degrees, so that she was sent flying, headlong into self-recrimination. Should she have guessed? What clues did she miss? If she lets her mind drift, Mary can still feel the four pairs of eyes boring in on her—Ted, Alice, Olive, Kit—their gazes laced with pity. No one likes feeling like the last person to know. Nothing else makes you feel quite such a fool.

A fool or a madman? Mary wonders. Weren't they two sides of the same coin anyway? She should have known that it was wishful thinking, imagining it was Jim on the phone. But seven years of waiting will do a lot to a person. It has been eighty-four months of hoping that this is a bad dream; two thousand, five hundred and fifty-five days of expecting him home every night—God only knows how many hours of unanswered prayers. To Mary, there was no other possible explanation for the calls.

Looking back now, it didn't help that Ted sounded so similar to Jim. Once she began to think about it, Mary realized there was a mere year in age between the two men, and nothing in their indistinct accents to tell them apart. The telephone line was never good quality, either. Then there was *what* was said. That he was lost, that he saw Mary as a safe place. Even the excuse of the drinking screamed "Jim." Maybe Mary wasn't so much delusional as surrounded by men struggling to seek help.

"Oh, I brought this, by the way." Ted shoves his hand deep into the pocket of his cargo shorts. It reemerges holding a Twix.

"Thank you," Mary replies.

For a minute or two they share the chocolate bar in silence. Mary tries to calm herself down by focusing on the little details outside her racing mind: the splinters on the six inches of spare bench slat between them, the crunch of an ice-cream wrapper beneath her restless feet, the dirt under Ted's fingernails. They are the same rough and ready hands that held Alice's makeshift sign just half an hour ago, albeit too high for anyone but a giant to see it.

Mary smiles, in spite of everything. The fact that Ted turned up then—needless to say, cripplingly embarrassed—meant a lot. Regardless of what he did, Mary knows that he has a heart of gold. She just wants to know his real reasons.

She looks over at Ted, who is busy fumbling with his thumbs. He has the demeanor of a wounded dog: meek, suppliant, chastened. She ought to put him out of his misery. Most important question first.

"Why?" she asks.

"Why . . . why did I call?"

Mary steels herself, gives a brisk nod.

"The first time was a mistake. Honestly." Ted turns to look at Mary but she is staring straight ahead. "I'd got back from my parents' place that day and, walking into my own house, it had never felt so quiet. The silence was . . . painful. So painful." He grips the tendons at the back of his neck. "I thought a drink might take the edge off, but it just reminded me that I missed you. And then the idea came to me, on the spur of the moment. Before I knew it, I'd called and you answered and suddenly we were talking.

"I haven't found it easy, since Bev. It devastated me, losing her so young, but even once I'd started to work on the grief, all I got was a new set of problems. There I was, working all day by myself, then coming home to an empty house. I missed being . . . I don't know—listened to, I suppose."

"But why?" Mary's voice is firmer this time. "Why did you want to speak with *me*?"

"Isn't it obvious?"

Mary stares at Ted. His brows are furrowed in confusion, the two lines that form at the center of his forehead like the legs on a wobbly coffee table.

"I like you, Mary."

She feels herself blush. Her anger dissipates, to be replaced by a sense of complete confusion. "Romantically?" she clarifies.

Ted nods. "I've liked you for a while now, Mary. I did try to get closer . . ."

She thinks back to all her previous encounters with Ted, focusing on those that took place in the last year or so, when she thought he was back to his usual self, his bereavement no longer the sole pole of his existence. He'd always made an effort to talk with her before the NightLine shift started, but Mary had put that down to the fact that she was the first one through the door. It would be rude not to exchange some small talk.

"There were our Sunday-afternoon walks—the highlight of my month! Then you took me on that fiftieth-birthday trip to Kew and I started to think the feeling might be mutual. You were so good at checking in on me when I was low, too. But I couldn't be sure. Were we just friends, or something more?"

Mary looks over at him, hoping this isn't a question he will expect her to answer. She can't process all this information. But Ted continues. "I know you don't see it yourself, Mary, but you are the most extraordinary person. You're so kind and interesting and you've always made me feel so safe in your presence. You keep my problems at bay for the hours that we're together. That's quite a skill, where my head is concerned.

"You've never wanted to talk about Jim, and I completely respect that. He's a part of you and you love him. I would never want you to feel that you had to change. It didn't stop me wanting to get closer to you, though. All I wanted to change was the way you *saw* me. And I know that it's possible: to love a person who is gone and still to grow feelings for someone else. The first call was a mad, drunken idea, but some part of me must have thought that maybe hearing my voice might shift things enough for you to give me a chance. I thought I'd exhausted all my other options."

"Why didn't you just say that you liked me?" Whatever is left of Mary's frustration has expired and her voice now is quiet, coaxing.

"I didn't want to scare you off. No, that's not quite it. I was scared. Too scared to tell you how I felt. No one likes an outright rejection."

There is a hard lump in Mary's throat. Turns out she isn't the only person who is happier to live in an uncomfortable hinterland of doubt than to deal with the blinding pain of confirmation.

"Although that doesn't make it any better, I know that now. Honestly, I knew that after the first call. That's why, the next time I called, I tried to apologize. But it didn't come out right. Things snowballed and I was so sucked in—so far down one road that I didn't know how to find my way out."

"And Alice helped you to the exit, huh?" Mary catches Ted's eye. They smile.

"She's quite something, I'll give her that." The specter of Alice's righteous anger, acted out among the paper cups of squash in Ted's garden, looms large. "It didn't even cross my mind that you might think it was Jim," Ted adds. "I never meant to mislead you. I hadn't considered it, which is so stupid and so selfish of me."

Mary reaches out and places one hand on top of his balled fists. "I misled myself. Don't blame yourself for that bit," she says.

A homeless man is making his uncertain way down the row of benches, a shorn-off paper cup in one hand. Ted fishes in his pocket and hands over a couple of pounds when he approaches. "Take care, buddy," Ted says with a familiar warmth. After the man moves on, they return to silence.

"I've got some work to do on myself," Ted says eventually. "I'm not in a good way. I thought I could cope, but this has shown me that I might need some proper support." He huffs. "I run a crisis call center—you would think I'd be better at all this, wouldn't you?"

"Not necessarily," Mary replies. Just because the volunteers at NightLine care for other people in their hour of need doesn't mean they don't experience their own.

"And I want you to know that I don't expect anything from you now. Not like that." Ted's voice is measured. "Trust me, I know I've blown my chance. I don't expect your forgiveness. I have to earn that. But I want you to know that I will, if you'll let me. Whenever you feel ready."

Mary goes to respond but the sound is lost beneath the piercing whistle that marks the end of a five-a-side tournament on the far side of the park.

"I said, I forgive you," Mary repeats. She has no idea how she feels about much of Ted's candor, his amorous intentions especially. But she knows that she means this with every fiber of her being. "I think we could both do with moving on from this."

If only it was so easy to let go of everything else.

29

2009

It was seven o'clock when Jim finally returned home.

"Mary?"

She was lying on her side on the sofa, her hands tucked under her head. If she had fallen asleep, the nightmares were sitting close enough to her new reality for her not to have noticed. Her eyes flickered open; the first thing they landed upon were two cheese sandwiches, sweating in their Tupperware. *The picnic. Jim. His unexplained absence from work. He hadn't been at the clinic all week.*

"What's wrong?" he added.

Slowly she sat up. The room spun and she felt the full weight of her head wobbling on her neck.

"Are you sick?"

Jim came to sit at her side and placed the back of his hand against her forehead. Mary wondered if the mental energy she had expended on tormenting herself over his whereabouts could have caused her temperature to spike. It seemed stranger for it not to have done. She inhaled deeply, a long breath to find the smoky scent of whiskey that she already knew would be layered there. How had she not noticed it earlier?

"Are you?" she asked. With one foot she kicked the package she'd collected from the clinic out from under the chair.

"What's that?"

"You tell me. Your receptionist gave it to me. I called by to bring you lunch."

"What did they say?" he asked, when the silence had ground so deep into Mary that it was all she could do not to scream.

"That you had been off all week."

Jim went to caress Mary's cheek, to stroke it, but she shot back out of reach. There was pain in his voice that she knew she couldn't let herself give in to. He'd lied about going to work. *Lied.* Even the touch of the man who held her heart in his hand couldn't undo that.

"I have," he said.

"Why?"

"Why what?"

"Didn't you tell me? Why the hell were you not at work in the first place? Why the hell did you lie, and let me go in there like that, making a fool of myself?" Mary could hear her voice rising an octave, so shrill it seemed to bite at her own ears. She stood and walked to the window in a bid to control herself. She had her back to Jim, but in the reflection she could see his head bowed, a broken man awaiting the executioner. She hated that it had to be her. "Huh?" She was impatient. If he was going to ruin her, he could at least have the human decency to make it quick.

"I'm not well."

"How? Why? With what?" She turned to face him.

"I don't know." The words stuttered out of Jim like the misfires of a gun.

In an instant Mary had reeled back over four years, to the moment when Jim had first confided in her about Sam. That was the most open he had ever been about the state of his own mental health. Since then, Mary thought that Jim had never said anything else about his mood, his mind, in the whole time they had been together because she had beckoned in a new era for him—one that was brighter and more hopeful. How could she have been so naive?

She had learned that the way into Jim's confidence was with the softest tread. She still believed it. Still wanted to exhibit it. But how? She felt angry, betrayed, disappointed. She was hurting too. Her mouth opened, but nothing came out.

"I don't know, Mary," Jim continued, when it was clear she couldn't supply the words for him. "Recently I've been feeling . . . lost. I thought I had outrun it. But I haven't. I can't shake the feeling that I shouldn't be here at all."

Jim decided it was for the best if he crashed out on the sofa that night. It was the first time they had slept apart while under the same roof. They hadn't resorted to that option when Mary had been floored by the flu last winter, sniffing and hacking her way through the night with such violence that she had begged Jim to sleep in the sitting room. Or when he had the norovirus the year before, either. Then, Mary thought they were in everything together. Now she wasn't so sure.

It was impossible to sleep, knowing Jim was just yards away. But emotionally he had never seemed further from Mary's outstretched arms. She couldn't work out how she hadn't noticed that he was in this much pain. What signs had she missed? Worse yet, she couldn't contemplate why Jim would choose not to confide in her. She wasn't judgmental, or so she thought. All she had ever wanted was for Jim to live a life as fulfilling as the one he had opened up for her. *Lost.* The word spun round her head like a pinball, loose in the machine. How was that possible? She was meant to be his anchor.

Mary must have drifted off in the early hours of the morning as she didn't hear Jim get up. For a while she contemplated staying where she was. Jim would come up to see her eventually, no doubt. There would be more apologies, more promises never to lie to her again. Ten, maybe fifteen minutes of idle waiting later, Mary heard a chair scraping on the floor tiles below. She kept her ears pricked for the accompanying sound of footsteps, padding up the small flight to their bedroom. Nothing. She picked up her glass of water and replaced it on the bedside table with enough force that she could guarantee he would hear it.

Still—nothing.

Mary headed downstairs. In the kitchen Jim was seated on the chair furthest from the door, mug curled in one hand, the other scrolling on his laptop.

For a minute or two Mary watched from the doorway. He might have acted like one, but this was no stranger. The cowlick beneath his right ear sprang at the usual forty-five degrees. She must have kissed him there ten thousand times.

"Morning," he said, when he finally noticed Mary lingering. He reached for the spare mug to his right and raised it in question. She nodded but stayed standing at the edge of the breakfast bar. "Did you sleep okay?" Jim asked.

"Yeah, not too bad. You?"

She couldn't understand how Jim was capable of small talk. Far be it for Mary to want to see him suffering, but some indication that he recognized the gravity of what had happened the night before would be nice. Necessary, in fact, if there was to be any hope of returning to normal.

"Yeah. As well as I ever do." Jim stood and walked to the toaster. Halfway there, with his back turned, he spoke into the settling silence. "I can't give you what you need."

Mary's heart stopped. She must have misheard. Or heard and misinterpreted. This was not what he meant. Jim was half-hidden behind the partition wall.

"What . . . what did you say?" There was a hollow thud as the foldout lid of the bread board collided with the countertop. A second later, Jim reemerged. He looked down at the floor tiles.

"I can't be what you need. I can't be there for you in the way I should be. Not in the state that I'm in right now."

"Wait, hold on. What do you mean? I never said——"

"I know." Jim raised one hand, pacifying. "But I'm being honest here. Or trying to be. I can't tell you how sorry I am for everything. The lying about my whereabouts when I should have been at work this week wasn't right, and I know that. It's bad enough that I've fucked up, without bringing you down too. You don't deserve this."

"Where were you?"

"What?"

"Where were you," Mary repeated, "when you should have been at work?"

She realized she hadn't actually asked, in the confusion of the previous evening.

"Just out."

"Drinking?"

"A bit," Jim admitted. "I needed some space. Work thinks I have a stomach bug. I couldn't be with patients in this state. I thought saying I was sick for the week would give me the time to think."

Mary noticed how quickly he brushed over the issue of the drink. And while part of her wanted to interrogate it further, another, larger part of her knew that it was nothing but a mask. A cover to numb a much deeper reality. Jim wasn't right in the mind. Not right at all. Mary had made a mistake by tackling the symptom, rather than the root cause. It wasn't alcohol Jim needed treatment for; it was whatever was going on inside that beautiful, riddled head of his.

"And I have been thinking," he continued. "All week. Mainly of you. I can't drag you down. I can't. I love you too much. So that's why I'm saying"—he inhaled, voice trembling—"That I want to set you free to find someone who can give you everything you deserve. Someone who will be better for you."

Mary went to reach for him but he inched away. "I don't want better, though . . ." Mary hated herself. The begging—it wasn't her. She could feel the desperation at work, transforming everything she thought she knew about herself. She wouldn't be okay if Jim left. Not now that she knew what it was like to be loved by him. "I want to help you! I want to make this better. Let me, please."

Jim looked up, his eyes glossy. Mary caught sight of her reflection waving in his irises. She was everything that she was now because of him.

"I can give you whatever you need—you just have to say." Mary could feel the complex fibers of Jim slipping through her fingers. "I can be flexible. There are things we can do. We could go speak to someone—get away for a while . . ." There was no chance she would let go of him, even if her efforts left her bruised and bloodied, flat on her face. "Please."

Just as Jim was about to speak, the doorbell rang, followed by a musical pattern of knocks, a car horn, and the unmistakable sound of Gus bellowing from the road.

A look of confusion crossed Jim's face. He balled his fists into his eye sockets, blotting whatever pain was there. Then he hesitated, as if considering whether or not to ignore his oldest friend altogether. But the lights would be visible from the street outside. Gus was persistent, too. Jim went to the window, cracked it open.

"Bloody hell, James old boy, I know the invite said 'smart casual,' but don't you think you might have taken the *casual* part a little far?" Jim was standing in his dressing gown, loosely belted so that the band of his boxers was visible beneath the cord. "We're christening a child, so don't scare little, er . . . what's-his-name already."

The christening.

Mary had forgotten that they had places to be that afternoon. One of Jim's friends had recently had a son. Olly, was it? Or maybe that was the name of his firstborn? She had bought a gift weeks ago—some stuffed rabbit with angel-soft fur, which had gone down well when she had bought it for Moira's baby back in January. That was three months ago. Mary hadn't spoken to Moira since. How had she let them lose touch? She needed her best friend's strength more than ever now.

"Er . . . right, give us ten minutes." Jim slammed the window shut. He turned to Mary, his lips pressed together in a poor attempt at a smile. "Look, can we talk more about this later? I don't think we can get out of the christening now. I don't know what we'd tell Gus."

Mary nodded.

"Yeah, let's get through today first," Jim added, more quietly.

She wasn't sure if he was speaking to her or to himself. Jim turned toward the shower before she could clarify.

If my heart can hold out that long, she thought, as he walked away.

30

2009

An hour and a half's car ride with Gus and his equally exhausting wife, Jillian, gave Mary a brief window to at least attempt to contain her panic. She was packed next to Jim in the back of the car, handbags and christening presents creating a barricade of sorts between them. How had things ended up like this? Awful as it might sound, all she wanted was for him to grovel, to announce that his unexplained absence from work—his lying about it—was the kick he needed to set himself back on the right path, to cut out the drink again and tackle whatever stress had caused this relapse.

But then things had spiraled so quickly, and suddenly it wasn't about the drink at all. Not really. Mary was confronting the reality she thought she would never see again, not after their heart-to-heart during her first trip to London, four years ago. Jim was depressed, wasn't he? There was no way around that now. He had used the drink to numb it, for God knows how long. And then he had cut that out, lasted a while in a state of equilibrium, and then had a relapse. Caused by what? Mary hadn't seen a trigger, not an obvious one at least. But then again, she supposed, if the state of anyone's mental health was as simple as cause and effect, it wouldn't strike the fortunate, the rich, the settled. It wouldn't touch someone like Jim.

All that nonsense about setting her free . . . His love was the expanse on which her life had been built. She couldn't go back to the husk of a woman she was before she met Jim. She couldn't. Mary imagined them arriving home later today and Jim heading straight upstairs to pack his bags. Or hers, as the case may be. It was his flat, after all—she didn't have a stake in it beyond the sentimental. Would she be able to stop him, at the door? She imagined throwing herself at his feet and clinging to his ankles, Jim shaking himself free of her shackling arms . . .

It was enough to make her want to stay out forever, much as she hated events with Jim's stuck-up friends. In any other circumstance she would have paid good money to get out of this day as well. Baby Oscar wouldn't stop crying, probably as a result of the gown they had subjected him to—some cream monstrosity, which was double the length of the poor wee thing. He looked more like a Christmas tree topper than an infant. To make matters worse, the church was freezing and Mary was seated right by the door. At least it gave her a chance to check that Jim wasn't bolting for it. The fact that he was already wavering on the threshold was bad enough.

The reception was held in the village hall, somewhere far enough in the wilds of Cambridgeshire that there was little mobile signal, and certainly not enough for anyone to be checking the football scores. The hall was too large for the number of guests and, as a result, they had clumped in the four corners of the room, an assortment of toddlers and unmanned babies sprawled in the central island between them. Keen to ensure she was giving Jim space, Mary forced herself to socialize by herself. Still, it was an effort not to keep her eyes solely on him.

She loitered at the edge of a conversation led by Jillian, with a few of the other wives. It was every bit as painful as she had anticipated. They all hung out together on weekends—that much was obvious from the shorthand they had developed to mention frenemies from Pilates by initials alone—and Mary tried to laugh along in the appropriate spots. Anything to minimize the risk of looking like a spare part.

Clearly she wasn't doing a good enough job to evade detection.

"We never see much of you, though, do we, Mary?" Jillian smiled, placing one hand on her shoulder to draw her in. "Don't you get bored, just the two of you?"

The women opposite—sprite-sized Bella and her sidekick Maudie, a corporate publicist, if Mary remembered correctly, although she had no clue what that was—both chuckled and Mary could feel her cheeks flushing.

Jillian slid into damage-limitation mode. "I mean I've never known a couple to spend quite so long in the honeymoon phase."

"Ach—you'd think that." Mary looked down at the floor. The irony seared. She prayed it wasn't registering on her face.

"How long's it been again—three years?" Maudie asked. Mary could have sworn she had only met her once, maybe twice, before; and here she was, keeping tabs on the pair of them.

"Coming up four."

"Wow!" Maudie widened her eyes. "That's quite something for James. Do any of you girls remember Evie?"

There was a chorus of ums and ahs, and a general conclusion of no.

"She was James's first serious girlfriend," Maudie continued, directing her explanation to Mary, the one person who had remained tight-lipped. "From university, but it lasted a couple of years after they graduated too. Total sweetheart. They met because they were both medics, so you would think she understood—you know, the lifestyle, yadda yadda . . ."

"So what happened?" Bella asked. Mary was overcome with the urge to punch her. *They wanted different things.* That was what Jim had told her when they covered the subject of exes not long after the two of them met. That had been all Mary needed to know. The past was the past for a reason and there was no point in dredging it up.

"Let's just say James made it pretty impossible for her to stay. 'Moody,' she told me at the time, but between us, ladies," Maudie leaned in, conspiratorial, "she wanted a ring and he made it pretty clear that forever wasn't a concept that he believed in."

"Anyone for a top-up?" Jillian squawked. It was a horrible noise, but anything was an improvement on Maudie's story time and the rush of blood it had sent thundering around Mary's head.

"No, no," Mary replied, setting her glass on a side table. "I've got to nip to the bathroom."

She locked herself in the cubicle and pressed her feet against the door, so no one would know she was hiding out in there. Away from the nauseating cocktail of perfume and judgment, she slammed her fists into her eye sockets. Of all the days for that conversation, did it have to be today? The last thing she needed was a bunch of new information to compute, and from a group of women who had previously treated her with the same grudging acceptance that they applied to the other necessary evils in their life, like their large tax bills or green smoothies.

But had Mary learned anything new? Jim had been *moody*. Well, find her a twentysomething man who wasn't and Mary would be the first to acknowledge the miracle. In the context of the previous day, though, the word seemed so thin, so inadequate, so . . . unfeeling. This wasn't a matter of moods. This was a man questioning whether he wanted to go on anymore—with Mary or without. She had never felt so powerless.

She tried to remember what other personal information Maudie had felt fit to impart. *Jim didn't want to marry Evie.* Well, he had been young. Mary didn't want to tie the knot now, aged thirty-one, when relatives and magazines and adverts wouldn't stop going on about her ticking biological clock, as if a bomb had been lodged in her womb without her knowledge.

But if Jim didn't believe in forever, what did that mean for the words he had uttered to Mary among the maps in Portrush, that he would be there to the ends of the earth, always? She had never questioned him on that before, had never had reason to. Now she found herself wondering whether some promises were too large to honor.

She drew back the lock and washed her hands, trying to avoid her face in the mirror. The sleepless night was written under her eyes and in the tension that was clamped around her neck like a vice.

"There you are." Jim was standing outside the bathroom door, holding two champagne flutes. He extended one to Mary. She didn't have the heart to try to argue him out of his. He looked sheepish, but otherwise a little more like himself than he had that morning. "I thought you might be here."

"Hmm."

"Can we talk? In private?"

Mary felt her stomach drop. He wouldn't be calling it off here and now, would he? The Jim she knew would never do that to her.

He glanced over his shoulder at the leering Stepford Wives, then steered Mary away from the bathroom door, through the entrance hall, and onto a bench in the front garden beyond. When he felt they were sufficiently out of earshot, he continued. "I wanted to say that I'm sorry. For earlier. I shouldn't have landed that on you."

"What do you mean?" The wind had picked up and Mary shivered. Jim shrugged off his jacket and wrapped it around her shoulders. It took her back to their second date in Belfast, walking to the Waterfront Hall. When she thought about the best days of her life, they always—*always*—featured Jim. Where had everything started to unravel? She could feel her eyes beginning to prick with tears.

"I mean that I'm sorry. Recently it feels like I've been stuck in a tunnel and it's like, I don't know . . . it's like the light at the end of it is getting dimmer and dimmer."

Her heart lurched. She couldn't shake the feeling that it should be her keeping the torch burning for Jim.

As if privy to that thought, he added, "I know you want to help me but I have to sort myself out. That was why I was . . . pushing you away, I suppose. I wanted to protect you from this." Jim gestured at his body; the shape Mary had come to know perhaps better than her own. "But this is something I need to fix for myself. If you can give me the time to work some things through, then we'll be fine."

Mary nodded. She so badly wanted to ask how much time—a month, a year? And when the allotted time frame was over, could he guarantee that it wouldn't happen again? No more drunken blackouts, no more unexplained absences.

"I love you, Mary. You're too good for me. I never stop thinking that. But I feel so guilty for bringing you down. I want you to know that I wouldn't blame you, for leaving me. For saying this isn't enough for you. I want to give you that option, now."

What option? The wisdom that Mam had shared before Mary moved in with Jim ricocheted around her head. *When you meet the right person, you need to be with them, no matter what. Through thick and thin. I have no doubt you'll do that for Jim.* There was no world in which Mary could conceive of walking away from the man who had brought her back to life, who every day showed her that she should expect only the very best from it. His behavior yesterday had fallen short of that, yes, but that was one day. One day they could put behind them, forgotten. She would never give up on him.

She turned to face Jim. "I want to be with you. All of you—the good days and the bad days. You will always be enough." Then, after a pause: "We'll be alright, won't we?" Mary wasn't in the mood for declarations of love. All she needed to know was that everything would turn out okay. That Jim believed it would, too.

"Yes," he replied. "We will."

31

2018

"Is this it?" Alice asks.

It is first thing on Monday morning. Here they are, about to embark on a road trip formed from Kit's research on the missing-persons forum and it looks unlikely that his choice of vehicle will get them out of the driveway. The first of the five potential Jim sighting spots is near Manchester. It will be a miracle if they get out of London in this scrap heap. Kit turns the key in the car door, simultaneously placing the other hand flat on the metal and shoving it so that the lock gives way. Secondhand this is not. Third-or fourth-, perhaps. Fifth-, most likely.

"It's had a few owners," Kit offers. "According to Freddie. But I've always admired its spirit."

Alice is not sure what sort of *spirit* a three-door Nissan Micra can have. She watches as Kit pulls a series of crushed cans out from around the pedals. When his hands are full, he shakes them toward Alice. A stream of amber liquid drops out of one that is dangerously close to her foot.

"I should have taken out life insurance," she mutters.

"What's that?"

"Nothing! It's fine."

She folds down the front seat and sifts through a pile of assorted plastic bags that lie behind it. True to his word, Kit has packed not one but five packets of budget spaghetti. The thought that they might be just days—hours even—away from finding Jim fills Alice with such trepidation that pasta is probably all her stomach will be able to hold down anyway.

"I'm looking forward to this," Kit says. When he sits down in the car, the whole carriage drops and there is a worrying rattle from under the hood. "Oh, by the way, I contacted NightLine last night, after we left the station."

"You didn't speak to Mary, did you?" Alice's pulse surges. "I thought we agreed we wouldn't tell her what we were doing."

"Oh no!" Kit flaps his hand at her but manages to clip it on the rearview mirror instead. "Ouch! Yeah, so I spoke to Olive. I had to tell her we wouldn't be at NightLine this week. I mean she wasn't thrilled, but you know how she is."

"What *did* you tell her?"

Alice cannot fathom how Kit, the antithesis of subtlety, will have managed to make their excuses without arousing suspicion. If Mary suspects what they are up to, then God only knows what she will think. Alice would hate to be the one to hurt her—not again. This is Alice's opportunity to make things right for Mary. To get her the answers that she doesn't believe it will be possible to find.

"I said that we were off on a holiday together. Málaga. Fleshed it out a bit by telling her I'd bought some new swimmers too. Olive said she wasn't expecting you again anyway. Apparently you didn't turn up to your sessions last week."

"Shit!"

In her despair, Alice had forgotten that she had made a commitment to NightLine, even if it was conceived as a conduit to Mary and the cryptic calls.

"Don't worry. I told her you had been sick and forgotten to cancel.

Arse-hat!" A van narrowly avoids turning into Kit, who is not very consistent in his use of the indicators. They haven't yet made it out of his road and Alice's heart is already lodged at the base of her throat. "Olive will forgive you. I tried to set her straight that this wasn't a dirty weekend or anything." The urge to face-palm around Kit is often strong, and never more so that now. "So I said, 'But I'm fastidious with my personal hygiene, Olive!' You get it? Hygiene, cleanliness. As in *dirty* wee——"

"Could we do this first bit in silence, please?" Alice interjects. "I'm getting an awful headache."

Kit, miraculously, complies and as they navigate the motorway network that leads to Manchester, Alice lets her mind wander down the roads she herself had blocked off, prior to meeting Mary. In this situation it is hard not to imagine what it would be like to be conducting this search with a different object in mind. Only that wasn't possible for Alice. There was no return address on the birthday card from her dad. Without needing to go to the trouble of spelling it out, he made it quite clear there was to be no further contact.

That was the hardest thing for Alice to wrap her head around. How did someone walk away from their own family? Was there not space in her dad's new life for one more? Four years after leaving, he must still have thought about her, if he had bothered to get in touch. But evidently not enough to offer any continued contribution to Alice's life. When she told her mum what had happened, the ash from her dad's burnt missive dusting her jeans, Mum was catatonic in her own grief, as ever. All Alice's mum could bring herself to say was that it was a "shame."

Well, she could say that again. A *shame* because Alice had lost a fight with two half-siblings she didn't know she had. A *shame* because she would pass through all life's milestones—first jobs and boyfriends, and babies and houses—without her dad at her side. A *shame* because what more is there to be ashamed of than the fact that your own father doesn't want anything else to do with you?

And while that disappointment has never disappeared, it has dulled. That, in turn, allowed Alice the possibility of building a life that doesn't require her dad's role as witness. Does Mary think that Jim sees her, day after day, with her sign? If not physically, then in his mind's eye? She must. These are extreme steps that Kit and Alice are taking, crossing the country on a hope and a hunch of finding a man who has been missing for seven long years. Alice wouldn't be going through with this if it wasn't for the slim chance that their efforts could similarly help Mary step out of the shadows and start living her life on her own terms.

"I'll need you in a minute, Alice."

Kit slams on the brakes to help a minivan off the hard shoulder. Alice's phone flies out of her bag and onto her lap. She wavers over whether or not to check her work emails.

"Alice?"

"Sorry." She slides her phone back into her bag. "Work—you know how it is."

"What happened to you being on annual leave? Leave it!"

Alice ought to be more careful; under no circumstances can Kit find out that she is a journalist. It would give him the wrong idea of why she is here—why they have grown close.

"You don't get endless work emails on your holidays, then?" Alice asks, in a bid to change the subject.

"It's not that sort of job." Before she can ask what exactly it entails, this being the twenty-first century and email being the bane of any office worker's life, Kit does some dramatic peering at the road signs announcing the upcoming junction. "I'll need some directions soon; I think we're near."

"The garage? Already?"

The three-hour drive has gone by in a blink. Kit looks over and nods at the very moment he pulls out of the middle lane, narrowly cutting ahead of a delivery truck. The car lurches to the right. Alice grasps the grab handle.

"Christ, Kit!"

"Just checking you're awake." He grins.

Sighting number one, of five, is located in Levenshulme; Kit's intel from the forums has directed them to an industrial estate off the motorway, where there are few signs of life. Metal pipes spew from a unit next to the parking bay, a single porcelain bathtub sitting out front. There is the sound of drilling and little else. The scene is not inspiring, but then again, Alice supposes, no one smart would try to fall off the face of the earth in an obvious location.

"I take it it's that one?" Kit cocks his thumb toward the garage next door. A sign above reads *Robin's Motors*—or would have done, had the *o's* not been nicked.

According to Kit's dossier, there were six separate posts that listed this as the location for recent sightings of a man matching the image of Jim that Kit uploaded to the forum. Alice tells herself that, confusion aside, it has to mean something. Jim could be inside now. Her palms begin to sweat.

It takes a while to see anyone in the garage. A car is raised on a hoist in the center of the space, its hood wide open and the four doors taken off.

"Can I help you?" A voice emerges from the back. A man, sixty if not more, makes his way slowly toward them, wiping his hands on a rag that dangles from his back pocket. "Tire change, is it?"

"We're actually looking for someone." Hearing Kit's voice in this setting, a heady mixture of testosterone and petrol, Alice is struck by how posh he sounds. It is easy to forget, when you consider his complete lack of polish and pretension. Easier when you have seen the place he calls home. But if Kit is self-conscious of his voice, there is no sign. "His name is James Whitnell."

"Or he might be using a different name," Alice adds.

"Might he now." The man takes a good look at them both. Alice is suddenly very conscious of how they must look: her in a baby-blue cardigan with big pearly buttons, and Kit with his plaid shirt buttoned down far enough to reveal the questionable tattoo of a snake on his right collarbone. "Are we the police then?"

"No!" Kit says. Alice cannot work out how he has managed to make it through his twenty-eight years on this planet without accruing the ability to detect irony. "James is a friend of a friend. We're trying to find him." Kit produces a printout of the photo from Mary's living room.

"Ben?" There is the sound of wheels rolling on concrete, and a low-lying creeper appears from beneath the car. The body on it slowly makes its way to standing. It belongs to a teenager who has yet to grow into his overalls or the facial hair that is making its first uncertain foray across his upper lip. "Get Mike from the storeroom, will you?"

Alice's heart hammers in her chest. She glances at Kit, as if to confirm that her fear is audible. They haven't had the chance to give any thought to what they would do if they found Jim—what they would say. If they were to strike lucky on this first shot, Alice would owe Kit. Big-time.

"What is it, Robin?"

Alice has to withhold the desire to stand on tiptoes and put herself out of the misery of anticipation. On impulse—one she will later deny—she reaches her hand out, nudges Kit's from its pocket.

The figure who emerges is tall. He has dark hair and warm hazel eyes with a scar on the left brow. He suits the overalls. He is handsome enough that Alice reckons he would look good wearing a trash bag.

"These two think they know you." The older man points at the pair of them and leans back on the bench behind him, taking his very own back seat to the action.

"Can't say I know them." There's nothing in Mike's voice to suggest that he isn't Jim, nothing in his face, either. But he looks as surprised as his boss that anyone is looking for him.

"We're looking for this chap," Kit says, reluctantly wiggling his hand free of Alice's and extending the image toward Mike.

"Well, I'm not that *chap*," he replies, in a very good impression of Kit's plummy accent.

"Are you sure? His name is James Whitnell." Kit perseveres regardless.

"I'm perfectly sure, thanks."

"And do you have anything to prove that?" Kit asks. Alice feels herself shrink with embarrassment. Kit looks across at her for encouragement, but there is little she can provide.

"Prove that? Bloody hell—I'll prove it with whatever it takes to get you to go away. A blood sample? A visit from my mum?"

Kit is finally aware that the mood in the garage has turned; he folds the image away and pinches the skin at the back of his neck, appears deeply engaged with the view of his own elbow.

Mike goes to put his hand in his pocket and there is a second when Alice thinks it is going to reemerge as a fist. She takes a small step backward, in the direction of the entrance. There is a rush of relief when Mike pulls out a wallet instead. Kit is wide-eyed as Mike flicks through the card pockets, before sliding one out.

"Right, here we are." He pulls out his driving license and thrusts it so close to Kit's face that there will be no way he can read it from there.

Michael Weston. Born 1983. If Mary is around forty and Jim is a few years older . . . Alice tries to do the mental maths, but only manages to get as far as realizing that Mike is about ten years too young to be Jim. There were six separate posts on the forum linking this location to a man matching Jim's photo—how is it possible for all of them to be this far off?

"Now can I get on with my day?"

"I'm sorry," Alice says, just before Mike reaches the storeroom. She thinks about explaining herself, but realizes there is a strong chance her crusade to exonerate their disruption will land on deaf ears. She is so crushed that it would be a struggle to muster up the energy. Mike doesn't stay to listen, either. Alice turns to Robin, who, at least, seems to have enjoyed the show. "Sorry."

He smiles. "Got a temper on him, has our Mike. He's been with me nearly twenty years now, if you can believe it. He was kicked out of school at sixteen and sent here as a warning to fix himself up. Couldn't get rid of him since. He's a sound kid, really."

"I'm sure. I . . . we didn't mean . . ."

"I know." Robin stands, knits his fingers, and pushes them away to crack the knuckles. "Don't mind him. And good luck finding your man. Looks like you'll need it."

Back in the car, Alice slams the door so hard that the side mirror wobbles.

"Careful, Al, I don't want to have to go back in there and get *Mike* to fix it."

If looks could kill, Kit wouldn't be long for this world.

"At least it's one lead off the list?" he says, quickly moving into full pacifying mode. He extends his hand to her knee and she shifts closer to the window. His hand drops into the dusty leather sack beneath the gearshift. "Allie?"

She refuses to meet Kit's eye. How could she have been so naive as to think that they would succeed with the first sighting? Still, there are few things in life worse than having your hopes raised, then dashed. It dawns on Alice just how dreadful Mary must have felt at the AGM.

"We have four more sightings to go, remember," Kit continues. "Chin up."

32

2010

"I thought we could do the Birling Gap walk," Jim said, steadying himself on the bannister as he pulled on his second trainer. "It's a bit hilly but only three miles. I've packed snacks."

It was March and the last day of a long weekend at Jim's parents' place in Sussex. Mary was sitting on the bottom stair, looking up at Jim. The fresh air had done wonders for him and the sun had given his cheeks, if not a tan, then at least the impression of good health. To think that they were five years in and still Mary felt she could never get enough of the sight of him. For once, it had been her trying to keep the two of them in bed as long as possible that morning, one thigh thrown over his to pin him there. But Jim wanted to get up and out, and Mary knew better than to deny his restless energy.

"Yessir." She gave a mock salute. She grabbed her anorak and tied it round her waist. Jim took her hand. "After you."

It had been a year since his unexplained absence from work and the near end of their relationship that had followed. Mary had said it at the christening: she wanted to be there for both Jim's good days and his bad. The last few had been some of the best. It was moments like this that had sustained her during rough spots over the past few months. She glanced over at Jim, a contented smile playing on his lips, and tried to commit the image to memory.

Because by now Mary knew only too well that it was never going to be a case of fixing Jim, more one of learning how to manage the uncertain fluctuations in that beautiful mess of his mind. What was going on in there, right now? More than anything, she hoped that he felt at peace. She had reconciled herself to the fact that there were things going on in his head that she would never understand, but that didn't mean she stopped craving his confidence or hoping that he would one day fully allow her into it.

After the christening, Mary lost track of the hours she had spent googling "depression" and researching the sort of help she felt Jim needed. There was therapy and medication, and more holistic therapies than she could shake a stick at. Two weeks or so later, with things between them back to normal, she presented Jim with a stapled pile of printouts with the relevant local services highlighted. He hadn't even riffled through them out of politeness. Instead he swept them to the side with the dirty dinner plates and smiled, taking her hand in both of his. *I can sort myself out. It's my job.*

And while he might have the relevant qualifications himself, as far as Mary was aware, Jim had never gone to see another doctor. There had never been a formal diagnosis. She had come to her own conclusions as to what was wrong with Jim—chronic depression—but she was an artist, for goodness' sake, not a medical professional. Still, she knew him well enough to understand why he was so reluctant to seek help. It went beyond his inherent sense of privacy. It was shame. It was stigma. Jim clung to the illusion of his normal, successful life, even when he was teetering on the brink of losing it forever. He hadn't missed a day of work since his stomach-bug lie.

"May I?" They had reached a stile and Jim extended a hand to help her cross, bending at the waist like a caricature courtier.

This was the old Jim. No one else could ever make her choke with laughter in the way he could. Two nights back, he had forgotten about the chicken he put in to roast and returned four hours later to present a blackened carcass. Mary's ribs hurt from the hysterics. They throbbed with wanting that moment never to end.

"With pleasure."

She dropped onto the other side, Jim shortly behind. He planted a kiss on the exposed patch of skin between the top of her sweater and the base of her bun. Her skin tingled.

They slipped back into a comfortable silence. Up ahead, four birds flitted in a huddle. They had black heads and rust-orange chests. Redstarts, Mary wondered? Da would have known—he was a great one for bird-watching. It reminded her that she needed to give Mam a call. Gavin had his first child a few months back and, while that had kept Mam busy, Mary knew that she never stopped fretting over her eldest and her only daughter, on the other side of the Irish Sea.

Of course Mary hadn't breathed a word to Mam about Jim's recent trouble. She couldn't bring herself to share information about his head-space when he was so painfully private about it himself. But it was more than that, too. Mary wanted to believe that she alone would be enough to pull Jim through his depression. All it would take was one wrong comment from Mam and Mary would slip back to thinking that if only she tried harder, Jim would be well. If only she was enough, he never would have felt like this in the first place.

At least, she conceded, there was her work to distract her from the increasing isolation that came from supporting Jim on his terms. In January it would be five years since she started her map business and, while she was no longer growing, turnover was steady year-on-year. By any metric, that was a success, and to have achieved it all from nothing was something to be proud of, however much Mary shied away from self-congratulation.

"Are you hungry?" Jim had spotted a bench on the horizon. It had always been a favorite of theirs, with a prime view of the chalk cliffs. Usually another couple would have beaten them to it, but not today.

"Always."

They nestled side by side and Jim pulled out two apples, a packet of Hobnobs, and a thermos of tea. He hadn't touched anything harder in three months, this time round. When he made a promise, he did everything he could to honor it. The drink was always going to be a struggle, but so long as he kept his word about being there for Mary, to the ends of the earth or Ealing, then she would see him through the rest.

Jim poured her a cup, passed it to her, and then threw his arm around her shoulders. Mary felt herself melding to him, as always. She could lose track of time staring up at his profile, at once refined and playful. She traced her fingers along his collarbones, imagined herself sinking beneath their roof and settling right where she belonged—on top of his heart.

"Nice of your parents to let us have the place," Mary mused.

They should come here more often. When it was just the two of them—work left behind in the smoggy confines of the city—everything seemed so much more manageable, surmountable. Mary was reminded that a love like this didn't come along every day. In fact, for most of the world, it never came along at all. It was luck beyond measure.

"It wasn't like they were using it."

There wasn't hostility in Jim's voice so much as an odd neutrality. Mary knew from the off that he had never been as close to his parents as she was to hers, had suffered from the pressure he had always felt they put upon him. Perhaps because of that, perhaps because of everything else Jim had on his plate, he had never confided in them about how much he struggled, mentally. Mary couldn't imagine what they would say if he did. They were the stiff-upper-lip type. If they weren't, then surely

Richard would have sought help for Juliette, who only ever seemed to have half her head in any given room, the other half with Sam.

"Well, I—for one—am very happy to be here." Mary kissed Jim's cheek. He hadn't packed his razor and the stubble was growing out into a beard.

"Me, too. I was thinking the other day, about us . . ."

Ever since that awful conversation last year, any mention from Jim of their relationship made Mary's pulse race.

"And it struck me just how much I owe you."

She frowned.

"I know things haven't always been easy," Jim continued. "Or that *I* haven't been easy. I know that I shut down about what is going on in my head, because I don't want to upset you or hurt you, or because sometimes there aren't the words for how I feel." Mary squeezed his hand a fraction tighter. "I was in a terrible place last year. Worse than before you came into my life. I don't know what it was, or where it came from, but I was at my lowest. I wanted to run away from my own head—the shit in it."

Mary wondered if it would ever leave Jim, this endless desire to run. He had first mentioned it not long after they had met, when he broached the subject of Sam. The restlessness that was a part of Jim had always worried her. But hadn't they committed to working through their issues, together, right where they were?

"And you stayed by me and you waited for me to get better. I can't thank you enough for not abandoning me."

"You don't need to thank—"

"No," Jim interrupted. "I do. Because you are too good and too patient to understand just what that meant to me. I didn't know until I hit rock bottom that I needed you to be a safe place to come home to."

"I love you."

"I love you too. You'll never know just how much, Mary. But trust me, I'd be a lost man without you."

She suddenly realized that up until now, she had been looking at love the wrong way around. She had approached it from the top and, in doing so, hadn't come close to understanding its entirety. Love wasn't about the moments when you were dancing on the ceiling, it was about picking each other up from the floor.

Before Jim, she had been stagnant, stuck at home and in a job that could never fulfill her. Jim gave her the confidence to fly. He rescued her by showing her that okay wasn't good enough, by removing her from the low of accepting your lot. Now it was up to Mary to continue to do the same for him, albeit in circumstances that were very different, with stakes that were so much higher. Losing Jim was an impossibility—he was everything to her.

When she spoke again, it seemed that her voice was loud enough, firm enough, to carry right down to the sea.

"I will always be your safe place to come home to."

33

2018

Over the past two days Alice and Kit have chased down three of the remaining four sightings, a journey that has seen them zigzagging across the north of England. They have accosted a postal-depot manager in Liverpool and wasted a further half day confirming that Stephen, the chartered accountant running a team of eleven practiced eavesdroppers in York, is categorically not their man.

Yesterday, thanks to Kit's persistence at a retirement home outside Newcastle, they were granted a two-minute audience with Owen, who had spent four decades as the groundskeeper of Tyneside Assisted Living. He could have passed for one of the octogenarians in his employer's care; when he swore blind there was no one matching Jim's picture who had worked at the premises during his tenure, they deferred to his superior wisdom on that.

That leaves one final sighting to check out—a farm near Alnwick in Northumberland. According to the information Kit gleaned from the missing-persons forum, three employees there reported having seen a man matching Jim's photo, six months ago. He was traveling with another guy, older apparently. Although that sounds plausible, Alice is losing hope. This is their last lead. Judging by the precedent set by the previous four failures, it is hard to see how this will be any different.

Kit insists on an overnight stop before the final push. Alice can't well begrudge him, given how good he has been about the chauffeuring. Besides, it is past 10 P.M. by the time they make it to a hostel, and Kit drifts off on the top bunk before Alice has even untied her shoelaces. She feels annoyed, however irrational she knows that to be. Without Kit as a sounding board, she is aware that the chances of her distress dissipating are next to none.

What if this last sighting turns out to be yet another no-hoper? What then? Return home and pretend to Mary that this mad excursion has never taken place? Try to coax her back to the present without the answers that have kept her trapped, statuesque, seven years in the past? No, there will be pigs flying over Heathrow before Alice returns empty-handed to Ealing.

She rolls onto her side, trying to block the sound of Kit's snuffling out of one ear. After so long spent shoulder to shoulder in the car, it feels weird to sleep near, and yet not next to, him. In a bid to extract the image from her mind, Alice reaches for her phone. It's now or never.

For a decade, since finding out that her dad had chosen another family over her own, Alice has avoided the missing-persons forum altogether. She has allowed it to take on the full shape and strength of her nightmares. But if she has truly grieved his loss from her life—then shouldn't she be able to face this last demon? For Mary's sake, if not for her own.

With uncertain fingers, Alice types the web address for the forum into her internet browser. She logs in with the username that might as well be tattooed on the inside of her eyelids: *AliceAlone92*. But this time it is not her father's page that concerns her. She types "James Whitnell" into the search bar and the page loads.

She avoids the outpourings of hope and support, which she trusts Kit to have combed through. Instead she types a brief message pleading for any final leads and clicks Post. Now she knows that she has done everything she possibly can. Before she turns her phone off, Alice tinkers with her settings to ensure that any responses come through to her as a text message.

After a patchy night's sleep, Kit and Alice begin Thursday by speeding up to the farm on the Scottish border, which, according to one of Kit's footnotes, runs a side business in training sheepdogs. In forty minutes they reach the point at which the GPS gives up on any further signs of human habitation, and where, conveniently, Kit believes their last location lies.

"Are we going to make it down here?" The Micra's suspension is shot and, with every bounce on the mud path, Alice feels the morning's cereal relocate itself in a different part of her digestive tract.

"*Absolutamente!*" Kit is busy trying to style the jolts from the road into some sort of dance routine to accompany the chirpy pop song on the radio. The result is more drunken uncle at a wedding than Ibiza tabletop.

In spite of the knot in Alice's bowels, she laughs. They could be the only two people in a twenty-mile radius—the moors rise ahead, not a soul in sight. Two weeks ago, when Alice first met Mary and was then forced to confront the uncertain future of her career in swift succession, she would never have imagined she would end up here. With Kit of all people, too. For the first time it dawns on Alice how lucky she has been with the company.

"That must be it." Kit points at a barn up ahead.

He stops the car and they clamber out. There is barking and Alice feels a pang of angst. Ever since she got floored by an enthusiastic Doberman in the park as a toddler, she has harbored what even she can appreciate is an irrational fear of dogs.

"Picking up or dropping off?" A man in a bright-red cap has

emerged. Behind him, Alice can see three young men in vests mucking out and refilling food bowls.

"Er . . . neither."

After four awkward encounters, she would have thought Kit's opening would be smoothly honed by now. Blame it on the fatigue, but there is a part of Alice that is beginning to see it as endearing.

"We're looking for a missing person," Kit says. "And we received a message saying there had been a sighting of him here, six months ago, with an older man. So maybe they were here to see one of your men about a dog?"

The man's tongue pokes to the edge of his mouth as he struggles to contain a laugh.

"Really now?"

Alice pulls the printed image of Jim out from her bag. It has been handled so many times during the week that his face is crisscrossed with deep, pale wrinkles. "This is the younger man—Jim or James. We have no idea who he could have been traveling with."

"Give me a second." He takes the image and heads to the barn.

Alice looks up at Kit. She wishes that he would wrap one of his gangly arms around her. Dancing may not be their forte, but comfort could well be. Four failed sightings, two hoax calls, and countless dead ends later, Alice feels as if she has vertigo. The stakes are so high that if she falls—if she *fails* Mary—then she doesn't know if she will have it in her to pick up the pieces of herself that are strewn among the rubble of this investigation.

"Yeah, the boys think they saw him. But you were right, they think it was a long time back. If you want, I can take a look at our records."

Alice is too gobsmacked to say a word. Did she hear him correctly?

"Please. Thank you. Both. Thank you." Kit looks as if he might be about to bow, and she jabs an elbow into his side. They cannot lose this glimmer of good news due to a fit of his gibberish.

The man leads Alice and Kit into a trailer at the back of the farmhouse. It is as hot as a furnace. "My office," he says by way of explanation. And Alice thought the *Bugle* was shambolic. There are empty cages stacked against all the walls, kibble ground into the carpet. Even the human visitors have left litter overflowing the bin. Wagon Wheels fans, by the look of things.

Kit offers her the chair and stands behind it, with his hands resting on its threadbare back.

"Alan, by the way. Owner of the mad doghouse."

"Alice." She cocks her thumb behind her. "And Kit."

"So this James is a friend of yours?" Alan is sorting through a pile of exercise books on his desk, discarding the majority on the floor behind him.

"Friend of a friend." Alice smiles. "It's a long story, but he disappeared and she . . . never got over it. And there's been a bit of interest in the case recently, so we thought we'd try and help find him. Bring her some closure."

Alan sighs. "Our Nick was the one who wrote to you, by the way." He tips his head toward where the men are wrangling leashes onto dogs. "My middle son. His best friend went missing after a night out in Sunderland. Nick was the designated driver and he left when Joe didn't turn up for the lift. Thought he had picked up a girl. No one's heard from him since. Police reckon Joe's dead. River fall, maybe. Nick's never forgiven himself."

"That's awful," Alice replies.

"You're telling me. Nick's a good bloke. But he feels like he let his mate Joe down. Won't forgive himself, no matter what we say. He tells me that's why he tries to help out on those missing-persons pages."

"We are very grateful." The tips of Kit's fingers brush the back of Alice's T-shirt.

"Now I might not have anything. Six months would take us back to

February and we don't trade much then. . . . Nick seems to think it was a sale. Right, I've got five that month." He turns the exercise book around to face Kit and Alice. *Peter Merton, Paul Purdy, Grant McInerny, Anthony Sifford, Scott McNaughton.* There is not a James or a Jim among them.

"Can I?" Kit points at his own phone. Alice is surprised to see that there is almost a full signal here.

"Be my guest. Just don't say where you got the names from."

"Course," Kit replies. "Burn after using—isn't that what they say?"

Reading, Alice thinks, it's *burn after reading,* but what use is that going to be, when she has spent a fortnight looking for one man and now there are another five to trace, with only three full days left on the clock before her article is due to Jack? She cannot tell whether it is the urge to cry or the urge to scream that is rising in her chest like the full crest of a wave. Probably both.

"Sorry that this isn't what you wanted to see." Alan directs his apology at Alice.

"Not at all," Kit says. "We'll get out from under your feet."

In the car Alice slumps forward, her head brushing against the glove compartment. Yet another time-waster. This is it—there's no way they can check out five new leads, when Kit needs to get the car back by Sunday night. Even if it was possible, what's the point? They are, literally and metaphorically, at the end of the road.

Alice feels the subtle pressure of Kit's palm between her shoulder blades. "Hey. We tried."

"It's not enough," she mumbles. She won't say this means that she has lost the one story big enough to save her job. The only reason it matters slips out instead. "Mary."

"What she doesn't know won't hurt her. In this case, at least. She doesn't know we're here."

Alice glances up. Kit is leaning over, close enough that she can see the exact point where his long, giraffe-like eyelashes cross. Her lips tremble. Her heart thunders.

And then her phone buzzes. A text message. Number unknown.

Alice clicks on it and realizes it is a new notification, sent directly from the missing-persons forum, as per her change in settings last night. All the text can show is the first line: James Whitnell: Location.

She clicks the embedded link to the forum, praying there will be enough signal for the web page to load.

"*Que pasa?*"

Alice finds the top post. There is nothing but two words and a number with a dialing code that she can't for the life of her place: Call me.

34

2018

The only thing convincing Alice that there is anyone on the other end of the line is the occasional low grunt of a labored exhale.

"Hello? It's Alice Keaton. I posted on the missing-persons forum about James Whitnell? We're looking for him right now. Not much luck . . ."

"I'd guess that's because you're looking in the wrong place." When it finally emerges, the voice is gravelly, the dusky baritone of a man who sounds exhausted by his lot in life.

"Are you Jim?"

There is a snort that could be a laugh or could be sheer irritation.

"I mean, I have to ask." Alice looks over at Kit, who is making a series of weird hand gestures and mouthing the word *speaker* so unsuccessfully that she has to cover the microphone with one hand to ensure the caller can't hear it too. She shakes her head. There is no chance she can risk losing this.

"No. Glad of it too, given the mess he's gone and caused."

"So, you know him?" Alice's next question holds everything in its balance. She takes a deep breath. "Is he alive?"

The man coughs, an awful bark so loud that it could have contained the sound of a cracking rib.

"Aye," he says, eventually.

Alice's head drops back in relief. "Thank God, so—"

"I can't talk much now. You'll have to come up here."

"Oh, okay, well, if you could give us the address . . ."

She scrambles on the dashboard for a piece of paper and makes a frantic scribbling gesture at Kit. He produces his mangled pen from his back pocket.

"You're not giving up on this, are you?" the man asks.

Alice toys with admitting they were just about to turn back and concede defeat. Strictly speaking, she and Kit had yet to discuss that, but they both knew where the conversation was heading.

"No," she replies. "I can't stop, I'm afraid, until I find Jim." Alice has no idea where she has uncovered these new reserves of energy. "For Mary's sake, for her peace of mind."

"I thought Mary would give up," he says. "It's not right, whatever he might say."

"We need answers." It comes out far more forthright than Alice had hoped, like an indignant child. She wishes she could draw the words back in, but it's too late. "I mean, Mary does. We're her friends."

"I gathered as much. Look, there's one thing I have to mention." There is a banging on the other end of the line. Alice can hear footsteps, another male voice. She is terrified the call will drop out and their one chance of finding Jim will be shot. "Got to go now. I'll write you."

"Wait, hold up—the address?"

He hangs up before she has the chance to finish her question.

"What is it? Who was it?" Kit's enthusiasm only makes Alice feel her failure more keenly. She throws the pen away. There is a stinging sound as the nib catches on the windscreen.

"I didn't get the address."

"But he seemed legitimate? Like he knew Jim?"

"I don't know." She catches a glimpse of herself in the rearview mirror. Her cheekbones are more pronounced than they've ever been—she's lost weight since knowing Mary, hours of sleep too. She doesn't know which way is up anymore; between the hoaxes and the dead ends and the letdowns, there are few certainties left in Alice's life. But she meant what she said on the phone: she will not rest until she gets Mary the answers she deserves.

Just as Kit is trying to work out what to say for the best, Alice's phone buzzes. He undoes his seat belt with such force that the strap whips up and catches his chin. He is still holding the throbbing patch of skin when she opens the message.

There is no acknowledgment of the call, only an address. Kit types it into the map app and the screen zooms out of their current location, before whizzing to the northernmost tip of Scotland and narrowing in on the coast.

Alice groans. They have three days left; two if you count the fact that they need one for the drive home, so that they can give Kit's friend his car back in time. She was hoping this would be closer to Ealing so that, if the worst comes to the worst and it didn't go anywhere . . .

"*Arriba!*" Kit jabs his finger at Alice's phone.

"Eureka, eureka, eureka," she mutters. Archimedes wasn't even Spanish.

"Whatever, Allie, you won't believe this." Kit zooms in, so that the forum username has been blown up to the maximum font size that will fit on the screen: tonysiff307@hotmail.com.

"A Hotmail account—groundbreaking."

One of Alan's four-legged charges is standing on his hind legs, looking at Alice through the passenger window. She shifts away from the door.

"Uh-uh. Tony Siff? *Anthony Sifford,* Al." Kit has brought up a photograph on his own phone. "Off Alan the sheepdog trainer's list?" He wriggles it under her nose. "And he bought one of your furry friends here back in February."

"Oh my Lord." Alice cannot believe it. God bless the internet and dogs and Kit—three things she never would have put forward for divine ordination before this very moment.

"Floor it!"

Maybe it's the winding Scottish roads or maybe it's the anticipation of what they might be about to discover, but Alice is feeling nauseous. She's not a good traveler, never has been. As a child, it was only ever lying with her head in her dad's lap that stopped her vomiting out the window at 70 miles per hour. Alice wonders what his life must look like now. Will he do the same for her half-siblings? She tries to imagine her dad stroking the baby hairs away from their clammy foreheads, in a bid to settle their sickness. But her mind comes up blank.

Strange, that. Since the day he disappeared, Alice has had no difficulty envisaging her dad's new life. Before she discovered where he had gone, she couldn't shake the encroaching images of him sleeping rough on the streets or under an archway. After she was forced to confront the truth, her imaginings were just as nightmarish, albeit in a very different way; she started to see him clapping for another child on the school stage, pulling his special faces to a crowd of smaller, cuter kids.

And now, nothing. How is that possible? Alice squeezes her eyes shut that little bit tighter and tries to hook onto a detail—the patch of eczema on the inside of her dad's wrists, the crook in his jaw where it had been set wonky, back in his twenties. No. Nothing. Does this mean that she has forgotten him, the way he has forgotten her? It has been long enough. Or maybe this is the first sign that her own issues have been eclipsed. Displaced, perhaps. Alice may have something to thank Mary for.

"Hey, Allie." Kit places a hand on her shoulder, gently, as if to check how much pressure he is allowed.

"Where are we?" It takes a while for Alice to rouse herself. When she does, she is faced with a concrete wall and, on it, a string of expletives spray-painted in a mix of sizes and styles. The word *knob* dominates.

"We'll have to stop for the night. The traffic was awful, trying to get into Inverness."

"Oh." Alice must have slept most of the afternoon and the best part of the evening too. She shivers. Where did the summer climate go? "I'm sorry you've had to do all the hard work."

Kit gets out and presses his hands against the roof to stretch his calves. His top rides up, exposing a fine snail trail of golden hair running between his navel and his boxers. Alice drops her gaze.

"I think this is going to be our best bet. There's a B and B over there," he says, pointing at a building on the other side of the car park. The lights flicker in the manner of a budget Christmas tree, less time on than off. Through the gray net curtains it's hard to tell what's inside.

The front door is open, despite the sign saying they will need to buzz after 10 P.M. There is a ripping sound, like tape being torn from a wall, as the receptionist, a woman in her midtwenties with her hair in a topknot, smacks her gum, and then tucks it behind her back teeth.

"Do you have anything for tonight?" Alice asks. She has waited for what she feels is a decorous amount of time for Kelly (according to the name badge) to set about greeting them. Kelly has many interesting texts to attend to, it would seem. She manages to tear her eyes away to examine the computer screen.

"We've got a double. No en suite, but the bathroom is only shared between two ro—"

"No," Kit and Alice both say at once.

"We'll need twin beds," Kit says. "We're, er . . ."

"Not together—like that," Alice adds.

The girl clicks the screen a few times. "I'm afraid we've only got that room."

"Really?" Alice is too tired to mask her skepticism in any convincing way.

"We're popular," she replies, shuffling an A4 sheet in a cheap wooden photo frame toward Alice: *South Inverness Best Stays, 2006.* It's typed in one of those handwriting fonts that does everything other than convince the reader of its authenticity.

"I can appreciate that," Kit swoops in, running one hand through his hair. He blinks and opens his eyes a little wider for his audience. They twinkle. Alice can see the receptionist's froideur melting; it feels like Alice has taken a sharp kick to her groin. When Kelly turns her body at just the right angle to block Alice from the conversation, it is all Alice can do not to scream. "And there's absolutely nothing else?"

"Sorry," she says, all sweetness and light. She squashes her lips together, slips the bottom one to the side, as if to say it is all out of her hands, instead of under the exact control of her mouse.

"We'll take it," Kit says. "Thanks for your help." He slides his card across the desk. Alice can't tell what she finds more shocking—the previously latent charm that is apparent in the wink she catches Kit giving Kelly, or the fact it's a gold Amex credit card that he's passing over.

He taps in his code and then Kelly hands over the key, a chipped wooden block hanging off it.

"Have a nice stay, sir."

Alice keeps the smile pasted to her face, and it is up to Kit to tug at the sleeve of her coat to get her moving. He drags her to the edge of the lounge, where there is a lift and, to the side, a set of stairs that look considerably safer.

"I'm happy to sleep in the car," Kit says, passing over the key. Part of Alice wants, churlishly, to let him. Maybe Kelly would want to join him. She swallows down her pride; a larger part knows she'll regret it.

"You don't need to do that." She takes her frustration out on the lift button instead. She presses the Up arrow so hard that the tip of her index finger begins to throb. "Honestly."

"I'll take the floor," Kit says, by way of compromise. In the low lighting of the lobby, his features seem to have taken on a new refinement. Alice tells herself that the tiredness is playing tricks with her eyes.

To Kit's credit, he doesn't immediately start to retract the offer when Alice gets the door to their room open. The carpet is green, but not of a dark enough variety to hide a cluster of blotches spreading like—and possibly as—a fungus from the skirting boards inward.

"Don't sleep on the floor," Alice says as they study the stain, side by side. "We'll manage."

She uses the bathroom first and by the time Kit emerges from his turn in there, she has taken the spare pillows from the cupboard and has lined them up on their sides down the center of the mattress, creating a wall of sorts.

"Nice work," Kit says.

She turns around and catches sight of the tip of Kit's tongue nipped between his teeth. Her eyes drift south. Kit is topless. He has one arm pressed against the doorframe, the other pulling the elastic of his boxer shorts a little higher, so that it now covers his hip bones. Alice has never seen such muscle tone in the real world. Aren't abs like that the result of a good airbrush? *Get it together, Keaton, save some face.*

"Ha—thanks," she mumbles, starting to regret her feat of engineering.

"Night, Alice." Kit slips onto his side of the barrier. He turns the light off and the mattress is soft enough for Alice to feel every movement of his body as he lies down, his back to her.

She hasn't closed the curtains very diligently and the floodlights from a fast-food shop across the car park creep into the room. He has a nice back, she'll give him that. She can see a cluster of freckles along the top of his shoulder blades, the subtle indent of his spine, the flat of his back, perfectly sized for a hand to guide, to steer. *Her hand?* It would be okay, wouldn't it, as a one-off, if she didn't get attached.

"You're watching me sleep, aren't you?" Kit says.

In Alice's shock, her knee jerks out and the pillows fall, wall destroyed. Kit goes to remove the one nearest his head. His hand brushes against Alice's and, on instinct, she takes hold.

Before she can think better of it, she loosens her grip and instead runs her fingers down his chest, hovering a centimeter above the elastic of his boxers. She nudges closer, her thighs pressed against the back of his legs.

She rolls Kit over. "Is this okay?"

Alice cannot, for the life of her, work out how it took so long to figure out that he is completely, absolutely, gobsmackingly gorgeous. The silence must have helped. Oh hell, why is he *still* silent—has she overstepped the mark?

"Very," Kit replies.

Then his mouth is on hers and it is as if every nerve ending is singed, aflame and alive. He tugs Alice's shirt over her head and begins to work his lips down her neck, her chest, her stomach, to the top of her thigh.

"Very, *very* okay," he breathes.

35

2018

When Mary arrives at NightLine, Ted is surrounded by paper, tiny rectangles of laminated cardstock scattered around his feet. A tattered box overflowing with the surplus lies to his right.

"What's all this about?" She bends and picks one up.

"Business cards," Ted replies. "Bit of a spillage. They are for NightLine, though, so not strictly 'business.' I thought it might be good to get the word out about us a bit more. My idea was that we would all take some and put them up at work, and ask the shops to display them. Maybe slip some through local letter boxes too. . . . You never do know who is having a rough time of it."

Mary watches his Adam's apple bob with an uncertain swallow. "How are you getting on?"

It has been four days since their chat in the park and, since then, Mary has reached her final resting place of understanding. Ted plastered such a convincing mask on his loneliness that it was little wonder she was so surprised by Alice's revelations at the AGM. And while Ted's decision to call her was misguided, it was never intended to be cruel. Mary knows how an excess of feeling, with no other outlet, can be channeled into unusual forms. She is no stranger to going to lengths that may seem odd to outsiders.

"Oh, you know—work has picked up again. A few big projects, which is good. Tim will be back this weekend, a new girl in tow . . ."

"I meant, how are you *really*?"

Ted pauses. Mary wonders when was the last time he was asked that question by someone who wanted the actual answer, not just a quick muttering of "fine" as an end to the necessary pleasantries.

"I made a call, you know," Ted says. "Not that sort, you'll be pleased to hear. But to, er . . . one of those professionals. Shan't call her a therapist because, well, I'm not American, but I'm sure you get my gist."

"That's great, Ted." Mary smiles.

Let that be the end of it, for now. When it comes to talking about feelings, troubles—whatever other euphemism there is for mental health—Mary has found that it is easiest to approach slowly. *With the softest tread.* Her eyes flutter shut, trying to blink away the memory. Why must the world make men so . . . guarded? It is to their detriment.

Although Mary knows that she herself is hardly one to talk, she wishes that she could crack the pressure in Ted's head enough to let him know that he didn't need to shoulder his problems alone. He is getting help now, though, which is more than Mary has ever sought for herself. If only he knew it isn't weakness in her eyes, this seeking of support; rather, it is something she cannot help but admire. She wishes she could find the same courage.

She grinds the toe of her court shoe into the carpet. "Let's get this lot back in the box, shall we?"

For the next minute or so Ted and Mary gather up the fallen business cards and slot them away. When Ted has aligned the last stack, he squeezes them into the spot that Mary has cleared and is holding open for him. Their hands touch. Mary feels as if she has been electrocuted—if that could be a pleasant experience, and one tinged with only the slightest pain.

A few days ago, when Ted first told her that he had romantic feelings for her, she was too surprised to consider, seriously, how she felt in return. She has never looked at him in that way. In truth, she has not looked at anyone that way since Jim. But during the nights that followed, she has started to allow herself to wonder, for once, what would happen if she wasn't so blinkered? If she could see beyond the disappointments of the past?

She doesn't move her hands, instead shifting her weight so that she is leaning in, just an inch or so further toward Ted. It feels, if not yet natural, then good. She looks up, meets his gaze.

"Am I interrupting something?" Olive shouts from the doorway. She has never had an indoor voice. "I would say I'd come back, but we're short on volunteers, as it is."

Ted jumps to his feet and Mary feels a ripple of disappointment.

"I've been quite enjoying being back on the phones this week," he says.

Tuesday was the first that Mary heard of Alice and Kit's curious holiday together. It got to 10:55 P.M. and there was just herself, Olive, and Ted at St. Katherine's. When Mary asked where they both were, she was met with a stony expression from Olive. "Málaga," she replied, by way of explanation, with her mouth so tight that Mary wondered if she might be doing some irreversible damage to the tendons in her jaw.

Ted explained how he had been roped in to cover for them both, then tried to lighten the mood with some joke about young love. But Mary was too panicked to listen to anything more. She knew an excuse when she heard one. She couldn't shake the feeling in her gut that their excursion had something to do with Jim. And her gut has never been wrong.

Part of her was furious; she had told Alice in no uncertain terms to give up on her fixation with finding Jim. Such arrogance, too! What made Alice think she would have more luck in locating Jim than her, the woman who has been waiting for him alone outside Ealing Broadway station for nearly seven years now? Mary had let Alice into her confidence and this was how she repaid her—first with an embarrassment at the AGM, and now a flagrant flouting of her wishes.

But another part of Mary admires Alice's obstinacy. And she is a busy young woman, what with her digital-whatsit job—she wouldn't be going to all this trouble unless she truly cared about Mary. And isn't the most likely outcome that Alice and Kit won't find Jim at all? He might be moving around or abroad or . . . *No,* Mary won't think like that. She would know if he was dead, in her heart, if not from Richard and Juliette.

But on the off chance that they do find Jim, what then? Mary tries to imagine what he would say to Kit and Alice, the sort of picture he might paint of her and of their relationship. Would he catch its beauty, the way it changed them both for the better? Or would he focus on its horrible, messy ellipsis of an ending? Mary prays that it won't be the latter. She has never stopped thinking about their last moments together, and how they reflected nothing of the precious, imperfectly perfect life they shared. If only Jim could remember that, then surely he would come home. That is what matters most to Mary—that he returns because he *wants* to.

"Well, shall we?" Olive is already at her desk, shoes off.

Ted looks over at Mary, a little shy. He seals the refilled box of business cards with a scrap of dangling duct tape. "Perhaps we could talk about how best to hand these out, after the shift finishes?"

"I'd like that," Mary replies, as she takes her seat and unwraps the Twix that Ted has left on her desk.

She begins to chew but the caramel refuses to go down. Mary imagines Alice on a beach, on the hard shoulder of an indistinct motorway, up a mountain bellowing at Kit to check out this location or that. She has Alice's number; she could drop her a text . . .

Just as Mary is about to reach for her mobile in the front pocket of her rucksack, her desk phone begins to burble.

"This is your first call of the night," Olive hollers from the far side of Ted's broad shoulders. "You ready?"

"Sure," Mary lies. She picks up the receiver. "Hello, good evening, it's NightLine. There're a few questions that I have to ask before we begin."

As the woman on the other end of the line sobs through her answers, Mary decides that there is no point contacting Alice. Not right now. She will wait for her return and, in the meantime, there is plenty to attend to here in Ealing. She keeps her attention focused on the caller. Every time she is on the phone, Mary never forgets that it is her duty to get the right words out. Words to comfort, words to help.

Because she failed Jim, and she cannot afford to fail anyone else.

36

2011

"What do you mean, *can't?*" There was a silence, then Mary added, "It's my mam's sixtieth." As if that would change anything.

"I'm sorry. I'm no company for it. You'll have a better time without me."

Mary had chosen Jim's starter, main, and dessert weeks ago. There was a seating plan. Now she'd be sitting with an empty chair to her right and a flurry of excuses to make to the twenty-three other guests. How could she tell them what had really happened? She could barely get the words out in a decent order in her own head. *James is too depressed to be here.* God only knows what they would make of that.

Another rap on the door, another call from the cab company lighting up on Mary's phone.

Neither moved. A swirl of dust, languid in the thick August air, swirled between them.

"You ought to go." Jim nodded toward the door. She heard the whisper of his socks on the floorboards as he shuffled nearer. He had taken his shoes off already.

"I beg your pardon?"

"I said that I'm sorry."

"It's not good enough, though, is it?" Mary could feel her volume spiraling out of control. She had lost all sense of sensitivity toward the person standing in front of her, the only man she had ever loved—let alone toward the neighbors. "None of this is good enough. What do you think you're doing, canceling on me at the last fecking minute, so that I have to lie to my own mam's face? How can you be so selfish?"

"Don't lie to her. Say I'm sick. She'll underst—"

But Mary did not want to hear it. For the first time, perhaps ever, her characteristic self-control had been perforated. She had no idea what would come out of her mouth next.

"Do you think this is what I want, huh? I'd be better off without all this . . . bullshit. Don't you think I deserve something a bit better from you?"

There was a silence, broken seconds later by Jim's voice, thin as a husk. "You do. I've always said that you do."

"Is that all you have to say for yourself? Is it? It's not enough! It's just not enough."

And with that, the fire in Mary's voice was extinguished. She leaned one hand against the wall to steady herself, the other clutching her carry-on bag. It had been—what, three months of bad days? It was all those long, dark days of struggle that had provided the kindling; the finality of his abandoned shoes that had ignited it; and now she was standing in the embers of her rage, already regretting her outburst.

Mary hated herself. She was patient, she was loving, she was kind. The frustration was a break from who she truly was. It was only a blip. Everyone suffered those.

She glanced at the window, where their best photos were lined up along the sill. In the center, one of the two of them at Birling Gap last spring, squashed on the bench overlooking the sea. It was taken just over a year ago. It had been the most perfect weekend. The bliss had extended through Christmas, through New Year's until Easter, when the depression had reared its head again, seemingly from nowhere.

For as many weeks as Mary could remember, there had been no space for her emotions in the quagmire of Jim's. But now she had voiced them, that would be an end to it. What is love if not patient? If not kind? There was no chance she would give up on him. The onus was on her to be more supportive. She would be the partner he needed.

Before she could apologize, Mary felt Jim's lips press against her forehead. In that instant she was back at the hotel on their first night together; at the pub in Portrush when she agreed to move to Ealing. She tried to remember every other time he had kissed her like that, but it was a blur. A messy, happy blur.

If nothing else, it reminded Mary that there would always be enough between them that was worth fighting for. They could always figure out the rough road to happiness again, together. Once she was back from Belfast, it would be the first thing she worked on.

"I'm so sorry," Jim murmured into her scalp. He opened the door and placed the flat of his hand on Mary's back, to steer her out. "I'm so, so sorry."

She chased down the taxi before she had the chance to apologize herself.

37

2018

"*Buenos días,*" Kit says. He is standing at the foot of the bed in just a pair of boxers, trying to tear open one of the teabag sachets. The minikettle next to him starts to shake as it comes to the boil.

Alice, who rarely pulls off nonchalance and has never been known to before midday, manages a small smile. For a moment she considers sneaking into the bathroom to sort herself out. But her makeup bag is buried at the bottom of her rucksack and she doesn't want Kit to think she is high-maintenance.

Instead she tries to distract herself from worrying about the state of her face by watching as he pours the water into the cups with their impossibly small handles. He is holding the kettle at hip height. An image of the night before—her thighs astride his, her nails raking down his chest—comes unbidden into her mind. *It was a one-off, Keaton,* she reminds herself. *That means one time only.* She averts her eyes to the relatively safe haven of the TV, which is balanced on top of the wardrobe, behind his head.

"What is it?"

"Nothing," Alice answers, rather too quickly.

"What are you looking at?"

"Oh, just the telly."

Kit looks up, confirms it is still off. "Okay." He has the tact not to make matters worse. Perhaps he is learning.

He climbs back into bed with the teacups, making slow, exaggerated movements to avoid slopping the liquid on the sheets. When he passes her saucer, she notices that he has taken two shortbread rounds out of their wrapping and left them on the side. Kit has given himself the digestives, which look hard enough to file teeth with. Unfathomable chivalry.

Alice deposits the tea on the small shelf to her left and begins to nibble the border of the biscuit. She can't bring herself to look at Kit straight on but, out of her peripheral vision, she is able to take stock of everything she glimpsed in the half light of the night before. He must have women falling at his feet back in London. By which Alice means ones who haven't yet been subjected to quite so much of his chat.

Kit moves a little closer and the mattress sags. He turns to kiss her, and Alice can feel her whole body jump to attention.

"So . . . ," he begins. His breath is a little milky. "Last night was fun."

Alice should have known this would happen. Kit is an idealist, through and through. If she'd had any sense, she would have laid out the ground rules, verbally, from the start: no affection, no attachment, no repeat performances. But then she was so caught up in the moment, and his mouth was on hers and it felt so *good* . . .

That doesn't matter now. What matters is making it clear that whatever they started last night ends right now. Alice isn't going to wait around on tenterhooks for his inevitable exit from her life two or three months down the line.

"Yeah. But I think that is all it was." Alice shuffles backward, so there is enough space to turn and face Kit. She never should have gone there, with him, because as much as she hates to admit it, she now knows that the thread of potential between them has the makings of something so much bigger.

Kit cocks his head. Alice realizes she won't get off that easily.

"What do you mean?" he asks.

"I can't do anything serious. Not right now."

"*Right now* as in right now in this B and B?" Kit glances up at the clock above the door, as if to assess how much they could fit in before checkout.

"*Right now* meaning generally. I'm not in the market for anything serious."

"You're taken?"

"Is it that hard to believe?"

"No." Kit puts his hands up in defense. "But you never mentioned anyone. It would have been courteous of you to say." With his ruffled hair, he looks more bohemian than ever. Alice hates it that part of her is tempted to reach out and smooth a capricious patch above his left ear. "Before." His voice is oddly neutral. It unsettles her. She would much prefer angry, then she might know where she stands.

"Well, there isn't. Things are complicated enough already; I don't think we should make it worse with this."

"Whatever you want."

"Sorry," Alice says.

She really is, but she doesn't trust herself to try and articulate the exact reasons for her contrition at 8:42 in the morning. It is a long story—the same narrative of abandonment and trust issues that have her out on this road trip in the first place. If she couldn't find the words to explain her personal circumstances to Mary in her flat, then what hope for Kit in a sketchy cheap hotel, when they have other urgent priorities? In just a few hours' time they could well have found Jim.

She doesn't have the chance to say anything more; Kit grabs a towel from the cupboard and heads for the shower before the apology has so much as left her mouth.

—

When Alice gets out of the bathroom, Kit is nowhere to be seen. There is a note balanced between her handbag and her rucksack, which demonstrates a particularly crisp use of the period: *Waiting in the car. Drop the key at reception, please.*

Key deposited and with the bill already settled, Alice makes her way to the car. Kit is sitting in the driver's seat, tapping his fingers against the steering wheel. Turns out she isn't the only one buzzing with anxiety.

"This could be it," he says, once she has thrown her bag in the back and shut the passenger door.

Whatever passive aggression Alice read into his note is nowhere to be seen. She quashes the thread of irrational disappointment that nips at the back of her mind, the one that says: *Well, he got over me quickly.* She should see his resilience as a laudable quality; without it, they wouldn't have made it this far in the search for Jim. But still . . . was she a bit hasty with her rejection this morning?

"Can you imagine if we found Jim today? That would be mega."

Is that prospect really *mega*? In some respects—yes. But to Alice it is also deeply, utterly, undeniably terrifying. It was hard enough to finish one of those shortbread rounds, because her stomach was churning with the prospect of what the day might hold. They now know that Jim is alive. Or at least they think they do, if this guy Tony (from the forum) is to be trusted. But they do not know anything else. How will Jim react to their arrival? And what on earth will he have to say for himself?

This is Alice's chance to unravel the mystery of Jim's disappearance once and for all, bring Mary closure, and perhaps salvage her job in the process, too. It should feel good, in the same way that productivity always does to Alice. But all she feels is dizzy with the tension and the pressure. To get here, she has compromised herself on so many levels: professionally, her neck is on the line; morally, she has lied to Kit about her real occupation, and to Mary about stopping her investigation; and emotionally, she has invested everything. If this doesn't work out, then Alice does not know how she will move forward.

"Exciting stuff!" Well, at least Kit is as hyped as ever. "It'll take about four hours to get there. Five, if there's traffic. I can't believe we're nearly there. That's teamwork for you."

As they navigate their way out of the city, Alice reflects on how much she owes Kit. He has thrown himself into this mission with his characteristic chutzpah. But more than that, he has been of *real* use too. It was Kit who found Gus and helped Alice build up a picture of Jim's life that was more complex and troubled than the image presented through the lens of Mary's adoration. It was Kit who suggested this change of tack too—from *why* to *where*. If they find out where Jim is today, Alice hopes that the answer to the question of why he disappeared won't be far behind, either.

And there is no denying that Kit is a good guy. As they speed up through the Highlands, the landscape wild and indeterminate, Alice finds herself wishing that she had spent less time focusing on Kit's foibles and more on admiring the rough fabric of patience, kindness, and loyalty from which he is stitched. She wishes she had it in her to give him a chance. To trust.

But this is categorically *not* the time to catch feelings. If anything, this journey has shown Alice that if there is one certainty in love, it is its very uncertainty. The odds would always be stacked against them.

"What was the name of the place, again?" Kit's voice cuts through Alice's slipstream of thoughts.

"Seacrest Cottage."

"Hmm . . ." Kit has moved the car into first gear, the engine close to stalling on the empty one-lane road. His brow furrows as he taps at his phone screen. "No signal—joy."

"This is it?" Alice checks her watch; they have now spent four hours on the road and Kit's GPS looks to have no further route suggestions.

Outside there are no road signs, no signs of life. A handful of white cottages pepper the landscape, but none are grouped together. It is quite literally the middle of nowhere. Alice cranes her neck out of Kit's window too. "What about that?"

"What about what?"

"That lake that's connected to the ocean."

Kit peers in the direction of Alice's extended index finger. "A sea loch, you mean."

"Sorry, I didn't realize that I was with the local expert."

Kit chooses to ignore that. "And you think Jim has morphed into a creature from the deep?"

"No, but he might be nursing one in the pub on the shore." Alice taps her finger a little to the right of a mucky splotch on the glass. A small building, almost camouflaged by its corrugated green cladding, is just visible, thanks in part to a sign swinging in the breeze above it. The name is too small to read, even with Alice's twenty-twenty vision.

"Fine," Kit concedes, making a three-point turn. "But you're buying."

Alice's vindication is short-lived. It is anyone's guess how they will be received. They reach the inn, park, and walk up to the entrance, weaving between picnic benches that boast a front-row view of the loch. In comparison to the rest of the week's heat, it is freezing up here. Alice wonders if the northernmost Highlands operate their own microclimate. Either way, no one is hardy or unhinged enough to brave outdoor seating in gale-force winds.

Inside it isn't much busier; a man in a raincoat is scrutinizing a paper at the bar, his back to the door, while two men at a side table—not obviously together but not obviously apart, either—seem to be searching for something at the bottom of their malt glasses. The bartender, a short, bald man wearing a heavy navy knit, looks surprised when the door creaks to announce Alice's entry.

"Afternoon," he says. The two men at the table look over. "Make yourself at home."

Kit, who has been keeping a good six feet behind Alice at all times, like a security guard, has now appeared at her side. Seemingly unaware of the cold, he is wearing a red T-shirt with a banana in peeling yellow paint on its front, the thread from the hem of both sleeves unraveling. Alice can see the bartender looking him up and down with palpable amusement.

"I was wondering if you could help us?" She tries to quash her fear and rustle up her last reserves of charm. They seem to be buried particularly deep today.

"Aye."

"We're looking for Seacrest Cottage. Are we near?"

The bartender raises his eyebrows. The voice that replies isn't his. It comes from the man at the bar, the one in the khaki-colored anorak. He doesn't turn around. At his feet there is a thump of a sheepdog's tail.

"Depends who's asking."

38

2018

Neither Alice nor Kit can think of an appropriate response. They look at each other, then at the back of the man in the khaki anorak. There is no way he can be oblivious to the tension that is building in the bar. Still, he is in no rush to diffuse it. Even the men savoring the last drops of their drams have looked up to see how they will respond.

No, Alice hasn't met Jim. There are no guarantees that she will *ever* be able to meet him. For all she knows, the latest forum message could be yet another dead end. She knows all this and yet still she cannot shake the possibility of getting to the bottom of his disappearance, for Mary's sake. The search has dredged up parts of her past that she buried for a reason. She has put her job, and her sanity, on the line. Now she can't think of a single thing to say to him.

There is a loud scrape as he finally stands and pushes his barstool back. He downs the dregs of his pint, smacks his lips.

"I take it you're Alice, then?"

The man in front of her has the same dark hair as Jim, striped with gray; the same height and lean build, too. Only when he turns around does Alice realize that is he is at least two decades too old to be him.

"Don't be too pleased to see me now," he says, with a chuckle. "I'm Tony—we spoke earlier."

While Alice tries to hide her disappointment as discreetly as possible, Kit steps forward, hand outstretched. Tony looks down, as if considering what to do with it. When he goes to shake it, it is with such force that the air between the two palms squeaks out as a clap.

"Kit—I'm . . . a friend. Along for the journey."

Alice has never heard the word *friend* delivered with such pointed deliberation. Tony, at least, seems not to notice.

"I'll put the two of you out of your misery. He's on a job. The boat's not due back until this evening. I'd make yourselves comfortable, if I were you."

"So . . ." There is something charmingly transparent in the way Kit thinks; Alice can see the cogs whirring, and she is worried about what will come out next.

Tony raises a hand, steps closer, lowers his voice. The rest of the clientele appear to have stopped listening but there is little background noise, beside the occasional clash of the waves breaking on the shore. "I'm not convinced I've done the right thing here. My wife swayed it. I swear she spends all her time on Facebook, and she saw that video from the station. Her heart is with Mary. That's why she's been following the forum—on at me to reach out. We thought Mary . . . Well, anyway, you'll find out soon enough. Strong lass, my wife is, and she's beaten me down. I'm not speaking for the man. He confided in me and I've done too much already. I have no idea if he'll ever forgive me." Tony kicks a beer mat that has fallen on the ground across the sticky floorboards to avoid meeting either Alice's or Kit's eye. "But sometimes you have to have a clean conscience."

Outside they are hit by a gust whipping in from the loch. Alice wishes she'd thought to bring something more substantial than a leather jacket with a zipper that won't go up. She readjusts her scarf to make another loop out of it and tucks the stubby ends down her jumper to try to retain what little warmth she can.

When she looks up, she realizes that Kit has wandered off back to the car, hands pressed into his pockets. She thought the two of them were back on an even keel, after last night's misjudged liaison. He'd better not be sulking. Belatedly, too! Men, they beggar belief. After everything that has just happened in the inn, Alice does not have the energy for anymore emotional upheaval.

"Where are you off to?" Kit doesn't turn round, and Alice can't work out whether he can't hear her or is choosing not to.

She refuses to follow him and instead sits down in one of the wooden chairs overlooking the trail of white-sand beach, burrowing her chin deeper into her scarf. The water stretches out ahead, clear as crystal, until the blue of the sky gives way to that of the sea, the horizon trembling between. If ever there was a place to disappear, then this is it. There's no way Mary would have thought to come here in a bid to find Jim.

Alice is interrupted from her thoughts by the smell of wet canvas, mingled with bonfire. A second later a wax jacket lands on the table.

"You looked cold," Kit says, by way of explanation.

"Thank you." Alice slides it on over her own jacket. There is something so universally comforting about being in clothing a size or two too big, like stepping into the arms of a parent. A boyfriend, perhaps. Not that she has any experience in that regard or would let Kit know it. She curbs the latter part of her thought before her face burns up with it. "That was quite something, wasn't it?" she continues.

Kit doesn't reply. He doesn't look miffed as such, more troubled. She can see him scrolling through his phone, and her mind winds back to the apology vigil—the way Kit was absorbed by something on his screen that clearly shook him to the point of distraction. She asked how he was, when that happened, but she never did get an answer.

"You said it yourself—there's no signal. I'd give up now, if I were you."

Still nothing. Alice's voice is tight with the effort of trying to lighten the mood. Suddenly, it's as if a switch has been flipped: concern shot down by indignation. So this is it, is it? She has endured *more* than her fair share of being ignored in her twenty-six years of life. It happens at work; it had happened with her dad. The very last person she has expected to make her feel this way is Kit. Is it so bad that once—just once—she wants to be seen?

"For fuck's sake, Kit, are you just going to ignore me?"

"Wow!" He drops his phone on the table and turns to face her. He is so close that Alice can smell the synthetic menthol of his chewing gum. "Not everything is about you, Alice. Can you comprehend that?"

Her heart is pounding so rapidly that it seems to have equaled out to one heavy beat. "If this is about last night . . ."

"I can get over the fact you're not interested, Alice. I wish you were. Really I do, but if you're not, then that's fine. It's not about that, though." Kit rubs his forearms, where rows of goose pimples are beginning to form. "I want us to be friends. But every time I try and get closer, you just shut down. Why is that? Huh? Why is that, Alice?"

Her mouth hangs open. It's as if she's been slapped, but without the righteous anger that might have tempered it. Maybe she doesn't want to be seen—not if it hurts like this.

Kit is still looking at her, his head cocked expectantly. *Because you will love me and leave me,* Alice thinks. *Because there is nothing that will hurt more.*

"It would be nice if this friendship felt like two-way traffic," Kit mutters as he picks up his phone and starts to scroll again.

"I thought you didn't have *that sort of job?*" Alice knows she is being childish, but it is always so hard to rein in the infantile behavior once her feelings take over. "Work needs you now, does it?"

"No. No, it doesn't." Kit stops and flips the screen around to face

Alice. He was on a weather app. "And do you know why? Because I was sacked."

If Alice is trying not to look shocked, she is making a poor performance of it.

"Yep, you heard me—sacked." Kit is getting increasingly agitated, his head juddering on the tensed column of his neck. Alice recoils. "Don't worry, it's not contagious."

"You said you were on annual leave. What . . . what happened?"

"I had a job in an investment bank that I hated. But it paid well and it made Mum and Dad proud, so I sucked it up. Until I couldn't anymore. I couldn't get out of bed; I couldn't get through the bloody revolving doors of the place in the morning. I felt so low I actually called NightLine. It was Olive that I got; do you know that? Not that she'd ever work out it was me."

Alice tries to imagine the call. The thought of Kit—happy-go-lucky, confident Kit—at rock bottom is enough to break even the hardest of hearts. Her hand reaches toward him, but he has his fists bunched in the pockets of his jeans.

"That night was the worst of my life. But it did something. I signed up with NightLine, thought maybe I could help someone else like me. It gave me something to do as well, once HR let me know that my absence record was impressive enough to get me fired. That was six months ago. My lease was up, so I moved to the cheapest place I could find, but I still won't be able to make my rent next month. Every time I look at my bank statement I feel sick. My credit card must be maxed out. And I can't go home, either, because do you know what?"

Alice has no idea what. She is starting to realize that the picture she has painted of Kit is in actual fact just a series of sketchy assumptions. What is that saying, about assumptions? It is flitting irritatingly out of reach of her memory. All she can remember is that it ends up with everyone looking like an ass.

"No?" Alice ventured.

"They don't know I got sacked. It would crush them. Or at least their expectations of me."

"So what will you do?"

Kit opens his mouth to respond, but before he can, a foghorn breaks through. Both of them look out to sea. A boat is approaching at high speed. There are three men on the short deck at the front, arms braced in inverted Vs along the railings. They are so stylized that they remind Alice of a child's drawing of a bird. Far too small to be identified, at any rate.

"I thought it wasn't due until this evening," Alice says. It's only just past 2 P.M. The door to the inn behind them swings open and there are footsteps.

"Well, looks like I was wrong," Tony says.

39

2011

As the taxi lurched right at the roundabout, Mary wondered if she would be sick. She had always had a strong stomach for car journeys, so it must be the anxiety to blame. She opened her handbag a little wider, just in case. It was cheap faux leather that was peeling around the straps. If the worst came to the worst, it could be chucked if she vomited in it.

The shamrock keyring that she had bought on a whim in Duty Free glimmered in the headlamps of a car streaking past in the middle lane. Mary picked it up and balled it into her fist until she could feel the metal edges biting into her palm. If ever she needed some luck, it was now. What would Jim be up to? In bed, doubtless. She wondered if he would have eaten anything. Mary was always buying microwavable meals for times like this, when she knew it would be too much for him to be cooking from scratch. The freezer was practically overflowing.

She should be furious. Of all the times for Jim to abandon her, five minutes before the cab arrived to ferry them to the airport and onto a flight to take them to Mam's Big Birthday was hardly it. But she had already expended her fury. Mary squeezed her eyes tight shut to try to block out the memory of how she had spoken to him. *I'd be better off without all this bullshit. Don't you think I deserve something a bit better from you?* The sheer scale of her own vitriol had stunned her.

Jim, meanwhile, didn't seem to register the outburst at all. His face was frozen. Numb. Perhaps that was the worst of it, Mary thought: that he didn't seem half as shocked as she was herself? Even when she had finished venting her frustrations, Jim still went in to kiss her forehead. She was a terrible person. To say those things to Jim, when it was clear as day that he was suffering? It made her a terrible person. There were no two ways about that.

The sooner she got home, the sooner she could start to make it up to him. She had typed a text apology to Jim at least twenty times over the course of the weekend—in the bathroom; when Mam was fussing with the teapot, while Mary was on the pretense of checking the cake— and deleted it every time. That sort of breakdown in sensitivity required some face-to-face contrition and Mary knew it.

"Chartes Road, was it, darling? Cos I can hang a right here, get us there a bit quicker."

"Yeah—forty-six. Thanks," Mary mumbled.

She had picked the moment for her outburst, as well. Two weeks ago Jim had reached an all-time low. It was his forty-second birthday. He hadn't wanted a celebration and, while Mary had heeded his wishes, Richard and Juliette hadn't. They had got caterers in to their place in Notting Hill, all for a supper for the four of them. Jim had pushed most of his duck-and-orange salad around the plate, and Mary had to stop herself shuddering when she saw the nice young girl who was there to serve the meal scraping the remains of it into the garbage.

"You know, I thought we'd have grandchildren by now," Juliette had said as she poured out the last of their (third) bottle of wine.

Jim had tried to draw a line under the discussion—"Mum, please"—but there was little to no conviction in his voice. Mary wondered if he had piped up out of habit alone. Both he and Mary had spent the last few years exhausted by everyone else's vision for their relationship. At that precise moment it was hard enough to keep the wheels turning on it, without contending with the constant reminders of the roads they had, mutually, decided not to take.

It was on the tip of Mary's tongue then to ask Juliette whether she had any idea what sort of pressure questions like that put Jim under. All those expectations for their boys—Sam and James—drifting from the spread shoulders of two sons onto the unbearably loaded back of one. Never mind that none of it was what Jim wanted. Not for the first time, it struck Mary that there was only so much living that one person could do for another.

They ended up taking two slices of cake home in a strangely un-scratched Tupperware box—Jim had feigned a headache to get out of dessert. Mary cocooned his hand in hers the whole Tube journey home, trying to stroke some serenity back into him. But he went straight to bed when they arrived, his silence louder than any actual protest at the state of the evening could ever have been.

The next morning Mary brought the cake up to bed for them both, along with a coffeepot. Jim brightened at the sight. But he made it quite clear that he didn't want to discuss what had been said by his parents. He kissed her and then it lingered, and suddenly the coffee was cold and they were under the duvet again, finding their way back to each other through touch and taste. Anything but talk.

She should have known that Jim's attendance at Mam's birthday was far from a given.

Mary was dragged back to the present with a jolt. The cabbie took a left turn on two wheels and she grabbed the handle of her suitcase before it careered to the far side of the vehicle.

"Alright, that will be twenty-nine pounds sixty, when you have a sec."

Without her realizing, the taxi had reached Ealing and the driver was now pulling up outside the flat. Mary brought the shamrock keyring up to her lips and kissed it once for luck, before tucking it into the inside pocket of her bag. She handed over the cash and climbed out onto the pavement.

The blinds were fully open and the late-August sunshine danced through the kitchen. She couldn't see much beyond the breakfast bar, but it was clear that Jim wasn't seated at it working, as he so often did. Maybe he hadn't moved from bed in the thirty-six hours she had been gone? One tiny part of Mary wasn't sure she had it in her to try to rouse some life out of Jim at nine o'clock on a Sunday night. All the other parts ached to see him again.

She turned her key in the lock and dumped her case by the door.

"Hello?" She wondered why she was whispering. If Jim was asleep, he'd be woken up by the sound of her clattering around in the en suite soon enough. "Hello!" Mary flicked on the light in the hallway. At the end of it, illuminated, the open bedroom door, the bed empty and the covers perfectly made.

Looking back, she would wonder if that was the exact moment when she realized what had happened. She had never known Jim to make the bed, and certainly not when he was in one of his dark episodes, when he'd be back under the duvet less than half a minute after he had straightened it.

As it was, Mary was still trying to keep herself calm. There would be a reasonable explanation for where Jim had got to. She opened the top drawer of his bedside table. The spot where he usually tucked his phone and wallet overnight was empty.

She tried to tell herself that he could be in the pub or with Gus, although she couldn't remember the last time he had seen any of his friends through his own volition.

The high-pitched buzz in Mary's ears surged in volume. It was becoming so loud that it drowned out even the heavy thud of her own pulse. Was this a repeat of the incident at the doctors' clinic two years ago? Or was it something worse? She slid back the door to Jim's side of the wardrobe.

While it wasn't empty, it was slimmer than it had been the day before. Two thick woolen jumpers had gone as well as his hiking rucksack, the one with the long straps that Mary was forever complaining trailed untidily across the carpet.

That didn't mean she wanted it gone, though. Not if it meant Jim was, too.

In the hallway, fumbling in the cabinet, the final piece of the nightmarish puzzle fell into place. Mary raised one hand to the back of her neck, as if that might help to withstand the weight of her world, crashing down around it.

Ten, fifteen minutes passed with her frozen in shock. She never should have gone to Belfast. If it hadn't been for the occasion . . . Duty was one thing, but what about when it was split between Jim and her own flesh and blood? Then she should have made the safer call and stayed in Ealing. There was no excusing what she had done. None whatsoever.

Jim's phone went straight to voicemail. Mary sent him a text— Call me, please—but in her heart of hearts, she knew there was little to no chance of a response. As she finally dialed Jim's parents' number, Mary tried to remember the last time she'd called either of them. She couldn't. Never by herself at least, beyond the customary hello when Jim passed the phone in her direction. She wondered if that was part of the nature of taking a number *for emergencies*—the never imagining you'll ever need it. The phone rang five times before there was an answer.

"Juliette Whitnell."

"It's Mary."

"What's wrong?" Her voice was sharp, but there was a quiver when she raised her voice to form the question that reminded Mary that she was a mother too. A mother who had already lost one son.

"I don't know where he is." Her words came out in dry heaves. Somehow saying them aloud suddenly made everything feel far too real. "He wasn't here when I got back."

"Got back from where?"

"Belfast. It was my mam's birthday. Her sixtieth. Jim was meant to be there but then he was . . . sick. He couldn't come, so I had to fly over alone. It was only the one night I was away, and now I've come back and he isn't here."

"Calm down. I can't hear you properly. Look, are you sure he isn't out? I don't know, at work or with friends or something?"

Mary pressed one hand against her mouth, the fingers of the other tracing the small rectangle of space where those same hopes of hers had just died. This was different from last time, with the aborted picnic. Awfully different.

"His passport's gone," she said, her tongue tacking, dry, against the roof of her mouth. It hadn't moved since their trip to Provence last summer. "He didn't tell me he was planning on going anywhere."

40

2011

Juliette arrived alone.

"Richard's away playing golf," she said by way of explanation when Mary opened the door. "He wasn't due until tomorrow night but he's on his way back to London now."

Mary hadn't had time to tidy anything up, or the inclination, and she saw Juliette scanning the kitchen. Jim may have made the bed, but there were still coffee granules sprinkled along the countertops, the plastic tray from one of her microwavable meals poking out of the lid of the garbage can. Mary wished she could deduce something of his mental state from the clutter, beyond his unwavering devotion to chicken tikka masala.

"I came as quickly as I could."

It was the first time Mary had seen Juliette without makeup or in a state that could be described as anything less than pristine. Her silk shirt was rumpled and looked as if it had been grabbed from the bottom of the nearest drawer as a replacement for her pajama top. Somehow it set Mary further on edge.

"Have you called the police?"

"Not yet," Mary said.

She stood by the window, staring at her phone, as if willing it to ring had any bearing on reality. Nothing made sense. This was Jim they were talking about, the man who promised he would be there for her to the ends of the earth. If he had meant that, then surely this had to be a fantasy, a delusion. Jaysus, why wouldn't someone shake her out of it already? She turned to Juliette, but her face was stony, her body unmoving.

"Shall I?"

Mary nodded.

"I'll need the details. Can you do me a sheet with the timings: when you last saw James, any plans he may have mentioned, the items you know are missing. They'll want to speak to you too, I'm sure." She was eerily calm. Mary would have wondered how on earth she managed it, were it not for the fact that there was little space in her brain for anything but terror.

Under Juliette's instruction, Mary felt herself revert to the role of child, albeit one devoid of its parent's touch. She tuned out of Juliette's call, without meaning to, responding to it like the background thrum of the television next door or the cry of the newborn in the flat upstairs.

Mary longed to be back at home, to collapse into Mam and have her tell Mary, in no uncertain terms, that everything would be okay, that there were no lengths she wouldn't go to make it so. But what would she say about all this? It was Mam who had told Mary the secret to maintaining a relationship—sticking to it through thick and thin. Mary could hardly claim that she'd done that the last time she saw Jim, storming off to the taxi without a word.

"Mary?"

"Sorry. Sorry." She turned back from the window to where Juliette was standing. She readied herself to take the handset, to give the police the answers to the questions she knew they would ask her time and time again, until she doubted every last syllable of them.

The phone dangled from Juliette's hand.

"They said they can't do anything yet."

"What?"

"He's low risk, apparently. They said we need to wait seventy-two hours. If we wanted, we could try the hospitals . . ." The word alone was enough to tip Juliette over the edge. Her reserve crumbled and, a second later, her chest fell forward, her teeth clenched together as if she was trying to hold down a wail that was rising from the core of her. Mary steered her to the sofa, putting an arm around the impossibly small curve of her waist.

They sat in silence, neither comfortable with the intimacy of the moment but too weak to seek an alternative. When the clock on the oven announced eleven with an impatient tick, Juliette prized herself loose and reclipped a strand of hair in its barrette.

"They asked me if there were problems, at home." Her voice was cold, clinical.

"What did you say?" Mary couldn't work out why the police would be after his parents. Jim was a grown man. Maybe Juliette hadn't made his age clear.

"I said I would ask you." The tears had dried in Juliette's eyes. It took Mary back to the first time she had met her, the strange distance in them that kept everyone outside the immediate family at an unquestionable remove. "They said there might be something he needed to get away from. A situation. A person, perhaps?"

"No, er . . . no. Not at all."

"See, the thing is, it doesn't make sense to me." Juliette had repositioned herself at the far end of the sofa, her body twisted to face Mary. Suddenly a police interview seemed preferable. "He was meant to be coming to this family party of yours in Belfast and then he . . . canceled. Why? Why would he do that?"

Because he's sick, Mary thought. *Depressed. Because he was so low he could barely move his head from the pillow.* Did Juliette even understand that concept? That mental health wasn't the sort of problem you could pay a staff member to fix for a wad of cash? Mary doubted it, otherwise why wouldn't Jim have told his parents before that he was struggling? They wanted their remaining son to be fit and healthy and well. They didn't want him nursed by the girlfriend who, in their eyes, had never been good enough for him. For all Mary knew, they would lay the blame for his struggles squarely at her door.

"He'd been stressed and, I don't know . . . I didn't want to push it. I thought it would be better if he had the weekend here, by himself, to recover. I wouldn't have gone, if it weren't for the fact it was Mam's sixtieth."

Of course Juliette didn't care about Mary's reasoning. She circled her fingers around a knot of tension in her brow. "So you are telling me there was no reason at all why Jim would walk out on all this?"

When she flung her arms back to gesture, Mary noticed that her hands were taking in the soft furnishings, the view to the tranquil neighborhood street. *This* categorically did not include Mary.

"There was no trigger at all, was there?" Juliette prompted.

Mary forced herself to meet Juliette's gaze. She felt guilty as sin itself, but the last thing she needed was Juliette to know it too. At the first sign of her implication in Jim's disappearance, Juliette would, no doubt, have Mary hauled in front of the investigating officers, handcuffed in an instant. It was no worse than she deserved, but right now Mary needed to be here. She needed to be at home, ready and waiting for Jim to return.

Juliette was in no rush to end the silence stretching between the two women. Mary's sole source of relief was the fact that Juliette couldn't hear the words careering, uncontrolled, through Mary's head. *Bullshit. Deserve something better than you.* Had it only been yesterday that they had spewed out of her? She would do anything to take them back.

"No," Mary answered. "Nothing."

"Fine." Juliette stood and brushed her hands down the front of her jeans. "I have to get back."

For whom? One son dead, one gone, and a husband still making his way down the motorway from St. Andrews. Anyone else would stay. Any other almost mother-in-law. Instead they would endure their insomnia apart. They would suffer, separately.

"I gave the police our contact details," she added. Then clarified, "Mine and Richard's. As next of kin. If there are any developments, we'll let you know. Keep your mobile on."

Juliette let herself out.

41

2018

"Are you sure we're doing the right thing?" Alice shuffles her chair a little closer to Kit's; she wants to offer him a hug, after everything he has just disclosed about his job and his mental health, but his body is rigid.

"It's a bit late for that—the man's over there." Kit points at the boat and Alice grabs his hand before anyone on the jetty catches sight of them. They are too far away from where the boat has landed to see whether any of the men unloading the nets bears a convincing resemblance to Jim. They are all wearing the same uniform of woolen hat, roll-neck, and waders. "Alright, alright." Kit wriggles his arm free and pulls it away. "Chill out, okay?"

To Alice, there are few things more annoying in life than being told to relax. She's come to the recent conclusion that she is physically incapable of it anyway. She is too highly strung. The fact that Tony told them that they would still have to wait three hours before there was any chance that Jim would be back at home didn't sit well with her in the slightest.

"Really, though, do you?"

"Do I what?" Kit asks.

"Think we're doing the right thing? I can't help but think it should be Mary here." Alice waves her hand vaguely in the direction of Kit.

"Cheers."

"You know what I mean. It's *her* Jim, right?"

"People aren't possessions," Kit replies.

"But they *possess* obligations."

He lets out a closed-mouth sigh and his nostrils flare. Alice cannot fathom how it is possible for someone to be at once so infuriating and so attractive in the same breath. And when did Kit start being exasperated with *her*? This isn't the right way around at all.

"You said it was better if Mary didn't know about our research—this trip. We agreed we didn't want to get her hopes up," Kit says.

Alice nods. That at least is impossible to deny, although Kit knows nothing about the conversation that passed between herself and Mary last time they saw each other, outside the station, with the rest of Night-Line packing away their signs. The last words that Mary said then, to Alice, have never been far from the forefront of her mind: *I'm asking that you stop looking now, for Jim.*

"What are we going to say, anyway?" Kit continues. "I mean, what does anyone say to a man who decides to disappear off the face of the earth without a word?"

Alice could provide reams of suggestions for what they could ask Jim. Because even though she knows that her dad is somewhere out there, with a family, safe and probably happier than he ever was with her and Mum—because even though she has moved on—there will always be one question that can never find a sufficient answer.

"Maybe just 'why?'," Alice murmurs.

"Yeah, that's bonza. Short. To the point. Bit like you, eh?" Kit smiles, but not as fully as before. Alice's heart hurts for him and his fear of disappointing his parents. Kit continues, "You're very good at this, Alice. Anyone would think you had done this before."

He bends his head so that his face, ruddy from the wind and sea air, is square on to hers. There is not a trace of judgment to be found among his features. He understands what it means to be vulnerable. What it means to hurt. So Alice could tell him, now, why she is here. She could explain to Kit that the same reasons why she cannot let him—or, indeed, anyone else—close are the very same reasons why she will not rest until she has found Jim. She could allow Kit to be the first one to know, to really know, her.

Her mouth opens.

"I'll get us some crisps, shall I? Don't know about you, but I'm starving." Kit bounds off to attend to their stomachs before Alice has the chance to find the words.

I t is past six o'clock by the time Tony is prepared to take them to Jim. He's been drinking all afternoon, by the looks of things, but he's surprisingly nimble as he leads them up the hill away from the pub. There are no streetlamps and it takes a fair amount of willpower for Alice to resist the urge to light the path in front of her feet with the light on her phone—the less attention drawn to the fact that they are outsiders, the better.

"So how do you know Jim?" Kit asks. They are walking in single file up a narrow stretch of a path hemmed in by fields on either side. Benji the sheepdog is taking the lead, followed by Tony, then Alice, then Kit.

An awkward silence descends. It is impossible to know whether Tony has heard or not.

"Jim, eh?"

Alice looks over her shoulder at Kit and nearly trips on a loose stone in the process. He reaches for her hand and does not let go until long after she is steady.

"That's not how we know him around here."

"Oh." Alice wonders if the cold has gone to her head. She's never been known to be short of things to say, but right now her mind is crammed to bursting point, chock-full of Kit's revelations, the potential proximity to Jim, childhood memories that she hoped never to confront again.

"Who do you know him as, then?" Kit, mercifully, does not seem to have fallen prey to brain freeze, despite wearing only a T-shirt. He has not so much as asked for his jacket back, even though he now has his hands tucked up under his armpits.

"Think it's best you ask him yourself."

"Have you known him long?" Kit is not taking the hint. Either that or he is as persistent as all hell. Alice thinks he would probably make a cracking journalist, if he has turned his back on banking for good.

"Long enough. He's been here a few years."

"Doing the fishing?"

Doing the fishing? Some of the things Kit comes out with baffle Alice. His turn of phrase is one part nineteenth-century novel to two parts Google Translate. She would be interested to know how, or rather if, he was socialized as a child.

Tony grunts in assent. *Doing the fishing* it is.

"And the two of you are close?"

It is all Alice can do not to kick Kit in the shins. They can't afford to have Tony back out on them under Kit's cross-examination. They have come so close to finding Jim. To return without answers for Mary now, with Jim in touching distance, would be unfathomable. Alice would never get over it.

Tony comes to an abrupt stop, and it takes a moment or two for Alice to register that they have reached the gate to a cottage. There is a small stretch of lawn, if such the unruly mass of wild grass can be called, a single-story house on the other side of it. It is low-key, to say the least. Alice can't imagine that she would be able to find it again, without Tony's help.

"This is it, then?" Kit asks.

Alice could not be feeling more uneasy. Her heart is hammering and there is a terrible pulling pain in her bowels. She needs the loo. Or a beta-blocker. Ideally, both. She momentarily wishes she'd never embarked on this whole sorry endeavor in the first place. "Are you coming in too?" she says to Tony, tapping him on the shoulder. She restrains the urge to cling onto it.

"I haven't the mind for a fight tonight, no. But it will come back to me anyway, no doubt. I'll get you to the door, no more."

The door has an old cast-iron knocker and, when Tony raps with it, the noise it makes is so loud there can be no doubt that whoever is inside will have heard it. Alice has that horrible telescopic feeling that always accompanies the major moments in her life—good and bad. Everything she has worked toward for these last few weeks, her highest hopes, are honed on the seconds that come next.

"Tony."

Benji bounds up to the man on the doorstep. He has a heavy beard, dark and flecked with the first strands of gray, and his hair reaches to his collar, the curls pushed back from his forehead and tucked behind his ears. He is older and he is weathered. But the other sightings had nothing on this. This is it. He is unmistakably the man from Alice's stolen photo. The slit in the eyebrow is there, the hairs still refusing to grow in the scar tissue.

"Who are . . ." They watch as the truth dawns on Jim. His eyes widen and he goes to slam the door. He exhales through his teeth, the sound of a train heaving in at the platform, when he realizes Tony's foot is in the way.

"Let them in, Sam. They won't stay long."

Even Kit is standing stock-still, too tense to move his head to nod.

"What the fuck? I thought you were looking out for me."

"I was. I am," Tony replies, his voice less than certain. It feels almost disrespectful to be intruding on such a personal moment, and Alice looks at her shoes. She notices that a small tear, the size of a five-pence piece, has appeared in the canvas on the top of her trainer.

"You lied."

"And you didn't? You told me everyone back home knew you were here. You told me that woman of yours knew, too."

"She does," Jim says.

42

2011

Juliette's last question hung in the air long after she had left. *There was no trigger at all, was there?* The implicit accusation made the whole flat feel tight, as if it had filled the very corners of the place, sucking the air out from behind the sofa and between the slats of the venetian blinds, until Mary could barely breathe from the panic. She had hardly expected Juliette to declare her previously withheld affection for her in these circumstances, but she hadn't expected her to place the blame at Mary's doorstep, either.

There was no chance Mary would be able to sleep. Her head was a turmoil of a hundred possibilities that didn't bear thinking about: Jim had been in an accident, the victim of a crime. She imagined his body on the side of the road, or down an alley, or bobbing in the river for an unsuspecting rower to find. If she had even countenanced the suggestion that this was, in some way, voluntary—that Jim had walked out of his own accord—it was fleetingly dismissed. She knew Jim. He wouldn't leave without saying goodbye.

It was clear that Juliette didn't hold the same faith. She had planted the seed of doubt and rooted it well enough to flourish. Mary tried to force her mind back to her final interaction with Jim. He was wearing the socks she had given him last Christmas, rainbow-striped from ankle to toe. Every time he wore them, it made her smile. With one exception: this time he wasn't just slipping off his shoes, he was slipping out of her life. He was letting her down when she needed him most. If only he had acknowledged that, then she never would have said what she did. She never would have lashed out.

As dawn broke over the city, Mary knew she had to be doing something to keep her guilt at bay. But what? It wasn't as if she could help with the investigation. Juliette had made that quite clear. "Next of kin," she had said, tightly, as if she were drawing the curtain on Mary's participation in Whitnell family life. Just because Mary wasn't first in the biological or legal pecking order, did that mean her grief was somehow less valid? That she was interloping on pain that wasn't hers to suffer?

She wondered if Richard or Juliette had ever made a comment to Jim about the two of them not being married, something that might have put him off? She could well imagine it. *Be careful, son. It's for life, you know.* Or perhaps that was Mary's paranoia speaking. The two of them were more than old enough to make up their own minds on the subject. The fact they didn't want the pomp and circumstance of a wedding was neither here nor there. It was all Mary could do not to call Juliette and scream "SIX YEARS" into the digital hum of the line. It meant something, with or without some legal formalities.

Terrified that she might, in fact, do just that, Mary occupied her hands by combing through the piles of paper in the kitchen, on the coffee table, under every jumbled pile of cables in his drawers, in the hope of finding a note. Nothing. She couldn't tell if that was a good sign or not. Perhaps it meant he wasn't about to do something stupid after all; that he had simply been called away and hadn't thought to let them know? That wouldn't be the worst thing in the world, she told herself. He would come home eventually, tail between his legs. All that mattered was that he was safe.

By the time it was dark, Mary was dizzy. Her anger was spent, the last of her hope, too. She hadn't eaten all day or taken so much as a sip of water. There was no way to get comfortable—not with her whole body tensed and her head so full that she couldn't get to the end of one thought before another snatched up its space. It was as if she were stuck in a time warp, or some awful alternative world where every bone of her rattled with urgency, but no one else could see the need to do anything at all.

One day became two, and two became three. Mary must have slept, but it was in scraps so short that she lacked the mental clarity to distinguish between her nightmares and the mirror image that was waking. Juliette texted to say that she had been to the police. The case was registered and officers assigned, and Mary could expect a visit to the flat very soon. Strangely, none of the details filled her with anything like the horror that Juliette's complete lack of interest in her own well-being did. Could she not bring herself to ask how Mary was doing?

When the police did arrive, she barely registered their presence. One officer was dispatched to the living room to ask Mary all the questions Juliette had already posed. *When had she last seen James Whitnell? And how did he seem, then, in himself? Was there any trouble she knew of, at work or between the two of them?* And while Mary answered every last query, she could have been pressing Play on a tape recorder of pre-recorded sentences. Her mind was far outside the room. It was far outside the flat, away from the policeman wiping a gloved finger along the surfaces of their bedroom and pushing objects, seemingly at random, into evidence bags. It was far outside Ealing. It was wherever Jim was. Mary hoped two sweaters would be enough.

The officers left with a small bow of apology. Mary wondered then if that was their way of conceding defeat. She knew that the odds of a missing person returning home in one piece decreased with every hour they had gone, and the week marker was rapidly approaching. What happened after that? They assumed Jim had a new life to lead and hadn't the heart to inform whoever had existed in the old? Mary texted Juliette to let her know that the police had come by. Two checkmarks announced that her message had been read, but there was no response.

She had never felt so alone. After five years in London, Mary was still using the excuse that she hadn't had the time to make her own co-terie of friends. She had her work, Jim, and the rare occasions they saw his set from university. But with Jim so cagey about his mental health and the way in which that isolated them both, it was hard for Mary to find the support network she needed. She couldn't talk to anyone they knew about Jim's depression, and it was hardly as if she could confide in a stranger at a Friday-night drinks event for the lonely self-employed of London, either.

Besides, it had never felt like a small life, or that her solitude was something to be rectified. Not until now. Mary thought about calling Mam—but what would she say? *I came to your sixtieth, and Jim left the min-ute my back was turned.* Mam knew her too well. She would ask the right questions, unlike the police with their fixation on time frames and pat-terns of movement. She would ask what had really happened. *Were there cross words, doll?* That was what she would say, and Mary wouldn't have the heart to disappoint her with the truth of her own behavior.

There were no visitors to the flat after the police and, when the knock came three weeks and five days later, Mary was so surprised by the sound that she almost didn't go to the door. Then another knock, and another. It was the bailiffs already—the clinic wanting to know how long they could keep Jim's contract going. She couldn't face that. More than anything, she didn't want to feel the ache in the back of her throat that was surely her body's way of telling her that it was impossible to cry and talk at the same time.

"Mary." A voice from outside. Mary pressed her eye against the peephole on the door. "It's me, Richard. Richard Whitnell. James's father."

Mary opened the door and Richard's gaze dropped from her face to her hand.

She was holding the gas bill, or rather the letter announcing that it was overdue. It had been tied to Jim's personal account. The two of them had never had a joint bank account, so there was no way to know what the state of his finances was. Had it just run dry? Or had it been empty for weeks by now? The fact that Jim could have been planning to break her heart over the course of the last few months sent a fresh, searing pain through her chest.

"Is it alright if I come in?" Richard prompted.

She nodded and shuffled aside. He led the way back to the living room, where Mary had the television on as background noise, some panel show where celebrities with dubious degrees of fame discussed the headlines. In the doorway, Mary watched with glazed eyes as they gesticulated toward the front pages, none of which featured Jim. If he was a child or a woman, there would be helicopters, patrols out in the neighborhood, sniffer dogs. People would look over their shoulder, walking back from the bus stop at night. But if it's a grown man who disappears, all anyone can think is that he has snapped—the woman in his life most likely responsible for it.

"Do you know where the, er . . . control for this is?" Mary's reverie was interrupted by Richard, busy in his search for the remote. She didn't have the energy to help him. "Don't worry, I've got it." Richard caught sight of its end, wedged between two sofa cushions. He aimed for the Off button but ended up muting it instead.

"How are you?" he asked, slumping down into the armchair.

Mary shrugged. "Awful."

"I know." He looked it himself. He was wearing tracksuit bottoms and his face had the sallow tinge of a man who had seen as little sunlight over the past few weeks as Mary. "I'm sorry we haven't been in touch more. It's Juliette, she's . . ."

Angry, Mary thought. *Vengeful. Wishes that I had never been born.* That would make two of them.

Richard settled for "Struggling. Sam, then . . . this. It's impossible. Look, Mary, will you sit down?"

Something in the atmosphere of the room shifted. She shook her head, a petulant toddler in the face of a father who stood to lose everything. Gone was Richard's booming laugh, the ill-considered comments about her background. Whatever he had to say, it was earth-shattering enough to have brought them parity.

"I'm afraid I have some news." Richard leaned forward, propping his elbows on his knees. Mary felt the rest of the room drop away, so that there was just Richard's voice and his hands, severed, floating in space. No good news ever came from someone being too scared to deliver it.

"Is he dead?"

Richard swallowed, his Adam's apple bobbing in the loose skin around his neck.

"Is he?"

He opened his mouth, licked the crusted corners of his lips.

"Is he? For the love of God, will you tell me?"

"He's not dead," Richard said, finally. "It's more complicated than that. The police have located Jim, but I'm afraid that he won't be coming home." Mary would return to those words every day for the next seven years. She would remember them for as long as she lived. "I'm sorry, Mary," Richard said, standing. He went to hold her, but she dodged his arms.

"You're lying to me," she hissed.

"I'm not, I swear." Richard took two steps back, hands raised, as if backing away from a feral dog. "The police will explain all this so much better than I can. They know to expect you. Please, Mary, call them." He rummaged in his pocket for a business card and placed it in the center of the coffee table. "The direct line is there whenever you need it." Then he added again, as if it helped matters in the slightest, "I'm so sorry."

43

2018

No one knows what to say. No one moves.

Eventually Tony clears his throat. "Look, it's a mess. That much is certain. But these two have come a long way, and I think the least you can do is offer them a cup of tea before you send them back again." Jim's hostility does not appear to waver. "Maybe this will be the chance to put it all to bed at last?" Tony adds.

Jim shakes his head. He couldn't look much more furious, short of having them pinned up against the wall. "No more than half an hour— okay?" he says, fixing Kit right in the eye.

"Yes. Thank you, we appreciate it. We totally respect that, too." Alice gives Kit a light kick with her trainer to stop him blathering on.

"There's a room in the inn for you both, when you're done. It's too late to be starting your journey back at this hour," Tony says.

"Thank you," Alice replies, restraining the urge to hug him. His generosity in the face of the situation they have landed him in is quite something.

Tony waits until they are over the threshold before raising a hand in farewell. "Safe trip back."

"You're not coming to enjoy the show?"

"Bitterness doesn't suit you, Sam. You know that." Tony refuses to rise to the bait. As the door swings shut behind him, Alice hopes that Tony won't lose whatever relationship he had with Jim on their account. They owe him a lot.

Inside the cottage is dark. Alice follows Kit down a short corridor: to the right, there is a small front room with a television perched on what looks to be a tree stump, two armchairs, and a circular table with two wooden dining chairs. To the left, a kitchen, where the kettle is whistling on the range. There is only one item on the worktop—a chipped cream beaker with some coast guard insignia painted on its front in cobalt blue.

"I do have another mug, if you'd like one." He has caught Alice staring.

"That would be great, thanks."

"You can go sit down through there." It sounds less like an invitation than an order and Alice heads to join Kit on the armchairs in the next room. When she sits down, Kit gives her a bug-eyed stare, as if to underline just how out of their depth they truly are. And there was Alice hoping he might take the lead.

Jim returns with two mugs of tea and extends them toward Kit and Alice. He takes one of the dining-room chairs and moves it so that they form an awkward triangle. He spreads his legs wide and rests his elbows on his knees, the whole weight of his body slumped into them.

"Well, then?"

Alice looks across at Kit, who is doing a very good impression of a rabbit caught in the headlights. It looks like she'll be taking the lead on this one.

"We're friends of Mary's. I don't know if you saw anything online, but she's been doing a vigil, for you. Every day she's outside Ealing Broadway with this sign." At the mention of the station, Jim's eyes screw shut. Whatever memory he is caught up in, there is no doubt it is shot through with pain. "It has your name on it. She's been doing it—the vigil, I mean—for seven years now."

Saying it aloud, Alice is struck by its gravity. *Seven years.* She looks at Jim to see if this is registering but he has his eyes closed.

"But it all escalated a few weeks ago. Someone videoed Mary when she was upset—angry, really—and then they uploaded the footage to social media. It got a lot of traction . . ." Would Jim have seen it? Up here, it would be perfectly possible to be cut off from the online trends. From the rest of the world.

Before Alice can ask, Jim interrupts. "I know. I saw the video. Only after Tony mentioned it, though. It was the first I'd heard of anything to do with Mary. Since I've been gone, I mean," he says. He still has not lifted his head.

"Oh." Alice was not expecting that. If he had seen the footage, even recently, why the hell didn't he get in touch? Just as she opens her mouth to ask, he cuts her off.

"And you're the lucky reporters who found me."

"No!" Alice is so quick to shut down his conclusion that the word comes out as a shout. She is not the same as them. She has turned her world upside down to find this man. However much she wants to keep her job, she would not have gone to these lengths were she not motivated by factors that run far deeper than the professional. "As I said, we're Mary's friends. We wanted to help her, and we thought that finding you would be the best way to do that. We had some annual leave. We thought we could use it following up the leads that the video threw up online."

"Well, congrats, then. You got me." Jim's voice is deadpan, his tone so dry it seems to suck up all the air in the room.

"Tony called you Sam," Kit says, in a bid to break the settling silence.

"Sometimes you need a clean break." Jim looks up and out of the small window behind them. Kit cranes his head to see what he is staring at, but there are no curtains, only the deep, unbroken darkness of the countryside at night. "A new identity. A fresh start."

His animosity has been replaced by something more nebulous, something altogether more unsettling. Neither Kit nor Alice knows what to say next. They have so many questions—too many perhaps—but none seem like a fitting follow-up. Before they can figure one out, Jim's eyes snap back to the room and focus on Alice.

"If you're *friends* of Mary's, how come you don't know what happened?"

"Mary's very private. We didn't want to push."

"So, you came here? To what? Bring me back? Like some sort of prize?"

"No. It's not like that at all." Kit puts his hands up, palms toward Jim, as if by way of placation. "We were just looking for answers. For Mary."

"She already has them."

Kit looks at Alice and is relieved to see that she seems every bit as puzzled as him.

"I suppose you want them spelled out for you, too?"

Alice nods. Her hands are trembling and she tightens them around the mug.

Jim takes a deep breath, stares at the floor. "I couldn't carry on with things the way they were. I'd fucked up at work—I was about to be fired. I was drinking too much, turning up at work under the influence. . . . Mary must have known; not about what happened at work maybe, but about me drinking again. Not that any of it is her fault. None of it was. It wasn't anyone's but my own."

He bites down so heavily on his bottom lip that Alice wonders if it will bleed. "But it wasn't fair that anyone else had to suffer for my mistakes anymore. There was no way I was going to fix myself there, in London, in that environment. There was only one way out for me. I had to cut all ties with my old life to survive. I couldn't live a life that wasn't mine."

"So why didn't you break up with her?" Kit asks.

For once, a sensible question, Alice thinks with relief.

"I tried. A few times. I felt so guilty for bringing her down with my problems. But she wouldn't listen. You must know what she's like— fierce, persistent. Christ, she wouldn't have been videoed like that, if she wasn't. I loved that in her, but it made trying to tell her that I had to leave impossible. It was like she was deaf to what I was saying. It seemed easier for me to give up on that and to stay, for a bit at least. But in the end, staying for her sake ate away at what was left of our relationship and I had to get out." Alice is stony-faced, unconvinced. "I'm not justifying myself here," Jim adds. "I'm answering the question."

"You just walked out, then? Left Mary to wonder what had happened to you for *seven years*?" The pent-up venom finally spews out from between Alice's words. There is nothing worse than being left in the dark.

"She knows."

"What?"

"The police caught up with me about a month after I left. I knew they would eventually. They said that my parents had reported me missing and their liaison officer would let them know I was safe. Not where I was; they promised they wouldn't share that. But they said they would pass on the message that I didn't want to be found. From what I understand, all the information was being relayed, through my parents, to Mary. So she knows. She must."

Alice's head is spinning. Did Jim's parents pass on the message? The picture Mary painted of them was cold, but no one could be so callous as not to share news that vital. But what of the alternative? If they did tell Mary and she kept her vigil in denial, then that is some faith in a relationship—in the ability of one man to change his mind.

Some people choose to see what they want to see. The words Gus spoke in his palatial banking office trickle icily back into Alice's mind. Was he keeping Jim's secret too? But still, it is Mary whom Alice has grown close to; Mary whose honesty she deserved. Perhaps selfishly, Alice feels a flare of resentment; she thought they shared a kinship—surviving the awful unknown of a disappearance—but now Jim is saying that Mary might not have been as blind as it seemed.

"Wow!" Kit says. "I mean, we didn't know or . . ."

"You wouldn't be here. Right."

"So, you don't love her anymore?" Alice feels as if it is her own heart breaking. There is an unrelenting tightness in her chest and the feeling that tears may not be far behind.

"No," Jim says, softly. "I did. Very much. There was a time when I thought we'd always be together. I believed it, too. But I should have known better than to say that. I've learnt the hard way that nothing is forever. Not even love. People fall out of it too."

Alice gulps. She will not let herself get upset. Rather, she will rage—angry, triggered, indescribably disappointed. How dare he move on, when Mary is wearing herself to rags night after night, waiting for him?

"Do you miss her?"

"Some days, yes, of course I do. She brought me more happiness that anyone else ever has. For a while I was settled. But my head got in the way, like it always does; and when it did, she couldn't fix me. It isn't for someone else to do that. At the end of the day I had to do what I had to do. I won't be coming back." There is a silence and then, "That's not what you wanted to hear, is it?"

Kit goes to protest but the reality is written all over both their faces. Alice may not have known where Jim went or why, but if there was one constant in her daydreaming, it was the vision of the reunion. There would be tears and there would be joy, but most importantly there would be Jim, arms outstretched, and Mary folded into them again, finally. Alice, the girl who has always prided herself on her pragmatism—the antiromantic herself—has found herself swept up in a love story that she cannot shake, even as it is crumbling to pieces in front of her.

Jim goes back to staring out the window, his face a cipher. Alice can feel herself shaking with the fury and the frustration. How some people think they can walk in and out of other people's lives is beyond her. It is cruel, heartless, the lowest of the low. It takes everything in her to bite her tongue, not to lash out at Jim for destroying Mary, for being so selfish. Sensing this, Kit places a hand on her shoulder as he stands, half hauling Alice up with him.

"I suppose we ought to get going," he says. Jim doesn't look up. "Is there any message you'd like us to take back with us? For Mary?"

For a minute there is silence. Alice is outraged. Jim has nothing to say for himself, and she can't say she is surprised. A coward through and through.

"Tell her that it was nothing to do with her, or what was said the last time we were together. I don't want her punishing herself over that. It was nothing; my decision was made long before then."

"What?"

Jim does not appear to have heard Alice. Either that or he does not intend to answer any more of her questions. "Tell her that I'm sorry. Tell her to move on." When he manages to tear his eyes away from the window and looks at Alice, they are glassy. "She has always deserved so much better than me."

44

2018

The bed in the inn is as uncomfortable as they come. The mattress springs jab between Alice's ribs and the cotton sheet is worn to transparency. But that is not the reason why Alice cannot sleep. Her head is fit to explode—what just happened at the cottage, with Jim?

She still hasn't come to terms with the fact that they located him, let alone the revelation that Mary knew he didn't want to be found. It didn't seem likely that Jim was lying. Everything he said tallied with what they had already gleaned: the fact that he jumped before he was pushed at work; as Gus said, it couldn't have been Happy Families at home, not if Jim was struggling to that extent. Even the mention of the drink made sense. Didn't Ted say that he had called Mary at NightLine after hitting the bottle? That would help explain how she confused the two voices and, as Alice can now attest, there isn't much else to tell them apart.

But no, Alice shouldn't—can't—believe the word of a man she has met for less than half an hour, over that of Mary. She needs to hear Mary's side of the story. But if she is to extract that, then Alice will have to admit that she ignored Mary's wishes and went behind her back to track down Jim. And what will Mary say to that?

Snatches of the evening play on repeat in Alice's mind, on a loop that she cannot mute. *Tell her that it was nothing to do with her, or what was said the last time we were together.* What did Jim mean? Alice wants nothing more than to ask Mary—to source the final, elusive detail in the puzzle of Jim's disappearance—but another part of her knows that she has already crossed bounds of privacy that feel ethically uneasy at best, downright wrong at worst.

Which leaves Alice feeling conflicted about her article for the *Bugle,* to put it mildly. With the information gleaned earlier in the day, she could well have an exposé on her hands. Jack would, needless to say, be thrilled. It might be enough to keep the threat of redundancy at bay. Why then does she feel absolutely no desire whatsoever to write the piece? By some mad paradox, it is as if the closer Alice has come to finding Jim, the less her investigation seems to be about him at all.

My head got in the way, like it always does. The words came from Jim, but they might as well have been from Kit, or Ted for that matter. All the men who have entered Alice's life in the last month, and not one of them is able to open up about his feelings in a way that might have brought him back from the brink of some terrible decisions. And then there is her dad. Alice was too young when he disappeared to have any real sense of how his mental health might have pushed him to leave. But if he was prepared to walk out without so much as a note, then the chances are that he was in a very dark place indeed.

It doesn't excuse what he did, abandoning his family, but it does help to explain it. Alice could never conceive why it was *her* burning with rage over her dad's disappearance, while her mum seemed to have skipped the anger and the ire and the fury, in favor of a crippling grief. Now she wonders if it was her mum's greater understanding of his headspace that set her apart. To confirm that theory, though, Alice and her mum need to talk, and that is beyond overdue.

At least her sleepless delirium makes her decisive. Alice types a text to her mum—Thinking of coming home the weekend after next, if that's okay?—and sends it before she can redraft herself into avoidance. A response arrives almost immediately: her mum will be delighted. It's a small step, but at least it is in the right direction. Alice has been so busy telling herself that she was fully over her dad that she never stopped to consider whether she had halted before clearing the final hurdle. It has taken meeting Mary for Alice to realize that acceptance isn't a competition. More of a not-so-Fun-Run race, perhaps? Her finishing line looks to be in sight. But everyone crosses it in their own time.

Over breakfast the next morning, even Kit is subdued. It is clear that neither he nor Alice knows how to broach the magnitude of Jim's admissions last night. The only certainty is that Jim will not be coming back to Ealing. Mary will have to find it within herself to move on, alone.

While Kit loads their bags into the car, Alice heads to the bar to settle up.

"On the house," Tony says. Turns out he hadn't been outstaying his welcome at the bar yesterday—he owns the place.

"Are you sure?"

He nods. Alice can almost hear her bank account weeping in relief.

"Thank you. That's very generous and we really appreciate it. Appreciate everything." There is no point in saying *see you soon,* not when Alice knows she will never be back. "Take care, then."

"Hold up—this is for you." Tony produces an envelope from beneath the bar and slides it over. "Not for you, but for you to take." Written in handwriting she does not recognize is just one word—*Mary.* "From Sam. Jim. James. You know what I mean. It was on the doormat when I woke up this morning. He left me a separate note saying he wanted you to deliver it as soon as you get back."

"I'll make sure Mary gets it," Alice says, slipping it into her handbag.

It is 8 A.M. by the time they hit the road. The GPS is predicting a twelve-hour journey home, and Kit is confident they will make it back without an overnight stop. He told Alice that his mate needs the car back by tomorrow, but part of Alice wonders if the appeal of sharing a room with her has all but dissolved after she pushed him away. She does not have the mental space to evaluate quite how this makes her feel. Hurt? Probably. Frustrated with herself? Absolutely.

Kit, however, appears to have already bounced back from the brush-off and, if he is nursing a bruised ego, it is impossible to tell. Once they hit the open road, Magic FM is blaring and Kit is singing along. Never have quite so many classic pop songs been butchered, or in quite such style. At one point he is so engrossed in his own karaoke that he nearly misses an exit and Alice's handbag skids across the footwell. Jim's letter to Mary falls out.

She turns it over, tests the seal. What can it possibly say? If it contains even so much as a fraction of what Jim admitted in his cottage—that he no longer loves Mary—then she will be floored. To have all those years of hope dissolve in the instant of reading? Alice can feel her throat struggling to choke down a sob. It is an unbearable, impossible sadness. No one deserves that—no one. Especially not Mary.

In the face of Mary's impending heartbreak, Alice has all but forgotten her frustration that they could well have been on a wild-goose chase. If Mary knew more than she was letting on . . . but it's a pointless thought process now. Besides, where does the blame really lie? Mary asked Alice not to try to find Jim. Only Kit could complain of being sent on a futile mission, and he said they shouldn't see it like that. They have a letter for Mary. And as Kit put it, it is a letter that could help Mary start to heal, however painful those first steps may be.

As for Alice, their week on the road has shown her that there is an awful lot she could learn from her unlikely choice of companion—his patience, his candor, his superhuman capacity for forgiveness. Just nothing vocal. She dozes off to the tortured sounds of "Bohemian Rhapsody," à la Kit.

By the time they reach the outskirts of Ealing, Alice is aware that she can't prolong the inevitable for much longer. She has promised Jack an article on Monday, and an article he needs, if there is to be any chance of salvaging her career.

She opens up her work email in-box on her phone and, once it has loaded, clicks on the new message icon.

Hi, Jack,

Can we set a meeting for 10 A.M. Monday? I will send my exposé by Sunday evening, latest.

Best,

Alice

She adds her footer (it's time Jack started to take her seriously) and is about to click Send when Kit has her check the inside lane as he pulls into a parking space near the station. It being a Saturday night, most spaces are taken, but Kit seeks out the final spot like a bloodhound. He narrowly misses taking out not one, but two side mirrors.

"Here we are!" He turns the engine off and there is silence in the car for the first time since they set off. The radio must be overheating.

"Thank you for coming," Alice says. Her right hand is itching to reach for his, to squeeze it tight. She loses track of all the little things Kit does that drive her around the bend—the pidgin Spanish, the foot-in-mouth comments, the complete and utter lack of irony—and yet she is struggling to see how she will manage without him when they part ways tonight. She checks herself. She cannot give in to these thoughts, and she sits on her hand instead. "I couldn't have done it without you."

"Nah!" Kit bats her gratitude away. "You could have, easily. You're determined—I like that about you." The temperature in the car seems suddenly to have doubled. Alice is keen to attribute it to the shard of late-evening sunlight piercing through the windscreen, but that is wishful thinking and she is beginning to realize it, too. "Will I get your bag?"

"It's fine—I'll do it." Alice drops her phone on the dashboard and gets out of the car. She pulls her seat forward so she can collect her rucksack, but one of the straps has got trapped and it takes her a minute and several firm yanks to set it free. "Finally! Right, I'd better be off. I'll let you know how it goes with Mary."

But Kit does not reply. He has a face like thunder, one that refuses to meet hers. Alice tries to work out what he is staring at—the awful personalized number plate ahead? That would usually make him laugh but, instead, it is as if his habitual good humor has been sucked out of him, an unresponsive zombie left in his place. Alice looks down at the dashboard. Her phone has moved a few centimeters to the right. The screen is still illuminated.

"*Exposé,* eh?" Kit says.

Alice's face is burning up and it is suddenly very difficult to breathe.

"Why were you looking—"

"I was trying to pass it to you. So you didn't forget it."

"Look, Kit, I can explain—"

The engine flares. "I don't want to hear it. I can put two and two together—I'm not stupid. I thought you were better than this, Alice. Or maybe I *am* stupid, because I never suspected this. Not once. I thought you genuinely wanted to help Mary. To do something 'worthwhile'? But no, it was all for a newspaper story. I can't believe you walked around telling people you were her *friend*."

"Please, Kit," Alice drops her bag at her feet and runs to the front of the car. She wants him to look in her eyes, to see that she is still the same Alice. The one he has spent 24/7 with for the last few days. The one he held in his arms, all through their one unforgettable night in Inverness. The one who is still a good person, contrary to what that email might have suggested.

Kit leans over to shut the passenger door. Before he does, he adds, "You were prepared to drag me into it too. I don't deserve that, Alice, I just don't."

"That wasn't the plan—please let me explain. That wasn't why I wanted to find Jim. Work wasn't the real reason . . ."

She wants to explain the irony that she hasn't checked her *Bugle* emails once since she embarked on their road trip, but the words are lost to the sound of the Micra reversing.

There is nothing she can do but watch as the car pulls out into the main road, its shape blurred by her tears.

45

2011

"So, Mary, why are you looking for a job with us here at SuperShop?"

Mary hadn't worn her suit since she moved to London. She hadn't had the need to find work that required one, and it had hung at the back of the wardrobe for six years now, the black sateen cover accruing a thin layer of dust. If it hadn't been for the trauma that was her new existence—the fact that she could hardly face the sight of the fridge, let alone stomach any food—she doubted she would have fitted into it.

In the three months that had passed since Jim's disappearance she hadn't been able to look at her sewing machine, let alone fulfill any of her existing orders. Three clients revoked their commissions due to the uncommunicated delay, and Mary hadn't responded to any new business inquiries. Last week the website company had emailed through an invoice for the renewal of her domain name and the associated software. Mary let it lapse. She would only ever associate her maps with Jim—his promise to go to the ends of the earth for her. It would be too painful to continue her work without him.

"I've had a recent change in circumstances."

Janet, her interviewer, gave a smile and clicked the nib of her pen away, placed her clipboard back on the desk. "Life's funny like that, isn't it?" She couldn't have been much older than Mary.

When she had greeted Mary at the help desk earlier that morning, Janet had inadvertently twisted her wrist to show three names tattooed in a thick script with sharp serifs, a font that reminded Mary of medieval illuminations. Her children, Mary assumed. If anything seemed funny, it was how fast and how far adult lives could diverge, once you were out of the starting blocks of childhood.

"Well, Mary. It's been a pleasure to meet you and I'd love to have you on board. You say you're available for an immediate start? We need all the help we can get in the run-up to Christmas."

Mary forced herself to nod. "That's great news."

It certainly didn't feel that way as she powered her way out of the automatic doors and up the incline to the main road. At the crosswalk she was held up by a man in an orange high-vis jacket pushing a snake of metal shopping carts back to their storage area. Maybe it would be great news if Mary wanted this life, if there was something wrong with her old one. But there wasn't. There was only a single flaw in it—an absence so large that she couldn't see a way for her life to carry on around it.

She hadn't got the hang of her new flat and it took a few attempts to get the key in the lock on the inside door. Once inside, she threw her bag on the sofa, and then herself. There was little evidence that she had lived there for the last six weeks. She'd accrued so few belongings during her time in London—so few that she could unequivocally claim were *hers,* as opposed to *theirs*—that she had filled only enough boxes to warrant a taxi, a small one at that. The four of them lay, still taped, in a pile by the kitchen garbage can in the corner. She had left her sewing machine in the back of a cupboard at the old flat. Maybe the new owners could get some enjoyment out of it, whereas hers had waned to the point of destruction.

When more bills had started coming in, Mary knew her days in the flat she and Jim had shared together were numbered. Part of her wanted to stay, so she could still breathe in the scent of Jim that lingered on the surface of his pillows first thing in the morning or in the unbearable wild between midnight and morning, when dawn seemed impossibly far away. The other part of her was tormented by the reality of waking up every day in a space that her mind and her body knew had been shaped for the two of them. There were two towels hanging on the back of the door, room for her clothes alongside his in the drawers.

In the end the decision was taken out of her hands. Less than two weeks after his visit, Richard called to say they were selling the flat. Those were the instructions and he was sorry, but he would give her as much notice as possible about when she needed to move out. Mary was about to hang up when Richard added that Juliette had decided they would be getting rid of the house in Notting Hill too. *She's always loved Italy,* he muttered. *We'll buy a place in Tuscany.* Mary tried to picture the pair of them surrounded by other expat retirees, out for lunch in the sole restaurant of a hilltop village. All she could see was the black cloud they would be bringing with them.

Two days later Mary left the flat and took the cheapest place she could find online. The deposit would pretty much wipe her out, but the landlady had been good enough to take a postdated check, which had left Mary just enough money to tide her over until she could get a proper job that would pay her a regular wage.

She had thought about going back to the hotels; from what she knew, they still paid better than working the tills at a supermarket. She had even gone so far as to research what was within walking distance, before she noticed that the nearest high-end venue offered wedding and conference services in the banner at the top of their web page. It would be impossible to work either of those without seeing Jim on the first day they met—dashing in that ridiculous collarless shirt. The thought of another wedding reception made her eyes smart.

Starting work at SuperShop wasn't too bad. The staff were kind, and Janet as good a manager as anyone could wish for. She took Mary under her wing, giving her the quieter tills at the far end of the concourse and never positioning her on the *Can I Help?* station, where staff were expected to provide compelling explanations for the inflation on risotto rice and the shape of the odd, unfortunate cucumber. Janet even invited Mary to supper at her house after a Wednesday shift, a few weeks in. Mary declined, although there was a part of her that regretted it. Janet was the sort to have a nice, welcoming home.

By far the hardest part of Mary's new reality was having to walk back from work past the flat they used to share. It was one thing to have to train your feet not to walk up to the front door on autopilot, quite another to see an unknown couple in situ, their arms draped around each other as they cooked in the evening, in full view of the street.

Once, Mary was watching when the radio started up. It must have been a song that held some special resonance because she could see them share a smile a split second before they began to shimmy along the side of the breakfast bar. Mary found herself confronted with an image of the future that had been snatched from her—or would have been, were it not for the fact that she simply could not let go. When the tune finished, the woman turned to open the window, breathless and giddy. Mary hurried away before she saw Mary staring.

It was best not to compare her old and new flats, for sanity's sake, or what little there was left of it. There wasn't much in the way of furniture in the new—a brown faux-leather armchair repurposed for the kitchen-cum-dining-cum-living-room and a sofa in crimson corduroy, which had worn away in shabby, pale patches. A phone poked out from under it, old enough for it still to connect with a spiral wire to a plug socket hidden somewhere out of sight.

That night Mary picked it up and, without thinking, dialed home. She hadn't expected it to connect, even less so to get an answer.

"Mary, is that you?" Mam had said, when it was clear the caller wasn't going to provide the introduction. "I've been so worried about you, doll. You have barely been in touch since you let me know you had landed back from your flight safely."

A small sob escaped Mary's lips and she knew then that she was done for. The floodgates had opened, the tears coming so fast and so thick that she couldn't get a breath out between them.

Mam said nothing, bar the occasional verbal equivalent of an extended hand to dry her eyes—*There, there, don't you worry now, I'm here*—the refrains of a stoicism that, in her suffering, Mary had left far behind. She cried until she retched. She rolled onto her side and a thin strand of bile trailed out of her mouth and onto her hand.

"Hush now, I'm here. Okay, it's okay. I'm here. You start me from the top now, Mary. Don't leave anything out."

Somehow she found the words. Most of them, that was. There was no way she could tell Mam what had passed between her and Jim before she boarded the flight for her birthday.

"I knew there was something wrong when he didn't come over with you."

"I should never have left him."

"Mary Kathleen, I will not hear you speaking like that. You have nothing to feel guilty about, do you hear me? Nothing at all."

"But, Mam, he . . ."

"I mean that. No more, Mary. We've got to get you back up on your feet. Will you come home?"

"I can't." Her voice shook but there was something firmer beneath it. She hadn't told Mam about signing the new lease—the only certainty in Mary's heart being that she had to stay nearby, in Ealing. "I can't leave here. He needs to know that I'll be here."

Because this was by no means the end. This was just another period. Another bad period to wait out until Jim came to his senses. He had said it, hadn't he? He needed Mary to be a safe place to come home to.

"Doll, come back to Belfast. What are you going to be able to do there now? Sure, haven't the police said there's nothing more you can do?"

Mary choked down a lump of snot in her throat. How to say that she had never followed up with the liaison officer, to confirm what Richard had told her? The business card he had left would be decomposing in a landfill site already. Better that than her last vestiges of hope.

"Are you still there?"

Mam rang back all evening. But Mary wasn't there to hear the calls coming so fast one after the other that the girl manning the chippy downstairs assumed a sticky CD had been left on.

No, Mary had somewhere far more important to be—outside the front of the station, sign in hand. Until Jim reached her outstretched arms, she would put them to better use. She would be the first thing he saw as he set foot off the train. Just like the old days, Mary told herself. Just like the old, happier days, when seeing Jim barreling through the ticket gates toward her after work was enough, in itself, to keep the world at bay.

He would see that she was sorry.

He would see that, contrary to what was said, Mary would never be better off without him.

46

2018

Saturday nights outside the station are never easy. While commuters travel alone, weekenders travel in packs and there is nothing that accentuates solitude quite like being alone in a crowd. The worst is seeing couples, unwilling to let go of their clasped hands even when the ticket machines demand it. When was the last time someone held Mary's hand like that?

She thinks back to Thursday evening, at NightLine. Ted came close to it. She knew he wanted to. And although she made no obvious move to reciprocate, part of Mary hoped that he would buck up the courage that she lacked, or rather lost, the minute Jim walked out of her life. But what is she doing, thinking like that? She is holding a sign for her first love, and there is no place and no space to be thinking about anyone else.

This little piece of cardboard is her last link to Jim and the best days of her life. When she first came to the station, sign in hand, Mary needed to feel that she was doing something—*anything*—to change Jim's mind. Seven years on and Mary still does not know how an action that she started as a means of survival has become the bedrock of her identity. Until she figures that out, her feet will keep finding their way to this same spot, whatever else she might have on her mind.

A group of drunken partygoers swing round the corner and almost smack right into Mary.

"Sowree," one slurs. "My bad."

When they move on, shrieking all the way to the escalators, Mary readjusts her footing and looks out to the road ahead. It is its usual indistinct blur, bar the sight of one very familiar traveler lingering by the traffic lights.

Alice smiles when Mary sees her.

"Do you fancy a drink?" Alice says, once she has reached Mary. She is wearing a battered wax jacket. She has a large camping rucksack in tow and her eyes are blotchy.

Mary's palms are sweating, slipping against the frayed edges of her cardboard sign. Her ears are ringing with such vengeance that the background hum and thump of the gates and the machines has all but disappeared. She knows there is no way out of what comes next.

For years she has shielded her eyes from the truth, and now there is a chance it is about to be hand delivered to her by a young woman who was but a stranger just a matter of weeks ago. And if that is the case, then life as Mary knows it will be over. She consoles herself with the fact that Alice still wants to speak to her. If she has discovered anything, it cannot therefore be that bad—can it?

"Sure," Mary replies. She hopes the tremble in her voice isn't as obvious to Alice as it is to her.

At the pub she finds a table outdoors while Alice buys the drinks. When she returns with two large G and Ts, Mary slurps a third of hers in one go—and it is a double.

"So how was your trip to Málaga?" she asks.

Alice's eyes flick between the exit and Mary. "Yes, well . . . the thing is, we weren't actually in Málaga."

Mary knew it. Her stomach gurgles. Gut instinct, indeed. She takes a deep breath. "You went to look for Jim, didn't you?"

"I'm sorry."

There is a pause when neither is certain quite how to proceed.

Because without knowing what Alice has found out, how can Mary know whether or not she forgives her?

"We found him," Alice says, eventually.

Mary looks surprised. So much so that, momentarily, Alice considers whether Jim was telling the truth.

"He said that the police found him, seven years ago. He said that he asked them to pass along the message that he was fine. That he didn't want to be found."

All Mary wants to do is slam her hands over her ears and deny the stream of words pouring out of Alice's mouth. But if she does that now, when will this end?

"The police told his parents that," Mary corrects. "They were the next of kin."

"And did his parents pass that message along?"

Mary just about manages a nod. "But I couldn't believe them," she says. "So they told me to confirm it with the police, but . . ." She digs her nails into her palm until the pain becomes unbearable. "I couldn't. I never confirmed it with the police, I mean. I thought it was better to live with the hope that his parents were wrong than to know for certain that they were right."

Alice closes her eyes, still swollen from her recent tears. That was what Mary meant when she said that the unknown was not the worst thing in the world. It is all falling into place.

"I'm sorry." Alice pushes her glass to one side and reaches across to place her hand on Mary's. "You could have told us; we would never have gone following those leads."

"I asked you not to go."

"I know, and I'm sorry. I thought bringing you answers would end all that awful uncertainty. I didn't realize you already had the answers, or that you didn't want to . . ."

"Comprehend," Mary says quietly. "I didn't have the strength to handle what the police might say. If they told me Jim wasn't coming back—that it was the end—then I would have died. So I never called. I let myself die inside, instead." Her voice has thinned into a reed of agony. "You're not angry, are you? That I didn't tell you? That you went after him?"

Alice shakes her head. "I have no right. I ignored your wishes. And I know it was wrong, but I genuinely thought closure was the best thing for you. There is some knowledge that you can't live without. It's impossible. In my life—in my own experience . . ." She stalls. The last thing she wants to do is belittle Mary's suffering by introducing her own. Or is that just another excuse for Alice to avoid her own issues? Before she has finished wrestling with herself, Mary interrupts.

"How was he?" All these years and she has never for one minute stopped caring.

"He was well. He looked healthy. You don't need to worry about that."

"What did he say?" Mary is thirsty for information. After a seven-year drought, one small, sweet droplet will do.

"He said that he wants you to move on," Alice says. Mary's head jerks downward, tears beginning to course down the bridge of her nose. "I'm so sorry, Mary."

"No." Mary removes her hand from Alice's and wipes at her eyes. "No, it's my fault." She tries to take a deep breath but it is an effort to get any oxygen in at all. Alice squeezes her hand and Mary rushes the words out with the last of the energy in her. "I . . . I couldn't accept it. That wasn't what we promised each other, Jim and me. We promised each other we'd be there, to the ends of the earth, but he . . . he changed his mind."

The tears are coming thick and fast now, and Alice gives up her seat on the other side of the picnic bench in favor of squashing next to Mary, one arm wrapped around her shoulders. She finds a tissue in her pocket, thankfully unused, and offers it to Mary. She can't hear what Mary is saying for her sobs.

"I understand."

"You can't." Mary's voice is raw from crying, the last syllable breaking out as a croak.

"Really I can." Mary turns to look at Alice, her brows furrowed. "My dad disappeared."

Alice realizes that she has never said those words before. Not aloud. Not to anyone other than her mum and, even then, she sometimes wonders whether the words have actually come out, such is the blank stare that meets her. To this day, her mum still refuses to acknowledge the reality of the situation. Denial—it's much more common than anyone would ever think.

"He disappeared when I was twelve. We didn't hear a peep from him, my mum and I, until I was sixteen. We had no idea where he was, if he was okay. Then, on my sixteenth birthday, I got a card from him. It said that I had two new half-siblings. Wherever he had gone, he'd made a new family, just like that. Never bothered to see the old one again. Never left a return address, either.

"And I've moved on now. Or, rather, I thought I had, until I started to try and find Jim and it took the trip to show me that I'm not there yet. I can't suppress the memories and hope they'll go away. At least you are expressing your loss. I can't say how much I respect you for that. But you need answers too. That's why I wouldn't give up on finding Jim. I know how awful it is to not know. I didn't want that for you too."

Mary lets herself collapse into Alice, so their foreheads touch, briefly. Alice can feel the cold of Mary's tears on her cheek and reaches up to brush them away, only to realize that they are, in fact, hers.

"You know what's even worse?" Alice continues. "I told myself it was my fault. If only I had done something more to keep him there, at home—for me and Mum—he never would have left. I told myself that I pushed him away."

Mary rubs her hand across the arch of Alice's back. "You were only a child, it had nothing to do with you. It's not your fault."

"You need to believe that too." Mary blinks heavily, and Alice knows that is as much assent as she can expect. Alice straightens up. She thinks of Jim, the self-loathing in his explanations. He said it himself: his mental anguish was never Mary's fault, but it nonetheless landed at her feet.

Then she thinks of Kit and Ted and her dad—no one had the answers to whatever they were going through. But it wasn't about solutions—was it? It was about support. And no one is better at that than Mary. "Whatever you think you might have said or done, it was bigger than you. Jim's problems were far greater than you could fix. At some point you have to forgive yourself. You have to let it go."

"What then?"

"What do you mean?" Alice asks.

"What do I do when I let it go? Who am I then?" Mary bites down on the pad of her thumb. "I started that vigil because I wanted Jim to know that I wasn't giving up. Not when I last saw him, and not afterward, either. Everyone else could abandon him: the police, his friends, his parents. But I loved him. I thought that meant something. And eventually, even when I realized that wasn't the case—that me standing there making a fool of myself was never going to be enough—I was too scared to stop because I didn't know what would happen then. I didn't know what I would be without it. Without him."

Alice waits until she is certain Mary's eyes will not wander from hers.

"You are so much else. Do you hear me? You are so much more than the woman with a sign."

47

2018

Alice watches as the second hand on the wall clock slides to mark one minute past the hour. *10:01* A.M. Jack has never been known for his timekeeping, but Alice had hoped that his punctuality would improve by nature of the fact he has some VIPs in the office today. Namely—the shareholders.

She restrains the urge to check her work email in-box for an early indication that he liked her article. There are no guarantees. Because what she emailed to Jack last night, in advance of today's meeting, wasn't much of an exposé. Not in the traditional sense, at least.

After she left Mary, Alice headed home for a grand total of five hours' sleep. Then, on Sunday, she was up with the dawn, laptop wobbling on her knees, a sheaf of notes spread around her legs, chronicling every stage of the investigation. There was a notebook detailing the particulars of the calls that transpired to be a hoax, all manner of research on how one could trace an anonymous phone line. There were printouts of search-engine results, pertinent tweets (Gus's highlighted), maps with red dots to show recent sightings, and Kit's own dossier. *Kit.* The thought of him was enough to send a horrible flush of shame through her body, along with the edge of another emotion that Alice hasn't the time to comprehend.

All in all, it was an awful lot of work to be swept into the garbage. But once Alice started on her new piece, the real story fell out of her. For years she had focused on doing the work that was directed toward her. With Mary, Alice finally found a story that she herself wanted to pursue. But the lengths she has gone to, in order to secure that piece, have taught her perhaps the most important lesson of all: that when it comes to telling stories, it isn't about want, it is about need. A journalist's job is to weave the narrative that demands to be told, not the one they wish they could steer. Alice may have found out where Jim went and why, but she *needed* to write a story that is altogether different. More authentic. More accurate.

She had typed five thousand words in no time and the rest of the day was spent polishing and honing the prose. By 9 P.M., as happy as she ever would be with her article, she emailed it to Jack. As soon as it was gone, she opened her personal account and sent it to Kit and Mary too. She has been so nervous about their response that she hasn't checked her email since.

"Alice." Jack is holding the door open for three tall men in suits. "Please meet Nigel, James, and Keith—the Bridge Media Group representatives who will be sitting in on all our staff consultations today." He arranges a pile of papers in front of him—on top, a copy of Alice's article.

A cold trickle of fear runs down her spine. The robotic formality of Jack's speech already has her hackles up—and that's before she begins to analyze what the hell a *staff consultation* is, anyway.

"Thank you for sending me your article last night," Jack continues. "I have shared it with the team here, and we are all in agreement that this is a wonderful and necessary piece." Alice wonders if she should interrupt with her thanks, but then she notices that Jack is avoiding her eye. Nigel and pals aren't looking any more engaged, either. "As I have emphasized to the wider team, you are a bright young talent and I have no doubt that you'll go far. I'm afraid, however, that it won't be with the *Bugle*."

"What do you mean?"

Jack finally looks up, his face contorted in a mixture of embarrassment and upset. "We are letting you go, Alice. HR will talk to you further about a redundancy pack—"

"But what about the article? You said that you liked it!"

Alice reaches across the desk for the copy that is sitting in front of Jack. She scans the opening again. No, she wasn't imagining it. This is a good feature. A *damn good* feature.

COME HOME, JIM

Male mental health—the silent epidemic enveloping Ealing's community

By Alice Keaton

If you are on social media, you will have seen it. Recently, local woman Mary O'Connor went viral after a video, taken without her permission, was uploaded to the internet. It showed Mary as she was interrupted from the vigil she has been keeping for the last seven years outside Ealing Broadway station. During it, she carries a sign that reads "Come Home Jim." Soon, everyone online was asking the same question—where was this mystery man? But it was what they *didn't* ask that was far more telling: What would make a successful doctor, with all the supposed trappings of happiness, abandon a gilded life?

Now, take a fifty-year-old single father, a twentysomething high-flying graduate, and a professional who has just celebrated his forty-second birthday. On the surface it might be hard to find a uniting strand, but give them space to speak and they will quickly find common ground in their personal struggles to break the stigma surrounding male mental health. Services such as NightLine, a local crisis call centre, do their best to manage the epidemic but, without council funding, their own future looks bleak. . . .

Alice doesn't read any further. She doesn't have the time to read the full five thousand words now, not with four pairs of eyes boring into her, awaiting her next move.

"Well, I'll be taking this with me," Alice says, standing up. Her chair legs screech against the floor. "Because, as you say, this is a very necessary piece, and I'm sure another publication will be able to provide a wider readership for it. Thank you very much for your time." She looks over at Jack. However frustrated and disappointed she may be, she owes him, for his faith in her. Alice knows he has fought tooth and nail to keep her in employment. "And for the opportunities you have provided during my time here. I am very grateful to you for that, Jack."

With that, she turns and walks away. Her heart is pounding, her legs are shaking and she is struggling to know which way is up. She knows that she should be feeling crushed, but somehow she has never felt quite as liberated. Even if the emotion is fleeting, she wants to cling on to its energy for as long as possible. She does not stop to talk to HR or to collect her belongings or to say any goodbyes. All of that can wait.

Out in the air, Alice feels like she can breathe properly for the first time in weeks. She said it to Mary: some problems are too big for one person alone to fix. It is not for her to convince the *Bugle* that they are making a mistake in not running her article. She will show them by finding it a better, bigger home.

That leaves her with two more manageable issues. She rolls her shoulders back with newfound confidence and heads for SuperShop.

Alice almost runs straight into Mary. She is unloading a crate of satsumas, her back to the automatic doors, but Alice would recognize that neatly pinned bun anywhere. As she approaches, she can see a pair of heavy, sand-colored boots next to her pumps. They are man-sized. Alice dives into the opposite aisle and pretends to examine a bunch of bananas. When she feels sufficiently inconspicuous, she glances up. It is Ted, deep in a conversation with Mary that is just out of Alice's range of hearing. Another day, then.

In the dried-goods aisle, she collects the items she needs and then goes to the checkout to pay. As she heads for the exit, she takes one more look over her shoulder at Mary, who is now rearranging some lemons while Ted acts out an anecdote in the manner of an amateur mime artist. For the first time since Alice met her, Mary is smiling. Properly. It is the sort of open-mouthed, teeth-and-all grin that suggests that the truth hasn't crushed her spirit. In the end, it might set her free.

One down, one to go. Alice jogs from SuperShop to her second destination, two streets away. The walk up six flights of stairs does not seem to be getting easier. Before she knocks, she wraps a ribbon around her gift and shoves the plastic wrapping into her handbag. It's now or never.

Kit may have been shoehorned into her life a short while ago, but the prospect of extracting him from it again looks very bleak indeed.

Alice raps her knuckles against the peeling paintwork and waits.

"What are you doing here?" Kit looks neither happy nor annoyed to see Alice on his doorstep. That is a good thing, right? She can work with startled.

In lieu of a response, she sticks her bouquet out in front of her. Five packets' worth of spaghetti, tied with a bow, brush against Kit's bare chest. It is probably a good thing there is a barrier of sorts between them. She wishes he had a top on. Or perhaps not. Either way, the sight is doing nothing to quell her nerves.

"What on earth is this?"

"An apology," Alice says. "Did you get my email?"

Kit nods. "It was a good piece."

"Thank you." Alice blushes. "They're not going to run it, though. I actually got made redundant today. Just now, in fact, so we'll have to see whether the article ever gets published. . . . But look, that's not why I'm here. You were right. You didn't deserve to be kept in the dark about my initial reasons for tracking down Jim. Not after everything you did to help me out."

"What were the real ones, then?"

Alice stares up at Kit blankly. Thirty-six hours apart and she has forgotten quite how sharp he is.

"You said *initial* reasons. So what were the subsequent and—I therefore infer—*real* reasons for wanting to find Jim?"

Would dating Kit be the intellectual equivalent of shacking up with a *University Challenge* contestant? Maybe some of his intelligence would rub off on her too, and she would end up curing cancer or finding the geopolitical solution to world peace. *Don't get ahead of yourself, Keaton.* He hasn't actually let her over the threshold yet.

"Can I come in?"

Kit raises one eyebrow, the hairs there as lawless as ever, then steps aside to allow Alice into the hallway.

Among the toppled shoes and clouds of mold, Alice feels her courage falter. Is she really going to tell Kit about her dad? She said it to Mary: opening up about her past is the final hurdle that she must vault, if she is ever to come to terms with her dad's disappearance. Besides, she can't lie. Not again. Kit deserves the truth. Especially after he was so honest about his own headspace. And she trusts him. More, perhaps, than she has ever allowed herself to trust anyone in her adult life. This last realization confirms Alice's decision. There is no hope of a future for the two them if she is not prepared to lay her true self bare.

Alice places her wheat-based peace offering on the coffee table. She sits on the edge of the settee and turns to face him. Any trace of hostility has been wiped from Kit's face. He gives a small smile of encouragement.

"There's a reason I don't let anyone close," she begins. "And it's the same reason why I was so fixated on finding Jim." She inhales as deeply as her palpitating chest will allow. "When I was a child, my dad disappeared, and for so long it felt like it was all my fault."

Ten minutes later and Alice has never felt quite as exposed. Not stark naked in the hotel room in Inverness. Not even when she broke down in Ealing's most public car park, two days ago. Kit has still not said a word. Alice tries to steady her breath. Maybe this is her cue to leave? But just as she is about to stand, the sofa groans. Kit shuffles forward until their knees touch.

"Thank you," he says. "For telling me."

Slowly, a little uncertainly, he removes one hand from his lap and places it on the back of Alice's neck. She feels the coolness at the base of her bob with all the relief of an oasis in the desert, the pressure on the most vulnerable part of her.

"For the record, I have no intention of leaving," Kit adds, running his thumb along the sinews of tension. "Not unless you ask me to. What do you say?"

Alice looks up. Maybe there is dependability and constancy yet. Because for every person who runs, surely another must stick around?

There is only one way to find out.

"Yes," Alice whispers, as Kit's lips brush against hers. "You can stay."

Six months later

Mary stands outside Ealing Broadway station, just down from the concrete porch and tucked to the left, where she won't be getting under the feet of the commuters. It is one of the first days of March and there is an admirable persistence to the rays that are still out at six o'clock in the evening. Satisfied with her spot, Mary takes in the view that she knows as well as her own reflection.

If she squints into the sun, she can make out the frontage of the pub where, six months ago, Alice confronted her with the truth that she had structured her life around avoiding. That moment felt so seismic that Mary couldn't understand how her body had continued with any of the motions of life at all. Her heart still beat, her lungs still inflated with ragged inhalations. But among the chaos of loss and shame and grief that ran riot through Mary's head, she knew this had to be it. The end. Her watershed, albeit one that had arrived seven years later than expected.

Now, as she waits outside the station with empty hands, Mary considers the peculiar way in which, despite our best efforts, life will always define itself into *befores* and *afters*. The dividing blow can only be delayed for so long. She feels this reality, perhaps, more than most—*before* she met Jim, *after* he disappeared. Then, with Alice, the most important distinction of all: before and after confirmation of what had happened to Jim.

Before, none of Richard's words had made sense and none of the sentences had tallied with Mary's understanding of the person who had been her rock, her all, her home. How could Jim have *chosen* not to come back? Whatever the police might have said, it was the decision of a man not in his right mind. A different man, a desperate man, and certainly not the man who had stood in a pub in Portrush and declared that he would be there for Mary, always, to the ends of the earth or Ealing.

After Alice's revelations, Mary was forced to revisit her past in a way she had never done before. She began by sifting through Jim's postcards. Whereas before, Mary found herself panning for gold—scooping up the sparkling fragments of their happiness together—she now forced herself to acknowledge the grit among those shards too. Had he been drinking on one of those business trips? Were the words laced with an apology for a loss that he knew might be to come? Although the exercise flayed her heart all over again, Mary needed to accept a more rounded picture of their life together. It made her appreciate the beauty of the golden days more because, without crushing lows, how can the soaring highs mean anything at all?

She made sure to commit to memory every compliment that had come from Jim's hand too. Then she forced herself to find as many examples of her own kindness and compassion and resilience as she could. Part of the reason she had never found the strength to confirm Richard's statement with the police was out of fear of how that knowledge might crush her sense of self-worth. But she is a different woman now. Stronger. She has walked through a blaze of pain every night outside the station and it has fortified her.

Finally she is tough enough to quash the voice that says if she were enough, then Jim would still be here; because, deep down, she knows it is never that straightforward. No amount of Mary's good qualities could balance out Jim's depression. We expect so much of love. And yet, like all of us, it can falter and it can fail. Mary has learned the hard way that love cannot always save the day. But it may well still show us how we can begin to save ourselves.

It is a process that starts alone, however grateful Mary is for the hard work Alice and Kit undertook on her behalf. Two days after their return, after forty-eight hours spent wrestling with the last of her deferred grief, Mary made the decision to hand in her notice on the flat in Ealing and at SuperShop. Then came the strange relief of a new set of concerns. Would she find a new job? How would NightLine manage without her? What of the friends she had made there? She told herself she would make it work—whatever that involved.

The new flat is less than an hour from London on the train but it may as well be half a world away. For her money, she has managed to rent a bigger space, on the ground floor too, so there is a garden. Now that there is nowhere for her to be after the end of her shift at the local co-op, she is coming to terms with the concept of free time for herself. She cooks elaborate suppers from recipe books that she sources from charity shops or after an afternoon's browsing in the local bookshop. Then she will move out onto the patio and watch the sunset from the inside of her own life, not the outside of someone else's. It turns out that the heart needs space to beat, every bit as much as it needs time.

Mary's first formal visitor to the countryside pad was Mam. Although there had been the odd trip to Belfast over the last few years and phone calls every few weeks, Mary had never told Mam what she said to Jim on the last morning they were together. She couldn't tell Mam what Jim's parents had reported, or that she hadn't the courage to confirm their story with the police. Mary had let Mam live in the darkness of Jim's disappearance, as she had with her colleagues and the team at NightLine.

But putting on a brave face is exhausting and it was only when Mary told Mam all this, her mug shaking between her hands, that she realized the toll her decision to shoulder the full story alone had taken on her. With every sentence, Mary could feel a load lifted. All the while Mam listened in silence. And then, when Mary had exhausted the story, her breath uneven as if she had returned from a long uphill run, Mam said, "I'm proud of you, doll."

Mary wasn't quite sure what she was expecting by way of response but that certainly was not it.

"What do you mean?"

"It takes a lot to do what you've done. To pick yourself up like you have. The past is the past and you're not to blame for a jot of it. I'm proud. And that's all I'll say on the matter."

Conversation closed, it was surprising how easily they fitted back into the patterns of their old relationship. They caught up on what was going on at home—the grandkids and Mam's hectic schedule juggling them all. They drank warm white wine on a picnic rug, attempted some weeding after half a bottle each. Ted had given plenty of instructions on how the flowerbeds were to be kept, but Mary found herself forgetting most of his tips. It was a nice excuse to text him now and again.

In the end, Mam and Mary had laughed so much they had to give up on their half-hearted gardening altogether. They made plans for Mary to visit Belfast more often—a chance to rekindle her friendship with Moira too—and then just before Mam left for her flight home, she handed Mary an envelope. *A wee thank-you note,* she said. Mary tucked it up on the mantelpiece to read once she had seen Mam off at the airport.

That night, when Mary opened it, a check for £1,000 floated out of the sandwiched sides of the card and onto the carpet. *Your da had a little bit stashed away for you all,* it said. *To buy something for yourself. That's what he would have wanted.* At first Mary was so moved and so grateful that she had no idea how to spend the money. She had never been one for fancy things, possessions even less. And then it came to her—the object that she felt the closest affinity with, the object that allowed her to create new worlds.

With her sewing machine, Mary has started work on her first fabric map since Jim's disappearance. She had built up so many layers of dread around how the sewing would feel, the memories it might evoke, that the reality could only ever feel easier. At the center of this piece lies Ealing Broadway station. From it stretch the arteries of Mary's life for the past few years: SuperShop, the park where Ted confessed his feelings, NightLine HQ. Connecting them all, the paths Mary has walked countless times, with each step wondering where disappointment ends and something new can eventually take root.

The answer to that lies in the finish: chain stitch. From afar, the overlapping threads look exactly like clasped hands. Mary did it manually. She owes Alice. She owes them all. After so many years thinking hers was a cross to bear alone, Mary needed a little hand-holding of her own to see a different, brighter future. Tonight the fruits of her labor will find a new home, but for now they sit in the inside pocket of her rucksack, the calico so much softer against her shoulders than the cardboard sign ever was.

As for the sign itself, well, by now it will be in a recycling plant, perhaps already converted into a cereal box or a kitchen-roll tube. The disposal was far from easy but it was another thing that was harder in anticipation than reality. Now, it mainly feels strange to Mary that she is standing here and not doing the vigil. But everything reaches its own, natural conclusion. Not dissimilar to love, Mary thinks. There are no guarantees that any relationship will last. The fact that people will still go for it anyway, aware of that risk, is perhaps the most beautiful part of it all.

"Mary!" Ted is jogging toward her, one hand raised in greeting. "I almost didn't recognize you—the hair!"

"Oh." She smooths her hand over the back of it, her fingers lingering over the point where the razored strands meet the skin at the nape of her neck. It is a pixie crop, something Mary saw when she was flicking through the magazines waiting for her appointment, and which she extended to the stylist in a moment of madness. "What do you think?"

"You're amazing." Ted coughs. "I mean, you look amazing. It suits you, it does."

Mary looks down at her feet in the hope it might help her blush pass faster. When she looks up, she is relieved to see that Ted looks as uncomfortable about his choice of words as she does.

"It's good to see you again," he says, as they pick their way through the crowds of after-work drinkers in their shirttails, pints in hand. "I'm sorry I couldn't make it over with the plants last weekend. Tim was back and he needed lifts and . . . Anyway, I missed you. It. The visit, I mean."

"Me too." She looks up at Ted and is surprised to see that he is wearing a shirt, a proper one—none of the polo business. He has the sleeves rolled up, his forearms exposed. Very shapely they are too.

"Do you think this is it?" Ted looks down at his phone, then up at the house in front of them. It is one of the huge detached properties a stone's throw from the main road, which he has most likely worked at before. "This can't be right . . ."

Before they have a chance to figure it out, the front door opens and Alice appears. She looks younger. As she approaches, Mary realizes that she is bare-faced, not a trace of makeup in sight.

"Mary! I've missed you." Much may have changed, but Mary's statutes on personal space have not. It takes a second or two for her to acclimate to the hug. She tries to focus on identifying the smell in Alice's perfume—is it grapefruit? Or something else with a punch of zest? "You are the guest of honor."

Alice leads Mary up the stairs and into the house, Ted following behind. The setting would be enough to overawe anyone—pillars on either side of the front door, impenetrable art in huge frames lining the walls of the hallway—but it is an effort for both Mary and Ted to keep their mouths from falling open and dusting the flagstone floor. They walk straight into the kitchen, where Kit is at the stove, a tea towel thrown over one shoulder. He comes over and kisses Mary on the cheek. He smells like grapefruit too.

Just as Mary's mind is making the connections, Kit returns from the fridge where he has deposited Ted's bottle and wraps an arm around Alice's waist. It seems their road trip wasn't a wasted journey.

"You never told us you lived like a king, Kit," Ted says, walking over to the glass doors at the back of the room and surveying the garden beyond.

"Could have bought some jeans without the holes." Olive is seated at the dining table, tucked out of sight from the door, flicking through a cooking magazine with glossy pages that give a satisfying thwack as she turns them.

"*Gracias,*" Kit says, rolling his eyes out of Olive's sight. "It's my parents' place, actually, but I thought it might do for tonight, given we're celebrating."

Ted's jaw drops and he homes in on Alice's ring finger.

"Not like that," Alice says. She brushes off the suggestion so quickly that even Kit gives a wry smile. "I got a new job."

When Mary read Alice's article, she was impressed. It was sensitive, yet hard-hitting, the anonymized portraits of Jim, Ted, and Kit faithfully represented. Should she have spotted that Alice was a journalist? It would explain her persistence and her chronic nosiness. Two days later Mary responded to her email, asking Alice why she hadn't run the simpler story: where Jim had gone and why. *It wouldn't have been right*—that was what Alice had said. Mary was pleased that her trust in Alice had never, truly, been misplaced.

And tonight they are celebrating a much bigger coup. Alice sold the piece as a freelancer and, on the back of its success, has earned herself a place on the features desk at a broadsheet. She found out about the role when she was at her mum's house for the weekend. The novelty of their closeness has yet to wear off on Alice. She has learned so much more about her dad—now his name is no longer *verboten*. Not all of it has been easy to hear but her mum made one thing crystal clear: he always loved her, even if he wasn't in the right frame of mind to show it.

Alice has been so busy with the new job that she has had to give up NightLine for the time being. It is a wrench, but one that is tempered by the fact that, in part due to the awareness raised by her piece, there are rumors of independent funding for the organization. As everyone keeps saying, it is early stages. Nothing is confirmed, but in the meantime Olive and Kit keep the lines open and Ted is back answering calls too.

After six months of stewing over how they would respond, Kit's parents took the news that he had left the soul-sucking world of banking surprisingly well and he has moved back home until he gets himself on his feet. Ted mentioned that Kit is looking into retraining as a counselor, which prompted Mary to ask how he himself was getting along. *Better,* Ted said, although Mary could already see that, from his renewed brightness. It is proof, to her, that "crisis point" is something of a misnomer—it doesn't have to point to continued crisis, not for everyone.

Even with the noise and the laughter and the wine, it is easy for Mary to zone out of their celebration supper. She knows that she will never be able to forget Jim. He is as much a part of her as the blood in her veins, the air in her lungs. She wonders where he is (Alice never told and she, in turn, would never ask). She wonders if he is alone or whether he has found someone new. She wonders if he ever found contentment—what that would look like for him.

She runs a hand along the table, haphazardly wiped down by Kit.

In the middle lies the map she made for Alice, a thank-you of sorts. It is Ealing, yes, but more than that; it is the network of roads and rail lines, of parks and plains and buildings that have watched her heart break, and which have seen the first steps toward putting it back together again. Mary looks up at the four faces beaming and bantering over the strewn cutlery. She may never move back, but the coordinates of this place are tattooed on her for life.

"I have an announcement." Kit clears his throat. Everyone looks nervous, Alice included. "If we could all assemble in the garden, I have prepared a bonfire. Done a bit of the old spring cleaning, haven't I, and I thought . . ."

He rattles a box of firelighters in his right hand, and Mary sees Olive's hands tighten around her wine glass. There should be a law against letting Kit loose with pyrotechnics.

Ted takes the offending item out of Kit's hand. "Why don't I do the honors, eh?"

Olive shoots Mary a glance that says they have narrowly avoided making an emergency call to the fire department. They share a laugh before Olive follows Kit and Ted outside.

"Are you coming?" Alice asks, as she lingers by the patio doors.

The rest of the group are already clustered around what Mary gathers must be the bonfire heap, their silhouettes illuminated by the moonlight.

"In a minute." She smiles to reassure Alice that she is alright, that she won't break down when Alice's back is turned. Not anymore. "I'll catch you all up out there—don't wait for me."

Finally alone in the kitchen, Mary pulls out the letter from the inside zipper pocket of her rucksack. Since Alice gave it to her on the night of her return six months ago, Mary has pored over the contents more times than she would care to admit.

She presses the paper flat against the table and begins to read, for one last time:

Dear Mary,

Tonight I met some of your friends. Kit, Alice—they're quite something. I'm glad you have people like that in your life. Ones who will protect you and buoy you in the way I wasn't able to. By the time you read this, they will have returned home. I hope one or the other is with you while you read. I have always hated to think of you alone.

I saw the video and, before you burn up in embarrassment, let me tell you that it was one of your finest hours. You have always inspired me. As for what I read, I couldn't believe my eyes. I was never worthy of you, let alone the dedication that you have shown over the past few years. I am sorry if the message didn't come through from my parents, and I'm sorry that I did not do more to ensure that it did so. You never should have waited for me, with or without a sign. I wish I could give you all those hours back but, seeing as I can't do that, let me say thank you. To have been loved like that, and by a woman like you, will always have been the greatest privilege of my life.

One thing still concerns me, though, and I wanted to use the opportunity of two messengers on my doorstep to clarify it now. If there was any element of atonement in your vigil, then please, _please_ let it go. I wish the last time we were together was a happy memory for us both. I wish I had held you properly. I wish I had told you how amazing you are and that you gave me, without a doubt, the best years of my life.

But neither of us was in a place then where we could see through the pain to the relationship we once had. No part of you was to blame for me leaving. Don't punish yourself. You are beautiful, smart, talented. I hope you will make many more maps and that they will find frames in galleries all around the world. If finding someone new is in the path that you want your life to take from here on in, then I hope they know just how lucky they are.

Know that I am safe and well. Know that you were never to blame. Know that you have only ever deserved the very best in life.

Take care,

Jim

When she has finished, Mary picks up the letter. Her hands do not shake. The paper is weak from months of folding and unfolding, so it tears into eight pieces easily. She slides them into the pocket of her trousers. She walks to the garden and the group shuffles to make space for her. Ted is attending to his inferno, but he glances up at the sound of approaching footsteps. He winks at Mary and the flicker of it is amplified by the flame.

Before anyone can bundle her into their conversation, Mary crouches and retrieves the final pieces from a period in her past that it is time to move beyond. She has no idea what the future will hold, but she has certainty over what—or rather who—it does not. She will always have been happy to have met Jim. She would rather have had those six years with him than ever erase the seven years without. She is grateful for everything he ever taught her, everything he gave to her, but now Mary has reached a place that may have been a long time coming but which has arrived nonetheless. *Acceptance*—wasn't that what she was always waiting for, after all?

She fishes the scraps of letter out of her jeans and throws them onto the fire, watches as they ignite. For the first time since the day Jim left, she feels no regret. Mary stares at the paper, noticing how the edges must crisp and curl, writhe in the heat, before they can crumble to ash and float up on the breeze. Jim is free and, now, so is she. Once the glare has faded from her eyes, Mary stands on certain feet and takes a step to her right.

Ted slips his hand into hers. Mary knows it is up to her to do the rest.

Acknowledgments

Thank you to my agent, the indefatigable Madeleine Milburn, who was the very first person to read my novel-writing and whose support and ambition for it has been unwavering ever since. Thank you for seeing the wood for the trees when my own vision falters. Thanks also to Giles Milburn, Hayley Steed, Liane-Louise Smith, Georgina Simmonds, Sophie Pélissier, Rachel Yeoh, Georgia McVeigh and Anna Hogarty at the agency for all your hard work on my behalf.

To my editor, Emily Krump, thank you for your belief in this story and for loving these characters so much from the start. Your ideas, shrewd comments, and willingness to brainstorm at the drop of a hat mean so much to me. At William Morrow, thanks also to Julia Elliott, Liate Stehlik, Jennifer Hart, Ryan Shepherd, Brittani Hilles, Stephanie Vallejo, and Ploy Siripant for everything you do to help my writing make its way into the world.

To the booksellers and librarians and bloggers and reviewers and readers—thank you. Your time is precious and I'm very grateful you chose to spend some of it between these pages.

To the family and friends who have taken such delight in knowing a real-life author, I hope you all know how much your joy has sustained me. Thanks for telling your colleagues and your neighbors and the poor soul who sat next to you at a party about my books. Thanks for live messaging me as you read and screenshotting your favorite passages. It makes the hours spent bashing my head against the computer seem worthwhile after all.

This book is dedicated to my parents—Stephanie and David Greaves—for their patience, but it could well also be for their faith or their pride or even just the fact that they allow me to boomerang back into their house without too much complaint. Thank you for showing me the meaning of unconditional love.

A special thanks to Emma Fairhurst for consulting on matters of wording and wardrobe. Your opinion means the world to me and I hope you know how grateful I am for your instantaneous replies to the inanest of questions. If that's not friendship, I don't know what is.

Last but not least, to John. It's always a challenge to say a nice thing about you, not because you don't deserve it, but because I know you can't stand the fuss. But I'm afraid you have to have one because your help with my messy, knotty writing head is invaluable. Thanks for spending hours trying to help me out of plot holes and to tie up my loose ends. You are the world's least likely muse, but I wouldn't have it any other way.

About the author

About the book

Insights,
Interviews
& More . . .

Read on

Meet Abbie Greaves

Charlotte Knee Photography

ABBIE GREAVES is the author of *The Silent Treatment*. She studied English literature at the University of Cambridge and worked in publishing for three years before leaving to focus on writing. She lives in the UK.

abbiegreaves.com
 @abbiegreaves1
 abbiegreavesauthor

Behind the Book:
The Art of Waiting

I am not proud to admit this, but I am a terribly impatient person. I would go so far as to say that it's my worst quality. I'm a toe-tapper, a handwringer, an obsessive phone-scroller. I eat on the move and rush for the bus. It annoys my family no end.

When it comes to waiting, my impatience is palpable. Whether it's at the doctor's office or in an airport or even in my own sitting room, listening to the twenty-ninth minute of the bank's hold music, you can guarantee that I'll be doing something to distract myself from the sense of time passing.

But it wasn't until two years ago that I began to reconsider my fraught relationship with waiting. At the time, I was living in London and had a friend visiting from out of town. I had arranged to meet her train at the station, but when I got there, I discovered that there had been a signal failure on the line, resulting in a delay of unspecified length. It would be too risky to head home in the interim. There was nothing to do but wait.

I moved away from the heaving station concourse, toward a row of metal benches at the edge of the hall, and, in doing so, found myself among a group of people all in the same boat. There was a suited man doing a crossword, two teenagers sharing headphones, a woman in a beret knitting, and a few ▶

3

others flicking through the assorted free newspapers. But it was those who were standing still, not reading or texting or fidgeting, who intrigued me the most. What did they know about the art of waiting that I so evidently did not?

Among the rush of commuters, my eye was drawn again and again to the examples of stasis around me. Whether that was because I was crying out for my own moment of rest after a busy day, or because I was worried about just what might happen when I stepped off the conveyor belt that is modern life to take it, I didn't quite know. What I did realize was that it was about time that I changed my own mindset toward the wait. It was part of my day's journey, as much as it was for everyone on the delayed train.

My friend arrived after an hour with profuse apologies, none of which were necessary. She had done me a huge favor. Personally, but creatively, too. Over the next few weeks, I sketched out a protagonist by name of Mary O'Connor whose defining characteristics are patience and persistence. I envisaged Mary in surroundings not dissimilar to the ones that had initially inspired me. I looked at her from every angle and asked her all the important questions. Who exactly was she waiting for? Did he or she materialize? If not, what then? How long would she wait? Where did her limits lie? And why?

From there, the finer plot points fell into place. In *Anywhere for You*, Mary has been standing outside Ealing Broadway station, alone, every evening for the last seven years, holding a sign that bears the words "Come Home Jim." No one knows who he is or where he has gone. Millions of journeys carry on around her, but Mary remains, waiting, until she finds the answers that will bring her closure.

Writing Mary reminded me that, by definition, waiting has an end point. We wait for, or until, the moment of change to arrive. And when it does? For Mary, it's the fortitude she gained through waiting that readies her to seize it. I know I have a long way to go until I can model Mary's composure, but meanwhile, I'll be biding my time—somewhat more patiently. ◠

An Interview with Mary O'Connor

First published on booksbywomen.org on April 29, 2021

First of all, Mary, I have to say a huge thank-you for agreeing to meet with me today. I know you've had a lot on your plate recently and that you're reluctant . . .

Mary: [quietly] Private.

Exactly, that you value your privacy. I suppose then, perhaps we could start with you explaining a bit about your own background? I notice you have a hint of an accent.

Mary: That will be the Belfast in me. You can take the girl out of Northern Ireland and all that . . . I've been in London for thirteen years now, but my Mam and my brothers are back at home. I don't get over to see them as much as I would like—they have their own lives— but I talk with Mam on the phone. She keeps me up to date with the goings-on.

It must have been a big leap, moving over here. What made you want to relocate?

Mary: Love. That's quite the cliché— isn't it? At any rate, it's true. I met Jim at work. Well, he didn't work with me, it wasn't an office romance or anything like that, but he was attending an event at the hotel where I used to work. We got chatting and then . . . I never looked back. I didn't think he ever would either, but if there's one thing these last few weeks have taught me, it's that there's no way of knowing someone else inside out, however much you might believe you do.

It's interesting you say that. . . . I gather that you're something of the local enigma, too?

Mary: [sighs] Depends who you talk to. That was never the intention, with my sign. I never wanted to make this about me. It was always about bringing Jim home. I wanted him to know that I would always be there, waiting for him, hoping he was well in the meantime. Whatever anyone else has read into it, that's their prerogative. I tell you what, though, you'd be surprised how few people even take an interest. All the commuters on their phones or in their own world. That's why when I met Alice . . .

Alice?

Mary: I presumed you knew her. Aren't all you writer types in one another's pockets? ▶

7

An Interview with Mary O'Connor
(*continued*)

Ha! Less than you might think. For the record, I don't know any Alices.

Mary: Well, I never caught her surname. Heaton, maybe? Anyway, she's young. And you'd know it, too—big eyes, glossy skin, enthusiasm like you wouldn't believe. If it had been anyone else to ask me all those questions about my vigil at the station, with the sign, then they probably would have given up with my first burst of short shrift. She's tenacious is Alice. She takes such an interest in Jim too, and it's been so long since I've had the chance to talk about him. I won't tell a lie—it's been nice.

That's great to hear. How did you meet Alice?

Mary: It was a complete coincidence the first time. She bumped into me when I was having a bit of a . . . of a moment, shall we say. That was at the station, and she bought me a drink afterwards, dusted me off as it were. I didn't expect to see her again, but then she turned up at NightLine, this crisis call center where I volunteer. She's been helping out there, too.

What got you into working for NightLine? It doesn't sound like you have much spare time on your hands, what with all the hours that you spend at the station.

Mary: It's bound up with the vigil in its own way—it's all reaching out, isn't it? Making sure that people know that they aren't alone, that there's someone somewhere who cares . . . I haven't always been the best at that. I've made plenty of mistakes, but I just hope it's not too late to make amends. If there's one thing that the last few weeks has shown, it's that you never know when there might be a bolt from the blue. A lead . . .

A lead about Jim?

Mary: [nods, then drops her head, gazing at the floor] I don't want to say too much. I don't want to jinx anything.

Okay, I appreciate that. I understand that, too. Is there anything you might feel comfortable expanding on here, though, before we go? I'm sure our readers would love to hear something more about Jim.

Mary: He called. For the first time in seven years, he called. ⌀

More by Abbie Greaves

THE SILENT TREATMENT

A lifetime together.
Six months of silence.
One last chance.

For readers of *The Light We Lost* and *Me Before You*, a life-affirming, deeply moving story about lies, loss, and a love that is louder than words.

By all appearances, Frank and Maggie share a happy, loving marriage. But for the past six months, they have not spoken. Not a sentence, not a single word. Maggie isn't sure what, exactly, provoked Frank's silence, though she has a few ideas.

Day after day, they have eaten meals together and slept in the same bed in an increasingly uncomfortable silence that has become, for Maggie, deafening.

Then Frank finds Maggie collapsed in the kitchen, unconscious, an empty package of sleeping pills on the table. Rushed to the hospital, she is placed in a medically induced coma while the doctors assess the damage.

If she regains consciousness, Maggie may never be the same. Though he is overwhelmed at the thought of losing his wife, will Frank be able to find his voice once again—and explain his withdrawal—or is it too late?

"The premise alone had me, but *The Silent Treatment* itself is just heartrendingly lovely. It's beautiful, so moving and clever. I truly adored it."
—Josie Silver,
#1 *New York Times* bestselling author of *One Day in December*

"A remarkably assured debut which doesn't go where you expect it to go."
—Jojo Moyes,
#1 *New York Times* bestselling author

"You won't be able to put down this tender and heartbreaking read."
—*Cosmopolitan* (UK) ꙮ